The Drummond Tradition

Books by
Charles Mercer

THE NARROW LEDGE

THERE COMES A TIME

RACHEL CADE

THE DRUMMOND TRADITION

CHARLES MERCER

The Drummond Tradition

G. P. PUTNAM'S SONS

New York

Library of Congress
Catalog Card Number: 57-11714

To Alma
as always

The Drummond Tradition

Chapter I

You can drive from Poggibonsi north to Florence in forty minutes, if you bear down, on a narrow macadam road which twists over the spurs of the Tuscan hills.

White oxen plod on distant yellow lanes lined by slim black cypresses, and in the lemon sunlight of afternoon the sky is dusty blue, which is quite different from simply a blue sky. It's all very picturesque, but if you're in a hurry to arrive in Florence, you're wise not to let the country distract you. For, around any curve, you might smash into an ox-drawn wain or a car filled with American tourists.

Drew Drummond, driving north fast on a late September afternoon, imagined an American family: call them Mr. and Mrs. Homer Q. Smith of Ponca City, Oklahoma, and their two daughters of appropriately spaced ages. How would their obituaries read in Ponca City? To say nothing of his own. But exactly what newspaper would bother to publish his obituary? Then, his speed unabated, he was around another curve without hurling into infinity accompanied by either the Smiths or a wain of straw.

The Tuscans work their fields and vineyards leisurely, not much surprised by anything. If you want to wax historical, the way south from Florence is an old invaders' route. Those who avoided the Via Francigena to the west, that Way of the Franks that led down across the Lombardy Plains and forded the Arno near Pisa and rolled on to Rome, have often entangled themselves in the hills of Tuscany. In our time the Germans came south through Florence and Poggibonsi and Siena to Rome, and after a while they went back north that way, and after them came the Americans and British, clanking north in tanks and half-tracks festooned with straw-covered flasks of good Chianti wine. To demonstrate that it was not a gay picnic, however, there lies midway of Poggibonsi and Florence an American military cemetery where the bodies hauled from the hills and draws have been interred under a geometric pattern of white headstones. Yes, the Tuscans have seen all manner of soldiers and arms and bloodshed, back to chain mail and sweat-blackened boar's leather, and they've engaged in a little marching themselves. So, Drew thought, only an arrant egotist would imagine that they'd be much dismayed if he cracked up the car and spattered his life on the road from Poggibonsi.

He was hurrying from a walled castle on a hilltop that afternoon because he had just learned that his father was arriving in Florence on the three-fifty train from Rome. The castle was the heavily mortgaged ancestral property of the Conte di Falcari. The yellow sports Citroën which he drove belonged to the Contessa, an American who had married the Conte only a couple of weeks previously. Although he drove fast, he had left regretfully, for he did not care whether he ever saw his father again. But basically, or perhaps only superficially, he was polite; he wished not to show how he felt, and he did not want to keep his father waiting. The Drummonds always had been a punctual family.

Drew's landlord in Florence had telephoned him at the castle and read the telegram which his father sent from Rome announcing his arrival. When Drew informed the Contessa of its content, she asked, "Who *is* your father?" She meant what did he do for a living and was he rich or poor, famous or obscure? He told her who his father *had* been. For some reason the information interested her, and she kept saying, "You didn't tell me who you *were,* Drew." It rather nettled him. She meant, of course, that he hadn't told her who his father was. When he said he'd better return to Florence after lunch to meet him, she said that she would go too. She became quite excited at the prospect, for her imagination was active. She imagined that she had read or heard of his father (though Drew doubted that she had), and she imagined he'd be "fascinating" to talk with (since she'd never met a distinguished member of his profession), and heaven knows what else she imagined. He did not encourage her to accompany him, however, and finally she announced that she would not go. He would take her Citroën and return to the castle that evening.

So he came alone, down the last inclines into the valley of the Arno, the silver olive groves falling behind, and he glimpsed the copper haze of Firenze with its cupolas and towers, the Cathedral and the Bell-tower and the Palazzo Vecchio, rising red and buff and white in the sun. He passed through the Porta Romana and down the Via Serragli, the speeding cyclists parting ahead, and he crossed the Ponte Alla Carraia into the chaos of traffic which hurls you by a kind of centrifugal force. At last he circled the Piazza Stazione and drew into the taxi line of the Central Station, which is modern and efficient and more worthy of Detroit than Florence.

His father was waiting. He stood at parade rest, his hat clasped in his hands before him, his luggage stacked in orderly array at his feet. When he saw Drew, his face lighted and he raised a hand and started forward, smiling. Drew hoped that his face lighted too, though he doubted it, as he went to him with lips set in a smile and took his hand.

"Drew. It's good to see you, Drew."

"It's good to see you, Father. You're looking fine."

He was six feet two and still spare and straight at the age of sixty-three. His hair had turned quite gray, much grayer than his brows, but his blue eyes still gazed at you with the directness that is called penetrating or cold, depending on how you feel about the man. His name was Andrew Jackson Drummond and he had retired a few months previously as a Lieutenant General of the United States Army after forty years of honorable service to his country. Actually his name was Andrew Jackson Drummond, 3d, after his father, Colonel Andrew Jackson Drummond, Jr., though in that small and select circle which outsiders sometimes irreverently call the West Point Benevolent and Protective Association he was known simply as Jack Drummond.

"Ready to roll?" asked General Drummond. "The people in Rome made reservations at the Excelsior. Is that okay?"

"Sure it's okay, if you mean they speak English there and have good service and all that."

"Harry's around here somewhere."

"Harry?"

"Why, yes." He looked at Drew as if seeking his approval of Harry.

Master Sergeant Harry Bannister came toward them now, a slight and wiry man with thinning sandy hair and a scarred jaw and neck. He was ten years younger than General Drummond and he had been in his service for many years. When the General retired, so did Sergeant Bannister, passing onto the personal payroll of the General and continuing to perform almost, but not quite, the same functions.

"How are you, Harry?" said Drew.

"Just fine, sir." Harry grasped his outstretched hand and smiled.

"How do you like Italy?"

"Just fine, sir."

They loaded the luggage and Harry crowded into the back seat.

"Looks like a beautiful city," General Drummond said as they swung into the traffic of the Piazza. "I've never seen it before, you know. Been in Rome before this trip, but never to Florence. Remember what Ike said about Florence?"

"No, Father."

"He said, 'All Florence must be regarded as a work of art.' That was in '45. Seems only yesterday, doesn't it? But here it is 1953." He looked about alertly. "A work of art. I have plenty of time now for looking at works of art. Interesting car. Citroën, isn't it?"

"Yes. It belongs to a friend of mine." After a pause, "A girl."

"Oh? A smooth car."

"She's a smooth girl," Drew said. "Woman, I mean."

"Oh? Italian?"

"American."

"Oh." Despite his effort not to, General Drummond sounded relieved.

When they reached the Excelsior, the chief concierge moved quickly from his desk toward the General, bowing—a gesture Drew never had seen in Europe by a member of that proudest profession.

"General Drummond," he said, "it's an honor to welcome you to Florence and the Excelsior."

It was flattering but rather incredible, since the General was not one of the widely photographed celebrities whom every good concierge would immediately recognize. Then Drew remembered his father mentioning "the people in Rome," who could only be the military people at the Embassy, or, specifically, a member of the Benevolent Association who would see to it that a fellow member received the proper tribute of courtesy, even from a concierge in distant Florence.

"It's a pleasure to be here," General Drummond said with the exact measure of reserve that showed he was accustomed to flattery and totally unmoved by it.

The concierge glanced at Drew, at his moccasins and dungarees and sport shirt.

"*Buon giorno,*" Drew said. "*Come sta?*"

"My son," General Drummond said indistinctly as he passed on.

The concierge knew and Drew knew that it was rude of him to speak Italian at that moment. Perhaps General Drummond knew it too. But Drew doubted his father understood the irritation that prompted his rudeness. Florence was his territory. And again, as so often in the past, his father had invaded his territory.

* * *

12

"I wonder," said General Drummond, "if it's possible to get a good Martini here."

He stood in the doorway of the living room which gave on a small balcony overlooking the Arno. He had removed his coat and his gold cuff links shone dully in the sunlight. They bore the initials A.J.D., and they were a gift from the staff officers of one or another command presented to the General when he moved to a new command. Drew did not know it as a special fact, but as a general truth; his father had piles of such loot garnered from many parts of the world.

Sprawled in an armchair and smoking an American cigarette he'd bummed from his father, he thought that the General's machine rolled as smoothly and efficiently as ever. He gave and he received and he knew the value of everything. He understood about the wine and fresh fruit arranged there on the table by the hotel management as a tribute to a leader of the most recent successful invaders; he knew that if he'd been a leader of the losers, a broken general of the Wehrmacht, he would not have been welcomed thus in Florence. He understood about his man Harry, who glided silently in the adjoining bedroom, hanging up the General's suits and arranging his shoes in inspection order and turning down the General's bed and putting out his pajamas and robe and placing a towel on the floor beside the shower and slipping a new blade in his razor. The General, standing there, reminded you of one of those dealers in a Las Vegas gambling hall; even when he was losing, you felt that eventually he'd win because there was an unlimited bank behind him trusting in his skill. He knows what to do about all things except one, thought Drew. Me.

"Yes, sir, I'd sure like a Martini," said General Drummond.

"You want to mix it yourself?" Drew knew that he did; he was mighty proud of his prowess as a Martini mixer.

"I wouldn't mind. I always like to know what goes into a Martini."

Drew called room service and ordered a bucket of ice and a fifth of Beefeater and a bottle of Martini Rossi dry and some lemons and glasses.

"You really speak Italian," his father said when he hung up.

It was close to flattery, and Drew thought guardedly, He wants something, what can it be? He said, "I only know a few words, but I'm working at it." He wandered out to the balcony and his father followed and slumped against the rail.

Slumping again, Drew thought drily. He himself was five feet eight and never had weighed more than one fifty-five; a comfortable

13

size, he felt, because you got around without creating any fuss. But obviously his height still troubled his father; he always slumped a few inches when they were together long. Drew did not know whether it was from deference to him or to his own ego for having sired only one child and that a runt by the standards of the Drummond stock.

General Drummond said, "You're taking it easy?"

"Yes, Father."

"Good." He looked away.

Drew suddenly was washed by one of those waves of pity he sometimes felt for his father, despite everything, because he was growing old and his personal life had not been happy. Staring across the Arno at the dusty buff dome of the church on the Piazza Costello, he wished he knew how to talk to him. But he did not, he could not, he had given up trying long ago.

Harry let in the room service boy and tipped him and came to the doorway and said, "Will I mix them, sir?"

"No thanks, Harry. I'll do it myself."

"If there's anything—"

"Everything's fine, Harry. I know where your room is. Take off. I'll see you in the morning."

Harry Bannister looked saddened. Then he said, "Thank you, sir," and left. It occurred to Drew that Harry, like many a thirty-year man who had spent much of his life in foreign travel, did not really like foreign travel.

"He's quite a remarkable guy," he said.

"Very remarkable." The General peeled the cellophane off the Beefeater.

"I'm surprised you brought him with you."

"Habit. I figured he might get a boot out of the trip. And he takes the travel details off me."

The General might have added, thought Drew, that he was accustomed to being followed and now he could not summon as much as a squad to his bidding, but at least there was Harry who could be commanded to fetch and carry and, when the going got very lonely, even ordered to play a game of pinochle with him.

"How does he like living at Burning Brook?"

General Drummond glanced at him, wondering why he should take such an interest in his man Harry, whose chief virtue was that he could be taken for granted.

"He likes Burning Brook. He's very happy there." He put the emphasis of finality in his tone.

14

Drew dropped the subject of Harry. He was inclined, he knew, to seem unable to stop thinking about someone like Harry Bannister, almost as if he were Harry himself, venturing out of the Excelsior now into the wilderness of Florence where there was neither a PX beer garden nor one of those ready-made bars in the wall where many men in American uniform naturally gravitate. But no stripes on his arms now, no sharply pressed suntans; no identity and no place to go and re-establish it with the men who still had it and with the women they could afford. He wanted to rush after Harry and tell him a place or two he might go, but he knew that Harry would think him patronizing. There was mystery about Harry Bannister, the old infantry-man who had fought and drunk and whored his way around the world and now served as gentleman's gentleman to Lieutenant General Andrew Jackson Drummond 3d, U.S.A., Retired. When a lady and gentleman or two came down from Nashville to visit the General at his country retreat in Burning Brook, did Sergeant Bannister pad softly and serve deftly and fade away appropriately? He must; other-wise the General would not have retained him in his service. But did Harry ever remember, as he passed the canapés, the time he beat up three Marines in Wahiawa and served his term in the Stockade? And was it fitting or odd to him that he should end his days passing drinks to landed gentry in the hills of Tennessee?

The General poured gin into the pitcher. Then he poured vermouth, measuring by eye one part to five of the gin. He dropped two hands of ice cubes into the pitcher and placed two glasses, rims down, in the ice bucket. While he stirred the drink quickly, his expression was rapt. He peeled two rinds of lemon and lifted the cooled glasses from the ice bucket and ran the rinds around the lip of each glass and dropped them, one in a glass. He filled each glass to the brim and only ice remained in the pitcher.

He handed Drew his glass in a steady hand, nodded, and sipped his Martini. "Not bad," he said.

It was a very good Martini. Drew told him so and they walked out to the balcony. When General Drummond sat down, a sigh almost escaped him.

Taking care not to look at him, Drew asked, "What are you doing in Florence, Father?"

"I decided to take a little trip. So I flew to Paris. And then I de-cided to come on to Rome. And being in Rome, I thought I'd drop up and see you."

His casualness was too elaborate, Drew thought. He had come with a purpose.

"You should have let me know in advance. I might not have been here."

The General turned his head and looked at him expressionlessly. He was thinking, Drew knew, that if he had given advance notice of his coming Drew doubtless would have absented himself from Florence. As always, surprise was the best tactic. But why did they persist in trying to kid each other—and themselves?

"Your back is okay?" the General asked. "You feel—all right?"

"Never felt better, Father."

"Good. It was a close one there in Korea, Drew, your back broken and your head split." He exhaled slowly. "But after all those months in the hospitals you *are* fit for general service."

So this was the game. The old man had come all the way from Burning Brook to Florence to make sure—yet how could he have known? How could the General possibly have guessed that he'd been toying with the idea of going home at the end of these three months and resigning from the Army?

"Three months' leave for rest and recuperation." General Drummond smiled slowly. "Rather irregular, you know. You must have charmed the medics. They declare you fit for general service and then they grant you three months' leave. Was it anyone I know?"

"The surgeon who made out my fitness report knows you, Father. The man who gave me three months' leave does not."

"*Touché,*" said the General. "But I would have granted you the leave, Drew—if you hadn't been my son."

"But you wouldn't have wanted me to spend it in Italy."

"Well—no, I wouldn't say that. It's your time and your life."

Then let me live it, Drew thought.

"I will say that I, personally, probably wouldn't have picked Italy. I'm more the Wyoming or Quebec type of vacationer." He made a wry face. "At least I used to be."

"Then what are you doing in Italy now?"

General Drummond said, "I wanted to talk to you about a book I'm writing."

Drew swore in surprise. His father frowned; he believed in saving oaths for crucial moments when they would be most effective. To Drew it was a crucial moment.

"Why should it be so extraordinary that I'm writing a book?"

16

"Perhaps it isn't," Drew said. "Can you tell me why generals always want to write their memoirs?"

"Maybe because they have so much to explain."

"So much to explain away, you mean. And you came all this way to talk to me about a book?"

The General nodded slowly.

"There's one book that never has been written, Father. It really should be because it would explain a lot about the nature of the armies in these recent wars. Only a member of the Club could write it. A kind of 'inside' book. About the generals and their—their frictions. You've known most of them. I could name one or two whose guts you must hate. Do a job on them and then square away into some other commands."

"Do a job on them?" There was revulsion in his tone. "I wouldn't think of it, Drew."

"Father, this is Florence, not the Army and Navy Club in Washington. The trouble with you brass hats is that nearly all of you turn pious after you quit the business."

"Let me put it to you this way," General Drummond said slowly. "Clausewitz, General Karl von Clausewitz, wrote that 'Everything is very simple in war, but the simplest thing is difficult. These difficulties accumulate and produce a friction which no man can imagine exactly who has not seen war.' Do I make my point?"

"Rather well, I'd say. To discuss only the frictions would be an unfair analysis of the accumulated difficulties."

"Exactly."

"You've become rather Olympian, Father. In the way that General Marshall achieved Olympia. What is there about so many of you guys with a lot of stars on your shoulders that makes you eventually see only big pictures?"

"I'm no George Marshall," General Drummond said quickly. "There is a truly great intellect. Did I ever tell you about the time— Well, he's a great man."

"Father, did you ever hear of a man named E. M. Forster?"

He looked at Drew alertly. "Can't say I have. Should I have?"

"Maybe not in your business. But he makes more sense to me than your Clausewitz. He's an Englishman. A writer I've started reading since I came to Florence. Anyway, he wrote that 'Hero worship is a dangerous vice, and one of the minor merits of a democracy is that it does not encourage it, or produce that unmanageable type of citizen known as the Great Man. It produces instead different kinds of smaller men, and that's a finer achievement.' "

"By Great Man," the General said, "I presume he meant Evil Man. A Hitler or Stalin or Napoleon. He surely can't have meant a Marshall or Lee or Lincoln." He nodded. "Still, that's pretty good. I'll have to read him. Forster, I mean." He stared across the Arno and smiled. "This is fine, Drew, sitting together on a balcony in Florence quoting various authorities on this and that." He drained his glass. "Let's have another Martini."

Sitting together on a balcony in Florence, Drew thought. Above all, he knew, the old man was lonely. He swam against another wave of pity for him as he followed him inside to watch the ceremony of the mixing of the drinks.

"Don't take my judgments too seriously, Father," he said. "If I knew so much about writing books, I'd have written a few myself. You have some swell material for your memoirs, going away back. Remember Uncle George coming to that dance in his purple uniform? That dance was in honor of old General March, wasn't it? Didn't Mother—"

"George always liked your mother," the General said.

"And Mother always liked Uncle George. They'd have made a colorful couple if he hadn't been a happily married man."

The General's hand was still and he peered sadly into the pitcher, as if it contained more than gin and vermouth and ice. At last he said, "If George Patton had ever had the misfortune to marry your mother instead of that lovely wife of his he'd probably have been kicked out of the United States Army. And the Second War in Europe would not have ended as soon as it did— Hold out your glass!"

He filled their glasses and put down the pitcher and faced Drew.

"The book I have in mind is not my memoirs."

Drew stared at him, surprised. Why, then, had his father let him rant on so? And then, grudgingly, he had to admire his method, his excellent military method, of drawing out his eager adversary into a thin line and finally—snip, snip, snip—capturing him.

Chapter II

There had been a leisureliness and simplicity about Drew's life in Florence that he had not found in previous and more vulnerable years. Coming to the city as a tourist and finding that he liked it, he decided to stay. Occasionally he went away for a few days, up to the hill towns and down to the sea, over to the Adriatic and down to Rome. But always he returned to the leisure and simplicity of his flat overlooking the river and the Piazza Niccola Demidoff.

With the arrival of his father, the simplicity suddenly seemed complicated, the leisure disrupted by a sense of duty. It was not entirely the General's fault. It was partially the fault of the Contessa. And basically, Drew knew, all of it was his own fault.

He started the complications quite innocently the evening before his father arrived. When he left the American Library, where he'd been reading for a couple of hours, he realized that he was low in cash and he remembered that an American painter named Jocko Webster owed him six thousand lire. Jocko was a bad painter, but an ingratiating salesman of his bad paintings. He spent a lot of time in Harry's Bar where he often met American tourists to whom he sold his strange abstractions. Only yesterday, someone had told Drew, Jocko had sold another painting to a woman from Houston, Texas. Thus it happened that he strolled down the Via di Parione from the Library to Harry's Bar looking for Jocko.

When he walked in, the low-ceilinged room appeared deserted except for the bartender, who said, "*Buona sera,* Signor Drummond."

"Good evening," Drew said. "I'm looking for the American genius, Jocko Webster. Has he been around?"

"Not today, Signor Drummond. Last night, yes. I heard him say he was going to Ravello for a week."

"Well," Drew said in English, "there went my ten bucks."

The bartender, who spoke English perfectly, smiled. But his smile faded into a frown as a woman called, "Hey!" Drew saw her then, leaning forward at her table around the corner of the bar. She was a beautiful woman, tanned, with cropped chestnut hair.

"Are you an American?" she asked.

"Yes."

"Then come and have a drink with me. Bartender, what's your name, come here and introduce us."

The bartender shrugged and followed Drew to her table. "Contessa, this is Signor Drummond—the Contessa di Falcari, signor."

He had an impression of strength, of physical vitality, as in a ballerina or a professional swimmer. If she would smile, he would be positive of it. But her face expressed melancholy. She wore a low-cut dress that revealed her wide shoulders and tanned arms. She was, he judged, possibly thirty years old.

"Martini?" she asked, waving toward the chair opposite hers.

"Negroni."

"Sissy."

"Oh, sure," he said, sitting down. "Sissy Drummond, Contessa."

She drained her glass and placed it far out on the table and nodded to the bartender. Then she folded her hands under her chin and studied him expressionlessly.

"Tell you what," she said suddenly, "I won't call you Sissy Drummond if you won't call me Contessa. What's your first name?"

"Drew."

"Okay, Drew. My name is Marcia. I'm an American too. Drew's a funny name."

"It's short for Andrew."

"Andrew what?"

"Andrew Drummond." He grimaced. "As a matter of fact, Andrew Jackson Drummond, 4th."

She said, "That's a hell of a name."

"It is. It's a secret I usually guard closely."

"Most disarming," she said. "Your personality, I mean. Are you rich?"

"No, I'm poor."

"I believe you," she said. "Your disarming personality shows you're poor. But the '4th' shows you're rich. I mean they must have been very proud of something in your family to go on naming one after another the same. At least there weren't any bastards for three generations."

"You're wrong, Marcia."

"But they were legitimate bastards." She raised the Martini which the bartender set before her and said, "Here's to all Americans everywhere."

"To some of them anyway." He sipped his Negroni.

She shook her head as he held out a cigarette. "I don't smoke. I don't even hardly drink at all. Not usually. But right now I'm pretty drunk. Do I show it?"

"Not at all."

"You said that too fast. You're very polite. What are you doing in Florence?"

"Just loafing."

"That's nice to hear," she said. "The trouble with Americans around here, they all pretend to be *doing* something. Writing or painting or improving themselves or something. And they're really just loafing. As a matter of fact, did you ever notice how Americans always claim to *be* somebody? They have to be drilling for oil or writing plays or *something*. I mean, why can't they just say they're loafing, like you?" She raised her glass again. "Here's only to the Americans who are loafing. Like you."

"And you." He raised his glass.

She frowned and sipped her drink. "I don't really want to loaf. I mean I don't think I do. Right now I'm sort of mixed up." She looked at him thoughtfully. "You remind me of somebody I've met in Hollywood." She mentioned a name unfamiliar to him.

He expected her to question him, but she didn't. She began, instead, to talk about Hollywood. It was a monologue, actually. Without her specifically saying so, he gathered that she had been an actress. Occasionally she'd ask whether he had heard of this or that person. Sometimes he'd nod and sometimes shake his head; it made no difference. He listened acutely, forming his opinion of her more from what she failed to say than from what she said. And what she failed to express, he realized, was pride or envy or malice, those deadly sins that were supposed to be the common vices of actresses. She talked, rather, with a faint nostalgia, as if she were turning the leaves of an old album in which each photograph reminded her of something else. But never of herself or him or her husband or life in Italy.

She finished the Martini and ordered another and insisted on ordering another Negroni for him. Then she said, "You're a good conversationalist."

"Oh, sure."

"You really are," she said. "Anybody would say so. You manage it by being a good listener. I'll bet lots of people are always telling you the stories of their lives."

His interest in her quickened, for what she said was true. Because it was true, he thought that she was astute. And he could not help but admire anyone who was able to make astute observations while drinking heavily. Furthermore, she was beautiful, and rarely had he met a beautiful woman who was astute, whether drunk or sober.

"I like to listen," he said. "I especially like to listen to what people refrain from saying."

She blinked slowly. "You sound like a head-shrinker, a psychiatrist I know in this town. "

"Not Mike Sabraccio?"

"That's the one. Are you a patient of his or something?"

"Just a friend."

"The things people refrain from saying," she said absently.

Now, he thought, the story of her life. But no. She resumed talking about Hollywood and motion pictures, her eyes insisting on his attention. Her voice grew so indistinct that he had to lean forward to hear her. He became bored. Harry's was filling with the evening tourist trade, and he wished the Conte or someone would rescue him. He glanced at his wrist watch.

"Am I boring you?" she muttered. "I'll have one more and then I'll stop boring you. . . . Yes?" She stared beyond him, as if she saw something ominous.

He turned quickly. The diners facing him grew still; a fat man, his expression astonished, held his fork halfway to his open mouth. He turned to Marcia. Her eyes were closed. She was sliding, sliding down her chair. Only her head was visible. Then she disappeared and he heard her sigh under the table.

A waiter and the manager moved quickly. "The Contessa has fainted," the manager said in a loud voice as he helped Drew lift her from the floor. They half dragged, half carried her into the kitchen and out a doorway into an alley.

"The Contessa didn't faint," Drew said to the manager, "but it was kind of you to say so."

"Thank you, Signor Drummond." He was panting from the effort of dragging Marcia. Each held her firmly under an arm while the waiter ran down the alley shouting, *"Tassi! Tassi!"*

"She has had seven Martinis," said the manager. "The last two have been very weak, but they come to seven. And usually she drinks little or not at all."

"If you can steady her," Drew said, "I'll pay the check."

"She cannot be steadied," said the manager. "Don't worry about the check, Signor Drummond. You have plenty on your hands tonight."

"Not me," Drew said. "Where does she live?"

"Many kilometers from here, signor. Perhaps she is staying in the city, but I do not know where."

"Where's her husband?"

He sighed. "In Rome, I understand."

"Listen, I—"

"Signor Drummond, let me tell you something. My boys and I have often remarked on your great gentleness of spirit. You have the soul of an Italian, signor. But you are an American. She is an American." He peered down at her swaying head. "You are an honorable man, Signor Drummond." He put his free hand on his heart. "One knows it here. You will help. She is in trouble. I can think of no one in Firenze whom I'd trust more to—"

"Well, thanks a lot," Drew said drily, "but—"

"Do you have enough taxi fare, Signor Drummond?"

"Yes, but . . ."

The waiter ran up the alley from the street where he had stopped a cab. They carried her to it and lifted her in. As the cab moved away, the manager raised his right hand after it in a kind of silent benediction.

Drew lived on the Via dei Renai overlooking the Piazza Niccola Demidoff. On the ground floor was a leather shop operated by his landlord, Luigi Delvecchio, who lived on the second floor with his wife and their five children. Drew was the sole occupant of the third floor, which was reached by a dark and narrow stone staircase that passed the Delvecchios' doorway.

When the cab stopped, he shook Marcia gently. She did not stir. He paid the driver and pulled her out.

"May I help you, signor?" asked the driver.

"Thank you, no." He heaved Marcia over a shoulder. "There's little dignity in this. But it's handy."

"It's also dark, signor," said the driver, "and the street is deserted."

After he'd climbed a few steps he began to wonder how a woman who looked so slim could be so heavy. He staggered on, passing the Delvecchios' doorway and hearing the chatter of the children, and finally he reached the third floor. Unlocking his door, he rolled Marcia off his shoulder onto the cot and turned on a light.

The flat consisted of a large front room and a bedroom and bath behind. In the front room, besides the cot, were a long low table, a couple of chairs and lamps, and a case containing many books. Above the fireplace he'd hung an engraving of a house that reminded him of

Burning Brook; he'd bought it in Siena, of all places, when in a nostalgic mood. Behind a curtain in one corner were an electric plate and cupboard. It was a bare room and often noisy, with sounds echoing across its high ceiling from the street and the Delvecchios' apartment below. But he liked the place, it had become home to him.

He smoothed down Marcia's dress and pondered what to do with her. Her mouth had not fallen open. She was still beautiful. She had passed out, but she had not come unglued. An admirable woman.

Never try to rouse drunks, he knew; they became sick or penitent or belligerent. When he'd recovered his breath, he carried her into the bedroom and put her on his bed and took off her shoes. He covered her and turned off the light and opened a window and closed the door behind him. He was hungry. If he went out to eat, however, she might awaken and, not knowing where she was, become frightened. So he went downstairs and gave young Vito Delvecchio money to run out and buy him a loaf of bread and a chunk of cheese. He ate bread and cheese, washing it down with some Chianti left in the cupboard, while he read a secondhand copy of H. O. Taylor's *Thought and Expression of the Sixteenth Century*, which he'd bought a couple of days before at a stall across the river.

About eleven o'clock it struck him as absurd to be reading while a beautiful woman slept in his bed. He went into the bedroom and looked at her. She was still beautiful and still asleep. He cleared his throat and shut and opened the window noisily. She did not awaken. The trouble with him, he thought, was that he wished to tack a happy ending on a not altogether pleasant occasion. It was a flaw of the imagination. Turning out the light, he shut the door quietly and returned to the sixteenth century. When he grew sleepy, he undressed and lay down on the cot.

He was awakened by someone calling, "Hey!" Sunlight poured through the open windows. From the street rose the snarl of a motor bike and the clatter of a street sweeper's wooden zoccoli. Marcia cried, "Help!"

He pulled on his dungarees and hurried into the other room as she raised herself in the bed.

"Where am I?" she cried.

"You're all right. You're in my apartment. It's me, Drew Drummond. Remember? Harry's Bar."

She stared at him wildly and wailed, "Oh, God!" Then she raised the cover and looked at herself and exclaimed wonderingly, "I'm all dressed!"

"Yes," he said, "I just took off your shoes."

"You mean—" Unaccountably her eyes filled with tears. "I remember. Harry's Bar. So I passed out."

"They were nice about it. They let the tourists think you just fainted."

"And you brought me here. And you—you took off my shoes and you—you just put me in your bed and went away. Didn't you?" Her voice rose. "Didn't you—I can't remember your name."

"Drew Drummond."

"Didn't you, Drew Drummond?" Her voice was resonant, and he thought that she must be a pretty good actress. "Do you know how lucky I am?"

"Uh—not exactly."

"Well, I am!" She clutched her forehead. "Oh my head! Where's the john?"

He pointed to the bathroom door. "Your purse is there on that table. I'll make us some coffee."

He took the coffeepot down to the Piazza and filled it at the fountain. When the coffee was ready, she came from the bedroom. She looked pale, but she had applied make-up meticulously.

"I feel terrible," she said. "I took three aspirin, but I still feel terrible."

"You look all right," he said.

"Do I?" She came to him and watched him pour coffee. "Do I really look all right to you, Drew?"

He said, "You're as tall as I am, I see. How much do you weigh?"

"None of your business."

"It was last night when I carried you up here."

She crossed the room to a window and raised her hands to the casing and looked out. "It's beautiful. What a beautiful place, Drew."

What an actress, he thought. But he said, "Here's your coffee."

She came back and took the cup of coffee from him. Sitting down, she watched him over the rim of the cup. Expectantly, he thought, as if he were supposed to say something.

"It's good coffee." She hesitated. "I want to ask you something. Will you tell me the truth and promise not to get mad?"

He nodded.

"Are you a fairy?"

"Good God, no!"

"Are you sure?"

"Of course I'm sure. I even was married once—for about two years."

"I was married too," she said. "I mean before this time. But being married doesn't prove anything. Homosexuals get married. Because what I wanted to say to somebody—well, Edoardo, the bastard, is a fairy."

"Edoardo?"

"My husband. The Conte di Falcari. The man I married two weeks ago. He went off to Rome a couple of days ago with a horrible man who—"

"How do you know he's a—"

"Because he told me. He cried like a baby when he told me. It was awful. I felt so sorry for him. I mean before I got mad. Before he went off to Rome with this— Oh, never mind. I just had to tell somebody and there was nobody to tell. He's gone and I hope I never see him again. You don't know how awful it is, that—that nothing happening. I mean you get married and then *nothing!* I was so sick and lonely with *nothing* up there in that castle that—well, I drove here to Florence. When was it? Yesterday, I guess. One thing I want to ask you. Last night, when I was lying in there, did you— Oh, never mind."

"I told you I'm not a fairy," he said. "Once I went in and made a lot of noise and hoped you'd wake up and— But you didn't and I—"

"Cut." She smiled at him. "Okay. That's that and that's fine. It's just that sometimes in a thing like this you begin to wonder, Is it me? But that's that."

She swung to her feet and went to one of the open windows. He followed and leaned on the sill beside her.

"It's beautiful," she said.

It wasn't exactly beautiful, he thought. But it was interesting. Beyond the Piazza morning traffic hummed on the broad Lungarno Serristori which follows the river. Beyond the street, below a wall, stretched green floodland parceled into small gardens where old men descended by wooden ladders on summer evenings and weeded their zucchini. Beyond the floodlands curled the river, low and flowing tiredly in late September. And beyond the river stretched the city.

"What a beautiful piazza," Marcia said.

It wasn't a beautiful piazza. But it was a serviceable and, at times, an interesting piazza. It was named the Niccola Demidoff because Demidoff had done something for the city, and the city, in turn, had done something for Demidoff. Its grass plots were green, its paths and yucca trees carefully tended. In its exact center the citizens of Florence had raised to Demidoff what surely was the ugliest memorial ever erected to a mortal. There was the raised figure of Demidoff and below, four square, stood the dirty marble figures of muses—presumably. Drew never was able to study the thing with much penetration because he always was distracted by the monstrosity covering it: iron pillars, set octagonally, supported an absurd peaked roof of leaded glass. The glass was punctured by many holes through which dripping rain had streaked the muses. One of these figures did sometimes bemuse him: a semi-nude female holding a lute. The lute and the hands were broken. Occasionally he saw symbolism in the fracture. But he never parlayed the symbolism very far; he always transferred his attention to any pretty girl who happened to stroll through the piazza.

"And this is where you live." Marcia looked at him, her lips parted.

He kissed her. He did not put his arms around her and she did not move. They simply kissed, without passion and rather tentatively, like children.

"You know what?" she said.

"What?"

"I feel sort of funny."

"It's the hangover."

"No. The hang is almost over. I just feel sort of funny. And all of a sudden I'm ravenous. Let's go to Doney's and have a big American breakfast."

He shaved quickly and she did not protest when he said they'd walk because a cab would bring them to Doney's before it opened. Apparently she had purged herself of babbling last night, for she walked silently.

After breakfast she said, "Drew, would you like to see my castle? It's a crazy place."

"Sure. When?"

"Today. I remember I left my car with the doorman at the Grand. We'll pick it up and you can get a bag at your place. Let's go now."

Chapter III

He had arrived expectantly at the castle with her and then, a couple of hours later, he had been forced to return regretfully to Florence. He thought of her now as he followed his father to the balcony.

General Drummond sat down and stared across the Arno. His Martini, raised in his right hand, trembled slightly, as if the wind had cast a seed in it. Then Drew saw it was the hand holding the glass that trembled. The General drank, quickly, and rested his hand on the chair arm.

"I want to write a history of the Drummond family," he said to the river. "And I want you to help me." He turned his head, lips drawn down, the old crow's-feet wrinkling about his eyes in an expression Drew never had seen on his face. Beseeching. Knocking, knocking, always knocking on my door.

"What do you think?" asked General Drummond.

Drew breathed deeply. How incredibly a family tradition could inflate the ego. Because his father cared about it, he believed the world could care. What a useless piece of work unless you sought the truth, and even then to whom was the truth important? To his father? No, for he sought glorification rather than the truth.

"You think it—foolish?"

"Not exactly foolish, Father. But what do you want to prove? That the Drummonds have been one hell of a great military family? Old campaigns and the flags waving and all that?"

The General frowned. "I don't especially want to prove anything about the family. Though it's not a bad family. I could demonstrate that from the record. What would you want to do? Demonstrate that it's a great disadvantage for a sensitive young man to have grown up in a military tradition?"

"It's the first time in years you've inferred I might be sensitive," Drew said. "It's not an insult."

"All right." The General's tone was weary and his shoulders slumped. "All right. Let's not . . ." His voice trailed off. He must be thinking, Why does this whelp claw so at my vitals? Then why, thought Drew, does he press me to his vitals so?

"Let me tell you *why* I'd like to see this book written," General Drummond said to the river. "It's not a spur of the moment idea. I've been thinking about it for quite a while. The last year before I retired I was rather on the shelf, you know." He smiled wryly. "What can they do with old infantrymen? But they gave me a project. A really interesting project, it developed. The Army of the future. The soldier of the future. What must he—and the Army—be? There's the Goddamned bomb and there's the Air Force and the admirals always will be standing three-deep on Pennsylvania Avenue while they wait on Congress. But what nearly everybody forgets is that there will always be a soldier. They'll never use the bomb, Drew. They don't dare. Maybe it's just as well that both sides have it. Because each side knows that the big knockout is impossible now without knocking out the world. The bombs cancel out and we're left with the soldier."

He sipped his Martini. "I'm wandering afield. The point is that in thinking of the future I had to think of the past. And naturally I began thinking about the family. After I went back to Burning Brook there was plenty of time to think. I began talking to Judd about it."

Judd was General Drummond's younger brother, whom Drew loved and admired. Twenty years ago he'd given up teaching and returned to Burning Brook. He had worked the land lovingly and intelligently and the farm had prospered. Drew's grandfather, who had not favored Judd, had willed the place to his father. But the General had made certain that Judd received all the profits from the farm and he had insisted that Judd and his wife Mildred, who were childless, continue living in the big house after he retired. He lived in the cottage, which had been the overseer's house in the old days. Whenever Drew thought about it, he was pleased with his father for insisting that Judd and Mildred stay in the big house.

"Judd has collected a lot of information about the family," the General continued. "It interests him."

"I know," Drew said.

"I began reading over the letters and diaries Judd has collected and making notes . . . I guess I still haven't told you *why* I want to write it, Drew." He looked at him slowly. "I guess I just want to see if I can find out what it's all been about."

Now, Drew thought, he's got me. He was inside the defenses. Because he always had thought his father knew what it was all about. For the right and the glory. Service under the flag. Death before dishonor. Duty before love. Pick your noble slogan and there was Father.

"When did you start wondering what it's all about?"

"A long time ago." Bitterness pressed General Drummond's rigidly controlled tone.

He must be thinking of Mother, Drew thought. He must be thinking of me. He must be thinking of the interminable afternoons of his retirement at Burning Brook when there was absolutely nothing to do but ask Harry to play a game of pinochle or Judd to play a game of chess. Once he must have had a dream. Drew did not know what it could have been, for his father never had confided his dreams in him. Perhaps it was a noble dream. Perhaps it was only of stars on his shoulders. But the dream had passed and now the dreamer was alone. And awakened.

"You feel," Drew said, "that by studying the past you can learn something about—yourself?"

General Drummond grinned, suddenly and self-consciously. He had said more than he intended, Drew knew. He wanted to sneak back into his disguise: the mufti of the affable, knowledgeable, retired general.

"Perhaps," he said. "But quite apart from that, there were some interesting ones. Not Father so much. Your grandfather was rather a— a frustrated man."

He was indeed awakening, Drew thought.

"I was thinking of Uncle Chad," the General said.

"The wild man?"

"He wasn't so wild. He was just in the cavalry."

"But he got himself killed."

"It was almost inevitable," the General said. "Like Custer. They were both romantic about the cavalry and so Custer got them both killed."

"And yourself, Father. None of them ever wore three stars except you. What are you going to do about the section on yourself?"

He was silent for a time. Then he said, "I'd hoped you would write that, Drew. I would tell you what I could and you would write it."

"But then it wouldn't be your book."

General Drummond looked puzzled. "*My* book? I don't have some special pride of ownership in it. It's only a—a hobby." His glass trembled again and he rested his hand. "Perhaps only a way to pass some time. If anybody ever wanted to publish it, which I doubt, I wouldn't let it be published in my lifetime."

He baffled Drew. To wish to write a book yet not to publish it was like wishing to fight a battle yet not caring to win it. It was—unprofessional. In the way that Drew had been largely unprofessional in the profession of soldiering by his failure ever to visualize stars on his shoulders. Why, then, had his father come all the way to Florence to talk about it and even, perhaps, try to start writing it? Why, except that once more, as so often in the past, the old man sought his time, his attention, the direction of his path. Like the Ancient Mariner and the Wedding Guest.

"How long do you plan to spend here working on it?"

"Well, let's see. You report back for duty in—"

"Father."

The General looked at him sharply.

"I might as well tell you now. I'm thinking of resigning."

General Drummond slumped almost imperceptibly in his chair and said, "I know."

"You know? How could you? I've told no one."

General Drummond tossed off his Martini and set the empty glass on the floor. "I *knew* all right. All this." His right hand indicated the dusty blue sky, the ancient city. "This Italy. Soldiers should not come to Italy—except to fight. I knew it would get to you, all this—this—I don't know how to describe it, but I've sensed it since I came. And you were ripe to be snared by the—the softness of it. But I want to remind you that the Army needs and wants you. It's a thing no civilian could understand because a civilian thinks the Army is just a big I.B.M. machine. Neither could the Army time servers understand, those well-marked men who only want to get by and weather these cutbacks that are under way now—the cutbacks you think you want to take advantage of. But there are some men the Army *wants* . . ."

Drew had an absurd, vivid image of one of those Army recruiting posters: THE ARMY WANTS *You*.

"When I was your age nobody was plugging for me to stay in. When I was thirty-one years old, like you, it wasn't the Army of today, and, let's hope, not the Army of tomorrow. You've broken just about every rule in the book, Drew, but you're still away out in front of it. Soldiering, I mean. You can't just throw it over. You were born to it. You're a natural at it. Your record proves . . ."

Drew would not listen to a recital of his 201 File.

"Listen to me, Drew."

He looked up slowly at his father.

General Drummond said, "I'm talking to you about only one thing. Call it the reason I came here to Italy on a hunch, if you will. I'm talking about *responsibility,* your responsibility in the world. Your grandfather and great-grandfather and great-great-grandfather all faced up to theirs. I believe that I have to mine."

The General breathed quickly and then he said, "You surely can't fail to judge these times. After all, you know them intimately. You gave plenty in both the Second War and Korea. But the times haven't ended yet. The troubles are only beginning. This is not a decade for a young man to spend in his back yard. In the brief space of my mature years America has become a world power, one of the two great world powers. And we do not have enough able young men who are willing to maintain the initiative of our power. It's as if nearly all the young men are tired these days. It's true that a good many of you have fought two wars. But why do so many now seem afraid of their responsibility in the world? Why do they just want to make money and be—secure?"

"It's comfortable in a back yard," Drew said. "Do you want us to be out selling tractors in Afghanistan?"

"Don't joke," said General Drummond. "You know what I mean. I'm not talking about being a colonial power, but simply of our responsibility to keep as much of this world as free as we can. And I mean as free as we are: self-autonomous, bellies reasonably full, some hope for tomorrow, the right to differences of opinion without violence. And the issue is not going to be settled by one more big war. It will be settled on many small points of stress around the world. And we aren't equipping ourselves to have the *force* where we need it."

The big issues, Drew thought wearily. His father, having settled so many little things, was now ready for the big things. Like where and when and how the wars should be fought and law and order established everywhere. Personally, he thought, I want to work on the little things. Like whom shall I love and exactly who am I anyway?

"I'll tell you something," said General Drummond.

Indeed, thought Drew, he will.

"As long ago as '47 I was plugging for three or four airborne divisions, with transport, which could be moved anywhere in the world in a matter of days. The potential of these divisions in readiness is tremendous. If we'd had them in '50 there wouldn't have been a war in Korea. But we didn't have 'em and now a lot more people are thinking the way a very few of us were six years ago. But it's coming, I believe. When our divisions are equipped with atomic weapons, it will surely come to pass. It's one reason I'm glad you followed my advice and took airborne training after you came back in '48, Drew."

A parachute comes in at a fast diving glide, Drew remembered. When you hit, your feet seem to split and a wave of pain flashes to your temples. You somersault and you almost, but not quite, black out. In that moment you are not really a man. You're nothing. Then you pick yourself up and try to remember who you are.

"I know," said General Drummond, "that you've thought what atomic weapons mean to the foot soldier. The skill and intelligence and judgment necessary in addition to ordinary soldiering guts. Certainly the Army is thinking about it. That's what I'm trying to get across to you, Drew, when I say the Army wants and needs you.

32

You're one of the most experienced field soldiers among our younger officers . . ."

I've seen too much of it, Drew thought. I've been brutal and subjected to brutality and, for the rest of my life, I would be gentle. I would soberly put the drunks to bed and lean from open windows to gaze on quiet piazzas. If I have been *something,* I now would be *nothing.*

General Drummond said abruptly, "I did not mean to rant."

"You've been ranting very hard, Father. But why do you try? Just a few minutes ago you admitted you aren't exactly sure what it's all been about. If doing what you've done and being what you've been hasn't showed you what it's about, how do you expect me to find any happiness and satisfaction in imitating you?"

The General raised his brows. "I don't want you to imitate me. I don't want you to be *like* me. I want you to be *better* than me. That's all I've ever wanted for you."

Drew, believing him, stared at him in surprise. Then how had his father failed so badly ever to make him realize that? Why had he always made him feel that he must be *like* him?

His father said it. "I've made a mess of trying to show you what I meant. If you ever have a son, which please God you'll have some day, you'll understand. These past few years I've seen that you're a better man than I was at your age. I—and many others in the Army—see what you can become."

"What can I become?" His tone was dry. "A tired and perplexed division commander pushing my troops across Outer Mongolia some day?"

"There are worse things." The General stared across the river. "If that was the way the dice fell, there could be worse things. Do you see"—he frowned—"I don't like to use the word, but do you see the nobility implicit in—in enduring the shape of your life? Do you see that you come of a certain tradition? You do a certain thing well, much as you've rebelled against it, but you do it well, and if you endure it long enough great satisfaction will come to you and you'll see there really was nothing more important than that. I said a while ago I wondered what it was all about. I guess I really know. I guess that's what it's all about."

Tradition, Drew thought scornfully. There must have been a time when a cult of nobility arose from carrying burdens on the head. And then someone invented the wheel. That was one trouble with a tradition.

"A father wants his son to be better than he has been," General Drummond said slowly. "But no man is Adam and every man remembers his father. Figuratively, if not literally. A man is a link between the past and the future, and it's no good to look at the past without seeing a future, and you never can see the future without looking at the past." He grimaced. "I'm becoming quite a philosopher in my old age. But I'm thinking of us, the Drummonds . . ."

At last Drew interrupted him. "Father." His voice sounded weary. "You really came here, didn't you, to make sure I share your view of things by glorifying the past to me?"

"Not glorifying," General Drummond said. "But examining. I want the truth of it. Yes, I suppose—I know that I want you to see things my way." He raised his head and looked at Drew. "Also there's the fact I'd like to *be* with you for a while. After all these years when we— I'd hoped you could find a little time."

Drew did not answer him immediately. Make him go home, he thought. Then he felt depressed as he imagined him passing the long afternoons at Burning Brook, sitting alone, staring across the hills in the heat haze.

It was dark when he left Florence. The Citroën plunged through the endless bright tunnel of its headlights. There was mist in the lowlands and wind on the crests. Above, the moon pursued its predictable course. Here below, on the twisting macadam which sucked at the tires, he felt confused. His father was not now as he always had seemed to him. In whom had a change been worked, or had change come to both of them?

He sped through the narrow street of a town, blasting the horn, seeing dark-garbed figures press against gray walls. And then he rushed downward. The road straightened and on the right sprawled the pale skeleton of the American military cemetery in the moonlight. He didn't want to think about military cemeteries or military families or military books. It was better to think of tonight's objective, the beautiful American movie actress—correction, Marcia, my love. But he was thinking of his father.

The General had ordered dinner served in the suite and he'd talked of plans. He didn't want to stay in an expensive hotel; he must find a flat where Harry would scrounge and cook and do for him. He was employing a secretary, some American woman whom he was bringing all the way from Rome, to take the dictation that bubbled in him and copy the family notes and letters he had brought with him from Burning Brook. And he wanted Drew nearby. Above all, he said, he wanted him there.

It was pathetic. His father was as incapable of writing a book as of swimming the ocean. And he knew himself that he could not write it; he tacitly admitted his incapability when he said he would not want to publish it. The proposed history of the family, Drew realized, was only a device which his father had thought up in order to stay near him and try to persuade him to remain in the Army. It would not work. To the contrary, the mere thought of the past generations hardened his determination to quit.

Beyond Poggibonsi he turned west and ascended a narrow, twisting valley whose hills shouldered out the moon. Soon, however, he climbed into moonlight that lay like snow on the uplands. The head-lights struck a mistlike curdling in which hoofs took shape. He slowed and halted behind a concentrated flock of bleating sheep. A dog glared back with yellow eyes and began quartering the flock. He sensed rather than heard the shepherd. Then he smelled him, garlic and sweat, as he stepped quietly beside the car.

"Good evening, signor." He wore an ancient cape; white teeth gleamed in the shadow of a broad-brimmed hat.

"Good evening."

"Do you have a light, signor?"

"Yes, indeed. And a cigarette too."

"Ah!" He sniffed the cigarette and held it up in the moonlight. "Americano?"

"Americano."

The shepherd struck the match, and by its light Drew saw that he was a very old man. He dragged deeply on the cigarette and handed back the box of matches in a curled, leathery hand. "If you will turn off the lights, signor, you may pass in a moment."

He turned off the headlights and the shepherd went ahead, calling to his flock, turning it from the road. In a moment his voice came dis-tinctly from a distance: "Pass on, signor."

He turned on the lights and moved ahead slowly. From the left the shepherd called, "God go with you, signor, and thanks."

He paused at a fork and heard wind singing in the telephone and electric wires which ran from the lower valley to the castle. Following the wires up the road to the left, he soon heard the rushing of a stream. A bridge rattled under the car and far ahead he saw the dim bulk of Castello di Falcari against the night sky. The steep approach was lined by cypresses which eventually opened their ranks and enclosed a gravel turn-around where he stopped the car and got out. Frogs croaked in the muddy moat. The castle walls seemed to exude a cold, dank breath.

Castello di Falcari had been completed in 1340, Marcia had told him. It was triangular, designed on the same plan as the well-known Castello di Sarzanello, north of Pisa, with three round bastions joined by high strong walls. Wide plinths rose halfway up the walls, which were defended by machicolations at the level of the battlements. Long ago an olive grove had been planted in its tumbled outwork. The bridge across the moat never had been widened to accept a carriage, but there had been stables near the outworks in the eighteenth and nineteenth centuries. When they burned down, no one had cared sufficiently to rebuild them; the Di Falcaris had become accustomed to living in more comfortable places. The bridge did not draw now, of course, yet it still was a stout bridge which echoed firmly to his footsteps.

A light bulb glowed at the first turning of the long bridge. No entrance was there, however, for you had to take another turn on the moat. In the old days one would have been under direct attack from the battlements of the main castle, the outwork and the keep. It was not surprising that invaders had failed to destroy the Di Falcaris; only time had managed it, with a sad and strange deviation in the last of them. He made the final turn and entered the gateway, a dimly lighted passage under the protection of the rectangular keep.

One of the later generations had installed a great pull bell beside a huge oaken door. He yanked it and listened to its distant clamor. In a moment Ugo, the caretaker, who lived on the first floor of the keep with his wife, opened a small grilled window beside the door. He looked straight at Drew and said in English, "Who's there?"

Drew laughed. "Frankenstein. Open the door, Ugo."

He scowled at Drew. At noon he'd been amiable enough, but apparently he took his castle night watch seriously. Finally, grumbling to himself, he opened the door.

Chapter IV

"Is that you, Drew?" Marcia called down the spiral stone staircase.

"It's Dracula." He laughed hollowly.

"That's real corny," she called.

"I can be real corny, Countess."

She wore a matching skirt and sweater and over her shoulders she'd drawn a cardigan. She had very beautiful legs.

"You have very beautiful legs," he said as he reached the top of the stairs.

"Tell me something I don't know. Like that I'm intelligent or something."

"And intelligent too." He leaned forward to kiss her, and she turned her head quickly. He pecked her cheek. "You remind me of my former wife. When I used to come home at evening I'd kiss her. If it had been a bad day for her, she'd turn her cheek. After a while she always turned her cheek. And eventually I stopped kissing her when I came home at evening."

She smiled faintly and her lips brushed his. "I was married too. Before this one. Remind me to tell you about it some time." She shivered. "It's cold as kraut in here. The fire keeps wanting to go out."

A small fire burned in the large fireplace at one end of the high-ceilinged, beamed living room. He built it up, feeding it carefully with chips and then laying on a large olive backlog. When he turned, she was seated on the sofa, legs curled under her. She smiled at him. "It's nice to have you here, Drew, building up the fire and everything. I was getting lonely."

"I should think you would." He strolled around the large room, which was half of what had once been the main hall of the castle. A full suit of armor, with visor closed, stood by the doorway in loving memory of the fourteenth century. Crossed maces were fastened above the fireplace, and under glass upon one wall was stretched a tattered, stained black and yellow banner of the Di Falcaris which once had streamed from the tower staff. In the center of the room hung a huge eighteenth-century glass chandelier. If the Di Falcaris ever had owned any good paintings, they must have sold them to pay debts, for all that remained were a few depressing efforts by some late nineteenth-century dauber to imitate the Umbrian painters of the fifteenth century. On tables and shelves there were many photographs from the past fifty years, each autographed: a Hapsburg prince, a former Queen of Greece, a noted concert pianist, a duke of the royal family. "Something from everywhere," he said. "Nothing for anybody."

"In a way I like it," she said. "Or I *thought* I did."

"In a way you bought it, didn't you, Marcia?"

She nodded. "When I was a little girl I loved stories about princesses and castles."

"And now, Princess, you have your castle. You found your fairy prince."

"That's a rough joke. I wish you wouldn't joke about it. I mean about Edoardo. Do you want a drink or something?"

"Do you?"

She shook her head. "But help yourself. There's ice in the pantry. I bought an electric refrigerator the day after we were married. They didn't even have a refrigerator here. Can you imagine?"

He didn't want a drink. Wind rattled the folding doors which gave on a broad balcony. He walked to the doors and peered out. The castle keep had been enlarged long ago to provide larger living quarters; there were eighteen rooms on three floors. The balcony of this second floor joined the battlements. You could walk all the way around them, as he had done earlier in the day, or you could descend by a curving stone staircase into the bailey and clamber among the grass-tufted ruins.

"Want to walk around the battlements?" he asked.

"In the dark? In this cold? I should say not." She hesitated. "But if you want to, Drew, I'll get a coat and—"

"I don't want to," he muttered. It was senseless to think of scrambling around the battlements in the dark when he could sit by a warm fire with her. He strolled to the sofa where he noticed a mimeographed script beside her.

"It's an old play," she said. "It was written by a man I knew. I came across it today and I started reading it again. It never was produced. There's no part in it for me." She stared into the fire. "I've never done a play. I never was good enough. I was always an also-ran, my name away down there in teeny type in the movie ads. They always cast me as a prostitute and things like that. I used to be pretty bitter about it. I used to say it was because I'm not flat-chested."

"Just be glad you're not flat-chested," he said.

She looked at him indifferently. "But it was because I'm not a very good actress. I'm really not. But don't think I'm bitter or anything. I don't remember exactly what I said last night in Harry's Bar, but I don't want you to get the idea I was famous or anything. And I'm not rich. In fact, before long I'm going to be broke. I guess that's why I started reading that old play. I was wondering if I can get a job when I go home. But it will work out somehow. The important thing is that I don't do something stupid again, like I did when I married

Edoardo." She grimaced. "This corny thing happened. It could only happen to people who are dishonest—or not very bright. I admit I was being sort of dishonest, but I'd hoped I wasn't *that* dumb. But I am, I guess, or at least I *was*. Never mind all that. Tell me about—"

"You tell me about the corny thing, Marcia."

"Well, I met Edoardo in Cannes. I was staying with friends of friends of mine for a while. They have a villa up in Super Cannes and they're an awfully nice couple. I was sort of putting on the dog and enjoying it. Buying that Citroën for instance, when I didn't need a car at all. So I met Edoardo, and because I was putting on the dog he thought I had a lot of money. And I—well, I thought *he* had a lot of money." She shook her head. "I'm really bad. I *liked* him an awful lot. He was so—respectful. He didn't make passes. Now I know why, but then I thought how grand it was to meet a *gentleman,* a guy who didn't make passes. Because I respected him I thought I'd come to love him and—" She breathed deeply. "At any rate, I thought *he* had money and he thought *I* did and—isn't that corny?"

"It's real corny, Marcia."

She nodded her head vigorously. "But that's the way it goes. You start getting into corny situations and it's awful hard to stop. I came to Europe three months ago because I finally could afford it. George, the man I divorced, paid off with twenty thousand dollars in a lump. No alimony. I didn't try to take him for any alimony. I felt so *sorry* for him—after I stopped feeling so sorry for myself. I'd loved him or thought I'd loved him, and he thought he loved me. We were married three years. His name is George Sadlerson, he's an agent in Hollywood. Then he got this awful thing on a girl in Hollywood and she got it too. He finally told me and I got mad, naturally, and—well, I won't bore you with the details. But after a while I just felt sorry for him and I knew I didn't love him and I settled for him paying me twenty thousand, because it was all he could afford at the time, and he married the girl and I hope they live happily ever after. Only the whole thing was so—so cheap and corny." Her voice rose. "What a stinking, corny life!"

Probably it would not seem so bad to her if she were not so candid with herself, he thought. Why, then, was candor supposedly a marketable virtue to be paid off in happiness? True, he admired her effort at complete honesty with herself, but he knew that she was not happier because of it. How did the soap operas ever have the brass to say that if you only would be candid with yourself life indeed would be beautiful?

Rising, she went to the fire and sat on the floor facing it, hugging her knees. "Tell me about your father, Drew. What's he doing in Florence?"

"He wants to write a book."

"About what?"

"A history of the family."

"Your family?" She looked around at him intently. "Do *you* have a family anybody could write a book about?"

"Well, *he* thinks so."

"That's wonderful. To have a family like that, I mean. To *know* where you came from. Doesn't it make you feel you *know* who you are? The way I feel I don't know sometimes. I grew up in Brentwood, that's near Hollywood, and I knew my mother, of course, and my grandmother. But my father died when I was three and I don't know where he came from. All I really know is that when my mother was growing up her father ran a coalyard in Quincy, Illinois."

"Don't worry about it, Marcia." He got up and sat on the floor near her. "The value of knowing where you came from is greatly exaggerated."

"That's because you know where you came from. A couple of times, when things have been an awful rat-race and I've gotten so sick of pretending—a couple of times I've wondered who in hell *am* I?"

Identity, the immemorial quest. Who am I, Lord? Whither camest I and where do I go?

"I guess all this"—she indicated the vast, shadowed room—"this castle—I guess all this was me trying to know who I am. As if I ever could be a Di Falcari. What a laugh! I'm an awful egotist, Drew. Tell me about your family. Who were they?"

"None was very famous. They were soldiers. It was a military family. There are lots of military families in the States. I mean a family where son follows father into service. Ours just goes back a little farther than some."

"Back to where?"

"There was one in the Revolution named Nathan. Nobody ever mentions him much. Apparently he wasn't respectable and nobody knows anything about him except that he was a mountain man. He slunk over the mountains with Nolichucky Jack and some others and they killed a few Englishmen at a place called the Cowpens. And that's all we know about Nathan except that he migrated to Nashville, or Nashboro as it was called then, in 1791."

"Who was his son?"

"The one we call General Sam. Quite a character. He fought in the War of 1812 and became a brigadier general in the Tennessee Militia. He died of fever on the way to Mexico City with Winfield Scott. By marriage and peculation he set up the place in Tennessee, Burning Brook, the place the family still owns. He had two sons and they were both educated at the Academy—West Point. They fought in the Mexican War and the Civil War, one for the North and the other for the South. The Confederate was killed. The other was my great-grandfather. Well, my great-grandfather had two sons and *they* graduated from the Academy. Gets monotonous, doesn't it? Uncle Chad was killed at the Little Big Horn, but nothing much ever happened to my grandfather during his long Army career. He spent the Spanish-American War in places like Tampa, Florida. Well, I hate to mention it, but *he* had two sons. All of them had other children who died young, but they kept dragging two sons to manhood—except my father. I'm the only child, and I think that has always bothered Father. Anyway, you can imagine where my father was educated. But you should meet my Uncle Judd. He had no use for a military career after serving as a sergeant with the First Division in the First War. He's a wonderful guy. He has great distaste for a life of enforced monotony punctuated by sprees of killing."

"You sound like a pacifist," she said.

"I've considered it. But I never had the guts to be one. I mean I don't have the temperament for it. At the last minute I always say, what the hell, let's fight."

"But you haven't followed the—tradition."

"In a halfhearted way I have. I'm in the Army."

"*You* are in the Army!" she exclaimed. "What an egotist I am. I blab on and I never even asked you, you never told me— What do you do?"

"I'm in the Infantry. But I think I'm getting out."

"Why?"

He shrugged. "I've had it."

"I should think because of your family— Are you an enlisted man?"

He tossed his cigarette into the fire. "Suppose I said I was? Would that make any difference?"

"Not to me. But maybe it would make a difference to you. I thought enlisted men always hated the Army and officers loved it."

"Not exactly. I'm a major, Marcia."

"Oh." She did not look impressed, and he thought, She's not a snob. Leaning forward, he kissed her cheek and said, "I love you."

"That's not true." Her plaintive expression reflected her mordant desire for honesty. "You couldn't be in love with me. People don't just go around falling in love with each other on sight. Even *I* know that. What you said is— It's immature."

She was right, of course. When younger he had frequently fallen in love; he could walk down a street and commit the rest of his life to a passing girl. But he hadn't fallen in love for many years now. He regretted it, he felt he was somehow emotionally impoverished. And sometimes he genuinely wished to do something about it. As now. By telling her he loved her, he hoped that actually he might.

"I don't see why you want to quit the Army," she said. "What's wrong with generations of a family being soldiers?"

"Absolutely nothing. Nothing more wrong than in generations of men being stock brokers. Except for the last generation. The only trouble with a rigid tradition of any sort is with the last generation. When you feel forced to do a thing because your ancestors were doing it, that is the trouble, that's the wrong."

"Fortunately," she said, "that sort of thing doesn't happen so often in America."

"I think it does," he said. "In America we're the prisoners of some pretty rigid traditions. But I'm talking about only one, the one the Drummonds fell prisoner to. The romantic tradition. In America we built it and we're still building it. We're a natural for it. Our mountains and skyscrapers go straight up and our prairies and streets go straight out, and when we've climbed as high as we can and traveled as far and as fast as we can, we like to say we're doing it like the old-timers. We're in the tradition. Living it up. Grab it while you can get it. Through the gap and over the mountains. But chivalrous, you understand. Great talkers. Great lovers. Great fighters. But always fighting for the right, of course. That's basic to the romantic tradition. Fighting's fair when you're for the right—and the tradition says we always have been." He frowned. "I'm getting as garrulous as my old man."

She rested her chin on her knees, staring at him. "Don't stop talking, Drew. Nobody ever talks to me this way. They think I wouldn't understand. But I do."

He smiled. "While I'm in the mood let me tell you something. Did you know that we've conquered more territory than any people in history except the British—counting our conquest of the Indians since 1800? The question is rhetorical because you did not know. Few do. But it's a fact. We're a fierce and warlike people, Marcia, and we've

42

slaughtered a few million to prove it. Our romantic tradition says we nearly always acted in self-defense. In order, for example, to protect the poor, defenseless, golden-haired women of the covered wagon trains against the bad, bad Indians. That's malarkey. Our men were simply horny for land, oodles and boodles of it, and they went sashaying after it with a bang-bang and God help the poor Indian who didn't move on. The romantic tradition protects the memories of these pioneers."

The telephone rang.

"You're saved by the bell," he said.

"Don't answer it," Marcia said.

It rang again.

"I'll answer it." She rose. "No, I won't either. You answer it, and if it's Edoardo I'm not here. I don't want to talk to anybody—except you."

He went to the phone and lifted it and said, *"Pronto,"* and a voice replied, *"Qui il* Dottore Sabraccio."

"Mike! What's new?"

"Do not tell me," Dr. Mike Sabraccio said in English. "It cannot be, but it certainly is the estimable Major Drummond. What are you doing out there, Drew? On second thought, perhaps you'd rather not tell me."

"Marcia and I are discussing the American romantic tradition. That is, I'm discussing it and she's listening."

"Who is it?" Marcia asked.

"Dr. Sabraccio."

"That head-shrinker!"

"She calls you a head-shrinker," Drew said to Sabraccio.

"Tell her I unfortunately cannot shrink them small enough. Ask her if she'd like to hear a report on Edoardo."

"You want to hear a report on Edoardo, Marcia?"

"Only if he's dead."

"Only if he's dead," he said to Sabraccio.

"There's nothing quite like the outraged sexual pride of the American female," Sabraccio said. "You might work that into your lecture on the romantic tradition, Drew. When she's in a mood to listen, tell her that Edoardo called me from Rome a little while ago. He's most distraught and ashamed, poor boy. It's an interesting symptom. Tell her as his physician I say it's an interesting symptom. He's ill and he needs her understanding."

"What's the matter with him?"

"I thought Marcia had probably explained to you. Edoardo has pronounced homosexual tendencies which—in fact—"

"I know that, Mike. I thought you meant he had the flux or the bellyache or something in Rome."

"Then everybody understands," Sabraccio said. "I won't detain you longer from your—ah—lectures. This is fine, Drew, very fine. I hope you two are enjoying yourselves. With abandon. There's nothing like abandon for two healthy young animals, if you'll pardon the description. Why don't you both come and have dinner with us tomorrow evening?"

"Thanks, it sounds like fun. My father arrived in Florence today. I don't know—"

"Bring him along," Mike said. "*Him* I want to meet. He has always sounded like an interesting repressive force. What's his purpose?"

"He wants to make sure I stay in the Army."

"You need allies, pal. Come tomorrow evening and bring him."

"I'll try. We'll be there unless you hear to the contrary. So long, Mike."

"We'll be where?" Marcia asked after he hung up.

"Mike invited us—and Father—to dinner tomorrow night."

She smiled suddenly. "I like that. I don't like Sabraccio much, but I like him asking us to dinner together. It's very settled and domestic like, you and me being asked out to dinner. Where did you meet him?"

"In the war, the Second War. He was a psychiatrist in our Army. His parents were Italian, but he was educated in the States. After the war he came back here to practice. Maybe he's basically the reason I decided to come to Florence on this recuperation leave."

"Recuperation?" She sank down slowly on the sofa. "Were you wounded in Korea?"

"Yes. But nothing permanent."

She clasped her hands together in a childlike gesture. "Tell me about Korea."

Tell me a story, Daddy, he thought. Tell me a story of the olden times and heroism and victory.

He sat down on the sofa. "It's not worth it, Marcia. Korea is a dreary place and you're a romantic girl."

"Romantic? Like in the romantic tradition?"

He smiled and touched her chin gently. "Like in the romantic tradition. The golden girl. The figure, the desire, the symbol men stencil

44

on the noses of their planes and paste under the lids of their foot-lockers . . ."

He paused, suddenly remembering. . . . Yes, the name had been Marcia. Strange that he had not thought of it before. Yet it was not strange, for you tried to forget rather than to remember, and there were many girls in the world named Marcia.

"Since we're finally getting acquainted"—he smiled at her—"you never told me your name. Before you were the Contessa di Falcari and Mrs. George Sadlerson."

"Marcia Dale," she said. "It's my real name and the name I used in pictures."

Marcia Dale. If the kid ever had mentioned the full name, he didn't remember it. He did not even remember the face of the photograph.

"Have you ever been in Fall River, Massachusetts, Marcia?"

"No. I've been in Boston, but I don't even know where Fall River is." She looked at him wonderingly. "What are you getting at?"

"Did you ever know a guy named LeRoy Tate?"

"If you're going to give me the third degree, you'll have to give me a clue. I've met a lot of guys."

"A kid aged nineteen in 1950. A big kid, with sandy hair and a lot of muscles he was proud of. From Fall River, Massachusetts."

"Did he ever get out to the Coast?"

"Only once. He passed through Bremerton, Washington, in a troop movement to the Far East. Could you have seen him there?"

"No. I've never even been in Seattle." She touched his arm. "Either smile or look sad, darling. It tears me up when you look both ways at once. What worries you about LeRoy Tate? I certainly never met him."

He could not smile and he tried not to look sad. "Nothing now. Nothing more than sometimes worries me about hundreds of other guys I remember." He stared into the fire. "Maybe that's one reason I want to get out of the Army. The responsibility you feel for so many LeRoy Tates."

"Darling, don't." She drew close to him. "Whatever it is, don't think about it."

"There's not some one terrible thing to be forgotten." He could smile at her now. "This is not a dramatic case on your hands, Marcia."

"Darling—I want to stop calling you that. Everybody calls every-body darling in Hollywood and I don't—" She looked at him, her lips parted.

45

Screen close-up of Marcia Dale, he thought, and he didn't want to think it. He kissed her. Her lips were warm. She kissed—expertly. He wished she did not kiss quite so expertly. And then he thought, But it's a part of her trade. He told himself to cut thinking that. He held her tightly, kissing her, feeling the fast beat of both their hearts.

She moved. "You must not say you love me, Drew."

"But—"

"Hush." She placed a finger on his lips and rose suddenly, tossing her head in a gesture that she must often have employed when— He told himself not to think about that.

"Let's not talk about us," she said. "Let's—"

Drawing an arm around her hips, he pulled her down beside him. He kissed her and gently touched her breast. Her breath quickened and her tongue touched his. Then she swung to her feet again, breathing quickly, staring down at him.

"You listen to me, Drew. Sit right where you are and listen. I have a long way to go and I'm not going to make it if we do now what both of us want to. In a few days it would be over and the whole thing would fall down in another lousy heap. There'd be nothing, and I've had enough of *nothing*. I want something that lasts. I want to be *good*. Do you understand? I never want to be bad again. But I don't want you to leave me. Give me a little time, won't you? I want to get out of this place. We're going up to Florence tomorrow and I'm going to check into a hotel. I want to meet your father and have him like me. I want everything to be *right* with us straight down the line. Now I'm going up those stairs to my room and I'm going to lock the door. It'll kill me, but that's what I'm going to do. You know where your room is, where you put your bag this morning, and that's where you're going to sleep."

Leaning forward, she kissed his forehead lightly. "Good night, Drew."

He stared after her, then followed her into the hall and watched her ascend the stone stairs. He put a foot on the first step and paused, listening to her receding footsteps, and then to the closing and locking of a door.

You're a pretty lousy lover, he told himself. Your record is definitely not superior in the love department, Mac. Except, sometimes, when the uniform has given you a boost. The paratroop boots, during the time you wore them, were helpful with the girls of Augusta too. But love, no.

He found himself sprawled on the sofa again, staring at the fire.

46

It had been a close thing with her. He had talked too much. A big talker could not be a big lover. But what was she driving at? The possible for them was a passionate, fleeting relationship. Yet she seemed to be seeking some permanence. Perhaps not with him personally, but *from* him impersonally. She seemed to wish love to do what love in their case could not: to wait without reason, to grow without roots.

Probably love was the wrong word for it, however. The word was desire. Yet desire could sustain you too. Look at LeRoy Tate.

Chapter V

It is highly desirable, as every soldier knows, to remain as far as possible to the rear in a war. But Drew's luck had not been good in that respect in the Second War, from which he had ribbons to prove his bad luck—or, as civilians foolishly view the bright bars of the military chest, his heroism. And then in November of 1950, he saw that his bad luck was unchanged. For they snatched him, flew him, hurled him with distressing rapidity from Benning to Korea.

On paper he was an infantry captain, trained as an airborne soldier, taken from the infantry school because the need for experienced combat officers was crucial. In person he was a worried man, with the occasional tinny taste of fear in his mouth when he remembered how unpleasant combat is. But outwardly calm and even, at times, displaying a fatalistic cheerfulness in a necessary pose of self-delusion.

He had asked for it. Not to be sent to Korea, heaven knew. But he had run the risk of being sent to die among Yahoos anywhere when, in 1948, he had done what would have been unthinkable to him in 1945. He had gone back to the Army. For a complexity of reasons, all quite vague to him as a C-54 bore him west, he had become a soldier again. He had said to himself, I will be a good soldier. And now he remembered that good soldiers often die.

In Korea he fell down, down the table of organization through the confusion of war. From Army to Corps (a paper organization which disturbed him greatly, for he believed the American tradition that in war a corps must be a strong command organization). From paper Corps to Division—and down to Regiment.

While he waited there he heard about the Big Picture, as enunciated by the old five-star general who had flown to Korea and issued a grandiose statement to the troops, pointing them north to the Yalu and saying it would be all over by Christmas. Then Old Five-Stars flew back to Tokyo while his tired Eighth Army began to form along the Chongchon River. Remember the emotions at Regiment on the morning of November twenty-fifth, a cold gray day in a hilly part of Korea where the land was the color of the moon seen through dark glasses. There was no jubilance along the Chongchon, for wise old hands knew that whenever generals said it would be all over by Christmas it never was. Old Five-Stars, who was a wise old hand himself except when dreams of glory clouded his vision, should have known better than to say it. It was bad luck. Only fools failed to realize it as the tired, underequipped Eighth groped numbly in the effort to form and move ahead. Many felt their luck was bad, but how bad they did not know. They did not know that three Chinese Communist armies, totaling about one hundred thousand men, were at that moment pressing south by night and fading into the land by day. Within a few hours the Chinese would pierce and sweep like a scythe.

So, at Regiment, Drew heard something of an old man's dreams of glory and saw something of the Army's depleted and overly dispersed strength. They would not let him stay. They flagged him on toward Battalion, up forward somewhere, up the valley, and they even provided a precious jeep and driver to take him there.

He came, through snow flurries that fogged the dun-colored landscape of late afternoon, to the Battalion Command Post. It was situated in a farmhouse between the river and a field of cornstubble and it smelled of manure and sweat. The Major commanding was staring at a map and gnawing on a turkey drumstick miraculously provided by a thoughtful government to all possible numbers of its troops in celebration of the national holiday called Thanksgiving. The Major had a tic in his left eyelid that bothered Drew because he thought it denoted nervousness, though it later developed the Major was an excellent officer who was simply exhausted at the time. He said he was glad to see Drew and asked him if he'd had combat. When Drew told him that he had in the Second War, the Major said this was different from anything he or anyone had seen.

He waved the drumstick at the map and started to brief Drew, but suddenly he abandoned the effort and began telling him what a fouled-up situation it was. He was as browned off as the lowliest private because his battalion had had it for a long time now, with little rest, and he blamed no one except Old Five-Stars in Tokyo, on whom he heaped obscenity. Which was taking a rather large view of things when you were in a farmhouse between a cornfield and the Chong-chon River. When he was out of breath, he said, "It's a lousy deal, Drummond, but you'll have to take over E Company tonight." Then the Major briefed him.

The companies of the Regiment were disposed widely in a semi-circle facing generally north, which was the direction they were sup-posed to go, regardless of the bad supply situation, regardless of every-thing except Old Five-Stars' Cortesan dream of planting his guidons along the Yalu. Easy Company, down to a strength of one hundred and twelve men, had moved north along the west bank of the river yesterday and taken up positions vacated by Fox Company, which now was in support to the south and close to the west bank of the river. George Company was a mile north of the Battalion Command Post and spread over three hills on the east bank of the river. Easy had run into a little trouble last night, the Major said, and its C.O., a first lieutenant, had been badly clobbered and carried back with three walk-ing wounded this morning. Its mission was simple (from the bird's-eye view): Stay on Hill 418 until advised of the coming kick-off. If forced out, which was unthinkable, pull back to Hill 412 on Fox's left and link up.

The Major sounded embarrassed in explaining the plan, so that Drew's respect for him increased, for both knew that disengagement and withdrawal is the most difficult maneuver, and that Easy might not be able to find Hill 412 in a country of hills which looked alike, and that Fox might not be there for linking. With increasing embar-rassment the Major explained that Easy had been out of communica-tion since morning when its Signal Corps Radio, a 300, had failed. He mournfully described the inadequacies of the SCR 300 and SCR 536 and SCR 619 in the hills. Drew asked if Artillery didn't have a spotter up there whose communications Easy could use. It did, the Major said, but Artillery was tied in with Regiment, which was very busy and presumably would forward anything important from Easy to the Battalion C.P., though it had not thus far today. The Major said he'd sent out two men to run a wire from Fox to Easy, but there was no light 130 wire available and the regular grade was too heavy for the men to carry over the hills. So they'd walked around hills until their wire gave out four hundred yards short of Easy's command post.

His luck was very bad indeed, Drew thought. And it grew no bet-ter when the Major said that Easy was out of rations and low on ammunition. A supply party of twenty Korean bearers was being organized now and he, Drummond, would leave with them and the enlisted man who had brought in the wounded lieutenant. The Major pointed the route: north along the east bank of the river by truck for three miles to a guarded ford and then wade the ford and follow a winding track which eventually led north to Hill 418. Drew looked out at the gathering darkness, and the Major said there would be a moon tonight, which was merely optimism and not weather forecasting.

Drew asked for food, for he knew that in war the most important thing next to avoiding combat is to eat heartily when you have the chance. He ate a heaping mess kit of turkey and mashed potatoes and gravy, forcing the glutinous mass upon the knotted dread in his belly with gulps of hot coffee. Then he drew a bedroll and carbine and ten clips, which he stuffed into his fleece jacket, and four grenades and a few extra clips for his .45. From his B-4 bag, so carefully filled in Tokyo, he took only extra socks and a first-aid kit and a couple of packs of cigarettes. Everything else he left in his B-4 bag in a corner of the farmhouse, and he went looking for his supply party.

A tall kid was cursing a gang of Koreans milling around a truck. He was, Drew saw by the light of a Coleman lamp, the all-American-boy type: tall and wide-shouldered and blue-eyed, with blond hair tufting from under his pile cap. The type, Drew thought, who sometimes is too big to fight well.

When Drew asked if he were heading for Easy, the kid grinned down at him and said, "Yes, sir. You heading for a fight, Captain?"

"Could be. I'm going to Easy. What's your name?"

"Pfc Tate. Sir."

"Okay, Tate, let's roll."

They finally herded the bearers into the truck on top of their frames of C-rations and ammunition and they lashed the tail gate and rounded up the driver, a corporal who left the command-post area reluctantly. Tate, who rode between Drew and the driver, wore a bandolier over his jacket and carried an M-1. When Drew asked him where his helmet was, he gave his all-American-boy grin again.

"You try to put that helmet you're carrying over that pile cap you're wearing, Captain, and it don't fit. Take off your pile cap and you'll freeze. That's why nearly all of Easy Company dumped its helmets before we took off yesterday."

No helmets, no rations, no communications and practically no ammunition.

50

"Where you from, Captain?" A big talker, Tate. Friendly and open-handed with his cigarettes. He wanted the world, or at least those members of it in the truck cab, to know he was from Fall River, Massachusetts.

Tate rattled on as they bumped north along the rutted road which followed the invisible river. Drew stared, troubled, at George Company's fires to the east, flaring beacons in the night to an enemy. But this was another war and presumably the men who had been here for a time understood how to fight it.

Tate interrupted his lecture on the glories of Fall River to say he'd sure enjoy a woman now. "But you know what's a fact, Captain? Even if it was lying all around asking for it, I wouldn't touch it."

"The hell you say," the driver said.

"I'm tellin' you what's a fact," Tate said. "I wouldn't touch it. I'm savin' mine. I got a girl, she's a movie star. If I told you who she is . . ."

Drew watched the road in the dimmed headlights. North, across the river, were the flickering points of other fires, presumably on Fox Company's ridges. It was incredible, he thought. And then he felt the cold night air and tried to understand.

Tate was taking a photograph from his wallet. "Lookit here. Look at her picture, Captain, and see what she wrote on it for me."

He suddenly thought he heard small-arms fire and he rolled down the window. The distant popping was unmistakable. Then, distinctly, the *thump-thump-thump* of a BAR.

Tate said, "It's this way every night, Captain. A few gooks crawling around. Lemme tell you about her . . ." And Tate was describing his prowess as a lover and the phenomenal, the insatiable receptivity of the girl whose photograph he carried, whoever she was.

Drew paid little attention. He strained to hear the distant popping of small-arms fire that faded behind them on George Company's ridges. He thought about the ford, which was about two-tenths of a mile ahead now, according to the speedometer. The Major had said it was guarded by an M-4 tank and a quad-50 and one squad detached from George Company. He tried not to think by the book and not to wonder why the Major had held George Company back instead of placing it to flank the ford, which was vital and yet dangerously exposed. The positions must be dictated by the necessity of holding the high ground, and when you had to hold the high ground how could you hope to retain the low ground too? Especially since your forces were incredibly small for the job to be done and you were here only as a token, a symbol of a unity of nations which did not care if you died —as long as you died a gallant internationalist.

"You ought to hear how it was in Bremerton," Tate said. "She knew I was shipping through and she flew up from Hollywood—"

"Hold it!" Drew cried to the driver.

A wire, strung with mortar shells, was stretched across the road at shoulder height. Drew knocked off the truck lights and flung open the door as a tommy gun chattered from the left and rifle fire opened from the right. The driver gagged and fell forward on the wheel. Drew tossed a grenade to the right and dropped to the ground, clutching his carbine, and Tate leaped after him. He crawled under the truck, feeling Tate behind him and hearing the Korean bearers howling and leaping over the tailboard. When he came out the other side of the truck, he pulled the pin from another grenade and lobbed it at the flash of the tommy gun in the darkness. As the grenade exploded, he sprang up and raced toward the river, weaving through a confusion of men. Tate galloped beside him. Then he tripped on a rock and fell and lay still for a moment, recovering his knocked wind. Tate halted and came back, muttering, "Geez, Captain, you hit? Geez, Captain . . ." Tate lifted him in powerful arms, muttering, "I'll carry you, Captain." But Drew shook himself free and said, "I'm okay," and they went on to the river where they dropped to the ground, panting and listening.

To the south, around the Battalion Command Post, there was heavy firing. Suddenly from the east came the faint *ta-ta-ta-ta* of a bugle, four distinct notes in the night, and then the *whump-whump-whump* of mortars stepping upward, seeking range. One of George Company's ridges flared with rifle and automatic fire. There was, somewhere, another faint sound, indistinguishable yet vaguely familiar. Drew put an ear to the ground and recognized the steady tramp of men, apparently along the road. The tank and quad-50 at the ford must have been caught napping. As they rode north in the truck, the enemy must have been moving south off the road and now they had overrun or invested every position on the east bank.

"We'll cross over the river," Drew said, "and try to join up with Easy or Fox." Following his example, Tate pulled off his boots and socks and pants and rolled up his heavy underwear.

The river, icy cold, snatched at them. They floundered on, holding weapons and clothing high, and trying to control their chattering teeth. When they reached the west bank, they dried their numbed feet with their jackets and put on socks and boots. The moon had risen and by its light they trotted north along the edges of rice paddies. From the area of Fox Company's position there rose ragged firing. It died away and resumed again, more heavily.

Drew paused at the end of the paddies and motioned Tate off a crest where he was silhouetted. Moonlight silvered the land, shining on the ice film of the paddies. It was very cold. Below them a dry creek bed curled toward the river and beyond the bed a steep, rocky hill rose whitely in the moonlight. Beyond the hill would be another, and then another, and somewhere to the north on a hill much like this would be elements of Fox Company. The firing indicated that they'd have trouble getting inside a friendly perimeter. But they had to get in, they had to join up with somebody, for the whole front was straining and it was not a night to wander alone in the moonlight.

From the gulley below them came a strange pattering sound, as of mice in the walls of an old house. Drew tugged Tate's arm and they sank into brush. From the direction of the river, around a bend in the gulley, ran a group of men, closely bunched. Drew counted six, unarmed, running up the creek bed. Tate fumbled with his rifle and Drew laid a restraining hand on his arm. Another group of six appeared, running unarmed, and after them, at an interval of about ten yards, six more. In a moment a man on a small, nimble-footed horse came into view, and behind him poured a column of infantry, trotting at double-time, carrying rifles and tommy guns at port. They were tall men, wearing heavy long overcoats which were crossed by white bandoliers. Drew counted hastily—about a hundred and fifty of them running up the gulley. There followed another officer on a small horse, and then another company. As he watched them, Drew realized his mouth was too dry to spit.

"Captain"—Tate's teeth chattered—"let's get the hell out of here."

It was a good idea. But where to go? He wished someone would rouse him from this nightmare and restore him to the peaceful mid-century, this twentieth which the soothsayers had promised would be the finest. At this very moment, somewhere in the old Catawba country of the southern mountains, there must be a poet (he did not know who or why he'd thought of a poet and Catawba) who shaped the finer emotions with chiseled phrases while he, consigned to the outer fringes of the earth, played at this weird game of cops and robbers, this riot of bang-bang and wild Indians. Angry then, angry at his lot and the whole Goddamned crazy world that let some men be sensitively superior poets and others only cops, he got to his feet, swearing. His mouth flooded with saliva and he spat. One for the eye of the superior, critical poet of old Catawba whoever he might be.

"We gotta find Fox," he said, saying it tough, playing it child-like since he had been assigned to play the children's game. And then, ashamed of his flash of self-pity and resentment, he strode into the gulley. Tate followed him. By the time they reached the creek bed he remembered the rules of cops and robbers and ran across the flood of moonlight into the safe shadow of the further hill.

They clambered upward over the boulders of the hill until they reached the crest where they lay down, panting and staring north across the frozen barren hills. They heard firing, but they could not see flashes to guide them across the wasteland.

"I wish I was home," Tate said as he followed him down the hill. In a few seconds he said, "But I'm gonna make home all right. I'm tellin' you what's a fact. I got a date with an angel. You remember that old song, Captain?"

"Pipe down," Drew said. And in a moment, "I know the song."

They slid into a valley over loose rocks and then climbed toward a saddle dimly visible in the moonlight. The silence was oppressive. A turned stone started a small rock slide and they froze. A figure rose against the saddle above them and descended silently. Another, and then another followed. Drew counted five descending quietly. He motioned Tate behind a boulder and then squatted, the barrel of his carbine steady on a rock before him.

Now they heard the scrape of feet and the turning of stones. Suddenly a nasal voice said distinctly, "My achin' back!" Tate rose from his boulder, saying, "For cryin' out loud, they're—"

There were two shots. Tate screamed. His knees buckled and he clutched his belly and fell forward.

Drew shouted, "Hold it! We're Easy Company."

There was silence above and then a warm, husky voice, "Come out with yo' hands up!" And he rose with hands raised, looking down at Tate who moaned, "Oh, Jesus, Jesus, Jesus, oh Jesus Christ!"

Above, the warm voice cried, "Oh, Jesus!" and there was the clatter of steel on rock as two, three men swarmed down and Drew knelt beside Tate.

"Captain," he whimpered, "did it get my—"

"No, Tate, no, it didn't get your—" It was in the belly, he saw, as he fumbled for his first-aid kit, but where or how bad or . . . A dark face, a Negro, pressed over his shoulder, groaning, "Oh, Jesus, I didn' know he was—"

"You're trigger-happy, Johnson," someone said.

"I didn' know," cried Johnson, "I didn' know! I was on the point an' I seen him stand up, I thought to throw, an' I jus' fired from the hip." He sank back on his heels and moaned, his carbine falling from his listless big hands.

Blood oozed from the hole to the right of Tate's navel. When Drew laid the sulfa dressing on the wound, Tate screamed.

"Shut him up," one said tensely. "Shut him up. This place—" "Ah, you shut up," another said. . . . "Okay, Tate," Drew said, "okay. You're going to be okay." But he knew that Tate would not be unless he had expert medical aid soon.

"Let's get goin'," one said.

Drew rose, turning to the voice, unable to make out the face in the moonlight. "What outfit are you men?"

"Jeez, it's a captain," one said. And Johnson, getting to his feet slowly, said, "We're Second Platoon Fox Company, sir. I'm Corporal Johnson an' I reckon we all that's left of Second Platoon. We tried to get in with Third an' we couldn't an' we—we goin' back. They's nothing left of Fox Company, Captain. We goin' back. We was pinched off an' then we was squeezed out, we's all that's left."

Tate whimpered, "Captain, it's killin' me, for Christ sake please get me outta here."

"We're getting out, Tate," Drew said. He asked if anyone had a blanket and one, surprisingly, did. He told them to make a rifle-blanket carry, and when they did not know how, he showed them.

"We're carrying *him?*" someone asked, and Drew said, "We'll take turns." "Then let's get *goin',*" another said urgently, "this place is swarmin' with gooks."

Johnson slung his carbine and said, "I'll carry his feet, I can't look in his face, I didn't know—"

"All *right,*" Drew said. "All right, Johnson. You"—he turned to a figure—"what's your name?"

The man told me his name, but now I can't remember it. I learned all their names, but now I only remember Johnson. And Tate, of course. There have been so many names and faces and it's better I can't remember all of them.

Tate cried out when they lifted him, and then he was silent as Drew led the way down the hill. "Gentle," Johnson kept saying as he carried Tate's feet, "gentle now, gentle."

55

In the valley Drew and another relieved the carriers. Tate, his lips tightly compressed, stared up at Drew as they began the climb up the next hill. He said, "I gotta make it, Captain, I *gotta*."

Drew said, "You'll make it." And then he added, forcing a grin, "Lover Boy."

Tate tried to grin too, but a groan escaped him. He said, "*She* used to call me—"

"Don't talk," Drew said. "Just think about her."

A man asked, "Who's he talking about?"

"His girl," Drew said, "a movie star."

The man said, "No crap?"

"No crap," Tate said, and then he groaned.

When they reached the summit they lay down, gasping for breath. About them rose the conical hills, yellowish white as snow in the moonlight, and silent now as a frozen waste. There must be hundreds of men scampering and scurrying in the valleys, Drew thought. But silently, with a strange silence. Then small-arms fire erupted somewhere and died. And then flashes on the western horizon were followed by the mutter of artillery.

They went down the hill and across the gulley where the two companies of the enemy had passed. When they reached the rice paddies it was almost three o'clock by Drew's wrist watch and clouds were obscuring the declining moon. He put his last dressing on Tate's wound, and Tate, who had been unconscious, suddenly raised his head and said, "Please give me some water."

"No water for gut wounds, boy," Drew said.

Tate said, "Okay, honey."

Someone said, "What's a matter with him, he queer or somethin'?"

Tate said, "Marcia, baby . . ."

Yes, he did call her Marcia. I remember now. But she was not his girl. She was something created, imagined from a found photograph, a phantom story. She was the symbol, the dream pasted under the locker lid of his desire.

The resting men raised themselves to hear Tate's monologue to Marcia until Johnson, hunching to his feet, said, "We shouldn' listen to him, he outa his head." But someone said, "This like tappin' the bedroom, this gal really somethin'." Johnson said, "He outa his head, I say, an' you shouldn' listen to a man outa his head."

But they did listen and whether they believed in his love or, like Drew, did not believe, they began to take a certain pride in him. Lover Boy, they called him, as they lifted him more tenderly and carried him on between the paddies and the river through the darkness. Once he cried out obscenely and one said, "He got to her that time," and Johnson said, "Shame on you fo' listenin', he outa his head an' it's my fault."

Drew told them to be quiet and they went on silently, tiredly in the darkness. Across the river they saw the flicker of fires where he believed the Battalion Command Post had been situated. Telling them to halt and rest, he went on alone cautiously until he saw the reflection of the fires in the river. He crept to the bank and watched and listened. He heard voices above the brawling of the river, and at last he saw men move close to the largest fire. They wore long coats crossed by white bandoliers.

Hurrying back to the men, he urged them on. Pressing them ruthlessly now, allowing no breaks, taking more than his share of the burden of carrying Tate, who moaned and muttered constantly. Light rubbed at the darkness and dawn cracked the eastern sky. They were on a narrow flat between river and hills. He pushed them to the thin cover of brushwood where they flung themselves down, sobbing for breath.

In a few moments he crawled to the edge of the brush and stared south at a gap which the river had cut in the hills. He remembered coming through that gap in the jeep yesterday. The Regimental Command Post had been a couple of miles beyond it. Johnson crawled to him and lay prone beside him. "Tate," Johnson said. "He hemorrhagin'." Drew crawled back to Tate. Blood had soaked his abdomen and crotch. His eyes were closed and his lips moved soundlessly.

"I'm starved," someone said, and none answered him.

Nothing could help Tate now, possibly not even a skilled surgeon in an antiseptic hospital. They could not carry him to safety and they could not leave him to die. They could only carry him until he died so that in the stillness of some future night, if they had any future still nights, they would not awaken with the guilt of having left Tate. He and Johnson, at least, had the fear of guilt.

Johnson crawled to them, his eyes wide and white in his black face, saying, "Look, look Captain!" Drew raised himself and saw river mist boiling across the flats. "It a sign," Johnson whispered jubilantly, "it a sign!" The mist thickened quickly, magically, and Drew and Johnson prodded the men to their feet. Then Johnson took the foot of Tate's litter and Drew the head and they went on south across the fields.

About a half hour later Drew heard the tramp of feet and murmured, "Hold it!" They sank down in the mist and Drew passed the litter rifles to the two unarmed men. Tate began to mutter incoherently and Drew pressed his hand tightly over his mouth. Dimly, then, they made out an enemy column marching north along a track they had not noticed before. Tate twitched his head, trying to free himself of Drew's restraining hand, and the column passed from sight.

Drew moved his hand and Tate looked at him clearly. He said, "She has a mole on her left hipbone, Captain, and it moves when she moves."

"Who is she?" somebody asked.

"I *told* you," Tate said petulantly. "I *told* you. Show 'em the picture, Captain."

"Later," Drew said. "We've got to hurry."

"Please, Captain."

"Later!"

They made up the litter and carried him toward the hills as the sun began to burn through the mist. When they reached brushwood at the foot of the hills, Tate was dead.

We left him there. We couldn't bury him in the frozen earth. Johnson cried, I remember, dreading his guilt. He needn't have. He died himself a few days later. We left the picture with Tate's body. I remember us passing it around. It was a picture of a beautiful girl, I can't remember what she looked like, but I remember she was beautiful. It was inscribed, To Roy *with passionate love,* Marcia. *I think that was the way it was inscribed. I'm sure of it. I knew he'd written it himself. Knew? Yes. He'd created something to sustain him and give him an identity. Her name is a coincidence. It could have been Helen or Isolde or Mary Jane . . .*

Chapter VI

Jane!

General Drummond awakened with a start. He must have called out her name. But he was alone, as always. Somewhere beyond the heavy curtains swaying on a morning breeze a church bell clamored. It was morning, it was Florence, and he had been dreaming.

His gaze swept the bedroom quickly, making sure that Harry, that no one had heard him call her name. He was alone. There was no sound except the church bell and the clopping of a carriage horse on the pavement below.

The bell and the horse's hoofs must explain the dream. These things happened instantaneously, it was said, an eon of dream in a few seconds of your life. It had been a good dream, too, for in it he had not been himself. Not exactly. He had been Grandfather. He or I, the person of the dream, had been riding west. West because there was a sun going down. And then it was morning and there was a river. The country of the dream was vivid, even after waking. Swamps and cutover timber, lonely little clearings and a twisting dirt road. And then the river where boats loaded with men floated motionlessly. There was a peach orchard where blossoms drifted indescribably.

Shiloh, of course. Shiloh on the Tennessee. He had been dreaming of Shiloh. Then why had he called out Jane's name?

Now he remembered. He or I, the person of the dream, had ridden through the peach orchard, which could only be the orchard so many men remembered after Shiloh, and there, on the farther side, walking toward him, smiling, came Jane Raleigh.

"Goddamn," General Drummond said softly.

What a case some quack could make of this. But it could have been anyone, he thought defensively. It had been she only because he'd been thinking about her last night. Naturally. She was arriving in Florence this afternoon. But this hypothetical quack, against whom he need not defend himself, but defend himself nevertheless he would under the circumstances just to prove his invulnerability, this hypothetical quack he would answer thus:

I am getting old, I am sixty-three years old, and I believe, I *know* that I have passed the age of emotional involvement with a young woman. For she is very young, she is twenty-four years young. I literally held her on my lap when she was a baby. She's the daughter of my good and dear friend Colonel Dave Raleigh, who asked me to look her up when I told him I was passing through Rome.

So he had looked her up in Rome. And the moment he met her—well, perhaps not the moment, but within five minutes he had formed his grand plan. She was beautiful and charming and intelligent. She was the girl for Drew. And Drew needed a girl, a wife who liked the life of the Army as much as Jane manifestly did. Her United States Government job in Rome was being abolished and she spoke of returning to her father. What luck! What a plan was taking shape. He

59

was going on to Florence with these few old family documents, impelled by an uneasy certainty that Drew might be thinking of quitting the Army again. The scheme he had conceived to prevent this was to interest him in the family tradition. Naturally he could not explain his scheme to Jane. He could only ask her to come to Florence and serve as his secretary in writing the family history. When she accepted at once, he was delighted.

To save Drew, he thought, is why I came all the way from Burning Brook to Florence. And I was right instinctively. He *was* thinking of quitting. He must be saved to serve a worthy cause for which he is eminently qualified. He has done many wrong things, but he has turned out to be completely right. I have not treated him wisely or well. I have done many wrong things toward him, but it turns out that I have been completely right. Now, I believe, if I do the one right thing, everything will be right forever.

Besides, I haven't long to live and I'd like to *be* with him for a while. Long to live? You have— Don't oil yourself. The most important muscle, the heart, is defective. Only Judd and Mildred know it. And Harry knows it, but it often seems that Harry is no one. Drew must never know it, for then he would only pity me. And pity is hopeless, pity cannot be the basis for anything. I'll say to myself now what I naturally can tell no one: I'm not afraid to die. That is not bravado. That is the truth. At times I rather look forward to it. I have hunted and failed to find a reason to continue living. My only immortality is in Drew.

Fortunately, he thought, there were others besides himself who recognized the qualities of Drew. He was both brilliant and kind, though he did not especially try to be either. Those were rare qualities, invaluable to the country today, especially in their trade, the soldier's trade. A truly good officer did not seek any special reaction from his command. But an officer harvested reactions down to the lowliest K.P. He would be liked or respected or hated. Drew was one of the few who was liked. It was better to be liked than respected. I know, he thought, for I was only respected.

There was, too, the quality of courage. Which was the quality that made you liked and even, under rare circumstances, beloved. God knew that Drew had the quality of courage. More important, the United States Army knew it. There was the strange, the almost incredible thing he had done in Korea. He had refused rotation when the system had finally been put into effect. He had stayed and fought the war until almost mortally wounded. Why had he done it? It was a manifestation of the Drummond tradition of courage and sense of duty. In him was the potential of greatness that none of the Drummonds had ever quite realized. In him had been bred all the strength of the past generations.

Drew should not have come to Italy. But he was here, and the problem was to bring him *back*. I cannot do it by myself, thought General Drummond. I cannot even write that book, even if I had the time left me to write it. I can only talk somewhat of the past and hope that he'll listen and understand that he is destined, as the best of the Drummonds, for great responsibility and unswerving duty. But I cannot do it by myself. I need Jane's help. If only he will fall in love with her and she with him, he'll find an immortality—

Eeek. The bedroom door hinges needed oiling. Harry had come silently through the living room. Damn Harry, he comes silently every morning of my life to see if I'm still alive.

General Drummond closed his eyes, trying to remember the peach blossoms of Shiloh, trying to remember the dream. If only he could dictate the story of Grandfather with the brilliant vividness of the dream. He'd better practice. He'd better *think* or he would seem only a maudlin old man mumbling about an ancestor when the time came to—

He opened his eyes and frowned at Harry.

"May I bring you some coffee, sir?"

"Hell, no." Since when had Harry decided to bring him coffee in bed?

"Would you like a tub this morning, General?"

Harry must have found an American movie somewhere last night and seen an English butler in it. "No, thanks, Harry."

When Harry went into the bathroom to check its order, General Drummond moved his feet over the side of the bed and sat up, waiting for a slight twinge, cursing himself for waiting, but nevertheless waiting. He glared at the bottle of pills beside the carafe of water, and then, making sure that Harry had not returned, he swallowed a pill and a little water. He felt fine.

It was exactly fourteen minutes to seven by his wrist watch on the table. He could do it in fourteen minutes this morning. Then he remembered old Colonel Blakeney saying, "You've got to take it easy, Jack. There's no rush. You've nothing to rush at." The hell with Blakeney! But Blakeney was right about there being nothing to rush at now. So he'd take twenty minutes. But the hell with Blakeney anyway!

It was ten minutes after seven when he emerged from the bedroom wearing the herringbone jacket and gray slacks he'd asked Harry to put out. He was rather proud of himself for having taken so long about it, for being so leisurely. But room service still had not delivered breakfast. Don't get mad, he warned himself, you're supposed never to get mad. Remember you're in Italy where they sleep half the morning and half the afternoon, finally getting down to a little work around a decent dinner hour.

He strolled to the balcony where the warm sunlight wrapped him languidly and made him want to stretch out in a chair. He resisted the weakness, clinging to the balcony rail and staring around the city which he hoped he would not like too much. He heard the room service boy with breakfast, and finally Harry, saying quietly, "Breakfast, sir."

The orange juice was cold and sweet. He smacked his lips with pleasure and said, "What did you do last night, Harry?"

"Just walked around, sir. I couldn't find a place where they had good spaghetti. Went to bed early."

Harry stood there, smiling timidly, his gaze averted, a man who could fight and drink and whore with the best of them. And he just smiled timidly. He'd picked Harry years ago because Harry was incredibly loyal and knew his *place*. But recently he sometimes wished Harry could manage to forget his place occasionally and be a little fractious or eccentric, be a problem, be a person. Once he'd even thought of dismissing him. But when he looked at him, at the scar resulting from inadequate surgery, he couldn't. For it was the one visible evidence of several secrets they shared: they were both to blame for it that time in the Normandy hedgerows, he for wanting to stand up like a bloody British grenadier in a mortar barrage and Harry for pushing him down and covering him. Both had violated old rules that time: he for acting like a hero with the troops, Harry for breaking the secret old Army rule that nobody's hide is worth more than your own. The trouble with Harry was that he needed something to worship. Having failed to believe in God or even very much in himself, beyond certain soldierly limitations, he fastened on me, General Drummond thought. He was impressed when I was a major and three stars is the whole firmament to him, even three retired stars in a world of many stars, both shining and clouded. That was the trouble with Harry and that was the good about him.

He finished breakfast, which was as close an approximation as an Italian kitchen could make of an American breakfast, the ham thin as shavings and the toast just a wild guess at the true nature of toast and the American coffee not really American, but the two fried eggs just right. Lighting a cigar, he retired to the bathroom with the Rome *American,* which contained an alarming report on Southeast Asia. He checked his thoughts on what he would do if he were in command of that situation and he turned to the sports pages and wondered what sort of a team Army would have this year.

When he returned to the living room he noticed that it was only eight o'clock. Jane was not arriving until three-fifty and Drew had been vague about the hour he'd see him today. Meanwhile, he should get cracking. That concierge was the opening to drive through. That fellow could get you anything for a price. He drew a five-dollar bill from his wallet and gave it to Harry.

"Talk it up with the concierge, Harry. You know the kind of apartment I want. Make him understand that if he finds it for me there's more in it for him. And double-check on Jane's—Miss Raleigh's reservation. And while you're down there get a decent map of this town."

After Harry left, he unlocked and opened the yellow leather case which contained the family documents he'd begged from Judd. He carefully unwrapped Grandfather's notations, bound in imitation leather and written in a scrupulous hand. It was not a diary, but a record of remembered events. Opening it, he read.

It was after much searching of my mind and heart that I came to take part in the War on the side of the Union. It was a painful decision which I was slow to arrive at. My younger brother, John Coffee Drummond, had resigned his commission in the United States 5th Cavalry and had become a Colonel of Confederate Cavalry; all except one of my friends and neighbors were persuaded of the justice of the Southern cause; even my dear wife was bitterly and unalterably opposed to the Union, having two brothers and numerous cousins under Confederate arms. I was a planter, born and bred in Tennessee, who owned slaves, and I had represented my neighbors in our State Legislature, so that I knew well and had believed I indorsed fully the fabric of my life. The intemperateness of the North troubled and often angered me, so that I was tempted by the Confederate Commission offered to me. However, I could not bring myself to accept it, and yet I wavered, often tempted and rejecting temptation. I wished, as did our Saviour, that this cup might pass from me, and I believed, for a time, that it would if I went my way about my acres. However, it did not pass, for I had been a soldier, educated by the Federal Government at the West Point Military Academy; I had served in the War with

Mexico and with the Army for a year afterwards before returning to Burning Brook; looking out at the great world I saw that the Union must be preserved and that we must persevere as one nation. Knowing that my name was Drummond, I likewise knew that it was Andrew Jackson Drummond, after our great General and President with whom my father served and who had been like a father to me in times past. I could not forget that Andrew Jackson had risen above sectionalism in the cause of Union and had acted fearlessly and forcefully in the case of the previous intemperateness of South Carolina. I came with great pain and slowness to my decision, arriving at it, in truth, on 1st April 1862. My dear wife cried out that it was indeed All Fools Day when I told her what I would do, and the poor tormented woman would not speak to me again.

On Tuesday, 2d April, my good friend and neighbor, Julius Niven, and I rode away together from Burning Brook and I confess that my heart was so heavy that I could not bring myself to look back at home. We rode south and west toward Waynesboro, with our ultimate destination Savannah on the Tennessee River. Having decided to serve, we went in the direction of anticipated action, else why should we serve? On 1st April there had passed near our homes a Federal Division, the advance of General Buell's forces marching south and west from Nashville. They were composed of regiments from the Old Northwest, wild and uncouth boys and men, many of them ill-kempt and ill clothed, walking along in ragged columns without fifes or drums or banners flying. We sat our horses at a cross-roads on that gray afternoon as they passed, hooting and jeering at us as —— rebels, when a young and amiable officer rode up and engaged us in conversation. He told us that they were going down to Savannah on the Tennessee to join the forces of General Grant, who was coming up the River. He was a most talkative man, even mentioning that under Grant was Brigadier General Sherman, whom I had known and admired, although he was somewhat given to temperament, in times past. I was greatly interested, whilst I felt it necessary to chide the young officer for giving military information so freely. He only laughed and said this was Union territory now and what harm could be done, and I vainly tried to explain that this country was strongly Confederate. Up he spoke, laughing, that though that might be so, I was Union else why did I chide him for speaking so frankly? He rode away and I sat my horse for some time, pondering that I was indeed Union to have spoken so and that I lacked only the courage of my convictions.

Before Julius and I parted that evening we agreed that we must in fact have the courage of our convictions, even though that meant flying in the face of nearly all that we held dear. We agreed that we should pass on down to the Upper River, for it took no military genius to see what was shaping there. It was a natural corridor into the deep South, for steamboats came up the River to a little place called Pittsburgh Landing. From the Landing there was a road south 20 miles to Corinth in Mississippi, a railroad junction from which the railroads ran out to Memphis and Chattanooga and down to the Gulf. Had I been a Union general intent on invading the South I would have moved in that direction. Had I been a Confederate general I would have tried to cover that exposure, and I had indeed heard that General Albert Johnston was gathering men in Corinth. So I knew there would be action shaping there, though I did not then know how bloody it would be. . . .

The bells of Florence pealed ten o'clock as General Drummond strode from the hotel, and paused, blinded suddenly by bright sunlight and the upward rush of pigeons and a vivid memory of Shiloh, lying dark and silent at this moment far to the west under an American moon.

He blinked at Harry beside him, narrowed his eyelids, and said, "Give me that map. Let's get oriented here." He took the map and walked across the street to the stone balustrade above the river. Spreading the map on the masonry, his finger prodded the X with which the concierge had marked the site of the hotel and then the X with which he had marked the location of the flat for rent across the river. He looked up from the map, this part of the city in clear perspective now. "Come on," he said to Harry and started along the river toward the Ponte Vecchio.

Shops and silver and good-looking women. It was like Fifth Avenue, except that there was a river. And it wasn't really much of a river. What did Drew see in this place? Easy, he told himself. Slow. You are, remember, an old potterer now. So potter.

He tried to. He walked slowly, staring conscientiously in shop windows, reminding himself that he must take something fine home to Mildred. She was the only woman he knew to whom he could take anything. Sad that you could live to sixty-three and have no child or woman, except a sister-in-law, to whom to take a gift.

He had heard, of course, of the Ponte Vecchio. His disappointment on seeing it was vast. No golden bridge of antiquity, linking old dreams. Just a press of small shops, with throngs of tourists. Too bad that silver looked like junk to him. He preferred gold.

After crossing the bridge, they turned left and made their way to the Via dei Bardi which slanted upward from the river. The address the concierge had given them was that of a large stone apartment house. There was a concierge expecting them. He was old and spoke a pidgin English. Corrupt, General Drummond thought. The concierge led the way up long stone stairs and turned through a corridor to another stairway. On the second flight he caught his breath and cursed his heart.

"It's no good, sir," Harry said.

"We haven't even seen the damn place yet," the General snapped and pushed doggedly after the concierge.

When Harry began, "Sir—" he said, "Shut up, Harry!" And then another flight. He was panting and his heart throbbed heavily as he watched the concierge unlock a door.

Stepping into a huge room, richly furnished in imitation of the Renaissance, the General exclaimed in pleasure. This dark strong wood, the splashes of red befitting strong passions, the big fireplace, and the wide wide windows reaching out over river and city to the hills beyond. It was his place.

"A hundred seventy-five dollar a month," the concierge said.

And cheap at the price.

"Any elevator?" Harry asked.

The concierge looked at him with a puzzled expression. Harry made pathetic motions of imitating an elevator until the General said, "Of course there's no elevator, Harry."

His Goddamned heart! This was his place and he could not rise to it, he could not come to it. But he would try. If he did it slowly, a step at a time, maybe once a day . . .

"It's no good, General," Harry said.

General Drummond eyed him coldly. "You're being rather presumptuous, Harry. I'm paying the rent."

"Five room and kitchen," the concierge said, opening a door.

The apartment was high and stout and unassailable. It was his place. And he cursed his heart.

"I'll think about it," he said at last. "I'll tell you this afternoon."

Steps going down so easy, but steps going up so hard. On the street Harry confronted him without timidity. "Sir, it's just no good. All those stairs."

He felt his rage swelling and recognized his childishness. He hated to feel sorry for himself, but he wasn't asking for the moon. He was

66

simply seeking a place to live that was right, and this was right, and—

"Hi."

He wheeled in surprise at the sound of Drew's voice.

"What are you two doing over here?"

"Looking for an apartment." General Drummond felt his anger ebbing. "What about you?"

"Just going home. I live a couple of blocks from here."

He carried a bag. The young rogue must have spent the night with that woman. And there he stood, looking fresh and undissipated. The young never knew what they had until it was too late.

"I'm not taking this apartment," General Drummond said to no one in particular.

"Want to see my place?" asked Drew.

He certainly did. They fell in step on the narrow sidewalk while Harry marched three paces to the rear.

"I just checked Marcia into your hotel," Drew said.

"Marcia?"

"The Contessa di Falcari. The girl—the woman whose car I was driving yesterday."

"Contessa, eh?" The General glanced at him quickly.

"Yes. She wants to meet you, Father."

Now what did that indicate?

"In fact, we're all invited to dinner at the Sabraccios' this evening. He's a psychiatrist I know. Met him in the Second War."

Jane was arriving on the three-fifty. It would not be decent to desert her on her first evening in Florence. "I'd like to, Drew, but I have a date."

"Oh? You get around fast."

"The woman I hired as a secretary from Rome. I'd hoped *you* could join *us*."

"Sorry." But Drew didn't sound sorry. Then he said, "Bring her along, unless she'd find it dull. The Sabraccios wouldn't mind."

The General repressed a smile. Drew meant, of course, unless they'd find her dull. He was in for a surprise.

"It would be very pleasant." The General injected the proper hesitation in his voice.

"It's a date," Drew said. "About eight o'clock. They dress for dinner. We'll meet you both at the hotel about quarter of."

"Thanks, no, we'll take a cab." Entrances were important. At least this entrance was. "What's their address?"

"It's up in Fiesole." Drew told him the address.

General Drummond prided himself on his ability to remember such details without making notes. "This Contessa what's her name—di Falcari—is she something special to you, Drew?"

"Rather."

"Is she a widow or divorcée?"

"She's going to get a divorce. Her husband's a fairy."

"Good God!" General Drummond fell out of step and did not try to recover it. "Why should you want to get mixed up in a mess like that?"

"No mess." Drew smiled at him.

"Then your intentions are—"

"Intentions subverted, Father."

"Oh?" He felt a smile gathering. "Oh." Perhaps this would not be so difficult after all.

They had cut off the Via dei Bardi and come to the head of the Via dei Renai. Ahead, at a distance, was green high ground. Drew said that up there was the Piazzale Michelangelo, commanding a fine view of the city.

"I'd like to walk up there and look around," General Drummond said.

Behind him, Harry spoke. "General, I think I'm working up a blister."

"Then fall out, Harry, fall out." He did not look around.

But Harry did not fall out. He padded along, in step and three paces to the rear.

When they entered Drew's apartment, General Drummond pointed to the engraving above the fireplace. "That's good. It looks like Burning Brook."

"Does it?" Drew said. "I hadn't thought about it."

The boy knew perfectly well that it looked like Burning Brook. Why wouldn't he admit it? The engraving indicated that he loved Burning Brook. And then General Drummond thought, There was a time when I wouldn't admit even to Dorothy, in fact, least of all to Dorothy, that I loved Burning Brook.

After a while, when he suggested that they have lunch together, Drew said, "I'm meeting Marcia. Why don't you join us?"

Perfect, the General thought. He said, "I don't want to interfere . . ." and he did not listen to Drew's protestation that he was not. He turned to Harry. "Meet Miss Raleigh at the station if I'm not back, Harry, and take her to the hotel. See that my dinner jacket's

in press. And work on that concierge to find me another place—
you know. In fact, if your *blister* will stand it, you'd better scout around
yourself. I want you to dig *in* on it, Harry. Understand?"

"Yes, sir." Harry's heels were creeping together and his back was
bracing.

Drew observed it and began to frown. He failed to understand,
thought General Drummond, that Harry was happiest when the commands were sharp and the burdens heavy; then his existence became
meaningful.

They walked along the Lungarno Serristori to the old watch tower
and then they climbed the hill slowly by the switchback paths, through
sweet cedar and beech and sycamores. General Drummond breathed
easily and his heart did not race. Enjoying one of those moments of
blind optimism, he thought, Maybe I'm better, maybe with careful
exercise the muscle can be strengthened. He knew it was not true.
But he told himself that for a time he would pretend it was. Pausing,
he gazed at a fragment of ancient wall.

"They had a problem with this hill all right. They daren't leave it
outside the walls, but they thought they couldn't take it all in. So
they tried to defend half a hill, and that's rough, if not impossible."

"They did the best they could," Drew said.

"Did they? I wonder. We always think the old ones did the best
they could. But often they didn't half try. Their failures make profitable study, however."

They climbed the last steep path to the vast paved *piazzale* and faced
a magnificent view of city and hills. Gazing down at the river and the
folding hills, the General realized he was studying terrain in the way
that had become habitual with him. As if some day he might fight
an army through here. But he'd fought his last battle, and he'd better
come off it.

As they crossed the *piazzale* to the Loggia, he felt a tug in his des-
picable heart. When they sat down at a table covered by a large green
umbrella, he fingered a pill from a pocket and swallowed it.

"Why the pills, Father?"

General Drummond grimaced, dreading discovery, dreading the
moment when Drew would simply feel sorry for him. He wanted these
last days of his relationship with the boy to be perfect.

"I have a—a slight liver condition. The quacks make me take these."
He stretched his long legs beside the table, waiting for the pill to work
its magic, wondering how long man could live by pills alone. "In your
letter, and I won't chide you for writing me only once since you came

abroad, you said your mother came through Florence. Did you bring her to lunch up here?"

"Yes."

"Where did you sit?"

"Where? Over there. That table over there."

General Drummond turned and looked at a vacant table. He could imagine Dorothy sitting there. Rather, he could imagine her as she used to be. With a past tenderness but without present sadness.

"I suppose that third husband of hers was along. What's his name? Goldstein? I never can remember it."

"Goldfarb."

General Drummond shook his head. "I can't get over the fact that Dorothy always said she hated Jews and then up and married one. Did you see much of them while they were here?"

"Not much."

"You couldn't stand Goldfarb?"

"No, I like Goldfarb. I couldn't stand Mother."

What a pity. Dorothy and Drew had always seemed so close. What had happened still was unfathomable to him.

"I suppose Goldfarb is rich," he said.

"Very."

"Smart?"

"Extremely."

"So Dorothy—your mother must have married him for his money."

"I suppose so."

"And he must be smart enough to know it. I don't see why he'd— yet I do too. Dorothy a member of"—he made his tone dry—"one of the finest and oldest American families. A Huntley. A South Carolina Huntley. And Goldfarb—I suppose that means something to him."

"I suppose it does. But her family history doesn't mean as much to him as it does to Mother. She's not very nice to him. She turns on that exaggerated southern accent. You know the way she could always turn it on and off like a faucet. She—well, she *patronizes* him, and it makes me so ashamed of her. Because he's smart and he's kind and he's taken his lumps. He . . ."

Drew's voice died as he gazed past his father. He rose slowly, smiling faintly, his expression abstract. General Drummond had seen the expression on many men; he must have worn it himself, though now he could not remember when. Wearily he turned and he felt that his heart constricted. That would be she, Drew's Contessa. There was little that one could do against such a woman. Her soul, her mind, might be as shallow as her looking-glass, but she was a beautiful creature who walked with a fine free stride, confident that nothing could be done against her.

Drew went toward her and General Drummond rose slowly, pushing himself up from the table on white knuckles.

"Marcia," said Drew, "this is Father."

General Drummond bowed. "It's a pleasure to meet you, Contessa."

She extended her hand. "I'm really a third-rate contessa, General, and I wish you'd call me Marcia."

It would be easier, he thought, if her voice were flatter, denoting a faulty ear. He called her Marcia and began a thorough search for flaws. But subtly. He knew all the tricks of saying nothing and making it sound like much: the attentively cocked head, the little smile, the build-up to the silent laugh. We old Academy boys, he thought, the best as well as the worst of us, perform effortlessly. As gentlemen, if not always as officers. Our training has been arduous, of course, beginning with lieutenants' brides and working up to generals' ladies, until we are socially indefatigable. But always predictable, we maneuver as exactly as in the precise figure of the waltz. Around and around, the smiles and the swirl and the music disguising the fact that it's really just one-two-three, one-two-three.

This empty-headed girl did not see it, however. Jane would detect it instantaneously; she came of a tradition, and it took a tradition to detect social emptiness. But this empty-headed, though most beautiful, girl was simply dancing with him, enjoying the smiles and the swirl and the music, quite unaware of the precise social steps on which she floated.

"What?" Drew asked vaguely when he spoke to him.

The General felt a frown gathering, and then he smiled as Marcia looked at Drew disapprovingly. "Dream on, Drew," he said.

"Drew is a lousy—I mean a poor conversationalist." Marcia smiled at Drew and her knee pressed his leg under the table, the General observed. "Aren't you, dear?"

"Oh, sure," Drew said. "Just a lousy conversationalist."

"Just a lousy dreamer," General Drummond said, smiling.

He knew that Marcia's knee beneath the table was more interesting to Drew than his conversation above the table. Naturally and inevitably. Leaning back relaxedly, his voice unstilled, General Drummond understood.

As he talked, he remembered a time. . . . It must have been exactly forty years ago, in 1913, when he visited his parents at Fortress Monroe.

There had been a girl. . . . He could not remember her name because nothing much had come of it, but there had been a girl who sat in the summerhouse pressing his knee below the table while his father had talked above the table. He remembered thinking then that the trouble was everyone always wanted to own everyone else. (She must not have been a very attractive girl.) But her knee under the table had wanted to own him and his father's voice above the table bore the pride of ownership in him. And then, from the void, the voice of the coach at the Academy, back God knew when, probably 1910, bawling, "All right, let's get *in* there, Drummond, let's get *going!*" They always wanted to own you and they always wanted you to *go*, and you weren't really well off until you accepted ownership and you *went*.

After the waiter served veal and zucchini fritto, Drew rallied, displaying the old social resources: the rapt attention, the smile, the quick reply. At last General Drummond began to understand that he was building up Marcia to him and him to Marcia and trying to weave a fancy bridgework between them. So perhaps this woman was not a mere target of opportunity to Drew after all.

He scarcely could believe he'd heard her correctly when she said it. "Has Drew told you I'm pursuing him?" She smiled at him across the deadly weapon of her candor. It was unfair that such a beautiful, empty-headed woman should play with candor.

He said, "I thought that Drew was pursuing you."

"Thank you, General Drummond." She bowed her head with irony. "You are truly a gentleman. But I'm really pursuing him. And I wonder if I have your blessing or if I'm your—enemy."

Smiling at her fixedly, he said, "My blessing would be fatal to whatever plans you might have." He nodded toward Drew. "If I approved, he almost certainly would disapprove. What I think makes absolutely no difference."

Drew grinned at him. "Go ahead, Father, and describe the perfect all-American girl. The one who has babies and shops thriftily at the post commissary on soldier's pay and is decorative and knowledgeable and flirts just enough with the colonel and is nice to the general's wife. The girl who can get tears in her eyes at retreat parade and can laugh at the corniest jokes of the most influential people."

General Drummond sank back in his chair, unsmiling. The whelp drove in hard. Yes, that was his idea of a woman, a part of his idea. Surely it *must* be Drew's idea too.

"Drew!" Marcia spoke sharply. "You don't have to be sarcastic."

"He feels he has some grounds." General Drummond decided he

would try candor too. "I've been far from the perfect father. I've pressed the Army on him. But that showed some good judgment on my part too. He's an exceptional officer. Do you know about him?"

She leaned forward, smiling, her hands clasped under her chin. "I know that he's fun to be with."

"You should know about him," General Drummond said. "He's broken just about all the rules in the book, but—"

"No kidding! What did he do?"

"He was kicked out of the Academy—"

"You never told me!" she exclaimed to Drew. "What did you do?"

"Chose suicide to slow death." Drew crumbled a crust of bread on the table. "Walked off limits in my plebe year and went down to a bar in Highland Falls. Ordered whisky, which they wouldn't serve me. Raised a big stink and that's where they found me—Drummond against the world. It just about killed Father."

"It didn't just about kill me," General Drummond said. "But I was greatly disappointed at the time."

Drew gazed at him reflectively. "I *told* you I didn't want to go to the Academy. And you *told* me I did."

"I told *my* father *I* didn't want to go to the Academy," the General said.

"I never knew that, Father. I thought— What did you want to be?"

"A mathematician. I had a flair for it and I had some crazy notion of going into pure mathematics. But my father *told* me I was going to the Academy, and I went and I never—I do not regret it." He looked at Marcia. "But I was telling you about Drew."

"Skip it, Father," Drew said wearily.

"You be quiet," Marcia said to him. "I want to hear."

"He was commissioned from the ranks in the Southwest Pacific and won the Distinguished Service Cross and was wounded," the General said. "He was one of the few living men who had the bad luck to be shipped to Europe after Pacific service and he arrived in time for one of the worst battles of this century. The Normandy Hedgerows. After the war he broke the rules by going civilian for three years. But he came back in out of the rain. He was number one in his class at the infantry refresher course at Benning and he has consistently maintained the rating of superior. In Korea, where he spent two years before he was wounded, he became one of the youngest majors in the field and his battalion won a unit citation and he got a cluster on his Distinguished Service. And that, by the way, means much more than a Congressional. But what's more important is the fact that there's a letter in his 201 File written by Matt Ridgway from Korea citing him as one of the most promising young officers in the Army. In another year or so he'll be sent to Command and General Staff School and—"

"End of obituary," Drew said. "Let me fill your glass, Father."

"Dear God," Marcia said, "you never told me."

"And let me fill your glass, Marcia . . . And let me fill my glass . . ." He looked from the General to Marcia and said quietly, "You can read the program notes and still fail to understand the play. That's something about me, but it misses *me*." He raised his glass. "Here's to sitting under an umbrella in Florence. And if you listen closely, to the one sparrow chirping in that cypress who has avoided slaughter at the hands of a bird-killing populace. Here's to thinking, as compared to detail. End of toast. End of theatrical gesture." He put down his glass without bothering to drink.

I'm licked, thought General Drummond. It was time to withdraw. A few minutes passed, however, before he could pull out decently. He walked straight across the *piazzale*, feeling naked, as on a wide fire field. He had almost reached the sloping path before he realized that he never would accept defeat so easily.

Chapter VII

Dr. Michele Sabraccio liked to shock by trying to shake whatever faith one professed. Sometimes he spoke so subtly that one was not aware of it until later reflection. Often, however, he spoke bluntly.

Thus, when invited to a party shortly after his arrival in Florence in 1948, he sat down beside a merchant who viewed a group of women with sad, sensual gaze, and said to him, "Let's talk about sex and get it out of our systems." Everyone realized that Sabraccio could not possibly have known the merchant had finally broken with an actress and returned to his wife, a harridan. Sabraccio's remark earned him a reputation for sagacity and he began to receive patients in his simple office.

In time he became renowned as a wit and savant among people who prided themselves on being cosmopolitan and not believing in much of anything. It brought him a huge yellow stucco villa in Fiesole which became the Mecca of many pilgrims of many nationalities. Besides being sagacious and witty and affable, Sabraccio could analyze his patients in English or Italian or French. Which was handy.

Sabraccio was not a charlatan. He could have, he knew, made more money in America. But he liked living in Florence and he generally preferred Europeans to Americans. He retained his United States citizenship for only one reason, he candidly told anyone. If the barbarian horde ever swarmed from the East again he planned to flee immediately to America where he had been born and educated.

His wife was French and named Gisèle, a rather plain little woman with gamine features and an abstracted manner who painted quite well and played the piano quite badly. She loved Sabraccio unpossessively, and sometimes, when Sabraccio looked at her, you knew that he loved her. He never spoke of her, but they had been observed at the Chez Moi, a night club, drinking and dancing and thoroughly enjoying each other's company.

As Drew and Marcia drove up to Fiesole that evening, he told her some of these facts about Sabraccio.

"Edoardo introduced me to him once in a restaurant right after we were married," she said. "He looked at me sort of lecherously."

"Don't hold that against him," Drew said. "That just means he's normal. I only wanted to warn you that he likes to shock people."

She patted his hand on the wheel. "Lamb-pie, you forget you're talking to a lioness. I've seen, heard and been propositioned on every known indecency."

"But let me tell you *my* proposition." He turned his head and smiled at her.

"Be gentle," she said. "Like when you were trying to break me in easily on Sabraccio. That was very nice, you running interference for me against imaginary tacklers. But don't worry. It's much more important to me than to you that I be a lady."

He turned the Citroën up the Sabraccios' drive to the huge yellow villa. When he opened the car door for Marcia, he paused for a moment, gazing out at the valley of the Arno, azure and gray in twilight under purpled cirrhus clouds. It must be fine, he thought, to be a craftsman of the psyche like Sabraccio and live in peace above this valley.

A maid conducted them to a large living room, sunken and modern in *décor*, with a carpet which clung to the feet like mud, and furniture growing on thin stems like enormous lily pads. Each time Drew entered this room he thought how, when he was younger and had the reputation of being somewhat of a clown, he would have exclaimed, "Look, fellas, I'm swimming!" Probably no one would have understood what he meant; he would have been thought odd; it would have pleased him that others thought him odd. But he had ceased making such remarks and, as a result, he was considered "mature," which presumably was merely a state of fearing to be thought odd.

Sabraccio came from the terrace. He was a thick-set man, with a blunt nose and heavy features exaggerated by heavy-rimmed glasses. Around his ample girth he'd wrapped a purple cummerbund and in the lapel of his white silk dinner jacket he wore a maroon chrysanthemum. Drew did not like the cummerbund or the chrysanthemum or the dinner jacket, but he liked Mike Sabraccio.

"Contessa. Drew." Sabraccio extended his small hands, the right to Marcia and the left to Drew. He seemed to look around them instead of directly at them. "Where are the General and his friend?"

"They'll be along by taxi," Drew said. "And this, by the way, is Marcia, not the Contessa."

Sabraccio passed a smiling, vacant gaze over her and said, "That being the case, I am Mike." He turned as his wife entered the room. "Very much on cue, my dear. And this is Gisèle—Marcia."

She approached, hand outstretched, smiling abstractedly. Her dress, like Marcia's, was expensive and fashionable. Drew did not like Marcia's dress, which was elaborate and disguised her figure. On Gisèle Sabraccio the similar fashion looked positively absurd to him, as if she were a little girl dressed up for the occasion. Why was it the fashion to dress up so? Don't be smug, he told himself, in your plain white shirt and snap-on black bow tie. Gisèle felt it important to draw attention to herself and Marcia felt it important not to draw attention to herself. And that encompassed the nature of fashion.

"Let's have a drink and exchange confidences before the old folks arrive," Sabraccio said as a butler appeared. He turned to Marcia. "Martini?"

"I"—she hesitated—"yes, thank you."

"Let's be frank." Sabraccio sank into a chair. "How may we help you with the General? Discuss his past or his dreams or his bank account? Brief me, boy."

"There's not much to brief," Drew said. "I've been thinking—" He paused, frowning. "I've just about decided to resign from the Army and my father somehow guessed I was thinking about it and came all the way here to try to make sure I don't."

Gisèle spoke in her heavily accented English. "But what is it that you will do, Drew, if you leave the Army?"

"That's a good question," Marcia said. "I wanted to ask you, but I—"

"It's not a good question," said Sabraccio. "It's just my wife expressing her Gallic pragmatism. While a man is sawing his way out of prison he should not be expected to be planning his future livelihood." He smiled. "But what would you do, Drew?"

"I don't know." And he did not know. He cared and he had tried to give some thought to it, but he did not know.

"That is too bad," Gisèle said. "If you wanted to do some one thing it would be easier to convince your father."

"But I don't want to convince my father," Drew said. "I couldn't anyway if I wanted to. I know that I won't go back to an advertising agency. I tried that once and—"

"I didn't know that." Marcia suddenly looked confused. "You—"

"You two should get acquainted," Sabraccio said.

"We're trying," Drew said. "We're working at it."

"You must work harder," Sabraccio replied. "You know so little about your future and Marcia knows so little about your past that it's difficult to see just what you *do* talk about when you're together." Catching Marcia's look of distaste for his remark, he smiled at her. "What do you see in the crystal ball for yourself, Marcia?"

"I—I don't know. One thing. You should be able to tell me. How do you get a marriage annulled in this country?"

"It depends on whether it was a church or civil ceremony. But I believe the marriage you refer to was civil."

"It was."

Sabraccio sighed. "It can be done. But it is difficult. In such matters the Italians are—" He spread his small hands eloquently.

"Dr. Sabraccio"—her voice rose with intensity—"you sound as if you don't *want* me to—"

"But I *do*," he said quickly, "if that is what you want. You must remember, my dear, that Edoardo is my patient. He is a most interesting, a most complex young man. He has an amazing imagination that in some would develop into a great talent but in him is a—a great misfortune. At some other time in history, perhaps in that age which we call the Renaissance, he might have developed some genius. But he is my patient, and the physician has a feeling for his patient, as the cleric for a soul to be saved or the craftsman for his bit of craftsmanship. So I—"

"But you know perfectly well," Marcia said, "that he isn't normal and—"

"I do not know what normal is," Sabraccio said.

She stared at him, astonished. "You don't know what *normal* is? What's your practice all about if it isn't to try to make people normal? What are you doing?"

Sabraccio smiled faintly. "Sometimes I wonder."

"What I'll do," Marcia said, "I'll get a divorce in Reno or Mexico or somewhere."

"I don't know whether those divorces are recognized in Italy," Sabraccio said, "but I believe not."

"Frankly, Doctor, I couldn't care less."

"Please call me Mike." He looked at her chidingly. "I'm not your enemy just because I'm your husband's physician."

"Don't call him my *husband*. You know damn well—" She lowered her head, and Drew feared for a moment that she would cry. She lifted her head, her eyes dry. "I'm sorry—Mike." She looked at Drew beseechingly. "Please forgive me."

"Do not ask forgiveness, Marcia," Gisèle said. "There is nothing to forgive. You have trouble and no one knows it better than Mike."

"You have trouble," he said in a kindly tone, "but it will pass." He raised his Martini to her and sipped it. "Let's pick on Drew for a change."

"Doesn't anybody ever pick on you?" asked Drew.

"All day long. That's why I work off my antagonisms in the evening. It's interesting how you never have a moment off in this trade. Just last week . . ." He paused, looking up at the sound of voices.

Marcia said indistinctly, "Oh-oh."

Drew glanced at her curiously.

"Just 'oh-oh,'" she said, gazing beyond him.

He turned and then rose slowly. He glimpsed his father, but he did not look at him. He stared at the woman—what was her name? It didn't matter, for she was not remotely as he had expected her to be.

"Jane, Miss Raleigh," General Drummond said, "this is Drew."

Dark hair and blue eyes, the two-edged sword of beauty. Slim, well-formed, and very beautiful. She stepped forward, smiling calmly. The pressure of her extended hand was firm.

Marcia gazed at her speculatively and searchingly; Gisèle was less abstracted now. Sabraccio, saying, "America produces more beautiful animals every day," almost, but not quite, shook her control. She flushed and her face reflected annoyance, less with Sabraccio than

78

with herself for flushing, Drew thought. Sabraccio gave a small and really understanding smile. "Sit here beside me, child," he said, "and let me tell you the story of my long and lecherous life." She laughed hesitantly, as he must have known she would. "Ah, General," he said heartily, extending his hand, "it's a pleasure to meet you, sir."

"Doctor." General Drummond's tone was equally hearty. He cruised gracefully to a place between Marcia and Gisèle and engaged them immediately.

"We have just poured some Martinis here," Sabraccio said, "but that means nothing. This house also serves the best Manhattan in Italy and we have all kinds of hooch lying around."

Sometimes, Drew thought, Mike was altogether too elaborate. "He means," he said to Jane, "will you have a drink?"

Sabraccio looked at him thoughtfully, then said, "Thanks for translating, pal."

General Drummond would have a Martini and so would Jane Raleigh.

"You really surprise me, Jane," Drew said. He paused, awaiting her reply. But she did not answer him; she gazed at him levelly, a trifle curiously. The others were still, looking at them. Feeling that he was about to embarrass himself as well as her, he glanced at his father and said, "I was telling Jane that she really surprised me. I expected someone—you know—old and—"

Sabraccio's laugh broke a strange, growing tension. "Someone—you know—old," he said to the General, mimicking Drew's gesture, and the General threw back his head in laughter.

Jane laughed too. "Plain Jane," she said, "old Jane, crazy Jane, Mary Jane. Everybody used to have an old Aunt Mary Jane."

"That's right," Drew said, grinning at her. "The shawl, the cap, Whistler's Mother with thick ankles." His gestures were eloquent.

His father was fairly throwing himself about with merriment, and Drew thought, He never found me so hilarious before, what's the matter with him? Marcia's lips were set in a smile, but her gaze was somber. Why, he wondered, was he suddenly so damned self-conscious?

He offered Jane a cigarette. She accepted it. He struck a light for her. She did not steady the hand that held the match. It was an old, secret test of a woman to him. When they tried to steady your hand, which was always perfectly steady anyway, they were possessive. One-handed steadiers were dangerous, but two-handed steadiers wanted to wrap your life in a protective blanket. It was, of course, just a superstition. For all he knew Jane might be the most possessive woman he'd ever met, even though she didn't try to steady his steady hand.

Father was talking. Blah-blah-blah. How respectfully they gazed at him. Even Mike. Especially Jane. She probably had to because he was Her Boss. Father had simply taken his Martini from the butler's tray and sipped it and pronounced it excellent. But the way he said it, the tilt of his head, the expression of his rather handsome old face, made you think he was Jove sipping mortal brew and pronouncing it Olympian. They went for that sort of thing. Even Mike. But perhaps that was not surprising when you analyzed the motives that made him wear a cummerbund.

Yes, sir, General, sir. The high command had addressed him.

". . . but if I'd reminded you of the Raleighs at North Post you might have remembered."

"Sir?"

His father started to frown, and then he smiled. "Dreamer," he said without asperity.

"Pardon me," Drew said to Jane, "I'm really not catatonic. They tested me thoroughly for it. But you, I gather, were at North Post. Meaning Fort Myer. When?"

"When you were a kid," the General said. "Don't you remember the Raleighs?"

"Oh, the Raleighs," Drew said. He smiled at Jane. "No, I don't."

"It's understandable," she said. "I had roller skates and you—perhaps you had a horse."

"Not exactly. I—"

"It's interesting you should say that, Jane." The General commanded everyone's attention. "I remember Drew at Myer doing one of the most courageous things I ever saw a kid do. It involved a horse. See . . ."

Blah-blah-blah. The incredible thing to Drew was that his father was not telling the incident accurately. Had he forgotten or was he purposely distorting it?

When he was eleven years old and his father, then a major, was quartered at Myer while on duty with the War Department, Drew believed that he liked horses. He liked the amoniac smell of the stables, the manure and straw and the leather. He liked to watch horses, their flexing muscles and shine of sweat and the rhythmic nodding of their heads as they pulled funeral caissons through the winter twilight of Arlington National Cemetery. But he had no particular ambition to ride a horse. He did not believe he was afraid; he simply lacked interest in riding. But he learned. His father saw to that.

An old sergeant named Sullivan gave him lessons for a couple of weeks. He liked Sullivan. It was natural, for Sullivan was a sentimentalist. He was an old 5th Cavalry man who had served in the Villa expedition into Mexico. The 5th was the oldest United States cavalry regiment, and Sullivan, always smelling faintly of whisky, would talk about it for hours. He was fond of recounting how Jefferson Davis had organized it in 1855 when Secretary of War and of its many noted commanders from Robert E. Lee and Jeb Stuart on. He knew the history of the eighteen battle streamers which flew from its regimental staff. An historian, Sullivan, much prejudiced against outfits such as the 7th and 8th and 12th Regiments. When Drew told him that his great-uncle Chad had served in the 7th and been killed with Custer at the Little Big Horn in 1876, Sullivan was not impressed. Custer was a horse's ass, said Sullivan, to have lost an entire squadron at the Little Big Horn; he diagrammed Custer's folly with straws on the stable floor.

Despite many interruptions for historical commentary, Sullivan taught him something about riding. Finally, on a Saturday afternoon, his father told Drew that they were going riding together. He picked the horses at the stable. As an enlisted groom finished saddling up, a colonel who was to become a four-star general swung onto his horse and smiled at Father.

"Your boy is pretty ambitious to handle that one, Jack." He nodded toward Drew's mare.

"He can handle him, Colonel," said Major Drummond.

Drew clambered aboard and the groom released her. She laid back her ears and reared. He clamped his knees and hung on. When she came down, she took off. He clung to her, fighting to keep his feet in the stirrups, sawing at the reins. His left foot slipped from the stirrup and he seemed to rise high in the air. When he came down, the mare was not under him. The earth turned over twice and he felt a sharp pain in his right shoulder. Looking up groggily, he saw his father pound past in pursuit of the mare. Major Drummond had merely glanced at him as he went by.

The Colonel galloped up and skimmed off his horse, looping his reins over a dogwood bough in one correct flowing movement. He squatted beside Drew, his gray eyes fixed on him broodingly. "Do you hurt, son?"

"A little, sir. In my right shoulder."

The Colonel's fingers moved expertly and Drew yelped in pain. "Your collarbone," the Colonel said. "They say you're never much of a rider until you break a collarbone. The Prince of Wales used to do it all the time. The surgeon will fix you up in a jiffy."

His father trotted back, leading the mare. "Well, Drew?" It was a question.

"He's broken his collarbone, Jack," the Colonel said.

His father frowned and dismounted. "Try your feet, Drew."

He got up dizzily, the Colonel steadying him.

"Well, Drew?"

"I can walk, Father."

"I'll send for a car, Jack," the Colonel said.

Major Drummond, ignoring him, stared at Drew. "It's not a question, Drew, of whether you can *walk*."

Drew looked at the mare and the mare looked at him. He knew what his father meant, but he had a great revulsion for that mare and he was in great pain. He knew, however, what his father meant. The Colonel opened his mouth to speak, then closed it firmly.

Resting on the Colonel's arm, he went to the portside of the mare while his father held her head. The Colonel boosted him up and then held the mare while his father mounted his horse and sidled close. Then the Colonel mounted and sidled his horse close to Drew on the other side. The mare walked docilely back to the stable.

At the time I merely felt scared and nauseated. Later I felt triumphant. But now it seems a pretty ridiculous thing for Father to have done in the age of the motorcar.

The General had finished his brief and rather fatuous story about his brave son who had clambered back on a horse despite his broken collarbone. The women looked impressed and Sabraccio looked at his empty glass deadpan.

It occurred to Drew that his father had not meant to distort the incident. All he basically remembered was that Drew had climbed back on the horse. He did not remember his own tacit will that had forced Drew to climb on the horse again.

Now the General thought of a little epilogue to his story. He'd forgotten it until this moment, but the colonel who was there that day had become a four-star general—he dropped the name casually. That interested them, especially Jane. She said she'd seen the general a couple of years ago in Washington. (Why, wondered Drew, does she sound so *excited* about it?) She asked Drew if he'd seen the four-star general recently and he said he had not.

He could have told them, had he wished, of another cadenza. When in the hospital after being shipped back from Korea he'd received a pleasant letter from the four-star general, who had retired. The general, curiously, remembered the incident at Myer and he inferred that there was some relationship between Drew's climbing back on the mare that time and getting his tail shot off in Korea. Drew, personally, failed to see how riding a horse was related to any other human activity. Ever since being thrown, in fact, he'd been a little frightened of horses. But then, he was frightened of combat too.

"Old range rider," Sabraccio said to him, "will you have another drink?"

He was aware of the butler beside him, with a tray of fresh Martinis. He took another glass and tried to wrench the conversation away from this service talk, a medium of exchange that tarnished quickly into dullness.

But Sabraccio would not let him change the subject. "In that story about Drew, General, I gather you rode after the horse."

"Why, yes," the General said, "yes, I did."

"And you *wanted* Drew to get back on the horse, didn't you?"

"Why, yes, Doctor, I hoped he'd try. But I didn't say a word to him about it. I certainly didn't command him to."

Sabraccio nodded. "Had it ever occurred to you, General, that you were thinking of the horse as well as of Drew? I mean, if that horse figured she could get away with throwing one human she'd figure she could do it again. Did you think of that?"

General Drummond examined the question thoughtfully, not sure that he was pleased with it. At last he said, "I don't recall exactly, but I rather imagine I did. It would be natural for me to think about the horse because— But you shouldn't infer that—"

"I don't infer anything, General," Sabraccio said. "I was just interested."

"It's the most natural thing in the world to think of the horse under circumstances like that," Jane exclaimed. The defensive tone of her remark made her cheeks color. "I mean—"

"You ride, Miss Raleigh?" Sabraccio smiled benignly.

"Why, yes, I do. That's why I—"

"Now I'm not needling you, but if you had been a man would you have gone to the Military Academy?"

"I certainly would." Her color increased. "I—"

"Very dull place," Drew said. "Very dull."

She looked at him. "I know. And I don't blame you at all for quitting it. But Dr. Sabraccio asked how *I* felt about it and I . . ."

Drew glanced at his father, who was almost imperceptibly nodding his approval. What went on here? It was extraordinary that in the course of hiring a secretary a man should tell the woman that his son had flubbed out of the Academy. It was, when you came to think about it, extraordinary that he should find it important to bring her here for dinner. But she was, when you studied her closely, an extraordinary girl. You knew how she'd look sitting a horse. You knew how she'd look doing a lot of things. Oddly, despite the impression of self-control she gave one, she was not as self-possessed as Marcia. But the result was charming rather than a fault. His father must have seen and sensed all this: the lovely girl, the occasional charming lack of self-possession that in her surely came from having been completely possessed by something—a family, a tradition. So what went on here? Sex was involved. Nothing overt, undoubtedly. But this girl made you think of sex, or at least she made him think of sex, and probably she had made his father think of it too. It was not to be defined by dwelling on her beauty; it was controlled, but not as hidden as she undoubtedly believed. This girl simply was passionate by nature. He knew it instinctively. And his father must know it. And Sabraccio unquestionably knew it. And so, in her oblique glance, did Gisèle. And Marcia—she certainly knew it as she sat there watching, for she was knowledgeable in such matters. Each, to some degree, knew it. Except Jane herself, Drew believed. And that was the charm that aroused in each of them a certain wistfulness.

Now Gisèle, with a remark, tried to blunt whatever sharpness the girl found in her husband. And Sabraccio himself surprisingly retreated, smiling kindly. And Marcia belittled her own self so that Jane laughed with pleasure at finding a kindred soul. And Drew said something innocuous and mildly funny. But General Drummond did not rally. He does not understand, thought Drew. Oh, he sees we are being nice to Jane Raleigh and he sees that she likes all of us now and he is pleased and really having a good time himself. But the situation has gone completely over his head. He fails to understand that we rally around the girl, not in any kind of pity, but with a mild envy. The girl—you fail to understand, General—is of a deeply passionate and dedicated nature, and we simply gather here around her in mute

84

testimony of the troubles that will come to her and with a mild regret for our own spent passions and lack of dedication.

After they left the Sabraccios' around midnight, Jane said, "What a wonderful evening. How wonderful everybody was."

"We are wonderful people, Jane," Drew said, "and you're very fortunate to know us."

"I'm not kidding," she replied from the back seat where she rode beside Marcia. "I certainly do think I'm very fortunate to know all of you."

"That should hold you for a while, Drew," said Marcia. "What can you think up to say about that?"

He could think of nothing, except how interesting that Marcia had decided to make a friend of Jane. They sat back there now, busily exchanging comments. Only a couple of confidences and perhaps a lipstick remained to be exchanged before they had cemented one of those feminine friendships that sometimes endure as long as twenty-four hours. In the front seat beside his father silence was golden. He pointed out the English Cemetery and General Drummond grunted, but Jane remarked that she had visited it. She drolly described a three-day week end she'd spent in Florence several months ago when she had tried to see nearly everything that the guidebooks recommended.

"But then I had only two days in Venice," she said. "I like Venice."

"I like Venice," Marcia said.

"I don't like Venice much," Drew said.

General Drummond, who rode with his head bowed tiredly, said, "I've never been there, but I'd like to go."

"Why don't you like Venice?" Jane asked.

"I've tried to figure it out," Drew said, "but I've never come up with a good reason. I just don't like it much."

They swept into the small square before the hotel, and the doorman sprang forward. Drew, feeling restless and not in the least tired, proposed a nightcap.

Three drunken and aging American males were whooping it up in the lobby when they entered. They were baying "Deep in the Heart of Texas" and they wore Stetsons and the heeled, tooled boots affected by amateur cowboys and professional cowboy singers.

"Americano!" one cried to them.

"Italiano," Drew replied gravely. *"Non parlo l'Inglese,* signor," and he turned the women toward the bar.

"These wops corner all the beautiful girls," one said plaintively.

As they sat down at a table Jane said, "At least they're having a good time."

"I don't think they really are, Jane," General Drummond said. "They're lonely. Their women must have brought them here and they're baffled and lonely."

"And their feet hurt from wearing those boots," Drew said, "and they're probably not really from Texas. Texans are growing more civilized, but some of the other states are sending quotas of males who like to masquerade as they imagine Texans are. It makes them feel big and strong in a foreign place."

The women ordered cokes and Drew and his father ordered brandy. General Drummond looked tired. When his brandy was set before him, he drank quickly. He lighted a cigarette and then mashed it out, crumbling it slowly in his fingers.

Marcia, who had been watching him, spoke suddenly. "Have you had any luck yet in finding an apartment, General?"

He shook his head slowly. "Harry was out on it most of the afternoon, but he didn't come up with anything. Tomorrow I've got to get *on* with it."

To Drew his tone lacked conviction that he would get on with it or that he had hope of finding what he wanted. Like the Americans singing in the lobby, he was baffled and lonely.

"There's something I'd like to suggest." Marcia spoke measuredly. "I have this big old castle. I mean Edoardo, my—my—he does—" She said to Jane, "My husband and I are separated." She looked at General Drummond again. "I mean how would you like to stay there for a while?"

He contemplated her gravely.

"I've decided to go back there and stay a while before I go home. There's plenty of room. There are eighteen rooms or something. Plenty of room for you and your man and Jane, and it's certainly plenty quiet, so you can work on your book. As a matter of fact, I'd be happy to have a little company out there."

Drew stared at her. This morning she had been determined to stay in Florence. Now she was going back to the castle. What was her motive? There was no answer in a vague generalization about the fickleness of women. For women, like men, always had motives; they merely seemed to change them more frequently. But why should she now have decided to house General Drummond and company?

"Thank you, Marcia," General Drummond said slowly. "That's

most kind of you. I—" He looked at Jane and then at Drew. "I—" At last his expression reflected decision. "I think it's a good idea. I— I'll wish myself—us on your hospitality for a week or so."

She smiled at him. "Good. Then it's agreed. Let's leave tomorrow morning. Say ten o'clock."

"Excellent." The General smiled, liking prompt action following a decision. "I'll have Harry rent us a car and we'll follow you." He rose. "I'm going along to get my beauty sleep. I'll leave you young people to yourselves. Good night." He turned abruptly and left the room.

In a few minutes Jane said she was going to bed.

"What's your rush?" Drew asked. "It's early. It isn't even one o'clock."

She flushed as she made excuses about being tired. Rising, she said good night and hurried out.

"A polite child. She thought we wanted to be alone."

"Maybe we do," Marcia said.

He looked at her. "If we want to be alone, let's be alone. May I come up?"

Her gaze avoided his and she frowned. "No."

He certainly was not a great lover type, he thought. If he were, he would be annoyed. But he was only amused—and puzzled.

"Whatever made you decide to ask them out to the castle?"

"I don't know," she said vaguely. "I just thought it would be an interesting idea. Besides, it's expensive staying in Florence and I've got to start thinking about expenses."

"It must be expensive at Castello di Falcari too, Mother, now that you've taken on so many extra mouths to feed."

"Not especially. I just give Ugo and his wife a little money and they do the most amazing things with it, and when they need more they ask for it. Edoardo's father left them some kind of an annuity or something when he died. I sometimes think it's really *their* castle."

"Well," he said, "I hope you have a happy time out there with your house guests."

She looked at him reproachfully. "You mean you're not coming too?"

"No, I'm not."

But he knew, with mild annoyance at himself, that he probably would. This had been his territory, a fine free place. Then his father had invaded it, spoiling its freedom. And Marcia, in a sense, had invaded it too. At least his awareness of her had invaded it, so that he could not be as content as he had been.

"I'm sorry to hear that," she said. "I'd hoped you would come too."

"Why should I?" He sounded almost petulant.

"But why shouldn't you?"

He gazed at her fixedly. "Have you the vaguest idea where we're headed?"

She smiled faintly. "That's rather surprising from you, Drew. You said yourself tonight you don't know what you're going to do. How can I tell you? You're sort of lost and lonely, like I'm sort of lost and lonely. I wish that you could enjoy just being with me as much as I do with you."

"That's fine, but . . ." He shrugged.

"Stop trying to play a role that doesn't fit you, Drew. I mean a—a rake. You're really not. That's why I—I like you. If you were just another one of those bores I wouldn't want to have anything to do with you. Now I hope that you're coming out to the castle tomorrow. I hope we'll meet you here in the lobby at ten o'clock. If you aren't here, I'll be very sad." She rose quickly. "Good night, Drew."

He watched her go. Then he raised a hand to the waiter and ordered another brandy. Sipping it, he found himself comparing Marcia with Jane. Each appealed to his senses. And there had been a time when he instinctively would have recognized the zealousness of Jane's nature and instinctively have believed, in his youthful egotism, that it could be dedicated to him, his pleasure and his profit. You've grown quite old and cynical, he told himself drily, to be wary of zealous enthusiasm for life in anyone. *Good Lord, I'm only thirty-one!*

Harry suddenly entered his abstracted vision. He came slowly from the lobby, planting one foot carefully in front of another, until he paused, swaying slightly, blinking around the bar. Seeing Drew, he closed his eyes and opened them, smiled stiffly, and turned away. He glanced back and Drew beckoned to him. He came to the table slowly.

"May I buy you a drink, Harry?" The offer was a disservice to Harry, he knew. But courtesy, if not friendliness, was involved.

"Thank you, sir." He spoke so carefully that his upper lip seemed frozen. "Guess I better not."

Drew smiled. "Okay. And Harry, you don't have to call me 'sir' all the time. We've known each other quite a long while."

"Quite a long while, sir. 'Scuse me, I'm so used to it. But I try to know my place."

"What is your place, Harry?"

"Oh, hell, you know—" Harry shrugged. "You know. I dunno." He dropped into a chair suddenly. "Scotch on rocks," he said. "I've

88

been drinking beer, but I'll have one Scotch and go quietly." He exposed his uneven, yellowed teeth in a grin. "I guess I call you 'sir' because when you get to be a general you might need a good man like me working for you."

"I'll never be a general, Harry. I'm probably resigning."

"You're nuts," Harry said.

"That seems to be the prevailing opinion."

" 'Scuse me saying that," Harry said. "Your father'd chew me out for talking that way to you. In fact, he wouldn't like me having a drink with you. You know the General."

"I know the General, Harry, but don't worry about it."

Harry picked up the glass which the waiter put down and peered into it with a crafty expression. "You'll be a general, I'm telling you. There's always a few generals who was enlisted men and you'd be one."

It was becoming wearisome to hear people say he could become a general. They believed it was bait, but it was not bait to him.

"The reason I say that," Harry continued, "is I remember Schofield. You remember the time . . ."

And he began distorting the past into the way he now chose to believe it had been.

Chapter VIII

It took Drew many years to realize that his father was an able fighting man whose nature would have been quite understandable to a thirteenth-century knight-at-arms. He believed that a man should find ways to develop and demonstrate his courage, that a man must learn to endure pain without flinching, that a man must learn to fight well without losing his temper. He believed that these virtues led to the greater virtue of what he called leadership. And leadership, he believed, was the quality of the superior man who led his weaker fellows through the travail of living.

Once he understood this dimension of his father's character he thought for a long time that that was all there was to him. For causes did not appear to trouble him. He simply believed in what he called "democracy," visualizing it, as far as Drew could ascertain, much as George Washington must have, with a slight Jeffersonian leavening. His politics he kept to himself. His church affiliation, at his wife's behest, was Episcopalian. But, like his wife's, it was nominal, and Drew never heard him mention God except when he requested Him to damn somebody or something. The theoretical, which included God, he shunned as a burden to his professed practicality.

This, then, became his fixed concept of his father, who, he realized, demonstrated virtues much admired by gentlemen of so-called western civilization for many centuries. As time passed, it came as something of a surprise to Drew that these very real virtues of his father had not led him to another ideal goal of civilization: personal happiness. But then, as Drew grew older, he learned (from personal experience rather than from reading philosophers) that happiness is relative and ephemeral and seemingly the result of accident rather than of the highly advocated virtues. Finally—very late, almost too late in their relationship for the discovery to make much difference—Drew began to sense other dimensions to his father's character that had eluded him all these years.

But knight-at-arms his father was, and recognition of that fact had come painfully to Drew when he was young. For he could not then see how his father was affected by the past. Item: His father's grandfather and great-grandfather had owned and whipped slaves, though it was doubtful that they had laid the rod on their slaves any harder than on their own children. Item: His father's father and grandfather and great-grandfather had ridden horses and fought with rifle and pistol, with fist and tooth and nail, thus generally asserting their sense of superiority over their fellow men by demonstrating what they considered their leadership. So it was handed down, from father to son. So it was handed from Andrew Jackson Drummond, 3d to Andrew Jackson Drummond, 4th.

It puzzled and worried his father that Drew did not become involved in fights when he was a child. He feared, of course, that Drew was cowardly. For all Drew knew, he was. He disliked pain, both to suffer and inflict it. Unconsciously he always temporized short of a fight. But so did the boys he played with around the posts. They horsed around and wrestled and yelled insults and threatened menacingly and squared off, but they did not stand up and fight each other.

When Drew was thirteen, his father was transferred to Schofield Barracks in Hawaii. In those days there was great interest and keen rivalry in boxing at Schofield. A good fighter was much pampered by his outfit. Major Drummond had one in his battalion whose name Drew never could remember. He pampered him and placed bets on him and generally displayed so much enthusiasm that Drew's mother remarked he was "passing through a physical education phase." Although Drew was not enthusiastic about boxing, he carefully simulated enthusiasm and went to the fights with his father and yelled for the right man (whatever his name was).

One evening as ground shadows lengthened under a rain-washed Pacific sky, he wandered obediently toward the Boxing Bowl where he was to meet his father. Children, stimulated by the anticipation of the fights, played near the Bowl. Drew had been at Schofield only a few weeks and school had not begun yet, so he knew scarcely anyone. He walked along, watching and waiting for the opening gambit that had become familiar to him: on the posts, two or more kids took in a newcomer; an individual never took up with an individual.

Suddenly he was hit behind the knees and went down. He'd met and become friends with a couple of boys after such an introduction. He got up, trying to grin, for he never had liked that old clip in the knees, and he faced a freckled and red-haired boy who was about his size. He waved his arms and made the old wrestling feint, which meant the boy could grin and close if he wished. But the boy didn't grin and he didn't close. He grabbed Drew's left arm and twisted it into a half nelson. Drew dropped to his knees. The boy kept twisting and Drew fell on his belly. The boy straddled him and Drew yelled, "Hey! What the heck!"

"Officer whore-hopper," the boy said.

The phrase, which Drew had not heard before, amused him. Although the boy was hurting his arm, he wanted to laugh.

The boy let go and sprang up and said, "What are you going to do about it, officer whore-hopper?"

Drew got to his feet, rubbing his arm. "Enlisted whore-hopper," he said.

The boy hit him hard on the chin and he found himself sitting on the ground, his jaw numb. A gang of boys had gathered in a silent circle.

"Get up, officer whore-hopper," the boy said, "and I'll do it again."

Drew was convinced that the boy would, and he did not wish to be hit again. What should he do?

"Get up, Drummond!" the boy yelled. "You yellow officer whore-hopper!"

The word yellow meant to Drew that he must get up and be hit again. As he gathered his legs under him, someone cried, "Beat it!" and the boys fled. The boy turned and faced Major Drummond, who stared down at him grimly.

"Get up, Drew," his father said without looking at him. To the boy he said, "What's the matter, son?"

The boy lowered his head and did not answer.

"I asked you what's the matter?"

"Just fooling around," the boy muttered.

"Your name is O'Rourke, isn't it?" Major Drummond asked him. "Which one are you? Bob? Dick?"

"Dick," he whispered.

"Well, Dick, let's see you and Drew square off again."

Dick O'Rourke stared up at him in amazement. Major Drummond looked at Drew. "All right, Drew, double 'em up and come on."

Drew wanted to run into the gathering darkness, but he dared not. He clenched and raised his fists and wavered toward Dick O'Rourke as his father stepped back. He swung wildly and missed, and he swung again and missed. Dick O'Rourke hit him lightly in the ribs and backed away. Drew rushed at him and fell across his hip and got up. Dick O'Rourke did not close, but stood, waiting Drew's next wild rush.

"All right," Major Drummond said, "call it off. There's no doubt but what you can lick him, Dick. You beat him. Take off."

Major Drummond did not mention the incident until they returned home after the fights. Then, on the bungalow steps, he said, "That kid is one of the sons of my first sergeant, Joe O'Rourke. Best Top I ever had." Inside, he went to the telephone and called O'Rourke's quarters. "Joe? Drummond speaking. Your boy Dick beat up my boy Drew this evening . . . Now wait a minute. He completely outclasses my kid, but they weigh in pretty close. It was fair enough. I'm calling you because you might hear about it and I don't want you to discipline Dick. Understand? You touch Dick and I'll beat *your* ass off. Understand? . . . Maybe some day we can arrange a return match. Good night, Joe."

The next afternoon, as Drew lay on the porch glider reading, his father strode in. Behind him came a lean, pale enlisted man wearing fatigues and carrying boxing gloves under one arm. Major Drummond frowned at Drew's book and said, "Get up, Drew, and meet Private Bannister. Private Harry Bannister. He's going to teach you how to box. You'll train with him until he's satisfied you *can* box. You're under his orders."

92

Major Drummond turned on a heel and walked out. Harry and Drew looked at each other guardedly. Then Harry said, "Let's go out back, Drew."

"I feel sorry for you," Drew said. "You got a lousy detail."

"It's better than K.P.," Harry replied.

"I mean you got a tough time teaching me. I don't *feel* like fighting. I don't want to learn."

"You'll learn," Harry said.

"Maybe I won't."

Harry looked at him shrewdly. "You'll learn because *I* want you to. You're my big chance, kid. You learn and maybe I'll even get a stripe back. I been in the stockade."

Drew whistled respectfully. "What for?"

"Beating up marines. You'll *learn*."

Drew did, fairly well. But he was not a natural at it, his heart was not in it. He tried, however, for Harry's sake. He wanted to like Harry and he wanted Harry to like him, but after a while he realized that he was only pretending he liked Harry. He did not dislike him; he simply could not get to know him well. For Harry raised a wall he could not cross. Drew was the Major's son and he was Private Bannister, wanting to be Corporal Bannister. He was Major Drummond's man, not Drew's.

Drew's mother protested strenuously the idea of his learning to box. "He's going to be a medical scientist," she kept saying to his father. "Why should he want to know how to box? He's going to discover the causes of all kinds of mysterious diseases, and *you're* going to look pretty silly, Jack, for having wasted his time."

Major Drummond invariably answered his wife's tangential arguments with mild amusement, a reaction that incited her more than the facts he mentioned: Drew had happened to read Sinclair Lewis's *Arrowsmith* a couple of months before and had begged money for a cheap microscope set. Now he was peering at rain water and other things and talking mysteriously of bacteriology and the like. "It means nothing, Dorothy, nothing." Hadn't he wanted to be a geologist for all of a month last summer? And before that it was an archaeologist and before that an airplane pilot. It was all meaningless. It was all inspired by the things he read. The trouble was that he read too much. He was neglecting the one thing he certainly would become: a *man*.

Back and forth, back and forth, until Dorothy Drummond hit on a taunting retort that reduced her husband to silence. "At least he's never wanted to be a damn Army officer, thank God! And I know him well enough to know he never will be one!"

Dorothy Drummond was a small, attractive woman with closely cropped golden hair. She was born into what used to be called the southern aristocracy, a loose description, and usually today a derisive description since so many novelists and playwrights have worked it over. If, however, aristocracy means privilege of station or place in a specific era, her family, the Huntleys, had been aristocrats. They traced (the word she was fond of employing) to the years before the Revolution in South Carolina. They were related to or socially familiar with families such as the Pinckneys and the Middletons, the Rutledges and Moultries and Mottes. They had owned a large plantation, and one Huntley had served his state briefly in the Senate, and another had been an Ambassador to Spain, and at least one had served in each of the wars through the Civil War—which seemed the end of historical time to surviving Huntleys. Dorothy's grandfather's brother had been killed playing cavalryman with Jubal Early, and her grandfather, who always was seriously referred to as "the Colonel," had jingle-jangled around for a time with that brave but slightly daft cavalier, Wade Hampton. To hear surviving Huntleys talk, life had not been the same since Sherman struck north from Savannah and Lee bowed his head at Appomatox.

I was twelve years old before Mother knew that Father's grandfather served with the North. It almost killed her. Isn't that crazy? But it almost killed her. And I think it helped to kill her love for Father. That's how much it meant to her to be a Huntley.

Dorothy Huntley Drummond's father had failed in business and practiced some law and died of cirrhosis of the liver at the age of fifty-three. Her mother and her Aunt Lucy lived together in an old house outside Charleston until they died in 1941. When Drew was very young his mother used to take him there sometimes. Although nearly broke, Grandmother Huntley and Aunt Lucy somehow managed to be served by an aged Negro retainer named Ivory Washington Jones who drove the ladies about in a 1910 Oldsmobile "Limited" and was forever dusting the books in the library, which contained such eighteenth-century rarities as Vattell's *The Law of Nations* and Sully's *Memoirs* and Grotius' *Questiones Publici Juris*.

In later years Drew came to feel that while there is nothing harmful in elderly women preserving illusions, his grandmother and her sister had worked great harm in what they did to his mother—or in what she had let them do to her. They had raised her to be a "lady," and it was a blow to them when she married his father. Doubtless they had expected that as a result of her beauty and vivacity and "breeding" she would capture some wealthy young blood who would both recoup the sagging Huntley fortunes and perpetuate the Huntley illusion—or, as they called it, the Huntley "tradition." Jack Drummond was passably respectable, of course, for he was southern and Army. But he was over-the-mountains Tennessee southern and he was Army poor and he had no rank to speak of.

Drew's mother and father had married, obviously, for the reason that most couples enter wedlock: they wished to legalize a romantic passion. His father was handsome and something of a hero because he'd picked up a Distinguished Service Cross in the First War. His mother was beautiful and something of a heroine because she'd picked up the title of a "Southern Belle" from her host of beaus and appearances at this and that cotillion. They were married in 1920, when he was thirty and she twenty-one, and they entered the anonymity of officers' row.

Anonymity was a state Dorothy Huntley Drummond abhorred. She was "somebody" in Charleston, as her mother and Aunt Lucy never tired of emphasizing when she returned there. But as the wife of Captain and then Major and then Lieutenant Colonel and finally Colonel Drummond she was, as she saw it, expected to be "nobody." Long afterwards she told Drew that marriage to his father had been a matter of her struggle to be important to him or to something against his determination to make her "unimportant." She liked to think of herself as a great rebel, but actually she rebelled only against those forces that made her life different from what it had been back in Charleston.

She waged her war of rebellion with a wide range of emotional weapons and an inexhaustible arsenal of notions. She was forever going off on self-improvement crusades. For a couple of weeks at a time she would seek to improve her mind by reading novels for seven and eight hours a day. Usually this was followed by an effort to "relax" her mind with murder mysteries, her favorite form of literature. Again, she'd try to improve her strong and durable little body by playing thirty-six holes of golf a day and abstaining from cigarettes and cocktails. After a while there would ensue a period of social self-improvement in which she'd entertain vastly and resume her daily consumption of four or five cocktails and two packs of cigarettes. She laughed a lot and she cried a lot. She loved to dance and she loved to flirt, so that among some of the older officers' wives she was considered a little wild.

Yet no scandal ever was attached to her name in those years, as far as Drew knew, because she was considered "basically sound." That is, she was patronizing to enlisted men and suspicious of Negroes and she scorned Jews. She was Episcopalian and a-political and a South Carolina Huntley—and to be a Huntley, she not so subtly let you know, was really to *be* somebody. But her pride of family was saved from social sinfulness by her candid claim to poverty and her prodigal spending of her husband's pay. For, quite unwittingly, she expressed herself fluently on certain matters that help you get along socially at any level of the Army: first, that you're broke; secondly, that you're worth much more than you're getting; and, finally, that you spend every cent you can lay your hands on.

Dorothy Huntley Drummond impressed Drew in his childhood as a good mother and he loved her deeply. For one thing, she was an interesting mother, always in a work about this or that and always taking him into her world. She loved him above all mortals, cared for his needs before her own, and gave him the impression that he was always right. She did not discipline him, but let him grow as the weeds grow, and she was indeed a weed with him.

In maturity Drew occasionally wondered if he would have been a better or a worse man had he remained totally under his mother's influence. Would his intelligence, which in children often assumes strange forms, have developed into a more creative purpose than had been his lot as policeman and professional killer and general roustabout in the world's upheavals? He could not know, of course. And to dwell on the plastic ages of childhood was futile.

To read the English language fascinated me, but to speak it bored me silly. I much preferred a kind of gibberish in which Mother sometimes joined me, though generally I was forced to imagine numerous people with whom to talk it. I remember Bud and Jake and I remember Hilo, who was neuter. "Depaddock me, gumpshaw," I'd say to Hilo, and Hilo would say to me, "Shaw, shaw, shaw, docked it." I do not know now what that meant, but I remember the words, and I remember that it was significant to me then.

He loved to draw and do water colors, but he shunned the usual subjects. In art, as in language, he preferred gibberish. One subject was a view between rug and floor, which no one ever had seen; it was dark and dusty and peopled with blastens, an invisible bug that drank

96

the sweet milk of rug fiber. His mother, to his everlasting gratitude, was an enthusiastic patroness of his art. He would, she said, become a great artist some day and he would live in Paris and she would visit him there.

Eventually he put aside art for composition. In the second grade in Manila, which he then preferred to think of as Grudo, he had a teacher named Miss Willow who inspired him to write the most popular composition of his life: "Miss Willow has hips like a pillow. It is round and soft and she can sleep on it all day. Once upon a time when asleep on her pillow Miss Willow woke up and found that school was over forever. She went home and never had a good sleep again." It was a smash hit (though not with Miss Willow, who did not see it because his mother intercepted it). His mother proudly showed it to everyone (except Miss Willow and his father) and eventually someone pinned a copy on the bulletin board of the Officers' Club. There his father read it and then cautiously removed it after learning the identity of the author.

In those days he liked to think of his father as Line. Line was long and forbidding and not filled in. You could walk all around Line, but you never could go into it and sit down and rock comfortably. Line quarreled with Mother over the Miss Willow composition. Line always started a quarrel in low tone and Mother pitched a high tone. Low tone rose and it became *ka-room, ka-room,* like field guns. Drew did not care. He lived his private life.

In later years he had great sympathy for his father in such matters as the Willow-pillow incident. His father understandably feared that Miss Willow would hear about the composition and be hurt. Furthermore, he did not like his son to receive such notoriety, for he clearly saw that he was a rather strange and egotistical little bastard, a show-off, a wise guy. His gibberish not only was nonsense; it was a symptom of something dark and unfathomable in his nature. So his father tried to kindly him out of it, for it was essential to him that Drew be manly. In trying to make him manly, he set out to *be* with him more. That meant their throwing and catching a ball together—a monotonous pastime, Drew thought. It meant that his father told him stories of men and arms and daring—dull stuff compared to the stories he could make up himself. In his own stories you could melt through any wall; in his father's stories you always had to strain yourself over a wall.

Kindliness failed one day when his father came home and found him lying on the porch floor doing numbers. He could write all numbers, but he liked to vary them, especially five, which looked better to him backwards. His father asked if such a big boy as he couldn't write numbers correctly. Let's see you do one through nine, he said. Drew wrote them down for him, making five backwards, as befitting his sense of the way it should be. Good, his father said, except for five. Like this.

"That's the right way to do it," he said.

"But it looks wrong," Drew said. "Why is there only one way?"

"Because everybody does it that way, Drew. Now let's see you do it." Drew made a five correctly.

"That's fine. Now do it again."

He scrawled it backwards.

His father yanked him to his feet, his face dark with anger.

"Don't squiddle me!" Drew yelled. "I done one for you and one for me!"

"Squiddle!" his father shouted. "What does squiddle mean?" He shook him so hard that his head wobbled violently. "What does all your pigheaded nonsense mean?"

"Oink Bud and Oink Jake! Don't squiddle me!"

Flinging him over a knee, his father laid on heavily with a hand. He'd never whopped him so hard before. Drew cried, less in pain or shame than in hope of release. His mother's shadow fell in the afternoon sunlight and she cried out more piercingly than he. What a row, but his father clutched him and would not let him escape it.

He found himself at the dining room table, a sheet of paper and a pencil before him, his father's hand gripping his shoulder, while his mother continued to cry out.

"Write five!" his father growled.

"You squiddled me!" Drew howled and then writhed under the pain of the grip tightening on his shoulder.

His mother screamed and struck at his father and raced out of the room.

"Write five," his father said.

He wrote five. Correctly.

"Write it again."

He did.

"And again."

He did.

"Don't ever say squiddle again. Understand?"

Squiddle, he thought.

His father shook him. "Understand?"

Squiddle, he thought.

"Answer me, Andrew!"

I burst into tears and buried my face in my arms on the table, think-ing, squiddle, squiddle, squiddle . . . But I suppose I had to learn some time and Father tried to teach me as best he could. I will not David Copperfield myself nor Mr. Murdstone Father.

The world was a public place, his father believed, and you had to live in it publicly. You could not merely get by in it. You must achieve above others. To achieve you must be strong, and to be strong you must write the numbers accurately and speak the language cor-rectly and ride a horse bravely and do the thousand things demanded in the world. But you must do them better than others. It was not enough merely to know how to box, for example. You must box better than anyone of your class.

So Major Drummond was greatly pleased when Harry Bannister reported to him that Drew was making favorable progress. He came home and watched when Harry brought a kid from the Y.M.C.A. in Honolulu to spar with Drew. He made a couple of suggestions about Drew's left and his failure to tuck his chin. But he made the sugges-tions to Harry, not to Drew, and when he left, he complimented Harry, not Drew.

Drew believed he was simply learning to box. He did not realize that he was being carried irresistibly on a carefully channeled current of events. But everyone in the battalion knew it. Once, as he cut through the battalion area, someone said distinctly, "Officer whore-hopper." He paused and turned around. Four enlisted men were dig-ging a drainage ditch near a barracks. They did not look up. Drew walked on, troubled.

Once, when he entered the battalion office to call for his father, First Sergeant Joe O'Rourke stared at him speculatively before his face creased in an unctuous smile. When he opened the door to the inner office for him, Major Drummond looked up and grinned. "What are you doing here, Drew? Hunting Dick O'Rourke?"

His mouth felt dry as Sergeant O'Rourke, still smiling unctuously, closed the door on them. Now he began to understand. He would tell his father that he didn't want to fight. But his father would dismiss as simple cowardice his plea that he did not hate Dick O'Rourke and wished only to forget him. He was expected—yes, it was demanded of him that he fight Dick O'Rourke. Honor, revenge, triumph. The men had set the stage and the boys must act like men.

As the days passed, he dreaded meeting Dick O'Rourke. A boy could not disguise his reluctance from the men, however. Eventually the men arranged it.

Harry said that he needed road work to improve his wind. After retreat one afternoon they trotted to the battalion office to meet Major Drummond. As they approached the office, Drew saw Dick O'Rourke sitting on the steps. He slowed to a walk.

Dick O'Rourke did not look up. He muttered, "Hi, officer whore-hopper."

Drew's heart pounded and he swallowed with difficulty. "Okay," he said, "let's get it over with."

Sergeant O'Rourke, a big man in butt and belly and chest, loomed in the doorway. Harry said to him, "Sergeant, your boy calls my man a whore-hopper and my man wants a fight."

"That's fair enough," O'Rourke said. "There's a pair of gloves in here somewhere." He looked at Drew. "You sure you want to fight, son?"

"No, I don't want to fight, you big fat bastard," Drew cried angrily, "but none of you'll die happy till I do, so let's get it over with."

O'Rourke threw back his head in a roar of laughter.

Major Drummond appeared behind him. "What's going on here, Sergeant?"

O'Rourke stopped laughing. "Your boy called me a big fat bastard, Major. And he wants to fight Dick."

Major Drummond controlled his smile. "You'll apologize to Sergeant O'Rourke, Drew."

"Like hell I will!"

The muscles of Major Drummond's jaw tightened. "We'll see about that later when you're not in such a fighting mood." Raising his hands, he removed his gold leaf insignia from the open collar of his shirt. "Let's go out back."

They went behind a barracks to a smooth clay square, a traditional fighting place. Men swarmed close silently. Major Drummond beckoned his famous fighter, the one whose name Drew never could remember, and said, "Referee 'em."

The fighter, a buck sergeant with a beaten face, came into the clay square and said, "Ya kids wanna shake?"

Dick O'Rourke shook his head.

"They's no rounds," the fighter said. "Ya gonna fight till one's had enough. Ya get outside dis ring ya's licked. Ya not back on ya feet by time I count ten ya's licked. No kneein', gougin', low-slingin', rabbit-punchin', other foulin', I disqualify ya. Lemme see dem gloves.

Harry tied the light gloves on Drew in one corner and O'Rourke tied on Dick's in the opposite corner. Drew did not listen to Harry's muttered directions. He saw his father standing, hands in his hip pockets, watching him. He heard a man say, "Drummond's kid called old O'Rourke a big fat bastard but that ain't why they's fightin'." He looked up and saw a Curtiss Hawk slanting down the blue sky toward Hickam Field. He was frightened and he wished his heart would stop beating so fast.

"Awright, awright," called the referee, "come on out."

They came out slowly and there was no sign of fear on Dick O'Rourke's face. They pawed and tried to feel each other out, as they had been taught. Drew swung and missed, and Dick swung and missed. Dick rained him lightly from belly to face, and Drew did not try to cover himself. He bore in and hit Dick's cheek. Dick stumbled back and recovered, then came in and knocked him sideways with a blow on the left eye. He hit the ground, his ears ringing. The ringing became the jubilant shouting of the men. The referee bent over him, yelling, "Tree, four, fie, six . . ."

He got to his feet and Dick was into him immediately, barely missing with an uppercut. Drew drove his left into Dick's belly and rocked him over with a right to his chin. Dick propped himself on his elbows, his expression stunned, while the referee screamed the count above the yelling. Dimly Drew heard Harry bellowing directions to him. Then Dick was on his feet and they pranced around each other uncertainly until the men began to boo. Drew went in hard, but he couldn't land on him, and he knew, vaguely, that Dick was the better fighter, he knew that Dick would beat him.

Dick's left seemed to come from nowhere in a long overhand that blotted out the sky. Pain stabbed his nose and he tasted blood. He was lying on the ground. The referee was bending over him, but he could not hear the count above the yelling of the men. He sat up and the referee still was counting slowly. He staggered to his feet, holding his gloves before his face, and there was no sound from the men.

Dick jabbed at him, circling, as Drew spread his legs and held out his gloves uncertainly. Someone shouted, "Call it!" The referee pushed back Dick and thrust his face close to Drew's. "Whada ya say, kid?"

"Whore-hopper," Drew said.

The referee grinned and cried, "He say, 'Whore-hopper!'" The men shouted delightedly as the referee stepped back and Dick drove in.

Drew weaved and spat blood off his lips. His left eye was closed, but with his right he made out Dick's bloody lips and cut cheek. Dick closed again and Drew weaved again, as Harry had taught him. Surprisingly, it worked. Then he smashed Dick's ear with a hard right hook. Dick staggered and slipped. When he got to his feet, Drew hit his face. Dick fell back and Drew followed, gasping for breath, throwing empty punches.

Suddenly Dick's fist seemed to explode on his temple and he felt he was drowning. He was lying on the ground and his father and Harry were bending over him. As his father lifted him to his feet, the men closed around them, calling out to him. He could not hear the words, but he knew the tone of pleasantry. O'Rourke pushed Dick forward and they touched hands without looking at each other, and then O'Rourke himself grabbed his hand and Drew muttered an apology through thick lips for having called him a big fat bastard. There were indistinct faces and voices somewhere beyond his throbbing head as he stumbled through the crowd with his father's hand on his shoulder.

They were in the car, driving fast up Waianae Avenue past the officers' quarters area, when his father spoke. "You fought a good fight, Drew. You got licked, but that doesn't matter, because you fought a good fight."

He started to cry, a child's wailing, his body shaking with sobs. His father did not tell him to stop. He patted his knee once and let him cry. Drew thought dimly, then, that he cried because his nose, his eyes, his entire head hurt so painfully. But later he thought, fleetingly, that he had cried because he'd lost more than a fight. He had lost a way he used to be, lost it so irrevocably that he could scarcely remember it.

At last he stopped crying and his father turned the car and came back along Waianae slowly.

"I want you to understand what's happened, Drew." His voice was low. "Your mother is going to raise hell over this, so I want you to understand. Because you and I will have to stick together. Some day you're going to be an officer." He felt of the gold leaf which he'd repinned on his collar. "You're going to have *privilege*. But you can't get by on that. A lot of officers try to—a lot right here at Schofield and everywhere else. Privilege is no good without strength. Do you understand? You have to be the strongest man in your outfit. You can't hope to lick everybody in it. You may not even be the smartest man in it. But you've got to be the strongest. By strongest I mean having the strength to take your lumps as well as dishing it out until everybody in your outfit respects you as a man. Because they'll never respect you for being an officer. They'll only hate you for that."

102

He was silent for a moment.

"You might some day wonder why it's worth the trouble. This being an officer, I mean. I'll tell you why. Because every few years the country would wash down the drain if it weren't for us. The officers, I mean. When the time comes, a good many of us aren't fit to do the job. But some are. Enough are. The ones who are fit when the time comes are those who haven't just been getting by on *privilege*. Do you understand why you had to fight Dick O'Rourke?"

"Yes, Father."

But he did not understand. For he did not want to be an officer. Of the many things he could become in the world, none would be worse than to be an officer.

Major Drummond turned off the Avenue to the quarters of a Medical Corps surgeon. He smelled of the whisky he was drinking before dinner, but his hands were gentle on Drew's face. He reset his broken nose and bathed his cuts with iodine and patted his head.

As they walked up the short path to their bungalow, Major Drummond rested his hand on Drew's shoulder. Dorothy Drummond sat on the porch glider, an empty glass in one hand, an empty Martini pitcher at her feet. She stared at Drew and then closed her eyes. "Go inside, Drew," she said unsteadily.

"Well, Dorothy," Major Drummond said, "what happened—"

"I know what happened!" she cried with her eyes closed. "I've heard all about it. Go inside, Drew!"

He went inside and sank down in a chair and rested his throbbing head in both hands. Next door in Major Duncan's bungalow the radio was blaring "Song of the Islands." The voices of his mother and father rose above the guitars whining *so-da-hee-ha-dee, so-da-hee-ha-dee* . . .

"I hope you're satisfied," Dorothy Drummond cried.

"Listen, Dorothy—"

"Shut up! You listen to me for a change. I said I hope you're satisfied."

The Duncans turned off their radio in order to listen.

"You forced him into doing a big thing for you, didn't you? The great democratic Major Drummond trying to show off for his battalion, the two-bit criminals and syphilitic little whore-hoppers you call the *Army*—"

"Now listen, Dorothy—"

"Shut up! Quit conning me. Quit conning *him*. You don't give a damn what happens to *him* as long as *you—you* make a hit with the stinking twenty-one-dollar bastards you call the Army. I *know* you,

Jack, I *read* you. Absolutely nothing makes any difference to you if only *they* would like you, the ones topside and the ones down under. Right now it's the ones down under. You want 'em to say, 'Drummond he all right, he okay, he let his kid fight one of *us* and *we* beat him up and *he* take it.' They'll talk about you in every bar on the island and you *love* it. You—"

"Listen, Dorothy—"

"Shut up! You're a killer, Jack, because you've got to be a *winner*. You've got to win even if it means him losing for you. You're a sort of baby-faced killer too. There's a lot of Goddamn Boy Scout in you, wanting to run around in a Goddamn uniform all your life bossing a bunch of small-time pimps and queers and mugs who couldn't even hold down jobs as clerks and waiters somewhere. And neither could you. You're *scared* to get out and make a decent living and *be* somebody. Look at you. Nearly twenty-five years of running around in a Goddamn Boy Scout uniform and what are you? A *major*. A lousy, stinking, two-bit *major* earning exactly—"

"Dorothy, Dorothy, please pipe down—"

"*You* pipe down! You pipe down and listen. I'm telling you now that the first chance I get I'm leaving you. I'm walking out on you and I'm taking *him* with me."

"So you're back on that tack," he said heavily. "You're back on the running-away tack. Every time you get a couple of drinks in you and something isn't just the way you want it, you're going to run away. Well, run away, Dorothy. I'm sick and tired of your clawing at me, so go ahead and run away. But take *him* with you and I'll come after you and I'll—I'll—"

He walked off the porch, slamming the screen behind him, and she began to cry. Next door the Duncans turned on their radio to drown the sound of her sobbing.

Chapter IX

"Let me buy one," said Harry Bannister. "That round was on you and this is on me. One for the road. Okay, Drew? One for the road and we go quietly."

Drew nodded.

Harry waved to the waiter and ordered their drinks. Turning to Drew he said, "I don't wanna p-presume on an old friendship, Drew, but I wanna ask you a p-personal question. I mean a sort of favor like."

"Sure thing, Harry."

Harry breathed deeply. "I hope you're gonna be nice to your father while he's here."

"I certainly hope I will be, Harry."

"Beyond that I cannot say. M-my lips are sealed."

Drew looked at him curiously. "Your lips are sealed? What do you mean?"

Harry slapped his face hard and leeringly mimicked a punch-drunk fighter. "Did I say that? I'm really punchy." Unaccountably his eyes filled with tears. "The General's a great man, Drew. He sure gave me the breaks. You wanna hear something? You know how I got my break with the General?"

"Back at Schofield, I suppose. When he took you on to teach me—"

"No." Harry shook his head violently. "In two, three years he was transferred Stateside, remember? But not me. I didn't see him again till—I dunno. Don't ever let on I told you, Drew. It was right before Pearl Harbor and I was at the Presidio. See, I was a corporal and—anyway, I had an overnight pass and I went into a place on Stockton Street in San Francisco for a beer and there was the General. Only he was a colonel then. A chicken colonel." Harry looked around the room carefully. "He was stinkin'. He didn't act it, but I could see it. He just sat there, drinkin' slow and steady. He sat right there at the bar. It's the only time I ever seen the General stinkin'—in just that way. I seen him sort a happy a couple times after something big in the war. But this is the only time I seen him stinkin'. See, this bar had a big long mirror behind it, you know the way they do, and I'm watching your father, I was a few stools down. I didn't wanna speak to him, natcherly. Well, he sees me in the mirror and he turns his head real slow and says real slow, 'How are ya, Harry?' It give me the funniest feeling, him remembering me. He says, 'Lemme buy you a drink, Harry.' I nearly fell off the stool. You know that isn't like the General. I mean drinkin' with enlisted men, you know."

Harry looked up and paused while the waiter put down their drinks. "*Grazie, camarado,*" he said and winked at Drew. He lifted his glass. "Here's to you, sir." He sipped his Scotch. "Where was I?"

"In another bar, Harry, having a drink with Father."

"Yeh. Well, I ask him about you and I ask him about his wife and he just nodded, nodded. P-pardon me for being p-personal, Drew, but how is your mother?"

"She's all right, Harry."

Harry shook his head. "The General never mentions her. But sometimes I think—I think it's too bad she and he—you know what I mean? I mean the General ain't no tail-hound. 'Scuse me saying that, but in the war and afterwards I seen him walk right by the stuff that's beggin' for it, and to him it's just like it ain't there at all. The General is a p-permanent sort of guy. I mean permanent about women, you know what I mean? Anyway I think it's too bad about your mother and him. I think maybe if she come back to him even now—I always liked your mother. I used to think she had a lot on a ball. That time in Texas"—he shook his head—"I was sorry, I didn't know what I was supposed to do—"

Drew stirred. "It's interesting you ran into Father in San Francisco that time, Harry. I never knew about it."

"Yeh. Well, anyway, your father just sat there drinkin' and not talkin' and I thought I better go. He says he's gotta go too. He was really loaded. He didn't stagger or anything, but he walks like he's in a brace. Outside he says, 'Good night, Harry,' and I salute him and he salutes me and he walks right out in the middle of Stockton Street, traffic coming both ways. He don't even see it and I run after him and drag him back. I ask him where he's staying and he don't know. So I get him in a cab and take him to this place I know, it's clean and safe and they put you up overnight for a buck and a half, this is before the war, and I put him in the sack and I sleep in the other bed. In the morning when I wake up he's lying there looking at me. He says, 'Thank you very much, Harry.' Then he says he's assigned down in the desert and he got a telegram yesterday, bad news, and he had a chance of a plane ride up to Frisco and he tied one on. Then he says, looking straight at me, he says, 'How'd you like to work for me, Harry?' It's funny, I know this is my big chance, even if it means the Goddamn desert, but more'n that, I know I'd like working for your father, I know he's one guy I wouldn't mind following anywhere. So I says, 'You bet,' and then I says I'm sorry about his bad news, and he says, 'I got a telegram from the Academy, Drew's booted out.' Ain't it funny how your bad luck was my good luck?"

Bad luck? It might have been the best of luck for him, Drew thought, if only he could have begun again when he boarded the West

Shore Railroad train from Highland Falls late that November afternoon.

There was nothing in his past to hold out promise for the future, it was true. A hell-raiser, a show-off, an academic failure. Booted from high school in Leavenworth, Kansas, for putting stink bombs in the ventilating system. Assigned to a small military academy in Tennessee run by an alcoholic headmaster who bore the title of "Colonel." Record there: Learned to smoke and drink corn whisky; improved fine points of cheating and lying; completed normal course in sexual experimentation by losing technical virginity to niece of "the Colonel." Comments: There was little distinction in the latter since she was the means whereby three students achieved the same end on the same evening behind the field house.

Assigned next to a better known southern military school which was called "The Jail" by most of its inmates. Record there: Abysmal. Learned the lock step of close order drill and how to survive as an individual under a totalitarian government. Failed to pass the entrance examination of the United States Military Academy. Comments: The Jail was an institution of rigid discipline whose goal was to make martinets of juvenile delinquents. That it produced some good soldiers was not to the credit of its faculty.

Assigned next by direct order of Colonel Drummond to a noted Military Academy cram school in Washington, D.C. Spent much time confined to Colonel Drummond's quarters, a small apartment on Connecticut Avenue where the Colonel's wife indulged herself with abstract painting while the Colonel was busy six days and many nights a week in the old Munitions Building, presumably helping to paste together a new paper Army. Record: Passed Military Academy entrance examination and received appointment. Comments: The cram course was so thorough and life on Connecticut Avenue so monotonous that any moron would have passed that examination.

At the United States Military Academy, he discovered, discipline was more stringent than at The Jail, but its faculty was more intelligent. He did not set out to be rebellious and collect demerits. He simply was appalled at what had happened to him. He was like one in a trance, like one suffering from shock at being sentenced for a crime he had not committed.

He baffled them. A test had demonstrated (he later learned) that he had the highest intelligence quotient of anyone in his class. They knew that he was an Army brat and that five members of his family had graduated from the Academy, his father and his great-grandfather with high distinction. They saw his obvious efforts to follow the rules and his incredible forgetfulness of the rules. He knew how to make a tight military cot, for example; but no matter how hard he seemed to try, his cot looked lumpy. They did a job on him, and then they tried kindliness. Finally, when he defied them and violated the fundamental rule by simply taking off, they had no recourse but to bounce him.

As the train descended into Jersey late in the afternoon of the day before Thanksgiving, 1941, he felt pretty good. He wore a gray Harris tweed sport jacket and he had forty-two dollars in his pocket and he was a free man. His mother would understand, he knew; she would even be pleased, for she'd fought his father all the way on sending him to the Academy. She had not gone to the California desert with Colonel Drummond. She had taken an apartment in Greenwich Village with the announced purpose of studying painting. He planned to go there. But he postponed his plans on the Weehawken ferry.

I remember going forward on the ferry and standing there in the dusk, staring ahead at the lights of Manhattan winking in the cold. I felt exhilarated. This was going to be my city. Here I would be good and great, as I had not been before.

A girl came out of the cabin and shrank from the cold and ducked back into the cabin. Wondering if she were beautiful, he went inside to investigate. She was not beautiful, but she was, he imagined, a college girl, home for vacation in one of the Jersey suburbs.

"Boy, it's cold out there," he said, hugging himself.

She didn't answer him as she strolled to a bench where another girl was seated beside a boy wearing a camel's hair coat. They stared at him. Ivy League kids, he thought, curdling with envy. He thought of Drummond at Yale. That was where he had wanted to go to school. Some place where there were people and books and a future. His eyes watered longingly.

He dug the heels of his hands into his eyes and said to them, "It's so cold out there it makes your eyes water."

The boy said, "Yeah."

The girl beside him said, "You need a coat."

"Completely forgot it," Drew said. "Walked right out of the house without it even though old Hudson was waiting there with it."

The girl he had decided was his girl asked, "Who's Hudson?"

"The butler."

She looked at him speculatively. Then she sat down on the bench and opened her coat and let him see the swell of her breasts under a white sweater. She crossed her left leg over her right, pressing the calf muscle against her right knee so that her leg appeared more shapely than it actually was. She did this very casually, but he knew that she did it for him, and he thought, What a pushover.

He said to the boy, "Did I meet you after the Princeton game at— No, maybe not."

"What Princeton game?" the boy asked.

"*What* Princeton game? Is there more than one?"

"Depends where you go." He raised his chin defensively. "I go to Rutgers."

The lucky bastard, Drew thought. But he looked at him sadly and said, "Oh."

"What d'you mean, 'Oh?' Rutgers is a damn good school."

The boy's date said to Drew in a tone she hoped was withering, "I suppose you go to Ha'va'd."

"God forbid. I'm at New Haven."

"New Haven? You mean Yale?"

She apparently had not read F. Scott Fitzgerald, Drew thought.

The girl whom he now considered his date spoke. "Where else?"

But he doubted that she had read Fitzgerald either.

Her name, I think, was Geraldine.

He told them he was going to the Biltmore. He never had been there, but he remembered reading a story in which some Ivy League characters met their dates under the clock at the Biltmore. But first, he said, he had to check his bag at Grand Central. Although not positive, he believed that trains to New Haven left from Grand Central. Geraldine said that she and the other two were meeting *her* date at the New Yorker. Drew suggested that they all ride to Grand Central where he would check his bag and then they'd go to the Biltmore and pick up *his* date and *then* they could all go on to the New Yorker. It was agreed, and in the cab Geraldine snuggled so close to him that he wondered if she really had a date waiting for her at the New Yorker.

At Grand Central he paid the taxi driver and checked his bag and proposed taking another cab to the Biltmore.

"A *cab* to the Biltmore!" exclaimed the boy from Rutgers.

"I *never* walk when I can help it," Drew said. "It's on me."

They entered a taxi and Drew told the driver to take them to the Biltmore. The driver looked around and said, "The *Biltmore!*"

"Yes," said Drew, sarcastically, "I presume you've heard of it."

How was he supposed to know that the Biltmore was only a block from Grand Central?

In the Biltmore lobby he looked over the crowd and said his date hadn't arrived yet, so why didn't they have a drink and dance?

"Look," said the boy from Rutgers, thinking of money. "Listen."

"It's on me," Drew said.

"Okay," Geraldine said.

Remembering a situation from a movie, he slipped two dollars to the head waiter, who found them a table despite their lack of reservations. The orchestra was playing "I've Got You Under My Skin," a tune he liked, and he asked Geraldine to dance. She began to sing the lyrics. He hated girls who sang while they were dancing, so he was forced to talk. Which meant giving her the third degree.

She was a freshman at New Jersey College for Women, but she was transferring to Vassar next year. At least she said she was transferring to Vassar. Her family lived in Ridgewood and her father worked on Wall Street. Did his?

"He used to," Drew said, "but now he's retired and just travels around all the time."

His father fascinated her; she kept asking questions about him. And Drew, of course, couldn't resist making it a fabulous story.

The floor was crowded with college students in town for the Thanksgiving holidays. Looking about, Drew wished that he could see some Joe or Bill from his school and meet their dates. He wished he were visiting a friend's house, a real house with a yard and a garage and a neighborhood, a place where they slept late on Sunday morning and then ate a big leisurely breakfast while they read the newspaper. He wished he were in a household where everyone knew what would happen on Monday morning—and a year from Monday morning.

Maybe Geraldine lived in such a household in Ridgewood. When he asked her what they did at her house on Sunday mornings, however, she looked at him as if he were crazy. When he plied her with questions, she gave him phony answers. He couldn't prove it, but he knew that she was talking phony, building up this and apologizing for that. Then he realized that she was talking so because of his own phony line. She believed him. He was stuck with his own story and he never would know how comfortable it was around her house on week ends. He began to feel sorry for himself. He even wished, momentarily, that he was back at the Academy where he was at least a recognizable part of a recognizable something.

"Let's sit down," he said to her. The other couple was dancing when they returned to the table. Drew sipped the Scotch he'd ordered and grimaced; he hated the flavor of Scotch.

"What's the matter?" asked Geraldine.

He started to tell her it was inferior Scotch. But he told her the truth, how his father was just an Army colonel and how he'd just been kicked out of the Academy and how he just couldn't see being a soldier. He did not look at her until he'd finished.

She stared at him with a kind of horror, as if the diamond she'd bought had turned out to be glass. Then she said, "I think you're absolutely the most horrid person I've ever met," and she rose from the table.

The boy from Rutgers and his date approached and Geraldine said to them, "Don't bother sitting down. We're getting out of here."

The boy from Rutgers stared at Drew oddly.

"Don't worry," Drew said, "I'll pay the check." Suddenly he laughed, high-pitched and hysterically.

They scurried away and people at adjoining tables turned and stared at him. He tried to drink his Scotch, but he couldn't swallow it. He paid the check and left. Stepping into a taxi, he gave the driver his mother's address. They had gone a long way downtown before he remembered his bag at Grand Central. But he did not ask the driver to turn back; he wanted to get home.

The taxi stopped in front of an old brownstone on a narrow street. By the faint light in the vestibule he made out four mailboxes, each with a card and a doorbell button. Printed in red ink on one card was *Dorothy Drummond*. He rang the bell frequently for two or three minutes, but there was no answer. Vaguely he wondered if he somehow could have come to the address of some other Dorothy Drummond. He pulled the card from its slot and turned it over. It was one of the engraved cards which his mother had required for formal post calls. Red ink lines had been drawn across *Mrs. Andrew Jackson Drummond, 3d*.

He returned the card to its slot and went outside. A strong west wind was blowing. Turning his back to it, he walked along the deserted street to a well-traveled avenue where he turned aimlessly and wandered through red pools of neon light. When he came to a brightly lighted cafeteria, he went inside. He was not hungry, but he told himself that he should eat. He ordered ham and eggs and coffee and sat down at a table where someone had left a newspaper. While he ate, he tried not to think about his mother or his father or the Academy or the future. He tried to concentrate on news of the war in Europe, which seemed remote and inconsequential compared to his own problems.

Restless, at last, from trying to kill time, he walked back to the brownstone where his mother lived. After he rang her bell several times, an old woman peered through the curtain of the inner door and shouted, "What do you want?"

"Mrs. Drummond," he called through the glass. "My mother, Mrs. Drummond."

"They's nobody home," yelled the old woman. "You go 'way or I'll call the police."

He tried to explain to her, but she kept yelling that she was going to call the police. So he went outside and stood in the lee of the stone steps. He knew that he should go back to Grand Central and get his bag and check into a hotel, but he could not bring himself to leave. He knew that he was like a child waiting there, wanting his mother to come home and comfort him. Several times he walked up the block to the corner, but he always returned and huddled out of the wind in the deep shadow of the steps.

He heard voices suddenly. Someone was walking up the steps. Then he heard his mother say, "If this isn' winte', Teddy, Ah dread Decembe'." Employing her exaggerated southern accent. The man said, "I'll keep you warm, Dotty." His mother said, "Then come on in an' wa'm me." They went inside.

He walked away blindly. He walked a great distance, trying to remember that he no longer was a baby, trying to remember there was no place left in the whole wide world for babies. At last, shaking with cold, he hailed a taxi which took him to Grand Central. He picked up his bag and inquired the coach fare to Nashville. Finding he was far short of the fare, he asked directions to a bus terminal. He walked there and found he had enough money to take him as far as Bristol, Tennessee, with thirty cents left over for coffee along the way.

In Bristol the bus driver directed him to a likely corner for hitching a ride. It was three o'clock on the morning after Thanksgiving, however, before a truck driver picked him up. Hearing his stomach rolling emptily, the driver bought him a plate of beans and hamburger outside Knoxville. He hitched another ride to Nashville, and then other rides south and west. The last mile to Burning Brook he walked. When his Aunt Mildred saw him, she threw her arms around him, and he felt that at last he was home.

Neither Judd nor Mildred ever asked him why he had come to Burning Brook instead of going to his mother in New York. And he, of course, never told them what had happened. Judd sent telegrams to both his father and mother, telling them where he was. His father did not acknowledge the telegram. But his mother telephoned Burning Brook as soon as she received the telegram. Tearfully she asked why, why, why had he not come to her in New York? He did not tell her that he had.

By the following Tuesday he decided that he'd like to enter Vanderbilt, Judd's alma mater. Judd drove him to Nashville on Wednesday to discuss college entrance with an old friend, a dean at the University. On Sunday a radio program of classical music was interrupted by a report of the Japanese attack on Pearl Harbor. On Monday Judd and Drew drove to Nashville again and volunteered for service in the Army of the United States.

Judd was rejected, but the Army accepted Drew.

Chapter X

In time of war, Drew learned, you can feel at ease in the Army of the United States by following its simple rules of housekeeping and maintaining a stolid indifference to your military fate. It is, no doubt, a state attainable only by men whose emotions or ambitions are unattached elsewhere. The few who attain it truly do (in the jeering words of the vast majority who fail to attain it) find a home in the Army.

Drew made himself at home. During basic training he was made a temporary corporal, a distinction he did not seek. After basic his stripes were made permanent and he was retained in the cadre, a fact that was unmeaningful to him since he did not especially care where he was shipped. He was promoted to buck sergeant and given an infantry basic training platoon. It was a role he enjoyed, for it gave him an opportunity to teach; and, since he felt that his life was an example of one who had been exposed to much bad teaching, he was instinctively a good teacher.

Eventually his company commander suggested that he apply for Officers' Candidate School. He declined because an officer's life offered nothing that he desired. After a while he was summoned to the office of a colonel at headquarters. The colonel knew his father and had taken the trouble to learn something about Drew. He had him sit down beside his desk and with his own hand, the hand that wore the Academy ring, he lighted a cigarette for him. The colonel asked what he heard from his father, and Drew was amused to watch his reaction when he replied, "Nothing, sir." For he had not heard from his father since he left the Academy nine months before. (His mother had written him, however, that his father had been promoted to brigadier general and was assistant commander of a division training in Texas.) The colonel wanted him to apply for OCS. Drew declined.

Two weeks later, at the end of a training cycle, he found himself on orders for the only place in the Army he did not want to go: the camp in Texas where his father's division was training.

After a delay en route at Burning Brook, he came to the hot and dusty plain where the Division sprawled. He waited resignedly in the enlisted pool to be summoned by his father. But his father did not summon him. Instead, he was ordered to B Company where he presented himself to Captain Jerome Stanley.

He instinctively liked Stanley, a handsome young man with a gentle voice. On his desk were photographs of a pretty woman, his wife, and a pretty little girl, his daughter, and a copy of *The Decline of the West* by Oswald Spengler. Stanley told him that he was assigned as sergeant of the second platoon. In dismissing him with a wave of the hand after a few minutes of conversation, he casually asked if he were related to General Drummond.

"He's my father, sir," Drew said, "but you can't help who you're related to."

Stanley laughed and turned him over to First Sergeant Panolski, an old regular who was not pleased to see so young a buck sergeant. Panolski introduced him to Corporal Joe Gannon of the second platoon, a thin young man with a curiously old, lantern-jawed face. Joe Gannon helped him carry his gear across the sandy waste from the company office to the barracks where the men, on noonday break, watched him guardedly. Joe Gannon closed the door of the squadroom which they were to share and sat down on his cot and stared at him solemnly.

"Well," Drew said, offering him a cigarette, "what's the pitch?"

"Okay," Joe Gannon said, accepting the cigarette and extending his lighter. "You're General Drummond's son, right?"

"Right."

"So you may not be around here long enough for it to matter. Maybe you'll go to OCS or something."

Drew told him that he never would go to OCS and that he expected to be around for a long time.

"This Company is pretty messed up," Joe Gannon said, "but battalion itself ain't so bad. It's Stanley's fault. Panolski sees it and he's wangling himself a transfer. Most of the other guys think Stanley is okay. Lieutenant O'Brian, who's in the hospital now, will never ship with us. He's bucking for a Section Eight or something. You can bet we're shipping soon. Some say North Africa, but the odds are the Pacific. I got that straight from a guy in AGO. Did Stanley tell you he went to Princeton?"

"No, he said—"

"He's saving that to wow you. He was a professor of sociology or something at some university somewhere. See, he's superior to the whole Goddamn thing. Now he's superior about having been a professor and when he was a professor I bet he was superior about having gone to Princeton. And I bet at Princeton he was superior about having come from a fine old New England family. You wait, boy, he'll take you all the way back to Plymouth Rock just to have you believing he's a great man. . . . Hey, did your old man put you on orders to come here?"

"I honestly don't know, Joe. I haven't heard from him in almost a year."

Joe Gannon rubbed his jaw incredulously. "What happened?"

Because Drew knew that he and Joe would become close friends, he told him about being bounced from the Academy. "But nobody around here knows that except you," he said. "I never put it on the record. And I don't want anybody else to know."

Joe smiled slowly. "Okay. So you trust me. I like that. Trouble with this outfit there ain't enough people trusting each other. You know what I think? Old Stanley caught your name on orders and made a grab for you. He figured an angle for him. But I bet it won't work. I don't think that as we sail into Tokyo Bay or somewhere and all hell's busting loose, I don't think your old man is the type who'll say, 'Let's see, now, my son is in Baker Company and—' Ah, the hell with it. But I mean I don't think it follows."

"It doesn't," Drew said.

"I'll tell you one more thing and then let's eat. The Division Commander is a foul-up. He was a big-shot insurance man or something while he was playing soldier in the National Guard. Anyway, I figure the Army made your old man his assistant to try to shake the lead out of the Division. But they ain't going to waste him under an insurance foul-up. And they daren't throw out the insurance man because he's got big political connections. I know that for a fact. So probably they'll yank your old man before we ship and give him something else to do. I'll tell you, I respect your old man. He's done a good job with us. He's rough, tough and nasty. But he's fair and he sure shook a lot of lead out of this Division. He pops up everywhere and talks to everybody. Week before last the battalion was on bivouac. It was raining and blowing and nobody paid much attention to guard duty. In the middle of the night your old man walks all the way into the battalion command post without being challenged once. You could hear him cussin' in Oklahoma. He chewed out the major and he had 'em turn all of us out into the rain and *all* of us stand guard duty the rest of the night. You couldn't see him in the dark and the rain but you could hear him reamin' out the whole Goddamn battalion from the major down."

"That's my father," said Drew.

A few days later Drew saw him as the company returned from the rifle range along a narrow road which wound through a gulley. He sat alone in a jeep at the side of the road, his arms locked over the wheel. He wore fatigues and a helmet liner stenciled with a single faded silver star. New lines were drawn in his tired face. At sight of him Drew's heart beat faster and he was tempted to fall out of the column and speak to him. The General watched the column intently, studying feet, faces, rifles, canteens. As Drew approached the jeep, the General's gaze crossed his abstractedly and then leaped back, his brows rising. Drew lowered his head quickly and instinctively. He stared at puffs of dust rising from the heels of the man in front of him and he did not fall out of the column, while he listened for his father to call after him. But his father did not call out above the foot-scuff and metal tinkle of the marching column.

In a few moments someone in the platoon said, "Hi, pop," and another said, "Hi, son." The first man said, "Where we headin', pop?" A couple of men laughed and Drew turned his head and said, "Hawaii, son." Fats Hibben, an innocent, called in his high voice, "No kiddin', Sarge, we goin' to Hawaii?" Along the column voices mimicked him, "No kiddin', Sarge, we goin' to Hawaii?"

The next afternoon following retreat Drew opened the squadroom door and paused in surprise. Harry Bannister sat in his chair, smiling at him. Staff Sergeant Bannister now, Drew saw by the stripes on his arms. He balled his fists and did the old duck and weave and said, "Who we fighting tonight, Harry?"

Harry grinned and got to his feet and they shook hands. "They got steaks at Headquarters Company," Harry said. "Come on over."

On the way to Headquarters Company Drew asked him what he was doing in the Division.

"I got a nice job, Drew. I'm working for the General."

"Which general?"

Harry looked at him. "Is there more than one honest-to-God general on this post?"

"So Father made you his number one boy. Can I pump you, Harry?"

Harry shrugged. "It won't do you any good. I don't know nothing, and if I did I wouldn't tell you."

They ate the thick steaks and crisp French fries of Headquarters Company. When they left the mess hall, Harry stuck a toothpick between his teeth, looked up at the lowering sky, and said, "Let's go over to the office."

They walked up the gravel drive to the sprawling white frame Headquarters as it began to rain. An M.P. seated at a desk inside the door glanced at them sharply and nodded to Harry. His steel-plated heels clicking sharply, Harry led the way along a corridor. He halted suddenly, faced Drew, and said, "Next door on your left. Just walk in."

The door was lettered BRIG. GEN. DRUMMOND. Harry's heels clicked down the corridor. Drew, looking after him, wanted to shout that he was sorry he'd eaten one of his damn thick steaks.

As he opened the door, his father looked up from his desk. He saluted smartly and said, "Sergeant Drummond reporting as ordered, sir."

His father's lips twisted as he stared at him. He got to his feet slowly and said, "Oh, can it, Drew." His hand extended, he came around the desk. With amazement Drew saw tears glitter in his eyes. He gripped Drew's hand and his left hand rested lightly on his shoulder. Turning quickly, he muttered, "Sit down, Drew, sit down." He paced to the open window and stood for a moment staring out at the rain. Then he faced Drew and returned slowly to his desk and sat down heavily. "Cigarette?"

"I've got one," Drew lighted his own cigarette while his father picked up a slide rule and turned it over in his hands, staring at it as if he never had seen a slide rule before.

At last he said, "I want you to know, Drew, that I had nothing to do with your being transferred to this division. It may have been chance, but I'm inclined to believe it was some—some—uh—well-intentioned person who—some well-intentioned person. I know it must be an embarrassment to you."

"And to you, sir."

"All right, all right." The General's voice rose, almost plaintively. "Forget that *sir* business."

"I'm just making like a soldier." Drew's voice rose too. "All my life you've wanted me to make like a soldier, so now I'm making like one and I hope you're satisfied."

General Drummond looked away, blinking. Finally he said gruffly, "Of course I'm satisfied. You're being a good soldier, Drew. I checked your record after—after someone saw your name on orders and remarked on the—the coincidence of names and—and I realized —I checked your record, Drew, and I'm proud of it. I—I understand you were recommended for OCS and turned it down."

"Correct."

The General, beating the slide rule softly in his palm, turned in his swivel chair and looked out at the rain. "I urge you to reconsider, Drew."

"You may urge me."

He tossed the slide rule on the desk and raised his hands helplessly. "Do you realize there is absolutely nothing I can do for you—"

"But I'm not asking you to do anything for me—Father."

"I know, I know. But damn it, I *want* to—to— All I can do is urge you to apply for OCS and I assure you your application will have the approval of this headquarters."

"And if I don't," Drew said slowly, "I'll ship with the Division. And that won't be pleasant. And there's nothing you would do to prevent it."

"Of course not."

"Check." Drew stirred. "You're doing a nice job of cleaning up the Division."

General Drummond frowned. "There's a lot more needs doing."

"And you won't be here to do it."

The General looked at him sharply. "Who says that?"

"A very smart corporal in my platoon who has no access to classified material. . . . What do you hear from Mother?"

He tried to smile. "Oh, she seems pretty wrapped up in studying painting. What do you hear?"

118

"Same thing. Well, you've laid it on the line, Father. OCS or be shipped. But if I tried to avoid the shipment you wouldn't like it. And if I went to OCS I wouldn't like it. So there we are. The old Mexican stand-off. It's been nice seeing you again, Father. I won't take any more of your time."

"Don't go." His voice rose urgently. "I've got nothing—there's nothing here—" His hands indicated the impersonal office. "Tell me, have you—have you got a girl?"

"No girl, Father, and no prospects."

"Well—how are Judd and Mildred? How's everything back at Burning Brook?"

"They're fine. Everything's fine." He rose.

"Listen." His father's eyes strained up to his in the dusk. "Listen, Drew, when you write your mother, tell her I was asking about her. She—she hasn't answered my letters in some time and—well, tell her I was asking for her, will you?"

"Sure." He held out his hand. "So long, Father."

General Drummond grasped his hand and clung to it. "Wait a minute, I'll have a car take you back to your area in this rain."

"Don't bother. What's a little rain?"

That same evening, I remember, I wrote one of my rare letters to Mother. I told her I'd seen Father and that he'd asked about her. I urged her to write him because he was very much alone and lacked even the dubious pleasure of my company since I was an enlisted man and socially untouchable.

A week later, in the late afternoon, there was a telephone call for him at the company office.

"Darling! It's Mother! I'm here!"

"Where?"

"At the Officers' Guest House. Come right over."

"Look, Mother—"

"I told Sergeant Bannister— Isn't it a coincidence he's here?—to pick up Jack." Someone must be listening to her, for she was employing her exaggerated southern accent. "Jack doesn't even *know* I'm here. He's away off in the woods or something somewhere. I'll wait right here for you, Drew."

When he climbed the steps of the Guest House, which was a wing of the Officers' Club, his mother hurried to meet him. She was heavily tanned; she looked—*different*. When she put her arms around him and kissed him, however, she still smelled of her familiar Chanel No.

5. Then she held him at arm's length and began to cry. He was embarrassed, for a group of officers' wives on the porch stared at them in fascination. His mother looked so young, he realized, that they were uncertain whether he was her son or her lover.

Drying her eyes with a lace-edged handkerchief and chattering incessantly in her southern accent, she led him inside. She ignored his protests that enlisted men were not permitted in the Guest House. But she was aware of the rule, for she had made an arrangement with the hostess: a small sitting room off the main lounge into which she led him.

Closing the door and abandoning her accent, she said, "Golly, I'm pooped. It took me nineteen hours to fly from New York. I got bumped in Memphis by a sergeant. No offense, darling, but a *sergeant!* I had them bring us some ice and glasses to go with this Bourbon." She drew a bottle from a paper bag and poured Bourbon over the ice in the glasses and let him light a cigarette for her. She raised her glass and said, "Cheers and stuff," and drank. "Now," she said, "tell me all about it."

"All about what, Mother?"

"Everything."

He quickly saw, however, that his mother had come to believe a good listener was a good conversationalist. She was telling him about the two months she'd spent painting at Miami Beach when his father opened the door.

He stood for a moment, staring at her. She cried, "Jack!" and leaped to her feet as he seemed to cross the tiny room in one huge stride. They kissed hard and his hands moved longingly on her back. Wishing to leave them together, Drew started toward the door. But his mother said, "Drew!"

"Drew." The General looked at him doubtfully and then they shook hands. He had taken pains, Drew observed, to slick up in his summer-weight uniform before coming to the Guest House.

"Here we all are together again after such a long time," said Dorothy Drummond. "Pour yourself a snort, Jack, and pull up a chair."

"Mother," Drew said, "I'm going to leave you and Father to talk for a while. I'll drop around after dinner. Say about eight-thirty—"

"You'll do nothing of the kind!" she cried. "Jack, where is the house that goes with that beautiful star of yours?"

"House?" He looked dazed. "Oh, well I'm living in the BOQ. I don't have a house, but—"

"No *house!*" she wailed. "I asked them at the gate and I thought they were just stupid when they directed me here."

"Yes," he said, "well, I wish I'd known you were coming, Dorothy. You—we can stay here for a couple of days until I—until we—" His face relaxed suddenly in a smile and he raised his glass and said, "Here's to everybody."

They simulated happy conversation in that tiny room, Drew thought, but their words hopped like wounded birds and would not soar. At last his mother said she was hungry and where did they eat? Drew rose quickly and said that he'd see them after dinner. No, said his mother, he'd see them *at* dinner or what was the point of reunion? Well, said his father, well. She turned on him.

"Jack, are you ashamed of your own son? Are you—"

"Good Lord, no, Dorothy, I was just about to say we're all going over to the Club next door and have dinner."

"All right," she said. "That's more like it."

As they passed through the Officers' Club lounge toward the dining room, General Drummond carefully introduced them to all ranking officers. Drew felt sorry for him. It was the General's absolute right to have his son, whether enlisted man or village idiot, as his guest at dinner. If one of them had simply been passing through the other's domain, there would not have been embarrassment for either. But this was a division, an institution as confined as a prison or a ship, and the General was its Chief of Staff and Drew a sergeant in its ranks. It would not be forgotten that the General had presumed upon the privilege of his rank to show a father's favoritism. If fate kept both in the Division, their relationship was an irreparable flaw to the General. *No privilege* was his motto. No privilege except to serve dutifully, to take the lumps of chance and circumstance. But now, with their relationship publicly emphasized, any good chance that befell Drew would be interpreted as a circumstance which the General had arranged. The General considered his viewpoint on this to be a matter of honor, the word he used to describe his pride. For proud he was, Drew knew, fiercely proud. His private image of himself must always be the public image. Let no one in the most remote outpost ever say, "Oh, Jack Drummond's okay, but he certainly set it up soft for his kid."

Dorothy Drummond knew all this, Drew realized. And she rejected it. What the General considered to be honor she saw only as his stubborn pride. She could not see, however, her own form of pride.

She sat at the dinner table, talking too loudly, showering her vivacity upon the stolid Club. She believed, Drew knew, that she was being like the South Carolina Huntleys, like the Southrons of yore, taking rightful advantage of her privileged place. Jack had achieved it and now she and Drew and Jack would enjoy it fully. That was the purpose of achievement, that was the right of a family. Had the Huntleys actually lived so, or did she merely choose to believe that they had? Could this moment on the Texas plains be traced far back to those who had stayed leisurely by the southern seaboard and to those who had pushed through the mountain gaps and gone down through the forests and canebrakes to find new land? Not actually, Drew thought. It could only be traced to the prides of a man and a woman which were fed by two pasts equally imaginary. In this moment each was living by a tradition.

For it was a moment. The General sat with his back to the wall, facing the latent hostility of the room. On his right, where he desired a loyal and subdued wife, sat a woman who came and went as she chose. On his left, where he desired a superior heir to his tradition, sat a stubborn youth who pained him deeply.

General Drummond knew that something was up. Dorothy had returned, wanting something. Had Drew prevailed on her to come and plead some special cause of his own or had she come at her own whim? And Drew knew that something was up as he waited tensely, toes curled in his shoes. After they'd finished dinner, he saw it coming when his mother said, "Let's all go over to your office, Jack. I'd like to see your office." General Drummond saw it coming, too. He nodded and rose woodenly and they filed silently from the Club.

Harry drove them to Headquarters in a sedan which bore a small, white-starred, scarlet pennant on a short metal staff. Inside the entrance an M.P. rose from the desk and stood stiffly at attention as they passed. When they entered the office Drew and his mother sat down on opposite sides of the General's desk while he rummaged through its drawers, muttering, "There's a pack of cigarettes here somewhere."

Dorothy Drummond lighted her own cigarette and said, "What's up?"

The General sank back in his swivel chair and smiled at her vaguely. "What's up? What do you mean, Dorothy?"

"I mean what's up with you and Drew and this division?"

"Well," he said, "I don't rightly know myself. I don't—"

"Of course you know, Jack. You merely don't want to tell us. This afternoon at the Guest House all the women were talking about the Division going to the Pacific soon."

General Drummond frowned. "You know how rumors float around a post. Those women shouldn't talk so. It's a definite breach of security."

"And I suppose," she said, "that you'd consider it a breach of security to tell us what you know."

The General nodded gloomily. "I would. And you should understand. The movements of a division in wartime are classified information. If I found anybody in my command discussing classified information, I'd have him court-martialed."

"Okay." Dorothy Drummond smiled tightly. "I'm not asking you to have yourself court-martialed for my sake, Jack. It's obvious that you don't think you can trust me—or Drew."

"Oh, look, Dorothy—"

"Skip it, Jack. Skip the Division. Let's take up Drew. What's going to happen to him? But first let's get it straight that he didn't ask me to come here to try to do something for him." She glanced sharply at Drew. "I don't hear from him very often any more. But you might like to know, Jack, that he wrote me a nice letter saying he thought you were lonely. You might put that down in your little record book."

General Drummond looked at him reflectively.

"What I want to know, Jack, is that now you've had Drew assigned to this division—"

"Dorothy, I did *not* have him assigned here. I had nothing to do with it. It's the last thing—well, I didn't want it to happen."

"I believe you, Jack. And you've answered my previous question. The Division is pulling out for the Pacific and you won't be going with it. But Drew will. That is, unless you do something about it. What are you going to do, Jack?"

He got to his feet and paced to the window and back. He sat down and said, "I've urged Drew to apply for OCS. I've told him his application will be approved by this headquarters. That's not because he's my son. It's because as an enlisted man he's showed himself eminently qualified to be an officer. And we need officers."

Dorothy Drummond smiled at her husband and turned to Drew. "Okay, darling, you're set. Have you put in your application?"

"No, Mother." Drew began curling his toes in his shoes again.

"Why not?" Her voice rose. "I know you think I'm an awful snob and all that, Drew, but do you think I take much pride in you running around as an enlisted man?"

General Drummond said, "Uh . . ." and slumped back in his chair.

"I rather doubt you do take much pride, Mother, but—"

"There," she said briskly, "I've said the wrong thing again. I take it back. *Why* don't you want to be an officer, Drew?"

"Apart from my sheer Drummond and Huntley stubbornness, the life makes no appeal to me. I don't want to be a *leader*. I like living in a platoon with other guys and I hate all the paper work officers have to do."

She stared at him, smoke curling from her lips. At last she said, "You mean you just don't want to be a soldier."

"That's true, Mother. I'm a natural civilian."

"And I think great things are in store for you in civilian life." Her tone followed her gaze to the remoteness of a ceiling corner. "I think it's a shame the way you've been forced to go in ways you didn't want to go. It's a shame what bad parents we've been. With a chance you can become something *great*. I've often thought what a fine career you could have in the diplomatic service. You remember I've told you about your great-great uncle Thomas who was Ambassador to Spain. That—that's in your blood more than all this soldiering." She looked solemnly at Drew's father. "We've got to help him, Jack. As his mother I've been a failure and I—"

"Yes." General Drummond added hastily, "I mean, no, you haven't. But"—he tried to make his tone humorous—"it's rather difficult to plan a diplomatic career for him in the middle of a war."

"Stop kidding," Dorothy Drummond said. "I'm deadly serious, and I know it's late for being deadly serious. But I am. He's bright. He has this wonderful I.Q. . . ."

Drew wished they'd stop talking about him as if he were a problem to be solved. He wished that they'd realize he was a living, thinking person and not just a dream that haunted them. He wanted to tell them that it was a mistake they had married and he had been born. And since he was a mistake, they should let him go off and correct himself in his own way.

"That student training program will be abandoned," General Drummond was saying. "Dorothy, there's a *war* on and a war needs soldiers, not students. From Drew's own record I believe that he himself would say—"

"Hey," Drew said, "here I am. I'm sitting right here. Can you see me?"

"What?" His father frowned at him.

"I *know* you're here, darling." His mother stretched a hand across the desk toward him. "And that's why I'm here." She looked at his father. "Listen to me, Jack. I've come back. Do you understand? I'm back. I want to stay with you. I want to live with you and be your wife. Do you understand?"

He nodded and lowered his gaze.

"I want—oh, I want us to be a family again, a family like we never were. But here I am and you're going off in one direction and you're sending him off in another. How can we be a family when—"

"There are quite a few families like ours right now," General Drummond said.

"All right. But I'm trying to get *through* to you, Jack. I'm trying to tell you that I want to be with you as long as I can. And if you must eventually go off, must you send him off too? Wouldn't you, for the sake of this family, do what was in your power to—to let it survive? Will you approve his transfer to some other place in this country where he has a chance to stay a while, where he has a little time?"

"Mother," Drew said, "I don't want a transfer anywhere."

They did not hear him. His mother's gaze charged his father and he fell back in his chair, eyes lidded heavily, defensively.

"Let me get this straight, Dorothy. You say you want us to—to *live* together again, as if there were some doubt that we were more than temporarily apart. And you say you want me to—to set *him* up some way so that he'll be *safe*."

She said measuredly, "I want you to do what any normal father would do who has the power to help his son."

"We'll set aside for the moment the question of what is normal behavior in a father. What I want to know, Dorothy, is whether these two desires of yours—to live with me as my wife and to give Drew some tenure of security—are in any way related?"

"If you'd listen to me for a second," Drew said, "I'd—"

"Please be quiet, Drew." His father did not look at him. "Are the two related, Dorothy?"

Her chin trembled. "They are not."

"You're sure then, Dorothy, that you aren't trying to strike some kind of *bargain* with me?"

"I am not." Tears suddenly flooded her eyes. "I *was* not!" she cried. "But you force me to! You pull and drive at me as if I was a—a horse or one of your enlisted men. You *kill* everything." Her voice rose higher. "All right, I *will* bargain with you. If you won't try to do this thing for Drew, I'll divorce you! Do you understand?"

His hands closed convulsively on the arms of his chair. "I think you would," he muttered.

"You're Goddamn right I would!" she cried. "I—"

"Please," he said, "these walls are very thin."

"All right," she whispered hoarsely. "All right, let's always remember the thin walls. Every place I've ever been with you the walls have been very thin and life has been a public spectacle. But I'm telling you, Jack, that if you won't do this for me—for *me*—I'll divorce you. And if you try to stand in my way . . ."

Her voice died and she rose hypnotically as he got slowly to his feet, his shoulders stooped, the knuckles of his hands pressed whitely against his desk.

"If you tried to stand in my way," she cried, "I'd put a divorce case in the newspapers that would make you the gossip of the Army and fix for all time that precious career of yours."

He hit her. His right hand flashed, palm open, across her face. She staggered. Drew had not realized that he was standing too, for he caught her as she stumbled against the desk. She began to cry, an uncontrollable low wail.

The General looked at her and then at his hand incredulously. Suddenly he raised both hands to his eyes, like a man blinded by fire, and he muttered, "I'm sorry. I'm sorry, Dorothy."

She rested against Drew, wailing.

"Dorothy," he said, lowering his hands and staring at her, "what's on your conscience that you must carry on so?"

"For Christ sake, *General!*" Drew shouted.

He led his mother out, holding her firmly by an arm. In the corridor a fat major pattered ahead, his perplexed moon face turned over a shoulder toward them. Harry, lounging beside the sedan, did not open the rear door.

"The Guest House," Drew said.

Harry rubbed his jaw. "Did the General—"

"Skip it!" Dorothy Drummond cried and plunged off into the darkness.

Drew said, "I'd like to remind you, Harry, in case you'd forgotten, that you're a son of a bitch."

When he caught up with his mother, she said, "I'm clearing out of here. I wouldn't blame you if you went awol and came with me."

"I'm coming with you," he told her, "but I'm not going awol."

He left her at the Guest House and trotted to the company office where he forged Captain Stanley's name to an overnight pass. Without asking a question Joe Gannon handed him the key to his car, which he kept off the post. He offered him cash if he needed it. Drew borrowed fifty dollars and hurried back to the Guest House.

A taxi took them to Joe's car. They scarcely spoke during the seventy-mile drive to the airport where she bought a ticket on a six o'clock flight to Dallas. They sat together on a bench in the small terminal throughout the night. She wished, he knew, to tell him something important, but words failed her. Eventually she fell asleep on his shoulder. He awakened her with hot coffee a few minutes before flight assemblage. She smeared on fresh lipstick and began to cry. He begged her not to cry and he gave her seventy-five dollars, which was all he had. "Buy something special for yourself," he told her. He kissed her good-by and gently pushed her toward the plane. In the plane doorway she stopped and looked back at him, crying and kissing her finger tips and waving to him.

He saw his father only once, at a distance, before General Drummond left the Division two weeks later. He was given a review parade on the Friday before he quit the post. As assistant divisional commander General Drummond had cannibalized the division band, sending its members into pursuits he considered more essential than music. So the division marched to the music of a small post service field band: eight fifes and eight trumpets and eight snare drums. The musicians, wearing white leggings and helmet liners, stood at attention below the reviewing stand where General Drummond towered above the slack-faced divisional commander.

I remember the drums crashing and the trumpets blaring and the fifes shrilling as the Division marched past in its cloud of hot summer dust. Through the dust you could see Father standing, straight and . . .

Chapter XI

Gravely staring toward the distant mountain line, which marched through clouds like a lumbering column in its own dust, General Drummond said, "Magnificent!"

Westward from the mountain clouds the blue sky arched until it seemed to rest on the sharp thrust of the castle keep behind him. He stood upon the balcony, his gaze traveling from the mountains to the hills that pitched beyond the battlements.

"It's beautiful," Jane Raleigh said. She was looking up at him, smiling, her eyelids narrowed against the glare of sun cast off the walls and the tumbled stones of the castle bailey below. How curious, he thought. There was pride in her expression, as if she were proud of him or proud to be with him.

"I wish—" He was silent. What did he wish? Now he decided he knew what he'd been about to say. Standing here, he'd been thinking of *The Scottish Chiefs,* a book he surely had not thought of in many years. But a book that very long ago had been his favorite, so devoured that he remembered long passages from it. Not now, of course, Oh, no?

Wallace married Marion Braidfoot, the beautiful heiress of Lammington. Nearly of the same age, and brought up from childhood together, affection had grown with their growth; and sympathy of taste and virtues, and mutual tenderness, had made them entirely one . . .

They didn't write of love in such a fashion any more. Love, they had decided, was not as simple, as gentle, as—chaste as the love of Wallace and the maid Marion. And they were right, of course. Look at myself! In those days so very long ago Wallace had been himself. But not any more, not for more years than he cared to remember. Though Wallace no longer was himself, an image had flashed from the indestructible trove of memory. So he had said, *I wish—* It was romantic, it was childish. But he had remembered the time when he wished that his life might be so.

She still looked up at him, wondering what he wished. She did not ask him. The question would have presumed a familiarity that, regrettably, did not exist between them.

He said, "I wish this good weather would continue." And then he regretted the circumstances that made him afraid to speak of more than the weather.

The gentle breeze this afternoon was from the east; it stirred Jane's dark hair. He looked away quickly, his gaze narrowing on the business that had brought him here to Castello di Falcari this morning. At the end of the balcony Drew was stretched in a beach chair, reading a book. Near him sat Marcia, wearing dark glasses and sketching on a drawing pad. They did not seem to understand the mystery and grandeur of the ancient castle in which they found themselves. Sometimes the young were too inclined to prosaic comforts, seeking popsicles in paradise. Here now, the General thought in some alarm. This Castello di Falcari must have somehow touched him in a tender place. For nothing could be better than that Drew enjoy prosaic comforts—at the same time that he remembered his duty, yes, his destiny of leadership. But the girl with him on the balcony should be Jane, not Marcia.

Jane was speaking. The General nodded, but he did not really listen. He was experiencing a small and momentary panic. He had set a stage. The players were on, but how would he maneuver them to the designed conclusion? Marcia the enemy to be removed. Drew the ally to be won. Jane the unwitting instrument of victory. Once he might have thought his plan fantastic. But now he must do something. The long promise of the family, never quite fulfilled, was forever doomed to be inconsequential if Drew . . . I must, he thought, do *something,* and this is all I know to do now that it is so very late.

"That's why," Jane was saying, "I think he must have been a very great man."

She had been talking of his grandfather. After lunch he'd given her Grandfather's journal. Copy it, he'd told her. But read it first. Then he'd gone to his room and dozed for more than an hour, not because the doctors had ordered it, but because he had lain down to *think*. Well, he hadn't done any important thinking. The stage was set, but he still did not know how to begin. He was improvising, and the only encouragement was that the best battles were series of improvizations.

She had taken the journal into the small library which Marcia had suggested as a good workroom for them. There she had set out her portable typewriter and notebooks and paper. A conscientious girl, she wanted to get to work and prove his wisdom in hiring her at the rate of one hundred dollars a week and expenses. (What would she think if she knew his basic motive?) In asking her to read the journal he wished to acquaint her with the Drummonds and also to spar for time while he decided where to begin.

"Let's sit down in the sun." He indicated two chairs near Drew and Marcia. "You have your notebook, I see." He smiled at her wrily. "I drop few pearls of wisdom."

He paced along the balcony and she walked beside him. Drew looked up, smiling at Jane, his gaze lingering on her pleasurably. Good, the General thought. Then, glancing at Jane, he saw that her expression was inscrutable as she looked at Drew.

Marcia, her lips pursed, did not glance up from the careful execution of a pencil line. Perhaps only she surmised his purpose. In the few seconds last night in Florence when he had weighed her invitation to come here, he had realized her motive was to keep Drew near her. And she had known his wish to keep Drew near him. She must have feared that in Florence he might absorb Drew and draw him from her. But here she had him under her eye. Woman-wise, she must have seen Drew's interest in Jane. Doubly woman-wise, she had preferred that his proximity to Jane occur within her orbit. In many ways, the General thought, she was a worthy opponent. But she maneuvered helplessly within his wings. He used her. He would envelop her. She was, however, a worthy opponent.

"What are you reading?" he asked Drew.

"*Thought and Expression of the Sixteenth Century* by H. O. Taylor. It's a good one."

"I had to read it at Wellesley," Jane said.

Marcia looked up from her drawing. "I didn't know you went to Wellesley, Jane. If I had an education like that I'd go around telling everybody about it."

"Why?" said Jane. "It's just a girls' school. It doesn't equip you for anything. Dad had to send me to Katherine Gibbs for a year afterwards so I could get a job."

"And then foreign travel," Drew said. "And here you are. That's a nice uncomplicated story."

Marica, holding up her drawing, cocked her head at it critically. "But Jane," she said, "is a nice uncomplicated girl."

"No, I'm not." She frowned and her tongue touched her underlip. "I think I'm pretty complicated."

"It's the way to be," Drew said. "Sit down and tell me about your complications."

The boy annoyed her when he spoke so, General Drummond observed. He did not blame her. Drew's frequent determination not to be serious abraded her underlying seriousness.

"Another time," she said drily. "I have work to do for your father."

"Well, now." The General spoke quickly. "I'd like to sit outside a while and talk over some things, Jane." Marcia stared at him fixedly; he wished he could see her expression behind her sunglasses. "We won't interrupt you two. I'll move these chairs up the balcony."

"You aren't interrupting us," Drew said. "Sit down and talk about the book." He smiled faintly. "It's what you came to Italy to do, isn't it?"

Marcia tore the sheet of paper off her pad and ripped it in half.

"Oh, don't!" Jane exclaimed.

"It stinks," Marcia said without emotion. "I'm a lousy sketcher and I don't know why I ever try."

"But maybe there's something you can salvage," Jane said. "Let me see it."

"Never." Marcia ripped the halves. "There's nothing to salvage it for." She smiled at her suddenly. "But you're sweet to care."

General Drummond said to Drew, "Jane has been reading your great-grandfather's Civil War journal." He moved a chair and sat down.

"What do you think of it?" Drew asked her.

"It's fascinating." She sat very straight. "I haven't finished it yet, but I suppose you've read it all."

"Yes, a couple of times." He looked at his father. "I'm surprised Judd would let you cart off all that stuff. It's pretty valuable. You could have copied what you wanted to bring along."

"Now that would have been intelligent," General Drummond said, "and it shows how stupid I can be. But I decided almost all at once to come over here. I suppose Judd thought of it when I asked him if I could bring this material. He knows, of course, that I'll guard it with my—my life, but— How far did you get with it, Jane?"

"The Battle of Atlanta. But I don't have to finish it before I begin copying, General. I can start copying right away."

"There's no rush," he said, "no rush, Jane. You've already read one of the best sections. The section about Shiloh."

"Why do you call that one of the best sections?" Drew asked.

"He told it well," General Drummond said. "Graphically, I mean. But Shiloh has been told well a hundred times. That's not the point. The point is that writing it in 1867, only five years later, he saw exactly its significance. Not just its strategic significance. The important thing Grandfather knew, as he recorded it in 1867, came long before the historians made it an accepted fact. He says, you remember, that eighty thousand men stood up and shot it out for two days at Shiloh, most of them hearing a shot fired in anger for the first time. And nearly twenty thousand of them got hurt or killed. After that, he says, he knew it would be a long and bloody war. And you remember he dwells thoughtfully and at length on the nature of his fellow Americans who could fight so hard with absolutely no knowledge of the strategy they were following or the history they were making. There was no glory and a lot of terror and not much realization of *why* they fought. But fight and fight they did. It reminds me of Normandy."

He fingered a cigarette from the pack he always carried. They'd told him he had to stop smoking and he'd obeyed them fairly well. But now he didn't care. He wanted a cigarette. He lighted it and stared at the mountains as a flight of swallows swept in over the battlements and wheeled, crying.

"They say that politics is the art of the possible, and I say that war is the art of the impossible. It seems utterly impossible that you can take this apparently passive animal man away from his home and everything he knows, take thousands of them and throw them together and cart them thousands of miles and tell them go ahead now, go ahead and get your heads blown off. And man does it. By the thousands. War is the art of getting him to do this impossible thing. The art of war is practiced by only a few thousand of the millions engaged in it. The millions merely try to imitate the artists. There have been many generals who were not artful at it. There have been many privates who were. I've seen true artists of war who never came near combat. And I've seen highly decorated heroes who were fools at war."

He looked at Jane. She had been making notes, he realized. Now she was looking at him, her expression rapt, her lips slightly parted. As if, he thought remotely, I were making love to her. He did not amend the thought, for it seemed so disembodied from himself that someone else might have thought it.

"Let me tell you a theory of mine about soldiers," he said to her. "I'm thinking especially of officers. The theory may apply to businessmen—and the arts too, for all I know. But I believe it especially applies to officers. A man, any man, is either intelligent or stupid. And a man is either energetic or lazy. Now the very best commanders are fundamentally intelligent and lazy. An outstanding example was

132

Grant. Napoleon, too, whether you believe it or not, was fundamentally lazy. Because such a man is intelligent and lazy he picks a brilliant staff to work for him, and that's one reason he's a great leader. A good staff man, as compared to a great leader, combines the qualities of intelligence and energy. There have been many, many good staff men. Sometimes a great commander has to function as his own staff, when for one reason or another he cannot obtain proper men. Lee was such a man; he had a couple of good field commanders, especially Jackson, but he had no staff. Neither did Washington, the only great commander who had to learn simple tactics as he went along; he had Nathanael Greene, but he never had a proper staff. Excuse me, I wander. There, in any event, you have the best types of officers. However, most officers, like most men, are stupid and lazy. There you have the mass of officers. And finally you have the most dangerous type of officer, the one who is both stupid and energetic. Beware of him, especially when his command is as high as a division or a corps.

"That is rather a parenthetical thought, Jane, but I'm glad you put it down. I think it should be put down. It was by way of saying that my grandfather was intelligent and energetic. He was a good staff man. He did very good work under General Thomas, who was brilliant. A fine accord existed between them, you noticed in the journal, because both were southerners fighting for the North."

Over the walls swallows broke their pattern of flight and scattered, crying.

"I'm putting myself into the record too. I feel I must. As an officer I was both intelligent and energetic, like my grandfather. I was a good staff man." He looked at Jane again. "And while you're about it, put this down too. Drew is intelligent and lazy. That is why—and put this down—he has the potential of being a great commander some day. A better commander than I was." He was careful not to look at Drew. "I've never discussed it with him, but I once talked with his regimental commander in Korea, an intelligent man who cannot help being energetic. Drew's battalion was the finest he had ever known, he told me, because it seemed to function as one complete staff. That, the regimental commander told me with genuine admiration, was because Drew is lazy. He selected the best men for the routine jobs and trusted them. However, though Drew is lazy, he understands *example*. It is not necessary for a battalion commander to go on patrols. But he went and was almost killed. A battalion, you understand, is a microcosm of an army.

"I truly am rambling. But let's get some of it down and sort it out later. Ten years ago I did not fully comprehend some of the things I'm saying now. I believed greatly in myself, and that is important in a man. I believed that I was fitted for the highest commands. That I never rose higher was partially a matter of chance—and something else too. Meaning my own limitations. Ten years ago I did staff work in the invasion of Sicily. I was begging for a division. They were right in keeping me at what I was doing because I was pretty good at it. Then I was sent to England. Staff work again for the invasion. The invasion came and a couple of weeks passed. One day The Man called me to his tent. He said, 'Jack, you've been crying for a division. You can have one, but it may ruin you. It's ruined two men.' I knew the one he meant. It was badly fouled up. I knew its trouble. There is always only one thing wrong with an American division that has had enough training and is still fouled up. Its officers. I took it, of course, on condition of unlimited housecleaning authority. And I went down there and cleaned house. I got men I wanted for replacements. There was no time for training. We had to go into line. Hedgerow stuff. Corps didn't want us for the job that had to be done, but Army backed us and Corps had to take us. It was rough." He looked at Drew. "You remember?"

Drew sat, eyes half closed in the bright sunlight, staring toward the mountains.

"Drew?"

"Sir?— Yes. Yes, Father, I remember."

"Drew was in the division on our left," he said to Jane. "He was a replacement, a second lieutenant. I had to go to Corps the day after the division on our left kicked off, the day before we were to push off. Harry was driving the jeep, I remember. We were balling along a road. A truck had skidded and bogged in the ditch. Twenty or so fresh-faced first and second lieutenants had climbed out and were pushing it. It was obvious who they were. Replacements. Casuals. You have to try to forget the human element in a time like that, you know. But I remember thinking, before I cut it off, that they were like cattle being lugged to market."

"That was a very accurate observation," Drew said.

General Drummond frowned. "You do not feel that way about officers and men who are in their own units," he said to Jane. "It's the replacements you're in danger of feeling sorry for. Though before it was over and we broke out, a replacement who lasted three days in some front line outfits was an old hand. Anyway, Harry suddenly swore and braked the jeep and I asked him what the hell he was doing. He told me Drew was back there. I thought he was crazy. I thought Drew was in the States. But I looked back and saw him. It gave me a turn. I jumped out and went back. He told me where he was headed and it made me feel sick. He had to go on, of course, and I had to get to Corps. But in the days that followed it didn't help me concentrate on what I had to do knowing where he was."

Marcia spoke. "May I interrupt with a question, General? Couldn't you have had Drew transferred to your division?"

He wished she had not covered her eyes with dark glasses. "Technically I could have. But it would have been an impossible situation."

"Impossible?"

"Maybe I can explain more easily, Marcia," said Jane. She glanced apologetically at General Drummond. "I think I understand because my father's an officer. I have a brother who graduated from the Academy five years ago and he's in the Army too. He and my father aren't too close. They're on the best of terms and all that, but not exactly the way Daddy and I are." She hesitated. "The point is that neither Dad nor Jerry would ever want to serve on the same post. The Army wouldn't want it either. Even if there wasn't any favoritism, which there wouldn't be, people would think there was. It would be the same with me if I were a man. Dad and I are very close, but neither of us would *tolerate* my serving under him." She looked at the General embarrassedly. "Excuse me for interrupting. I—"

"You put it very well," he said quickly. "Heaven knows I need interpreters for what I'm trying to say. I'm not trying to take our family chronologically. A tradition does not grow by exact chronology. And that is the important thing, the tradition. There are differences, but great basic similarities between my grandfather and me—and Drew. If—"

"Father."

He looked alertly at Drew, who sat with his hands clasped behind his head.

"You speak a great deal about your grandfather," Drew said. "And you speak of yourself and me. But what about your father? Why don't you ever mention him?"

Not him, General Drummond thought. Let's not talk about him.

"I mean," Drew said measuredly, "he certainly was a very important part of the—the tradition, whatever that word really means. He spent over forty years in the Army. More than any of the others before him. Old General Sam served a few years after the War of 1812 and then married himself a 'plantation,' as he liked to call it. He got his brigadier's commission in the Tennessee Militia by political pull and finagling. Except for militia drills, and you've heard what drunken brawls those were, he had nothing to do with the Army until 1846 when he talked his way into a command of volunteers in the Mexican fandango. Then—"

"But—" General Drummond frowned. "Pardon me. Go ahead, Drew."

"His son, your grandfather, got out of the Academy and went off to the Mexican War. He stayed in the Army only two years after that before going back to Burning Brook to be a farmer."

"You forget Grandfather's younger brother, John Coffee," said General Drummond. "He served in the cavalry from 1846 to 1861 when he resigned his commission and entered Confederate service."

"I forget him, Father, because nobody knows anything about him. He never married. Apparently he never wrote letters. He was in the West and suddenly he was in the East, a Confederate colonel. He rode up the Shenandoah one day and was killed. End of John Coffee Drummond. He's just a—a kind of myth. Like your Uncle Chad, who was killed with Custer. We call him 'the wild man.' Why? Did he chase girls and get roaring drunk every Saturday night? Or . . ."

"I don't know how he came to be called that." General Drummond paused, remembering an old story. Where had he heard it? Perhaps from his mother in her later years. Something about Chad getting drunk when home on leave and— It did not matter.

"So we're left with your father," Drew said, gazing at him.

Why, wondered the General, does he look at me so searchingly? Does he suspect or possibly even know the enormity of Father's failure? There was a stone in Arlington lettered Col. Andrew Jackson Drummond, Jr., 1853–1926. It told nothing. In a way, however, it told everything. The last time I visited it, many years ago, I heard a mockingbird singing.

"My father," he said slowly, "had the misfortune to serve in the Army during long years of military stagnation. Let me tell you something that Father often told me. When that incredible mob of volunteers and regulars assembled at Tampa in 1898 to go to Cuba, a good many of the regular captains—Academy graduates, mind you—were Civil War veterans. I remember Father saying that in the Tenth Infantry—I think it was the Tenth Infantry—the youngest company commander was promoted to captain after serving for twenty-two years. Well—"

He paused, scowling at an infernal racket rising from the bailey below. A dog barking and voices shouting in Italian.

Drew rose and went to the balustrade. Marcia followed. General Drummond, still scowling, got to his feet.

A man and a woman stood on a huge stone in the bailey, staring in surprise as Ugo and his wife stormed at them angrily, accompanied by their small mongrel dog. The man was stocky, bespectacled and bareheaded. He wore a sport shirt and slacks, and a camera was slung around his neck. The woman, a strong-limbed creature with dark hair, clutched his arm in fright.

"Non capisco Italiano," the man cried at Ugo. He grinned suddenly. "Americanos—uh—*ici* Americanos."

"What's the matter, Ugo?" Marcia called.

Ugo spluttered angrily and flung his arms downward. The man and woman turned to the balcony in amazement.

"We didn't mean to trespass," the woman called. "We thought it was a deserted castle."

"It practically is," Drew called down. "Just a few old ghosts and us chickens."

The man smiled and led the woman toward them. "You're Americans. Do you have to pay or something to see this place? It's fascinating."

Drew rested his elbows on the balustrade and said to Marcia, "I like those people. I don't know why, but I like them. Let's ask 'em up."

"Okay," Marcia said.

Jane frowned. "Shall we go inside, General?"

Why should Drew wish to interrupt him by taking up with two bumbling American tourists? Why did he do things like this?

"No," he said wearily. "I guess I've already talked too much for one day."

Chapter XII

"You've got to admit," the man said, "that from the outside it doesn't look inhabited. We saw the cars out there and thought they belonged to sightseers."

"We really didn't mean to trespass," the woman said. "We left Siena to drive to San Gimignano and we got lost and Hal saw this place away up on the hill and said let's—"

"And here you are." Drew smiled at them and extended his hand. "My name is Drew Drummond. This is the Contessa di Falcari. And Miss Raleigh. And my father, General Drummond."

They stood close to each other at the head of the stone stairway from the bailey, their eyes wide with interest. A contessa! A general! They had a story to tell the folks at home, Drew thought. "See, we left Siena to drive to San Gimignano," the woman would be saying years hence, "and . . ."

"Our name is Davidson," the man said. "This is my wife Dora, and I'm Hal Davidson." He gripped Drew's hand strongly and bowed awkwardly to the women. He started forward to shake hands with General Drummond, but he fell back when the General nodded coldly. "We're from Chicago," he said, as if that explained something, and then he looked embarrassed.

"Won't you sit down?" Marcia said.

The Davidsons looked at each other, torn between politeness and curiosity. "We really must be getting on," Mrs. Davidson said. "We want to reach San Gimignano in daylight. We have to leave for Rome tomorrow to take a plane home. We're high school teachers and we're late for school already. But since Hal teaches European history and we taught summer school this year and we've been saving our money for years to come to Europe, the principal approved . . ." She turned to her husband in confusion. What did a contessa and a general care about such matters?

Drew was glad they had blundered in, two natural people interrupting his father's curious mystique of war. Like warmth entering a cold chamber.

"Let's show you around the place," he said, aware that his father was gazing at him with annoyance. "The castle was completed in 1340. The place where we are now was originally the keep. It's been enlarged over the years—"

"Come inside," Marcia said. "You can see how the original hall has been divided into rooms."

As Marcia and he led them in, the General and Jane sat down again. The Davidsons, interested deeply, asked intelligent questions as they wandered through the rooms and Marcia obviously enjoyed conducting them on the tour. They returned to the balcony and walked around the battlements, the Davidsons exclaiming at the beauty of the country which rolled down from the castle walls. Davidson insisted on taking their picture. "Stand right there facing the sun," he said, backing from them and opening his camera. "I'll send you a print. I'll take your address and send you one."

Marcia took off her sunglasses and Drew put an arm around her. They looked at each other, smiling.

"Perfect!" Davidson cried and snapped the shutter.

"Now we'll take one of you people," Drew said. He took a picture of them, arms around each other, smiling gravely. "Now let's do a corny one for the folks back in Chicago. Marcia, get up there with Mr. Davidson."

She stepped to Davidson and put an arm around him and gazed at him adoringly. Drew snapped them in Davidson's moment of surprise while Mrs. Davidson laughed delightedly.

Davidson became extraordinarily active with his camera, rushing here and there, snapping fragments of tower and walls and country-side while his wife kept reminding him to save enough film for San Gimignano. They were fine people, Drew thought, for a single reason if no other. They must be very curious about Marcia and his father and Jane and himself. Who, they surely asked themselves, *are* these people and what are they doing here and where is the Contessa's husband and isn't she an American? But they did not ask questions. And he did not try to explain to them, for explanations seemed tiresome. So leave it at this, pictures snapped on the walls of a castle in Italy with no false promises of enduring friendship in Chicago.

Yet he disliked to leave it so. For he felt that he *knew* the Davidsons. Long ago, in the Army, he had hoped to become a teacher after he was released. He had not, for reasons that had seemed imperative at the time and now seemed merely foolish. He envied these Davidsons their modest ambitions and he sensed, in their manner, a great accomplishment. They liked people; they had made friends of young reluctants; they had inspired in a few the desire to learn. This truth about them was implicit and did not require the magnified announcement of examples. He would be sorry to see them leave.

As they returned to the balcony along the wall walk, he thought that some explanation was due them after all. If for no other reason, to dispel the mystery of the people in the castle that certainly would assail them some evening in Chicago when they sat looking at their European photographs.

"My father has retired," he said to Davidson. "Miss Raleigh is his secretary. We're visiting the Contessa, who is an American. The Conte is away on a trip."

Davidson nodded. "It seems to me I've heard your father's name somewhere."

"You may have," Drew said, "but I doubt it. He was just another American general. There are hundreds of them."

General Drummond and Jane rose as they approached. There was something glacial in their manner, Drew thought. In hers as much as his. Why should she choose to frost the Davidsons, except in imitation of his father? It was annoying. And yet there was something attractive to him in her manner. It was a weakness, he thought, this Old Adam conviction of his that passion dwelt behind a cold front. He had spent some time investigating it, but he was not certain that his conviction was right.

When Davidson inquired the way to San Gimignano, Drew said, "It's not far, but it's a little complicated. I'll lead you down and set you right."

"Take that English Ford I rented," General Drummond said. He looked at Jane. "Have you been to San Gimignano?"

She shook her head. "I wanted to go on that first trip to Florence, but I didn't have time."

"Drew, why don't you take Jane there with you?"

"Why not?" He looked at her, but her expression was inscrutable.

General Drummond smiled at Marcia. "I suppose you've been there."

She smiled in reply. "Yes, I have, General."

"Then you can help me prepare Martinis for the returning travelers. I wonder where Harry stashed that case of gin I brought from Florence."

She turned her fixed smile on Drew. "Have a nice time in San Gimignano, pet, and don't be late for dinner."

As they drove down the road between the rows of cypresses, Drew sensed Jane relax beside him.

"Does my father make you tense?" he asked.

"Of course not." He glimpsed her looking at him. He saw her moist parted lips and he was aware of her warm body glow. This time his Old Adam conviction surely was right. She lighted a cigarette. "Want one?"

"Thanks." He took the lighted cigarette, slightly smeared with her lipstick. The gesture was not extraordinary, and he wondered why he took extraordinary pleasure in it. The lighted cigarette indicated she'd been around. Though how far around he could not guess. Like himself, she was different when she was with his father. Dress parade for the General and off duty in his absence.

"Why did you ask if your father makes me tense?"

"I just wondered. He makes a lot of people tense. Including me sometimes."

"I like him terribly," she said.

"You don't have to like him," he replied.

"You must be very proud of him."

He nodded non-committally.

"He's certainly very proud of you."

He grunted. "It's the first time he's ever carried on so. It's just his pitch to try to make me stay in the Army. I'm considering resigning."

"You won't." Her confident tone startled him. She was looking at him intently. "You can't. You don't even have a choice."

"Sure I do. My term is up in a couple of months. They've started another cutback. It's a cinch."

"I don't mean that," she said. "I mean you don't really have any choice but to stay in. How old are you?"

"Thirty-one."

"What are you going to do? What can you *be* at that age?"

He grinned. "I'm not quite your grandfather. I can be—well, I was thinking a few minutes ago, I've saved a little money, I can go back to school and become a teacher, a high school teacher. The Davidsons started me thinking about it again."

"A teacher!" she said scornfully. "You mean you could stand being a teacher in a place like Chicago?"

"Quite happily. And I'm not romantic about it either. I know how monotonous it can get. But what doesn't? And I don't think kids are little cherubs, but I like the look on some of their faces when they learn something. You have a job like that and read books and make some friends and go to the zoo on Sunday afternoon. Things like that. What more do you want?"

She stared at him incredulously. "You're crazy."

"Crazy as they come," he said.

She touched his knee; her hand was warm. "I could understand that for some people, Drew. But not for you. That's what I mean when I say you're crazy. It's—it's symbolic suicide."

"I'll bet you learned that term at Wellesley," he said. She withdrew her hand and looked hurt. "I'm kidding," he said.

141

"About what?"

"About Wellesley. I'm kidding."

Watch it, he told himself. You have an affinity for entangling alliances with women of strong convictions. Better to commit your life, like so many men, to a series of amiably available women. But the trouble with those women was that their blood did not speak to yours. There you were, Havelock Drummond on love and sex. It was all in the imagination anyway, someone had said.

"Is Wellesley all you're kidding about?" she asked.

Yes, she was tenacious in her convictions. Let him say, "I'm kidding about everything, I'm not quitting the Army." What then?

He said, "I'm kidding only about Wellesley." He had some strong convictions himself, it seemed. If in these times one must pay a price to live in peace, he had paid his in full.

Clouds floated their dark island shadows across green valleys and olive hills as they descended to Poggibonsi. In golden columns the afternoon sun struck white villages and feudal sentinel towers. The road dipped steeply, then rose again, and finally dropped to the lower valley.

From Poggibonsi the road curved out and up, climbing through fields scarlet with poppies, crossing a rushing stream lined by silver birch and poplar, and then rising into dazzling sunlight. Jane exclaimed excitedly and pointed. Ahead and above them the slim towers of San Gimignano stood against the azure sky. Her excitement pleased him; he stopped the car at a turnoff and they got out as Davidson halted his rented car behind theirs.

Jane turned from the town above them to the valleys below, her eyes bright. "Can't you imagine it, Drew, the way it was six hundred years ago? Wasn't there a lot of fighting through here?"

He glanced at her in surprise. Yes, there had been. But he had been thinking of Dante, whose acquaintance he had made quite recently; he had been thinking of Dante walking up this steep hill one day in 1299 on his worthy but futile effort to bring peace to the two great warring families of San Gimignano, the Salvucci and the Ardinghelli.

Yes, he told her, there had been much fighting. The valleys below there had run with blood. The Sienese would come out over Monte Maggio down there to the southeast, that long gray ridge which stood before Siena like a rampart. And the Florentines would come down the Valley of the Elsa. The people of the hills and valleys would hole up on their fortified hilltops; they suffered most because it was their land which was being fought over. And up here, in the thirteenth century, stood San Gimignano, proud and free. Though not really free.

She did not understand. "Not really free?"

Up in San Gimignano, as below in the country, he told her, there were partisans of the two great powers. The Ardinghelli and their friends were for Florence, while the Salvucci and their friends were for Siena. Within the walls of San Gimignano their bickering led to bloodshed. Hatred grew. They took to building towers in which they locked themselves, shooting arrows and slinging boulders and pouring boiling oil on their enemies. What a mess.

"It must have been very messy," said Davidson, aiming his camera at the distant coastal range.

"Oh, I don't know," Jane said. "They were fighting for what they *believed* in."

Davidson glanced at her quickly and then frowned into his camera.

"Your father should have come with us," she said. "He'd enjoy it."

Yes, Drew thought, Father would have a fine time here. He and Jane could commune on the glories of the past, the march and countermarch and clash of old wars. They did not see it as it actually must have been, he thought as they got in the car and drove on up the hill. Rape and pillaging and burning, the arrow in the groin, the sword thrust through the neck; and the ordinary perpetual discomforts— foot blisters and saddle sores, phlegm and dysentery, heat and piercing cold.

"Can't you imagine how it must have seemed to a knight in one of those towers?" She pointed to San Gimignano.

"It must have been pretty monotonous," he said. "No penicillin or central heating. I think of a guy on guard duty up there, maybe one lung gone and his bladder enflamed."

"Oh, really, Drew!" Her tone despaired of him. "Why do you bother to come to such a place?"

"I like to feel how it must have been, the bad as well as the good. Did you ever think what life must have been like for old knights?"

She did not answer; she gazed up at the towers of San Gimignano.

"I have," he continued. "It must have been rough when you got to be forty-five, which was old then. All your victories behind you and the young men no longer would let you ride the best horses and they took your falcons from you. What did you do?"

She smiled. "You're really amusing. I think it's wonderful to be old in any age and have all your victories behind you. It's—I don't know. But I do know that I look forward to growing old."

Her remark was significant, he knew. He was at a loss how to interpret it, however; never having heard a young woman say it before, he lacked a precedent for judgment.

Now they were on the summit. The road felt its way along the crumbling walls of the town, seeking an entrance. When it finally widened, Drew stopped the car and they got out. A strong wind bore the barking of a distant dog. Before them the sky and Italy stretched infinitely. In the suffused light of the declining sun the mauve sweater and skirt Jane wore seemed to glow redly; her hair took on a bluish cast and her skin was the color of ivory.

"You should have brought a coat," he said. "It's always cold up here."

"I'm never cold." She glanced toward the Davidsons as they stepped from their car. "Let's shake them. Let's go on our own."

A small dark man wearing a lettered cap came toward them from a public urinal, buttoning his pants and calling, "Good American guide here."

She looked at him distastefully. "And I don't want to follow that dirty old man around."

Davidson, unslinging his camera, called, "I want to get one more shot of the country before the sun goes down."

"It won't look like anything," Jane said to Drew. "All that country he's shooting won't look like anything on a little photograph. Come on."

He followed her, calling to the Davidsons, "See you at the Church of San Agostino." To the guide he said, "No thanks." The guide looked so crestfallen and he was such an old man that Drew took a couple of frayed hundred-lire notes from a pocket and handed them to him, saying in Italian, "Have a drink on us." The old man crowed exultantly and inundated him with a torrent of gratitude.

"You spoil them doing that," Jane said as they strode toward a cleavage in the walls.

"I know it," he said. "I try not to, but sometimes I can't help myself. It's their faces."

"What's at the Church of San Agostino?" she asked.

It was one of the places where the Ardinghelli and Salvucci continued their war after peace was officially declared in 1353, he told her. Officially the Ardinghelli won San Gimignano for Florence in that year. But the Salvucci didn't really give up. They started a cold war—with art. Although no one was sure who had started the cold

144

war, he personally was convinced the Salvucci had. And the Ardinghelli retaliated, of course. He was pretty sure that the Salvucci had started it at the Collegiate Church. From Siena (where the Salvucci surely would go for their artists rather than to Florence) they brought in two painters, Barna and Bartolo di Fredi. Go to it, gentlemen, the Salvucci told them, gesturing grandly to the cold blank walls of the church. So Barna fell to it on the right, telling the life of Christ in immense frescoes, and on the left Bartolo splashed away at scenes from the Old Testament. It was not exactly to the single glory of God and His Son, you understand. Most of the glory went to the Salvucci, who demonstrated by this grand gesture that even though San Gimignano had fallen politically to Florence and the Ardinghelli, the Salvucci still were the noblest, most powerful and patronizing clan on this high mountain top. Well, the Ardinghelli smarted for a while under the insult, and then one night they sneaked in a painter from Florence named Benozzo Gozzoli and shut him up in the Chapel of the Choir of San Agostino.

"The critics say," Drew continued, "that old Benozzo was a slick and clever painter rather than a great one. The type who'd do *Saturday Evening Post* covers in our time. But wait till you see what he did with the life of Saint Augustine in the Chapel of San Agostino. There must have been something in his spirit that made him understand Augustine. I'm no great judge of art, I've only recently begun to be aware of it. But seeing Benozzo's work the first time I came here made me start reading about Augustine and trying the *Confessions*. That's another story, of course. What I was telling you was that Benozzo must have made the Ardinghelli very happy after he finished his work. They must have felt that they'd proved their superiority. But nothing was final in those days until the last ounce of energy was drained; that's a point about the Renaissance. There are other works by other painters brought here by warring families. One work led to another, a series of frictions creating a chain of life. That's what the history of Tuscany and the period we call the Renaissance is all about, I think. We haven't time to visit more than one place so I thought . . ."

She had not been listening attentively, he realized. They had passed through narrow, shadowed alleys into the town. Hewn stone, so brightly mottled by sunlight at a distance, was dark and oppressive here. It towered above a labyrinthine winding. Hemmed in by it, she looked up at walls, her expression baffled.

"You're really quite interested in art," she said absently.

He did not know what to say to her, for he had hoped she would understand that he was interested in life. I speak to her, he thought, but she does not hear me.

Looking back, she said, "Here come the Davidsons. Come on." She plunged on along a narrow street where dark-garbed women scurried before the wind. There were many barbershops where men looked out, ogling her with sensual smiles.

"This town is full of barbershops." She sounded angry.

"It is. I've never seen so many." He smiled. "It's a commentary of some sort, isn't it? Still populated by the descendents of the Salvucci and Ardinghelli, they say. Barbers and shepherds and tourist guides. Wine makers and olive growers. Shows you what a proud tradition can lead to. Not that there's anything wrong with it. They look most content, don't they? Wine and pasta and a little mutton on feast days. Church for the women and a little quiet gambling for the men. Love for everybody who wants it, as much here as anywhere. I can see it. There's probably a poet or two and at least one scandalously rich man lurking around somewhere. They have opera here in the summer too. I've heard it's poor—but energetic."

She halted and stepped out of the wind into the lee of an abutment. Why did she look so angry? He remembered thinking only last night that it would be fun to take her sightseeing.

"You're cold," he said. "Shall we go back?"

"No. I told you I never get cold. But where are the towers?"

He stepped out and pointed. "There's one. There's another. There are thirteen. Nobody knows how many there were originally. Fifty-six, some say. Others say seventy-six."

"I'd like to climb one and look out," she said. "Frankly, this place disappoints me."

"Well," he said doubtfully, "most of the towers are abandoned. I don't know . . ."

She strode on, leading him now. Looking back, she said, "We can't seem to shake the Davidsons." She hurried faster and suddenly darted to the right into a narrow alley.

Turning and waving cordially to the Davidsons, he followed her. "What's the hurry? It's a long time yet till dark."

"I don't know." She slowed and forced a tense smile. "I—I'm sorry, but I don't like this place very much. It's so—hemmed in."

"That's what makes it interesting," he replied. "It's the way all the cities were back then. Didn't you get into the back alleys of Venice? This is the way Florence was in the age we romanticize. The people

146

were turned in upon themselves and they— Sorry, I'm even worse than the guides. They don't bother with theories."

"Look!" she exclaimed. "A tower!" The alley widened into a tiny deserted square. Above it soared a slim tower, its upper stones faintly pink in the declining sunlight, its walls slitted by numerous narrow apertures. Across its gaping entrance a long rail had been placed. Tacked to the rail was a crudely painted sign, VIETATO L'INGRESSO.

She went to the entrance and looked in.

"Vietato L'Ingresso," he said. "No admittance."

"I know." Her tone was sharp. "I've been in Italy a while too and picked up a few words." Ducking down suddenly, she moved under the rail and stepped inside. She smiled back at him. "But we're Americanos and we don't speak Italiano." She looked up. "Listen." She cupped her lips and cried "Ha!" Off the walls the echo came: *"Ha . . . ha . . . ha!"*

She troubled him vaguely. But interested him too. Somewhere he had known someone. . . Maybe some daredevil girl around one of the posts when he was a child. He stepped over the rail. Above, shafts of light entered through the narrow apertures.

"Listen," she said. "Hey!" And the echo: *"Hey . . . hey . . . hey!"* She started up a stone stairway which ascended into darkness. "Come on. Let's see how far we can go."

"No," he said.

"You're scared." Dimly he could see her smiling down at him. She made her tone good-naturedly jeering. "Hero, holder of Distinguished Service Cross twice, scared of dark."

"It was an accident both times," he replied quickly, "and I don't want any more accidents."

"Then stay there," she said. "I'm going up a little way. I'd like to look out from the top of this tower."

"Jane!" She was crazy. He sprang up the steps and grasped her arm. She shook it free and climbed slowly, staying close to the wall. Light flooded through an aperture. There was a solid stone landing and the flight turned.

"All right," he said. "It's my turn to go ahead." He squeezed past her. Carefully testing each step ahead and keeping a hand on the rough stones of the wall, he led the way. If heights didn't bother you, he thought, there was really nothing to it. The stairs were as solid as the mountain itself. That sign must have been put up merely because the stairs lacked a rail.

At the next turning he halted. "It's a long way yet. And probably not worth it. Let's go back now."

"I like to climb," she said. "I was an awful tomboy. Go back if you want to."

He looked down. Fifty feet below, the light of the entrance glinted on rubble.

"Ha!" she called down suddenly, and her voice echoed back to them.

"Ha yourself," someone called. She gripped his arm. A figure moved against the light of the entrance. Davidson stood down there, peering up.

"Can't we *ever* shake them?" Jane whispered.

"We're up here, Davidson," Drew called down. "But I don't recommend coming up."

"Okay," Davidson said. "What does *Vietato L'Ingresso* mean?"

"No admittance."

"Golly! Maybe you'd better come down. I hoped it meant men's room."

"Hal," his wife called, "what are you doing in there?"

"Not what you might think," he replied. "Mr. Drummond and Miss Raleigh are climbing the tower."

Jane started ahead of Drew, but he forced himself past her and they climbed the next flight. Another shaft of light revealed a wooden ladder rising from the landing. Above, he made out a network of wooden platforms joined by ladders rising to the top of the tower.

"Okay," he said. "We've had it. I'm no Tarzan."

Wordlessly she brushed past him and tested the ladder. "It's solid as iron," she said, putting a foot on the first rung.

What was the matter with her? The hazard simply was not worth it. Seizing her arm, he pulled her roughly off the ladder. "Listen—"

"All right. I'll make a bargain." He could see her smiling at him. "I think this is loads of fun. But if you're scared on that next landing we'll go back."

"You'd better be careful," Davidson called up.

Drew did not answer him. His hands on the ladder were suddenly sweaty. The ladder was angled forward beside one wall of the tower. It was, he judged, fifteen or eighteen feet to the wooden platform above, which rested on stone abutments of the walls.

He was crazy to try it, but she had challenged him. What an adolescent she was. But so was he to respond.

"Stay here until I reach the platform," he muttered. He climbed slowly, testing each rung ahead of him with the full strength of both

148

arms. At last the platform came level with his eyes. He hitched himself onto it, testing it cautiously. It did not feel solid to him. He rolled over on his belly quickly, spreading his legs, distributing his weight as best he could. Far below, directly beneath him, Davidson stood peering up.

A plank creaked and he swore.

"What's the matter?" Jane asked calmly.

"I just wondered how I got myself into this mess." His voice was dry with fear.

"I got you into it," she said.

"Don't come up, Jane. This thing isn't safe."

Already she was halfway up the ladder, however, her head close to his thrust over the lip of the platform. "All right," she said. "I'll go back. I'll steady the ladder. Be careful."

There was a sickening creak and then a loud crack. He gripped her right wrist as the ladder broke and plummeted down. She swung in space, held by his grip, raising her left hand, fumbling for his right hand. He groped and found and grasped her left wrist, digging in his toes as her weight dragged at him. Dimly he realized she had not cried out. She was trying to say something to him. Now he heard her.

"Swing me closer to the wall!"

As he inched painfully along the platform, he thought of Davidson. A woman was screaming down there. Mrs. Davidson. He didn't have the strength to call. He inched toward the wall, hanging to her, wondering how long he could hold her. She was swinging her legs, groping for the wall, trying frantically to find a rough stone on which to rest and relieve the strain. At last, incredibly, the strain on his arms was less.

"I have a stone!" she cried. "My left foot's on a stone. Can you hold me now?"

He didn't try to answer her. "Davidson!" he shouted in a choked voice.

"Yes, yes!" roared Davidson. "What can I do?"

"That rail across the entrance. Bring it up! Watch the stairs. Come fast as you can!" He closed his eyes, his arms throbbing. "All right," he muttered. "All right, Jane. I can hold you now. You'll be okay." He opened his eyes and saw her white face, eyes straining up to his.

Davidson's feet clattered on the stairs. It seemed to take him hours. And then, at last, Drew heard him panting on the landing below. He cried up to them incoherently.

"The rail," Drew gasped. "Will it reach this platform close to the wall? Careful of Jane."

Davidson yelled, "It reaches, thank God," as he placed the rail against the lip of the wooden platform.

"Get your feet on it," Drew said to her. "Now your hands. I have your wrists."

"It's all right," Davidson called up. "I'm holding it steady. You're only a few feet above me. I'll grab you."

"Let go my wrists," she said calmly to Drew. "Hold the top of the rail."

He let her go and she slid down slowly. Brushing sweat off his eyelids, he stared down at them on the stone platform. Davidson was speaking to him, but he paid no attention. He lay for a moment, rubbing his sore arms, wishing he could still his racing heart.

Then he crept across the platform and moved the upper ladder, lowering it over the edge until Davidson seized it. He climbed down it and blindly followed them to the ground.

Chapter XIII

"My shoe!" Jane's voice trembled as she groped in the rubble. "I can't find it. I kicked them off up there. I've found one, but I can't find the other."

A swarm of children, who had been drawn by Mrs. Davidson's cries, stood in the entrance staring at them. Drew, turning suddenly, gripped Davidson's hand. "Thank you for saving her life. If you hadn't been here and—"

"Heck." Davidson still breathed heavily. "Heck, I just—"

"My shoe!" Jane wailed. "Help me find it."

The children cried out that the lady had lost her shoe and they began to laugh delightedly.

"All right," Drew said, "I'll look." But in the failing light, which was obstructed by the children in the entrance, to search was futile. "I'll send one of these kids for a light."

"Never mind." Her voice shook. "Let's get out of here. I can't stand this place any longer. I—*quieto!*" she cried at the children, and their laughter died.

She turned to Davidson. "Thank you. Thank you so much." She wheeled suddenly and plunged to the entrance. Quickly, silently, the children made way for her. The Davidsons and Drew followed her into the pale light of the tiny square.

She hobbled a few steps on one high-heeled pump and then faced them. Her stockings were rent by runs. Her sweater had torn and raveled. Dirt was smeared on her hands and face.

"Look at me!" she cried. "I'm a mess!"

"Wait a minute," Drew said. "I'll—"

"Thank you," she said to Davidson. "Thank you so much."

"I didn't do anything," he said. "I—"

"Good-by." She hobbled away. The children began to laugh again. Angrily she kicked off the pump. It arched upward and, as it fell, a small boy darted after it. She ran up the alley.

"Thanks again," Drew said. "We'll see you later. If you have the time, go to the Church of San Agostino and look in the Chapel—" Davidson turned his astonished gaze from Jane to him.

"See you later," Drew muttered and ran after Jane. When he caught up with her and grasped her by an arm she slowed to a walk. He looked back. The Davidsons still stood at the foot of the tower, their expressions astonished. The children raced about the square, throwing and catching Jane's shoe.

As they turned the corner, two young men stared at her feet and laughed. A woman halted in surprise. Jane tore her arm from his grip and ran.

It seemed that they never would find their way from the town. At last, however, they came out and hurried to the car.

She sat for a moment, gasping for breath. "Drew!" She raised her hands to her face and sobbed.

He pulled her to him and she pressed her face against his chest, clinging to him and sobbing. Like a child, he thought, as he gently stroked her hair. Then he thought, Yet not like a child, for her body pressed against his stirred him. Desire, yes. But also the ineffable mixture of strangeness and recognition that was more than desire.

She raised her face. "You saved my life."

"No. Davidson did that."

"No," she said. "*You* did."

He lowered his head to kiss her lips. She turned her face quickly and her body stiffened.

He did not kiss her. He said, "I ought to go back and speak to the Davidsons. I ought at least to get their address and maybe send them a gift of some sort. I—"

"Please." She moved from him. "Please take me away from here."

He would. He knew that he would do anything she wished. Something had begun between them when he clung to her in the tower, and he did not know how it would end.

He started the car. Silently, taking care not to touch each other, they rode away from San Gimignano.

When they had gone a short distance, she suddenly said, "I'm sorry I made that sarcastic crack in the tower about your being a hero. You *are* one."

No, he thought, there is not such a thing as a hero.

She said, "I know *why* you are. You don't do impetuous things. You're very cool—and strong. That's why you won medals."

"No," he said, "you're wrong, Jane. Heroism is an absurd abstraction. Everything is chance."

When she disagreed, he replied, "If you aren't careful, I'll tell you how I won a medal."

"Oh, tell me." She rested a hand on his arm, her eyes suddenly bright. "Please tell me, Drew."

Tell me a story, Daddy. How war loving women were.

"There's not much derring-do in it, Jane. It's sort of a funny story."

"But tell me," she said impatiently.

And so he told her the story.

Where the hills of Tuscany pitched into deep blue shadows now there had been then the oily calm of the Southwest Pacific and ships moving in the amber glow of early morning mist.

Operation Scarsdale, the Army called it, in that late autumn of 1943. Nine destroyers and three destroyer-transports moving off a group of Japanese-held islands. Specifically, Scarsdale Reconnaisance Force, an initial landing group composed of elements of the untried division that had been rotting to the south for many months.

At 0415 on D-Day, as the Army phrases these matters, the Force Commander informed Captain Stanley that B Company would lead the assault on what was called Red Beach. At 0420 Captain Stanley, pale and shaking and speechless, lay down on his bunk. Drew, his first sergeant, crouched beside him, trying to find words that would comfort and arouse him. He was baffled. In their months of living and training in the island jungles to the south he'd found Stanley a pleasant companion, thoughtful of others, always demonstrating integrity. But now he lay inertly on his bunk.

The Company exec, Lieutenant Mason, a spidery little man whom Drew did not like much, took the news calmly. At first he laughed at Stanley. As time passed, however, and Stanley did not stir or speak, he grew angry. Finally he yanked him from his bunk. Stanley, his expression dazed, sank to the deck. Mason kicked him, but he did not stir.

Drew left and found Sergeant Joe Gannon, who had made his confession to the Roman Catholic chaplain on board and was in a jovially resigned mood.

"You should be a Catholic," Joe said. "Then you'd have nothing to worry about."

Drew envied him. "It's a little late, Joe. But I'm going to look into it if I'm still around tomorrow."

"You'll be around," Joe said. "But you won't look into it."

They took up their landing boat stations, badly frightened men, muttering to each other, smelling of sweat and vomit in the stifling heat of dawn. Before them a flat, yellow island grew in the overcast. The hands of wrist watches seemed to crawl and then leap forward. H Hour was 0745. The destroyers turned sluggishly to their fire support stations and at 0710 their five-inch guns belched flames. The crews of the destroyer-transports jostled the standing troops and swung the ramped Landing Craft *Personnel* outward on shrieking davits. Each of the four LCPRs of the three transports was to carry thirty-seven men ashore in the first wave and then return for more.

As the boats were lowered, Mason yelled at Drew to hustle Stanley on deck. He found him lying on his bunk, his lips set in a smile, his hands riveted to the bunk stanchions. Drew cursed him, furious now, feeling betrayed. He seized his wrists, but he could not shake his grip from the stanchions above his head. The boatswain's whistle shrilled and he ran above. He never saw Captain Jerome Stanley again or learned definitely what happened to him, but he never forgot the fixed smile on his rigid face.

Clambering down the landing net, he took Stanley's place in the lead LCPR. In a moment they put off and curved toward Red Beach, crouching low and staring back at the orange flashes of the destroyers' guns and then ahead at the distant blur of beach stretching between the slate sea and green coconut palms. A B-24 came in and made its run, its bomb bursts muted by the roar of the LCPR engine. It disappeared in the overcast and they did not see another plane.

The LCPR gained speed, moving ahead of the others. No man looked at another, each seemed transfixed in his individual dreams. Forward, beside the Navy gunner who crouched below his 30-caliber machine gun, Drew felt lonely and not at all resigned to death. His mouth was dry and sweat trickled from his armpits. His bowels stirred loosely and he feared he might retch. It seemed such a hopeless cause, a handful of inexperienced men thrown against God knew what fortified positions, with their ultimate goal an airstrip away up forward somewhere. It was bad to be the first, he thought, and he cursed Stanley aloud.

Ahead, there was a sudden ripple on the surface of the sea, a white series of leapings such as a skimmed pebble makes. The Navy gunner, cursing steadily, stood up to his gun and opened fire. Drew suddenly felt detached, as if he were watching a movie. And then detachment left him as he saw two small figures moving on the beach, two men running before the machine gun's tracers. He waited for a blazing wall of fire as the LCPR seemed to move with painful slowness. There was no movement anywhere except the pitching of the small boat as it approached the beach at agonizingly slow speed. There was no sound except the hacking roar of the boat engine.

They were waiting, that was it. They were waiting until . . . The engine slowed, the flat bottom crunched gravel, the ramp whinnied down. Gripping his rifle tightly, he leaped forward and ran swiftly through the shallows and across a narrow black sand beach toward the wall of palms which seemed friendly now. He tripped over a shell-fragmented palm trunk and fell sprawling in kunai grass. Raising his head, he looked around. The others were fanning out behind him, running low and spreading in an orderly fan as they had been taught. He got to his feet and moved forward cautiously through the kunai and deadfall, shouting to spread out and move ahead, look ahead and watch the man on your left and your right, but look ahead.

In a few minutes they emerged into the park of a coconut plantation. Drew halted the platoon there, spreading the men out under cover, and waiting until he heard Mason's voice shrilling somewhere in the kunai behind. Platoons formed on their left and right under lieutenants Pawetski and Carr, and then Mason took over. The three platoons moved forward abreast, a squad scouting ahead of each, the fourth platoon following in reserve. They felt pretty good now. They had not seen an enemy or heard a shot fired. It was going by the book, as if they were on the plains of Texas. He walked on the point of the lead scouting squad, going there at no one's order and without any desire for heroics, but leading because he was the company first sergeant, a very young first sergeant. You could not drive men into battle but had to lead them, it was said. So he was leading, unwilling to be shot, but willing that men approve of him.

They came to the edge of a heavily shelled deadfall where, according to plan, they set up their automatic weapons under cover and waited. Then, according to plan, the second wave passed through them. The Force Commander, a slight and sandy-haired colonel, plunged along with the lead platoon of the second wave. By noon the Force Commander had three of his four rifle companies and half the heavy weapons company disposed along the airstrip. Scouting parties which ventured onto it were driven back by mortar and machine-gun fire from brush-covered revetments on the farther side. When the platoon of field artillery still had not come up at 1230, the Commander ordered B and C Companies to attack abreast across the field.

They ran forward reluctantly into the hot glare of the noon sun, ducking into and weaving out of the Navy-laid shell craters. For the first time Drew heard the shrill screaming of a desperately wounded man. He felt sick and wanted to turn back, but he went ahead until they reached the farther side.

Through the stifling heat of afternoon they fired at and were fired upon by an enemy they seldom glimpsed. You moved forward and were pinned down and sometimes stumbled over the doll-like bodies of the enemy dead. There was an objective and then another objective, and you never were certain that you actually killed anyone. The sun shifted and directions shifted until, quite suddenly, there was no opposition.

The line of battle had turned ninety degrees since they took off across the air strip. It was the way the Commander had intended it to turn, it was a victory—for the moment. Drew dimly admired the ingenious planning that had brought it about. He was glad he was not an officer; although he might have managed the forward movement, he could not have turned the force and pushed it to its limit and then pulled it back to the line where they were ordered to dig in for the night and establish their perimeter. In the hard fighting you easily forgot the careful planning, the forward movement and the turning and the push to the farthest limit before the pullback to the dig-in with the flanks safely hemmed.

As he was digging his foxhole, Mason told him to report to the Force Commander.

In the Command Post, established in an abandoned palm log hut, the Commander frequently interrupted his orders on the night defenses to tell his signalman for Christ sake to keep trying to contact the command ship on the 284 Radio. At last his sergeant said, "Here's Drummond, sir."

The Commander, whose fatigues were soaked black with sweat, looked up at Drew, blinking, and said, "What?" A captain said, "They're *waiting,* sir." The Commander said for Christ sake let them wait, he was busy. But he broke off in a moment and said, "Come on, Drummond," and trotted off through the palms toward the beach. Drew trotted after him. He looked back and said, "Come up here, Drummond." So Drew trotted beside him, admiring the Commander's durable wind that allowed him to carry on a casual conversation while trotting.

The Commander asked if he knew what this was about, and Drew told him that he didn't. He questioned him closely about B Company until they came through the kunai grass to the beach. There he stopped and frowned at sight of an officer, wearing suntans and a peaked cap, wading out to a beached LCPR.

When the officer reached the ramp, a couple of Signal Corps movie photographers called, "Okay, General, okay, come on down, sir." And the officer, who was an Old General, strode down the ramp and waded through the shallows to the beach while the movie cameras whirred. Then a photographer called, "General, please sir, be talking to the Admiral," and the Old General smiled benignly and began talking to an admiral, gesturing authoritatively to land and sea.

"By God," exclaimed the Force Commander, "it is an admiral, but how the hell did he get ashore without getting his feet wet?"

"Watch your language," someone said behind them, and they turned and faced a man who wore general issue fatigues and leggings and cap, with the three stars of a lieutenant general pinned on his cap. They saluted him hastily. He smiled grimly at the Force Commander and called him by his first name and began asking intelligent questions. Finally he declared, "I'm going up there."

"General," said the Force Commander, "there's just plain nothing to see and already we've been annoyed with some sniping and—"

The General uttered an obscenity and said he sure as hell was going up there.

"First we've got to get *this* over with," the Commander said, ges-

156

turing to Drew. Then he introduced him to the General, who smiled and shook his hand and said, "You must feel it's pretty safe here, Sergeant, with so much brass around."

Drew said, "Yes, sir," and the General, cocking his head and looking at him closely, said, "You have the deceptively angelic smile and handsome face of a born heller, son. What are you really thinking? Anything with which I can amuse the rear echelons?"

Drew said, "We'd be happy if you'd all come up and spend the night with us, sir."

The General smiled and said, "That's pretty good. I've heard better, but it's pretty good."

At last the photographers were finished with the Old General and the two-star staff general and the division two-star and the admiral and a Navy captain and a colonel wearing command pilot wings who wandered around trying to explain to everybody what had happened to the B-24s in the overcast. The Old General asked some questions of the three-star General and the Force Commander while the others listened, nodding, nodding. Then the Force Commander presented Drew to the Old General.

He returned Drew's salute gravely and shook his hand and asked where he was from. Drew had not then learned always to snap the name of the crossroads hamlet near Burning Brook, which was simply a convenience rather than a sentimentality, for he felt rootless and not *from* any place. The Old General believed his hesitation was caused by shyness and he patted his shoulder kindly. Drew blurted the name of the hamlet in Tennessee and the Old General briefly extolled the virtues and fighting traditions of the Volunteer State.

Taking a medal from a case held by an aide, he pinned it over Drew's heart. Sergeant Andrew Jackson Drummond was receiving the Distinguished Service Cross, he intoned, for bravery displayed as the first American soldier to land on the islands.

The Signal Corps photographers' bulbs flashed while the Old General held his fingers to Drew's medal. After he returned Drew's salute and pivoted away, a signalman and a *Yank* reporter wrote down Drew's name and age and serial number and the hamlet he claimed as his home. The *Yank* man asked questions, trying to get a story about the invasion, but Drew couldn't give him much of a story because it hadn't been much of an invasion yet.

The Old General and his party returned to their ship and Drew and the Force Commander returned to the airstrip. The medal troubled Drew, for it was mere chance that he had been the first ashore and he had not displayed extraordinary bravery during the day. There must be many others, he felt, who had been more heroic than he. Merely by rising from his bunk and falling into the landing craft, Captain Stanley could have received it. Instead, he would be shot or incarcerated or psychoanalyzed or whatever it was the Army did to officers who funked out under stress.

"There you have it," he said to Jane as they entered Poggibonsi. "That's how I became a hero."

"And after that you were commissioned and wounded?"

He nodded.

"How did it happen?"

"They just ran out of officers." And that was all he would tell her. Since he could not describe it to her as it actually had been, he would not mention it at all. But he could not dismiss the memory of those terrible days and nights in the islands after the airstrip was secured.

After a brief rest B Company moved to another of the islands and to its assigned mission on Number Three Road. The road, so designated on aerial photographs, twisted up a spur of the island's main ridge to a strong enemy concentration. It was a narrow track flanked by deep, jungle-locked ravines. The company which they relieved in the assignment had lost half its officers and forty men without gaining more than two hundred yards toward the ridge.

B Company did not have better luck in the fight against hidden bunkers along Number Three Road. Air strikes were ineffectual. Artillery, firing time fuze on snipers and delayed fuze to penetrate bunkers, failed to develop close co-operation with the infantry. As casualties mounted, the survivors became more tense.

You never get used to the screaming of wounded men, either your own or the enemy. You never get used to not taking prisoners, even though an enemy has proved he'll kill you and himself with knife or grenade. You may kill so many men that you even stop trying not to count them, but you never get used to it.

On a single day the company lost two lieutenants, one killed and one wounded. The next morning Mason was killed and Drew was left in command of B Company. He walked back to the rear C.P. with the two men who carried Mason's body. When he radioed Battalion, the S-3 told him, "Don't get your bowels in an uproar, Sergeant. Pull back for thirty minutes while we give them an artillery douche and then go on in again."

Late in the afternoon word was passed up to him to report immediately to the rear C.P. There he found the Reconnaissance Force Commander who had been promoted to brigadier general and was now assistant divisional commander. With him was a strange captain. The captain listened attentively as the general spoke.

"What's your biggest need here, Sergeant?"

"Closer liaison with artillery, sir. The spotters can't get in close enough. And we could use a couple of heavy tanks."

"Does the Company need relief?"

"Yes, sir, but I assume we'd get relief if it was available."

"Do you think you can make the ridge without reinforcements?"

"I wouldn't make a guess, sir. We'll keep trying."

The Brigadier General smiled slowly. "This is your new skipper, Captain Hawley. Hawley, this is your new exec, Lieutenant Drummond." He took a couple of tarnished gold bars and a U.S. insignia from a pocket. "You just passed your officer candidate examination, Drummond."

"I don't *want* to be an officer," Drew said. "Sir."

"I don't give a good Goddamn what you *want* to be," the Brigadier General said. "We're short of company officers and you're now a lieutenant—Lieutenant." He pinned a gold bar and the insignia on the collar of Drew's dirty, sweaty fatigue jacket. "And that's permanent. Division already has your records. They'll have you fill out some forms and crap. From what I see there's no point in my going farther forward because I might get myself shot."

Drew always admired the man, even though he had made him an officer. He was killed eventually, but he allowed himself to be shot at only when he deemed it necessary.

Two days later, while working along Number Three Road, Drew was hit in the right leg and side by machine-gun fire. It spun him around, but he did not fall. He did not feel pain. Somewhere he heard men yelling at him to hit the deck. Crazily, he did not want to flatten. He stood, his right hand pressed tightly against his side. He lifted his hand and stared at blood dripping from his fingers. He took a step and his leg crumpled under him and he fainted.

They carried him back to battalion aid and then on, quickly, to the evacuation hospital. The next day a C-47 transported him and other wounded to a base hospital in New Guinea. His thigh was smashed and his gut perforated, but it was not serious enough to remove him permanently from active duty, the doctors said. Accepting this depressing news philosophically, he resigned himself to another rainy season in New Guinea.

*   *   *

Aware now that Jane had spoken, he glanced at her.

She frowned. "I said, aren't you going to tell me about it?"

"There's nothing to tell," he replied.

"All right, have it your way. But you must have been a very good soldier to be a company first sergeant at that age."

He shook his head. "I was able enough. But I was no better than Joe Gannon. Stanley merely picked me for his first because my father was a general. And then there was the matter of luck. Instead of getting killed, I was wounded. Joe was wounded, too, shortly afterwards and sent to the same hospital in New Guinea. We saw a lot of each other there. We believed in luck. My luck held, but Joe's didn't. He was killed a year later. One day in January the hospital chief called me to his office and said I was being shipped back to San Francisco for reassignment. The Colonel said, 'They've put out a call for heroes for TDY with the Treasury Department. War bond stuff.' He said, 'It turns out this theater isn't adequately represented by heroes back home. They're scraping the bottom of the barrel and here you are with a D.S.C. You're lucky, son. You won't see the Pacific again.'"

"You must have been elated," she said.

"Not exactly. Oh, I was glad enough to get out of New Guinea. But I couldn't help feeling it would be better if Joe was sent home instead of me. He came from Orange, New Jersey, and I never tired of hearing him talk about Orange and his home and family. I knew how much it would mean to his parents and sister and brother—and even to the people of Orange—if he came home a hero. But I—well, I felt I didn't have anything to go back to."

"There was your father. He must have been very pleased."

He glanced at her. "Yes, Father was pleased."

Yes, indeed, the General had been highly pleased. Someone on the Association grapevine must have told him that his son had been decorated and wounded and commissioned. He wrote Drew from an undisclosed place, presumably in England. The divorce which Dorothy Drummond had obtained six months previously he casually dismissed with the remark, "I suppose you've heard that your mother received a Nevada decree." Principally he expressed exultant praise of Drew and said something about courage.

Chapter XIV

"Courage," Andrew Jackson Drummond, Jr., nearly always said when he poured a slug of Bourbon into a tumbler. Then he'd thump the red glass decanter on the sideboard and turn slowly, the tumbler clenched in a hairy hand which rested on his paunch. "Above all, courage," he'd say, his heavily scalloped nostrils twitching as his expression became sardonic. And then, usually, he'd drain the tumbler at a gulp.

Whenever General Drummond took a drink, he remembered his father. He had tried a variety of psychological devices to prevent the recollection, but all had failed him. The only recourse, he sometimes thought, was to stop drinking. To stop now, however, was pointless.

As he poured himself a Martini, he muttered wryly, "Courage. Above all, courage."

Behind him Marcia said, "Courage?"

He started nervously, spilling some of his Martini, and cursed himself. When he faced her, however, his expression was bland, his hand steady. "I didn't hear you come in." And then he censored himself for the stupid remark.

She smiled and raised the glass of tomato juice she'd gotten for herself after refusing his offer of a Martini. "To courage then," she said.

"I'll drink to that."

As he sipped his Martini, he observed her glance at her wrist watch. Wondering where Drew and Jane were, no doubt. Personally, he'd be delighted if those two stayed out together until midnight. "To courage." He made his tone wry. "I'm getting old, Marcia, but not so old that I don't know when I'm talking aloud to myself. Although I'm all for courage, I'm not in favor of going around being sententious about it. I've been known to extol the virtue, but not while drinking alcohol."

She sat down slowly, keeping her gaze on him, and he thought that his explanation was growing altogether too elaborate.

"My father used to say that whenever he poured himself a drink." He dropped into a chair and smiled bleakly. "I don't know why."

But I do know why, he thought. Or do I really know? And what do I care this half-century later? I want to forget about it. Why did Drew ever bring up the subject of Father this afternoon? And why did I make that inane remark aloud just now?

"Oh?" Marcia said. It was all she said.

"Yes." He crossed his legs restlessly. "You see, my father used to say that—sardonically. Not that he was opposed to courage. He had plenty of courage, you understand. He—uh—well, as a matter of fact, he picked up that phrase from Teddy Roosevelt. He hated Teddy Roosevelt with a passion that was—well, an unfortunate obsession."

He wished she would ask him why, but she did not. She looked at him with interest—with, by heaven, a kind of compassion, so that he knew he must be acting a very old man. He wished he could stop explaining. But explanation seemed necessary.

"Most of the regular Army hated Roosevelt after the Spanish-American War. I suppose they had plenty of reason after the way he disobeyed orders and grabbed the spotlight and generally used the war to put himself on the national political stage. After all, he was only a civilian."

She smiled. "Only?"

He smiled too, feeling better now. "I guess you'd expect me to say that, wouldn't you? But let me say, on the other hand, that the Army was poorly led and organized with its morale pretty low in 1898 when the politicians suddenly decided we must become a world power. But to come to the point, I think my father had more reason than most regular officers to hate Teddy Roosevelt. Because Roosevelt literally prevented him from seeing service in Cuba. It happened in Tampa. You remember that's where our expedition gathered and sailed to Cuba."

"No, I don't remember, General. I don't know much history, but I want to start studying it."

"Tampa was the place they sailed from," the General said. "I've often heard Father describe it as it was then. A sandy waste with a few shacks, steaming hot and swarming with mosquitoes and the water bad. Suddenly it was teeming with thousands of soldiers and volunteers in one of those states of military confusion we've been famous for until recent years. There was one railroad track down to Tampa. It was built by a fellow named—Plant, a real estate speculator. At the end of his railroad, among the shacks of Tampa, he'd built a magnificent hotel. Father used to like to talk about Mr. Plant's hotel, the miles of piazzas and the ornamental silver minarets and all the gingerbread outside and the statuary and overstuffed sofas inside. The Army held a regular reunion there, renewing old friendships and rocking on the piazzas while they drank vats of iced lemonade—and plenty of Bourbon too, I daresay.

"It was like Chatauqua there, I guess. Ira Sankey, the evangelist, came down to preach and pray and sing to the soldiers. Clara Barton showed up in a funny hat with several ladies of her Red Cross organization. And, of course, there were newspaper correspondents and politicians from everywhere, all parading around and around the piazzas of Mr. Plant's hotel."

General Drummond smiled reflectively at his Martini. "Mr. Richard Harding Davis was there. I don't know exactly why, but Father hated Mr. Davis almost as much as he did Mr. Roosevelt. Maybe it was because Davis called the life at Plant's hotel the 'rocking-chair period' of the war. I remember a few years later he came into the house one day and found me reading one of those tropical romances by Davis. He flew into a frightful rage and snatched the book out of my hands and threw it right out the window—which fortunately was open and screenless. And then he roared, 'Don't you ever bring a book by that idiot into this house again!' So I went outside and retrieved the book and took it out to a woodshed we had behind our quarters —it was at Fort Hancock—and finished reading it."

His smile faded slowly until his expression was solemn and he looked around the living room of the Castello di Falcari as if it were totally unfamiliar to him.

"I wander badly, Marcia." His gaze appealed to hers.

"No," she said, leaning toward him, "no, you don't, General. It's an interesting story."

"I wander," he replied briskly. "The point is that from the military viewpoint the situation in Tampa was badly fouled up. The whole war was fouled up. The Navy tried to whitewash its role in bottling up Admiral Cervera's squadron at Santiago, but you should read the record on that some day. At any rate, the force assembled at Tampa was commanded by Major General William R. Shafter." He shook his head. "Poor Shafter. He's been much maligned, chiefly because he weighed three hundred pounds and couldn't get along with the newspaper correspondents who were trying to run the war. But he didn't have a proper staff and his supply and transport were all messed up.

"For instance, my father's branch was Coast Artillery. His assignment on the expedition to Cuba was with the siege train. But the parts of the siege train and ammunition for it were scattered through hundreds of freight cars on sidings all over the state of Florida. They worked hard at trying to assemble it." He hesitated. "I'm sure Father didn't spend all his time at Mr. Plant's hotel. I've heard him say how he was out scouring for his battery's equipment. I've heard him—it doesn't matter.

"One night at the hotel Father saw Mr. Roosevelt in the lobby. He was—to use Father's word—'haranguing' another officer and some politician. Father was quite vivid in his description of *Mister* Roosevelt, as he always insisted on calling our lieutenant colonel of the so-called Rough Riders. The puttees he was wearing, the vehemence of his gestures, the fervent shine of his glasses—those things that were to magnetize so many Americans simply failed to magnetize Father. He heard Mr. Roosevelt exclaim to the two men he was addressing, 'Courage! Above all, courage!' Well, Father believed in courage. I'm sure he did. That is, I *know* he did. But he turned away from Mr. Roosevelt with what he said was disgust there in the hotel lobby. To him it seemed wrong that such an important quality should be bandied so. At least I think that's what Father meant—I *know* it is."

There was a dull throbbing in his left arm and he moved it carefully and sipped his Martini.

"My father was scarcely capable of judging Mr. Roosevelt objectively. As Teddy Roosevelt later demonstrated, he was a man of tremendous personal courage, an inspiring leader who expressed something basic in what I'd call the American character. But consider my father. He'd graduated from the Academy in 1874. For twenty-four years he had diligently pursued his profession. Drill, inspection, paper work, discipline, routine, up and down our coasts in the often unpleasant places where the Coast Artillery was stationed. After twenty-four years of what he felt was a dedicated career, he found himself a captain. And as a captain he saw in Mr. Roosevelt a rich New York politician who merely by asking for it became overnight a lieutenant colonel. Furthermore, he heard him ranting about 'courage.' It was too much for Father. He turned away with loathing.

"Probably he would have forgotten the incident in time if something else had not happened. The time had come for action. The country, the politicians, the newspapers, the War Department, even Mr. McKinley himself demanded action. There was great delay and scurrying and chaos in Tampa. A weird fleet of ships and tugs and cockleshells was assembled offshore. Mind you, there was one rail line down to the bay and one pier into the bay, and down the railroad and onto the pier our expedition plunged in a wild confusion that's hard to imagine.

"There were orders and counterorders. As a methodical man, accustomed to five copies of everything, Father found it frustrating. He was used to the slowness of the Army. The sudden speed-up must have baffled him. As he used to tell me, the siege train was supposed to move on a single transport, and then its elements were broken up. His battery was assigned first to one ship and then another, and finally—the last orders he received—they were to go aboard a transport called the *Yucatan* with the 2d Infantry—that's the regular Army —and the 71st New York Volunteers.

"Well, on the eighth of June Father's battery crept down to the pier by train into the cheering, yelling confusion of the mob. Father, by the way, was a tall, heavy man with a voice that could bellow like a bull's. He also could cuss more fluently than any man I ever knew. I've always had a vivid picture of his disentraining his battery and pushing them up through the press of troops along the pier, cussing heartily, I'm sure. He saw the *Yucatan* at the pier and he was happy. The big adventure, you know, after twenty-four years of waiting.

"The confusion at the gangway to the *Yucatan* was incredible. His battery could not move. Then he realized there was some kind of trouble. Men were trying to board the transport and being shoved back by men aboard. And then, up on the deck of the *Yucatan,* he saw *Mister* Roosevelt, barking and howling and flashing his teeth and prancing around. Father found a captain in the 2d Infantry he knew who was fairly frothing with rage. At last Father calmed him down enough to learn the reason. *Mister* Roosevelt and his Rough Riders had seized the *Yucatan* and would not let anybody else aboard."

General Drummond smiled faintly. "At this point in his story Father always began pacing. His language became—eloquent. His voice thundered and crackled like an electrical storm. I wouldn't attempt to repeat his language as he pushed to the gangway and raised his voice and addressed the future President of the United States on the deck of the *Yucatan*. He waved his copy of his orders while the men on the ship under Roosevelt and Colonel Wood hooted at him. He used to say, 'I made Mr. Roosevelt fairly dance with rage.' Personally, I doubt it. I think it was Father who danced with rage while Roosevelt held the *Yucatan*.

"The way Father told it, Roosevelt yelled at him, 'What's your name, Captain?' And Father roared back, 'I'm Captain Andrew Jackson Drummond, Jr., of the United States Army, *Mister!*' And Roosevelt, according to Father, made a note of it. I doubt that he did. But Father chose to believe that his personal animosity for Roosevelt was reciprocated personally. And he believed that when Roosevelt became President he personally obstructed Father's promotion. That's ridiculous, of course. It was mere coincidence that Father finally attained his majority in 1909 after Taft became President.

"Roosevelt had his own say about that day in his book, *The Rough Riders*, which I took the trouble to study at an early age. He doesn't mention Father or Father's battery, but only the 2d and 71st Regiments in connection with the *Yucatan* incident. He was much more restrained than Father, I remember. He simply wrote, 'There was a good deal of expostulation, but we had possession.' I came to admire that simple sentence more than all of Father's eloquent passages."

"But how could Teddy Roosevelt prevent your father from sailing on another ship?" asked Marcia.

"He couldn't. He didn't. He merely prevented him from boarding the *Yucatan*. Later the Rough Riders permitted four companies of the 2d Infantry on board when they found they had room for them. I, personally, admire Roosevelt's initiative. He felt he had a date with destiny in Cuba and he was trying to keep it." General Drummond frowned. "Other outfits scrounged around and got transportation. The 71st, having captured a railroad train to take them to the pier, sent a small boat out in the harbor and seized a transport. So it went. Good initiative, such as you expect of soldiers when the system breaks down."

Still frowning, he scratched an ear. "I *think* I know what happened, though Father was always incoherent about it. He became enraged, he lost his head after the system broke down. He became embroiled in a quarrel with the port quartermaster, a Colonel Humphrey. The expedition's fleet hung off Tampa for a week before they sailed. Basically, it wasn't Father's fault that he didn't get his battery aboard a transport. Orders were changed somewhere, orders that had nothing to do with Father personally. It was decided to reduce the size of the expedition's coast artillery force. If Father's battery had been on a transport out in the bay it would have sailed. But it wasn't. It was in Tampa while Father ran here, there and everywhere trying to clarify orders. The next thing he knew he and his battery were on their way north to protect Boston Harbor against invasion."

"And he never went anywhere in the war?"

General Drummond shook his head. "He never went anywhere at

any time. When he was sixty-four years old they put a colonel's chickens on his shoulders for the last six months of his Army career."

"It's a sad story," Marcia said.

Yes, he thought, it was a sad story.

"And so he just went along all those years? You'd think he'd have resigned and gone back to Burning Brook."

"There was a certainty about the life." The General hesitated. "The pay was poor, but it was certain. It's to his credit that he didn't sell Burning Brook. If he hadn't had such a sense of tradition, he would have sold it. Fortunately, most of the time he had a good tenant farmer who managed to meet the taxes."

Marcia leaned toward him. "Is it really a dull life, General, living on those posts?"

He smiled faintly. "You'd probably find it so."

"Why would I?"

"It's not very—glamorous."

"Then I'd like it," she said emphatically. "From now on I like anything that isn't the least bit glamorous."

"But it's not exactly un-glamorous either," he said slowly.

And then, hesitantly, he began to tell her about the life. It was much the same in one place as in another, and in one year as in another. Although an Army post was supposed to be a man's place, women were the most important element in it. A man's wife made a post either pleasant or unpleasant for him; she was even more important than his commanding officer. His own mother had made life pleasant for him and Judd, he said, trying not to think about his father. His mother had liked Army life.

He heard himself talking about his favorite post when he was a youngster, a post abandoned now. Fort Hancock on Sandy Hook, where he had lived from 1904 to 1907. But he could not describe it to her as he remembered it.

Merely to mention the name of that post was to lift memory to an ear, like a conch shell, and hear the long roar of the Atlantic on the curving white beaches. The sibilant whisper of wind in the dry grass of the empty dunes. The crying of gulls in the morning and the long bleat of the lightship on foggy nights. Smells, too. Of stables and bayberries in a hot sun and always the tang of the sea.

There, on the tip of sand dunes at the entrance to New York Harbor, the world passed in ships of all nations. There were sailing ships, too, in those days, beating out to sea; on a clear day you could hear the cries of sailors on the yardarms. And always, on any night, you heard the blast of whistles when pilots were dropped. Yes, the world went by, but there on the Hook was a smaller and more orderly world.

They were on the Hook to man the huge rifled coastal guns which raised black muzzles from concrete emplacements toward the open sea. It did not matter that their presence was tactically or strategically unimportant, that the guns never were fired at an enemy and finally—many years later—were dismantled and moved away. They did not care about the higher scheme of things. It only mattered that they lived on the tip of the Hook, in an orderly world which no stranger entered, surrounded by sea and gulls and ships and sand.

I'll forget the red decanter on the sideboard, General Drummond thought, as he haltingly described the Hook to her. I'll forget how much Father drank and try to stop wondering why he drank.

"I remember," he said to her, "I had a pony I rode down the Hook to high school in Highland every day."

But I'll forget, he thought, that when I was seventeen they gave up teaching me more mathematics there. I knew as much as they did and I was trying to teach myself calculus—and succeeding pretty well. I remember wanting to live in a world of pure mathematics and pure sea and sun and wind. I remember it, but I'll forget it because now I know there is not pure anything. Just as I've forgotten the time when Father had tilted the red decanter too often and slapped my face because I argued a problem in logarithms with him. Yet he didn't strike me because he was drunk; he struck me because I was right. And he had to be right that time because I threatened his authority over Judd and me. I understand that now and I forgive him.

"We lived in a yellow brick house on a row of houses all alike," he said to her. "There were some swamp maples and a grassy area and the bay beyond. The day began with the sunrise gun and it had a definite termination at retreat when the flag came down."

And each day had a pattern which his mother threaded confidently and cheerfully. Quilting parties and carriages then, as there were bridge parties and autos now. Circumscribed, yes; but so was any way of life you could name.

"I think," Marcia said slowly, "that I'd like the life."

She alarmed him, curiously. She must not like it, he thought. Jane liked it, but she must not. In some devious way she might convince Drew that— He did not want to think about it. She was, in one respect, a worthy opponent. But she was not worthy ever to be Drew's wife, as Jane was worthy.

"You would not like it," he said heavily. "It's best if you grew up in it. Not so many have, of course. But failing that, it's best to come from some—disciplined way of life before you marry into the service, some—well—"

"Tradition, General Drummond?" she asked sharply. "Tell me, did your wife have in her background what you'd call a 'tradition'?"

He stared at her for several seconds. Then he muttered, "Yes. Yes, she did." He got to his feet heavily. He wanted to leave the room, but there was no place to go. He turned, wearily, to his improvised bar. "I think I'll have one more. Won't you join me?"

"No, thanks," she said quietly.

He began mixing another drink, trying not to think of his father, trying to remember the roar and thud of the waves on the long beaches of the Hook. Instead of the waves, however, he heard his father saying sardonically, "Courage. Above all, courage."

Chapter XV

Jane and Drew climbed toward the castle under a clear sky. Behind them the sun rested at the horizon, sending its light flat across the heavens. A star winked in the east. Below, the valleys were wine dark, while on an upland an ancient sentinel tower shone whitely.

"Forever dreaming, your father says." Jane smiled at him. "You haven't said a word since we left Poggibonsi."

Suppose he told her that he'd been thinking of her? She did not understand many important things about him, and he failed to comprehend her in many ways. Nevertheless, they were much alike. His tenuous grip on her in the tower had created a bond between them.

It was not new, this sense of bonds—or bondage—between him and a woman. And he found himself, with a vague regret, remembering other women.

When a C-54 landed him and other casuals of the Pacific at Hamilton Field on a cold evening in February, 1944, he still had to walk with a cane. To his annoyance it caused people to treat him solicitously.

He checked into the BOQ and ate a big dinner at the transient officers' mess and then walked down the hill to the PX where he bought toilet articles and paper-backed books and drank a malted milk. In the midst of his shopping spree he suddenly thought of his mother. She had written him when he was in the hospital in New Guinea that she'd married again. Her second husband's name was Clarence Huddel. "Darling, he's a darling, a wonderful man, a dealer in *objets d'art*." In other words, an antique dealer. She enclosed a picture of Clarence taken in a night club. He had a long, goatlike face. He looked pretty drunk to Drew.

He conscientiously inquired his way to the telephone exchange. But hard as he tried, he could not remember his mother's address in New York or the name of the goat-faced man she'd married. So he couldn't very well place a call to her. But he could call Burning Brook.

He stepped into a booth and sat for a while with a dead telephone held to his ear. Finally he opened the door and yelled to the exchange operator, "What's the matter with this phone?"

She yelled back, "Did you put a nickel in it, stupid?"

He could have kissed her for calling him stupid, it made him feel so much at home. Then, however, she noticed his cane and said, "I'm sorry, honey, can I help you?"

He slammed the door shut, liking it better when she called him stupid.

When he returned to the barracks, he was tired from so much unaccustomed walking. He lay down in his single-deck bunk and read until he fell asleep. Quite a crashing return to the States after all that Pacific big talk.

He was awakened by someone saying, "Lieutenant. Lieutenant Drummond." A young Special Services lieutenant stood beside his bunk. Bright sunlight poured through the windows. The lieutenant was most persistent and cheerful and helpful in his duty of official greeter. He greeted Drew all the way to the shower and greeted him while he shaved. He wore him out before breakfast. He took him over, worshiping him, expediting him, spoiling him. By ten o'clock he had him believing he actually might be a hero.

Clearing him quickly from Hamilton Field, the lieutenant and his driver swept him to the Presidio in a sedan. There the lieutenant smoothed his pay problems with the finance officer and bought him the proper ribbons and showed him how to pin them on. Blouse and greens and pinks and shirts and socks and ties and shining leather shoes—all were produced quickly by post tailor and salesmen. His private room was opened to him and the mysteries of obtaining a car and driver were explained. Then, after lunch, the most helpful lieutenant directed the driver to a downtown office building and saluted ceremoniously.

In an upper-floor office Drew explained his mission to a red-haired secretary who smiled at him fetchingly and said, "Yes, *sir,*" and walked off with an interesting twitch of her little buttocks. She looked back. "*This* way, Lieutenant. Mrs. Davis is expecting you." He limped after her into a small office.

A blonde, pretty woman rose and extended her hand. "My name is Mrs. Davis." She indicated a chair. "Frances Davis. You might as well call me Frances because we'll be seeing a lot of each other. You see, I'm your ghost and you're the first house I'm going to haunt."

It was a joke she'd thought up, he knew, so he gave her the old innocent, boyish grin.

She smiled too. "What do they call you? Andy?"

"Drew," he said. "What do you mean, Frances, a ghost?"

Her brows rose slightly at his promptly calling her Frances; she had believed that he was shy.

"I'm your writer," she said measuredly. "I'm not a professional, but I've always enjoyed writing little things for my own amusement. Now with the war we're all volunteering to do what we can to help. My *hus*band suspended *his* career to serve in the Navy."

She indicated on her desk a large Bachrach photograph of a man presumably handsome. The two and a half stripes of his left shoulderboard were tilted into the camera so that you could not possibly overlook the fact he was a lieutenant commander.

"What are you going to write for me, Frances?"

"I'm not going to write *for* you," she replied. "I'm going to help *you* write some of the brief speeches you'll make at rallies and on the radio . . ."

He was startled. He had not considered how he'd have to pay the price of public adulation. But public speaking seemed too costly.

"I wish," she said, picking up a pad and a little gold pencil, "you'd tell me something about your experiences in the Southwest Pacific."

He froze, his mind benumbed at the thought of how the guys in Baker Company would roar at that question. He started trying to figure what time it was now in the islands and what the Division was doing.

She was looking at him worriedly, her pencil poised. "I know this may be painful to you." She spoke hesitantly. "I know you've been wounded—"

"That's not it," he said, frowning. "There's nothing to that. It's just that my winning the D.S.C. was a lot of crap."

She grimaced faintly and he realized that she was a woman who preferred two-syllable to one-syllable words. A fine and wellborn lady, who had volunteered to do her bit for democracy, and he must not tread on her sensibilities. In short, an amateur. He never had known a professional writer, but he bet none of them had gold pencils or asked you to tell your experiences in the Pacific. They were supposed to be ulcerous, cranky men, addicted to drink and carnal pleasures, but he sure could use one to help him now. She was, however, a fine and wellborn lady, and he felt sorry for her.

"I mean," he said, changing his tone, "that it was by the sheerest coincidence that I, instead of many fine and probably better soldiers, received that medal."

She smiled hopefully. "There's a dualism in you, Drew. Or do you understand what I mean?"

"Yes, Frances. I have a certain ambivalence. But don't we all?"

She looked at him strangely. Reaching in her mesh bag on the desk, she took out a silver cigarette case and opened it to him. He lighted their cigarettes ceremoniously.

No integrity. That was his trouble, he thought. He would have liked to talk to someone about what had happened to him in order to get to the truth of it. But he could not talk to her. This was merely an assignment, a detail to her. As he, for example, had made Number Three Road an assignment, a detail. But, now that you began to think about it, you might as well get to the truth of the Number Three Roads if you were going to discuss them at all. Why, for instance, had some men funked out and others kept going? What was courage anyway? Above all, what was wrong away topside in the nature of man and the running of the world that caused the agony and cruelty and killing on the Number Three Roads away down below? The truth would not sell war bonds, however. And he and she were here to sell war bonds.

So he began to make up a pretty little speech for her to type and him to record on tape tomorrow. He had absolutely no integrity, he thought, for he merely tried to make her smile pleasurably at an apt phrase and to take delight in her own smoothing transposition of some of his sentences. But he tired of it.

He interrupted the pretty little speech. "On this Number Three Road job there was one guy who had been pretty timid all along and he cracked up and we had to keep him on work details in the bivouac down below. Nobody minded much. They felt kind of sorry for him. There was another guy who'd been going along regular and *he* cracked. Everybody was sore at him. He took an awful beating. We finally had to ship him to the evacuation psychiatrist. All along I thought those were two of the best guys in the company. I still do. I'd like to find out what happens to them some day. I mention it because something just occurred to me. Maybe I'm trying to make what happened in the islands sound important only because I was there." He smiled. "You know, self-justification. Everybody would think that what happened to those two guys marked them for life. But maybe it turns out that what happened is completely unimportant. Do you see what I mean?"

She shook her head, frowning. "There's nothing more important than—than being courageous when the chips are down."

Oh, sure, he thought. You should know in your heated office with your mink hanging over there and your diamonds on your fingers and your little gold pencil in your hand.

"It's—it's"—she groped for the words—"being willing to take a chance. My husband and I are enthusiastic sailors. One of the great things about sailing is those chances you take. You know, cutting around a buoy, you run the chance . . ."

Oh, sure, he thought. Hard alee, lady. You may go over and get your bathing suit wet. But you should see a man who took a chance and is trying to hold his intestines in his hands.

"I think," she said, "that it all comes down to breeding. If you have the right stuff, you're just naturally going to . . ."

Sure, sure, sure. He returned to the pretty little speech they had been composing.

She bored him, he began to realize. It was simply that she thought she knew the answers to everything and so refused to think. She could not help it. She was a lady. And, presumably, she could not help that either.

Perhaps he bored her too. She began to shift restlessly in her chair. Rising, he suggested that they call it off for the day. He opened the office door and glanced out, thinking he might ask the receptionist with the twitching buttocks to have a drink with him. But she was not there. He turned to Frances. Could he buy her a drink somewhere?

Why, yes, that would be fun. Visitors to San Francisco usually wanted to go to the Top of the Mark, but it was terribly crowded with servicemen these days, so why didn't they go to the St. Francis? They rode there in the Army sedan and then he dismissed the driver.

She enjoyed being seen with him because he wore an officer's uniform and ribbons and limped on a cane. He observed that. He observed how she smiled when a couple of young and fashionably dressed women stopped and spoke to her archly. She introduced him and almost preened when one of the women said that there certainly was more glamor in selling war bonds than working for the Red Cross. They made him feel uncomfortable.

She dismissed the women and concentrated on him. He gave her a reasonably accurate and tastefully edited account of his life, and he saw regretfully that she was greatly interested by the fact his father was a general. Which was not really displaying any interest in himself. He did not like her much, he thought. She was pretty and well formed and she used a pleasant perfume and she smiled at him; she made his guts stir when he thought about it. But there were probably twenty or thirty million women around the country who, if in such close proximity to him, could make his guts stir when he thought about it. He certainly didn't dislike her, but he didn't like her much. She was proper and restrained and she questioned nothing. She was like somebody's mother. He looked around the room, wishing he could meet a younger and more vivacious woman. He'd like to tie one on and maybe throw aside his cane and try to dance somewhere. But she drank sparingly and talked of her home and two young daughters, two little dolls, aged six and four.

At last she looked at her wrist watch and said she really must be running along home. He asked her to have dinner with him. What a screwball he was. He didn't really want to eat dinner with her. But neither did he want to eat dinner alone. She demurred. He pressed the invitation, outwardly urgent, inwardly indifferent. All right, she said, but first she must call home. When she returned, he had paid the check. She said that she had wanted to pay it, and since she hadn't, she was taking him to dinner at a place she knew. She would have asked him home, but it would have meant eating with the children, and while they were dolls, it would be a delightful change to eat out just once.

They ate in a French restaurant where she knew the headwaiter. She was one of those people who considered it estimable to know headwaiters by their first names, and she presented the young and heroic Lieutenant Drummond to the great man with a flourish. One character to another. He must have the bouillabaisse, it mattered not what he wanted. The headwaiter attended to everything but eating dinner for them. And no check presented, of course.

He took her home in a taxi. Home was a large house of Spanish architecture on the side of a hill. He must come in and meet her daughters. A stout, pleasant woman servant let them in. When Frances went upstairs for the children, he looked around the large, expensively furnished room. There was another Bachrach photograph of her husband, the wartime lieutenant commander, and a family group, and a large picture of Frances and her husband on the canting deck of a racing sloop. A solid house, a serene life.

The little girls, hair braided identically and wearing matching bathrobes, came down the stairs with her. They curtsied in unison to him. It was something. He wanted to hug them and tug their pigtails tenderly. But he could not because they already had assumed the roles of ladies; they had curtsied in unison to him and he'd never seen two little girls wearing bathrobes curtsy together. Polite and self-confident little girls, already able to pitch a conversational line. They asked about the war and he told them it was going along fine. They asked if he'd seen their father in Pearl Harbor, and he said no, but he'd heard that he was doing fine.

Soon Frances said they must go to bed. They went up the stairs with her docilely, each holding her by a hand. She called back to help himself at the bar. He poured a short brandy at the breakfront bar and meditated on the happy life of Frances Davis. She declined a drink when she came down. He admired her home and she belittled only a few of its details. Before the dim-out there had been a beautiful view of the Golden Gate Bridge from the den, she said. He followed her into a small adjoining room where she turned on a desk lamp.

She drew back an arm, accidentally brushing his shoulder. He would ask her, he thought dimly. Anyone back from the islands would have asked her. He had virtually no experience in finding out such matters. Probably forthrightness was the best way. Then, at least, it would be over with.

"Frances." His tone was strained. "Would you go to bed with me?"

Her eyes widened and she stepped back from him. "No," she said.

"Okay," he said unevenly. "I just wanted to be direct and simple about it. So forget it. I hope you're not—insulted."

She stared at him. "I'm not," she said slowly. "I should be. If anyone had told me this could happen and I'd not be insulted, I'd think —I'd think there was something wrong with me." She looked away. "You're not very—experienced, are you, Drew?"

"Not very," he said uncomfortably. "Are you?"

"No." She sat down. "I'm not experienced at all. I love my husband and it never would occur to me to be anything but faithful to him. It wouldn't occur to anybody I know that I'd be anything but faithful."

"That's fine. That's the way it should be." He was, he thought miserably, a terrible salesman of himself.

"I miss him. But I don't really miss . . ." Her gaze wavered and she could not say the word.

"You mean sex," he said helpfully.

"That's right." She looked up at him. "How old are you, Drew?"

"Twenty-one."

She managed to smile. "I'm thirty-three. When you're my age maybe you'll see it's pretty overrated. So I'll just say I'm complimented by what you said."

"It's too bad you don't enjoy it much," he said. "You're very beautiful." She wasn't, but she was quite pretty. "And you're very—desirable." Like twenty or thirty million other women.

Her smile remained fixed. She was not looking at him, however. He turned his head and saw another photograph of her ubiquitous uniformed husband, this one posed on the deck of a Navy ship. But neither was she looking at the photograph. She was smiling fixedly at her reflection in a mirror on the wall.

"Let's talk about your speech," she said.

It was an effort for both of them, however. He had placed a strain on their relationship that neither could quite remove, he thought. He tried and she seemed to try. But he was glad when enough time had elapsed that he could leave courteously.

She told him she'd call a cab. Then, turning from the telephone, she said, "Why go all the way out to the Presidio? Why don't you take a room at the St. Francis? You won't have any trouble getting one with—" She nodded at his cane. "We really ought to get to work early in the morning finishing this speech and you'd be handy to the office. You can borrow some toilet articles of my husband's."

She went upstairs and returned shortly with toilet articles in a leather traveling case. The cab was waiting. "Good night," she said and held out her hand. He took her hand and bowed awkwardly and left.

176

A clerk at the hotel looked at his cane and his ribbons and found him a room. He wandered into the crowded, noisy bar. A fat man wearing a dinner jacket seated beside a blonde woman in evening dress looked at his ribbons and cane and offered to buy him a drink. He declined, saying he was looking for someone, and passed on. Yes, he was looking for someone, he thought, but not for a fat man and a blonde woman to buy him a drink. And not for the two carefully made-up girls who smiled at him. He was looking for someone or something not to be found in the bar of the St. Francis Hotel.

He had been a fool, he thought, to make that proposition to Frances. A double fool, because he had not really wanted to do it. But he had felt, somehow, that it was *expected* of him. Not by Frances, naturally. Rather *they* would expect him to. Yet who were *they*? The men in Baker Company, yes; but more, every big-talking lover in the lonely islands. More than that, war and soldiering had expected it of him, as war and soldiering had expected him to plug ahead on Number Three Road. He had done it according to the book of war in which it was written that the only good thing about war was that it gave everybody a chance to raise a little hell. The book was crazy. You had to do things because *you* wanted to, not because the mythical book prescribed standard operating procedure. I must not, he thought, be afraid to be a lousy lover until the time comes when I cannot help being a sincere lover.

Discouraged, he went to bed.

The ringing of the telephone awakened him. It was a bright morning, ten minutes after eight by his wrist watch. He answered the phone.

"This is Mrs. Davis, Lieutenant." Her tone was formal. "I'm in the lobby."

She must be kidding. "Well, Mrs. Davis," he said drily, "if you'll wait a minute I'll come down and we'll have breakfast."

"I have the material, Lieutenant," she said in the same formal tone. "I'll bring it up. What's your room number?"

He told her the room number and asked her to give him a minute. Baffled, he pulled on shirt and trousers quickly. Then it occurred to him that she must have decided that they should not continue working together as a result of his proposal last night. Well, so be it.

There was a tap at the door and he opened it.

She stepped in quickly and passed him without looking at him. Going to the window, she stared out at the lemon winter sunlight.

Then she turned, her face pale, and she said tensely, "I've changed my mind."

"Now Sin was a place in Egypt, it says in the 30th Chapter of Ezekiel, which I have read to you. But the Lord says and I say to you that sin is everywhere. It lurks close at hand to strike the pure heart, to poison the bloodstream, to blind the eyes, to smite the clear mind and drag you down, down, down to the perdition that awaits all who fail to heed the one true God . . ."

Thus spoke the Tennessee preacher.

And I, his definition of a sinner, having broken all the Commandments, sat there listening to him and feeling strong and good and untroubled. But he, a good and aging man whose years of sinning were all behind him, was much troubled.

Spring came early to the Tennessee bottomlands that year. It stretched outside the clear glass windows of the hamlet's Methodist church where he sat between Judd and Mildred. The clear violin notes of a hermit thrush were sweeter than the preacher's voice. Killdeer and red-winged blackbirds called along the banks of the stream which flowed behind the church. Only yesterday he'd heard a grouse drumming at Burning Brook and at evening the little frogs began their music in the ponds above the creek.

Kill-dee—kill-dee—kill-dee-dee-dee. Damn that bird that put the preacher to shame with his raucous, triumphant cry of the teeming, spawning spring earth. Drew thought how his father and his uncle had often sat here and failed to listen to the words of preachers. So had his grandfather and his great-uncle, Chad the wild man who was killed with Custer. His great-grandfather had been shunned here after the Civil War, but he had come without embarrassment and probably failed to listen. And *his* brother, Colonel John Coffee Drummond, who had chosen to fight with the Southrons and paid with his life in the Shenandoah, he must have sat here and failed to listen. To say nothing of the Drummond infants and children, boys and girls who were merely names in the family Bible, having been taken by the preachers' God while they were still too young to know wars and passion. Maybe (as he did not then yet know) even old General Sam himself, the patriarch of all these brawling generations, had sat here unlistening when this was only a slab log church.

They had sat here, all of them, basically unregenerate and unpenitent, as he sat now. What interesting sins had they committed? As the killdeer cried above the warm spring earth, so must cries have echoed in their memories, of rapture in the warm flesh, of agony from a dying enemy, of reproach from a betrayed friend, of all the sinful prides and passions on which their worlds had turned.

He thought of Frances. He did not long for her now and he doubted that she longed for him. They had attained what was attainable during four weeks and it was ended forever. Whether she would resume being a faithful wife or become a faithless wife he did not know. They had taught each other something. He heard her voice more clearly than the preacher's: "You must never try to rouse me because you don't have to. I see I'm quite a different person than I thought I was. I didn't know and I'm sorry to find out. But not very sorry."

Sin, as the preacher was describing it in the pulpit now, he did not honestly feel he had committed. And she did not, she had told him at parting. That, he knew, was because she had not been caught. He heard her voice again after their first time together: "The important thing is that nobody knows and nobody must ever know. That's why it's wonderful. The excitement of nobody but us knowing. We'll be very careful and it will be very good and exciting because nobody will ever know." If she had been caught, however, she would have thought her sin enormous. Which was a fact about sin and human nature that the preacher was neglecting to mention.

The service was over at last and they passed from the church, speaking to the preacher, speaking to the few devout farmers and their families who were willing to expend precious rationed gasoline in order to hear such a gloomy definition of their sinful lives.

"I like to go three or four times a year," Judd said as they drove toward Burning Brook. "I think his diagnosis of the patient is brilliant. By the patient I mean the human condition. It's the medicine he prescribes that I can't take. So joyless. Pray, tithe and be good. It took a lot of honest-to-God sinning to get man out of the Neanderthal Age."

"Is he out yet?" asked Mildred.

"That's a searching question, Mrs. D.," said Judd. "I'm not sure. But every once in a while there are signs he's trying."

Drew, looking at them from the back seat, thought how much he loved them. They were the only people he knew who sometimes could stir him to a closer look at what the preacher would call his sins. Which was one point up for the preacher. Or, more significantly, it was a whole series of points up for genuine love.

Judd was looking at him in the driver's mirror, shrewdly and kindly. He had the Drummond blue eyes and the thick Drummond hair. He was five years younger than Drew's father, but his white hair, his leisurely way of moving, his crow's-footed and seamed dark skin made him appear older. He conveyed, however, a sense of great strength and vitality in his heavy frame.

"What do you think, Drew? Is man trying to shake the Neanderthal off his back?"

"Not trying very hard," Drew said. "At least *I'm* not."

"You!" Mildred turned and smiled at him. Dark haired and dark eyed, she was fifteen years younger than Judd, and sometimes, to his amusement and her embarrassment, she was taken for his daughter. "You aren't half old enough, Drew, to know how Neanderthalic man can be."

"Objection," Judd said. "You aren't addressing a callow youth, Millie. Don't be patronizing at your ripe age. I'm sure Drew could tell us some fascinating sins. Right, Drew?"

"Right." Drew spoke without relish.

"Just keep them to yourself," Judd said. "Never mention them. It's good to raise a little hell when you're young. It gives you something to enjoy or regret when you're old."

Mildred was thirty-three. Exactly Frances's age, Drew thought. It troubled him. Not that Mildred was anything like Frances. Yet many people must think of Frances in the way that he thought of Mildred. Including, of course, Frances's husband, the lieutenant commander. What had happened did not make any difference, he and Frances had agreed at parting. And only a few minutes ago in church he'd been thinking that it made no difference. Not to him and not to her—and the hell with her husband and her cousins and her aunts. It was *her* life. Yet Mildred's life was her own too. Just as he finally had come to see that his mother's life was her own. But with Mildred, who was closer to him than his mother, who was thirty-three and married to Judd rather than an anonymous lieutenant commander, it would be different. If she ever became involved with a man, as Frances had become involved with him, he would be crushed. As others who knew Frances would be crushed if they ever found out. He was sorry he'd thought of it. He did not like to think of it. He was troubled.

They were driving fast along the black-top road then. You could see where the farm began. Peeled wooden fences began to divide clean fields and then white fences sprang up and you glimpsed a splash of white on a distant rise. A yellow clay lane passed between white stone pillars. There was a mailbox lettered DRUMMOND; the words Burning Brook existed only in the minds of the family. The lane ran straight between rows of sycamore until it split, one fork leading to the five-room cottage and the other rising between ancient thick-boled beeches until you saw the white house before you. It was square and substantial, without pillars; it was a farmhouse which demonstrated that the land, rather than an imagined romantic tradition, had held the Drummonds here for this century and a quarter.

I always loved Sundays at Burning Brook.

It was the last Sunday of his leave; on Tuesday he would start for Governor's Island. At Burning Brook time was suspended and there was certainty.

He poked about the library until Mildred called him to dinner, always a hearty meal on Sundays. Chicken and rare preserves and a great choice of vegetables and flaky pies, while outside the wide windows the land stretched green and yellow under the warm spring sun.

He liked the Sunday ritual of a horseback ride in good weather. Always, when he first returned to Burning Brook, he approached a horse reluctantly; but once he had mounted and ridden forth, he rode nearly every day. After dinner he and Judd pulled on breeches and went to the stable and saddled up. In spring the stable cats dozed in the sun; stroke one's head and you were rewarded by a deep contented rumbling. The horses knew it was spring, of course; they nudged eagerly for the bit. And then Mildred came from the house, wearing jodphurs, her thick dark hair tied by a bright red ribbon. Then they were up and away, the horses prancing expectantly.

The farm was a finer place than it ever had been, thanks to the efforts of Judd and Mildred. When he quit teaching and brought her to Burning Brook as his bride in 1932, the place had gone to rack. The fifteen hundred acres which Sam Drummond had accumulated by 1840 were reduced to six hundred acres a century later, the lost land having gone to pay debts and taxes. For there was no money in the family. There was nothing but the old house with its paint peeling away and the outbuildings fallen into disrepair and the six hundred acres which had become too much for an aging tenant farmer; mullen and hackberry and chokecherry had marched in and the fences had fallen. Whatever grandeur had once marked Burning Brook was forgotten by even the oldest inhabitants of the countryside.

Judd went to work with scythe and ax and paintbrush and plaster, and Mildred helped him. He assumed debts and pushed on with knowledge acquired from pamphlets and the County Agricultural Agent. He learned by trial and error, aided by a Federal Government which had begun to cast a benevolent eye on the farmer. After jettisoning most of the traditional ideas of how this land should be worked and taking up the raising of beef cattle, he began to make money.

Now they cantered across clean, free acres, riding up the lane and taking the trail along the rushing brook. They passed through the woods and the upper pasture, walking their horses to breathe them, until they came to the height of land and halted.

Resting a hand on his horse's rump, Judd looked back at the farm. He said, "It's interesting how I used to live in the cities and pity the poor farmers. And the poor souls in the cities support us."

"Why did you do it?" Drew asked. "I mean, Father owns the property because Grandfather was stupid enough to—"

"Don't hold it against your father," Mildred said. "We're perfectly happy."

"We certainly are," Judd said. "Your father and I have an understanding. And don't hold it against your grandfather either. There wasn't anything promising about me as a youngster. Don't forget, I wouldn't go to the Academy. Willing your father the farm was a matter of primogeniture, which is very much a part of the tradition. And you know what tradition is."

"I certainly do know," Drew replied. "But I'm surprised you ever came back to it. You were well on your way as a history professor."

"I didn't exactly want to teach history, Drew. I wanted to be a historian." He looked at the reins between his fingers and then at Mildred. "But the more I studied the past, the more I desired an active present."

"And you wanted to come back?" Drew asked Mildred.

She smiled. "I certainly did. Even though I was a damn Yankee I wanted to come to Tennessee." She looked at him closely, her eyes narrowing in the sunlight. "Some day you'll come back here, Drew. You'll want to."

He turned his head, feeling vaguely troubled. Some day he presumably would inherit the land. He loved it, but he would not feel it was his. It was theirs, Judd's and Mildred's, for they had created it as it now was. He must create something of his own and not merely insert himself into another's creation.

"There's something we should tell you, though you must know it perfectly well, Drew." Judd turned his horse and faced him. "You're like our own son. Nothing would make us happier than if you came here and lived forever. I'll teach you all I've learned about farming

182

and you can take on all the responsibility you want. You could marry and take the house and we'd take the cottage."

"The cottage would suit us better anyway," Mildred said. She smiled slowly. "You'll come back and live here, Drew. I know you will."

He wished she would not be so positive. It troubled him. Why, he was not certain—except that he did not want to move into their lives as he had recently moved into Frances's. Let established lives remain established. And let him establish his own.

"I know," he said at last. "I appreciate it. I love it here." He wanted to tell them that he loved them, but he could not quite manage to say it. He said, "Let's gallop across the ridge to the side road."

Chapter XVI

He had been assigned to Governor's Island almost three weeks before he could bring himself to visit the Gannons in Orange. Finally, on a Saturday, he decided that he must call on them for Joe's sake. He would visit with them for an hour and go away, his obligation fulfilled.

I remember feeling that I wanted to live on the outside of people's lives and not even look in.

He had glimpsed the inside when he spent a night at the Manhattan apartment of his mother and Clarence Huddel. It had been painful. Booze and bickering. On an economically high plane, to be sure. Clarence had money, but that was all he had, and in his presence Dorothy Drummond Huddel acted foolish.

Drew hoped that he would not be at Governor's Island much longer. He had made a formal request for reassignment. He was sick and tired of being a hero, of standing before the vacant faces and hearing the empty tone of cheering. Although he did not want to return to combat, he sometimes thought it would be preferable to this playing the golden calf.

Joe's sister, Eileen, met him at Pennsylvania Station in Newark. She was a slender, dark-haired girl of eighteen who carried herself well. In her thin, grave face there was to him a certain beauty. Joe had said many times that he'd like Eileen. He did, immediately and instinctively.

As he rode beside her toward Orange in the Gannon's old Dodge, he remembered Joe's descriptions of the suburbs and he grew interested in the complex of cities and towns. There were not definable boundaries. There were mergings—and interesting conflicts: a garish filling station laid against an old clapboard house with a carriage-stone in front; the economic deterioration of a block and then the sudden social hopefulness of a new garden apartment. You could trace a lot of history here. People pushing toward the periphery and people trapped in the interior; people content in the interior and people trying to create new interiors on the extreme periphery. Also, there was the land itself. It had been gouged and hacked and smoothed, but it still rose to the west inexorably until it swelled in a line of low hills.

There I was, getting back inside of things again, not at all content to be an outsider.

As if he were a social historian, he asked her questions about this interesting fluid change in the suburbs. She did not seem to think it odd, but answered his questions as best she could. The streets grew narrower, the houses more closely huddled together, and she said, "It's a pretty old, tired neighborhood we live in. But I like it. I guess because I've never known anything else."

"Hey," he said, "that must be the cemetery Joe told me about. The place where old Thomas A. Edison is buried."

"Did Joe tell you about it?" She glanced at him in surprise. "That's the place all right."

She stopped the car in front of a brown clapboard house with a wide porch set in a small yard. There was a sign: J. GANNON, *Job Printing*. In a window was one of those service flags with a single blue star for Joe. The door opened and a gray-haired, tired-looking woman stepped out. When she looked at Drew, tears filled her eyes. Joe instead of him should be coming home, Drew thought, and momentarily he was sorry he had come.

"Mother," Eileen said, "this is Drew."

She took his hand. "It's nice to see you, Drew. Joe has written so much about you."

The furniture of the living room was cheap and old, but it was a comfortable, an immaculate room. From a distant part of the house came a steady thumping that jarred a small vase on a table. Eileen went through the hall, calling, "Dad! Dad! Drew's here!"

184

The thumping stopped and in a moment a stocky, balding man came in. He looked at his inked hands and thrust them in type pockets in his short apron. "It's nice to meet you, Drew. Excuse my hands. I'm trying to finish a job. You're staying for supper and the night with us, aren't you?"

"Thanks," Drew said, "but I planned to get back to New York."

They looked distressed.

"I mean," he said, "this is pretty short notice to drop in on you people."

He knew, then, that he would stay, and so did they. Eileen told him that he'd have Joe's room. She led him upstairs and showed him the room, which Mrs. Gannon kept exactly as Joe had left it. Pictures of girls on the dresser. A photograph of the Orange High School football squad of 1937 with Joe frowning fiercely. A crucifix. A pair of dice left in a Niagara Falls ashtray.

When they came downstairs, he followed Eileen through a passageway from the kitchen to the printing shop where Mr. Gannon was running off a job of business cards. The smell of ink and the whump of the press were curiously pleasant. Eileen sorted clean type into a tray of boxes while he sat and studied one of the cards Mr. Gannon had run off. Herman Glutzman, Painter & Interior Decorator, and an address in Bloomfield. "We Offer You Unexcelled Home Beauty At Unexcelled Moderate Rates." How long had it taken Herman to reduce paradise, really something for practically nothing, to two lines of type? And why did he wish his cards finished on a Saturday evening? Maybe because he wanted to hustle for jobs on Sunday; maybe just because he liked to feel his identity in a pocket. Drew watched Eileen's slim hands moving dexterously. He looked at her father's hands, square and strong, with the second finger on his left hand smashed flat. She glanced up at him and smiled.

After the job was finished they went to the living room and Drew began telling them everything about Joe that he could remember. Joe's brother, Francis, a quiet boy of sixteen, came in from his Saturday job in a supermarket. Herman Glutzman called for his cards. But Mr. and Mrs. Gannon refused to let anything interrupt at length their questions about Joe.

After a roast beef dinner which must have cost them a week of meat ration points, Drew insisted on drying the dishes while Eileen washed. Once her mother called her to the telephone. When she came back, he asked her if she had a date. "I broke it," she said.

Francis went out, despite his mother's protests, and they played a couple of rubbers of bridge. After Mr. and Mrs. Gannon went to bed, Eileen turned on the radio. She told Drew she hoped it hadn't been a boring evening for him, and he replied that it certainly had not.

"It reminds you of home?" she asked.

"Home was never like this," he said. "I never had it so good."

"Now I see, Drew. This is all—different to you."

He didn't try to explain how different. They talked for a while until he yawned—and apologized. Rising, she remarked drily that the Army had better get its rest, there being a war on. "Sleep as late in the morning as you want to, Drew. There will be coffee on the stove. We go to eight o'clock mass."

"I want to go to mass too," he said.

She glanced at him quickly. "Are you a Catholic?"

"No. But I want to go to mass."

She frowned. "Why?"

"Why? Just because I want to go, that's why. Do they object to agnostics like me going to mass?"

"Of course not. Are you a—an agnostic, Drew?"

"There's a P for Protestant stamped on my dog tags. But I'm really nothing. I mean I don't believe— It doesn't matter what I don't believe."

"It only matters what you believe," she said. "And you just believe in yourself, I guess."

"I don't even believe in myself much," he said. "But that doesn't matter either. About mass, how am I ever going to believe in anything if I don't go to the place where they do believe?"

Her eyes widened. "I never thought of that. All I meant was that I don't think it would be right if you went just to be *nice*. Just to try to please Mother and Dad. Do you understand?"

"I understand. But waken me for mass, Eileen."

Church bells awakened him, ringing across the towns in the bright spring morning. When they assembled in the kitchen for coffee, he said that he wanted to walk to church.

She wore a funny little hat and a dress that rustled like silk when she walked. It was good walking with her in the Sunday morning stillness until the rustle of her dress began to bother him by making his thoughts not altogether pure, as he wished them to be. His sensual nature depressed him and he tried not to glance at the swell of her breast and the roundness of her legs under the dress that rustled like silk as she walked. He wished to be pure, like the little children who hopped along in new straw bonnets and bright spring coats, like the

186

fresh smell of the first cut grass and the young green leaves which had a couple of seasons to go before they tarnished in frost, the earth's desire for change. But he was not pure, he had broken all the Commandments and probably a few others that had eluded Moses. He was not pure, but he did not believe he was damned for his impurity. For, since he did not believe he could be saved from anything, he did not see how he could be damned for anything. He was simply going along to church with Eileen, wishing hopelessly that he could recover his irrevocably lost innocence. They entered the church and into the ceremony that was meaningless to him. He saw, however, that it was meaningful to Eileen, that she believed. And seeing that was enough for him. Seeing it was a form of believing too. Then they walked home, hearing the bell-clang of churches of many faiths in the still, warm air, and he did not listen to the rustle of the dress which was not silk but only sounded like it.

On the way he bought newspapers, and when they reached home he announced that he would scramble eggs. They ate them hot, with toast and coffee, and they read the papers at the table as the morning sun streamed in.

When Drew said good-by to them at the Newark station, after taking them out for dinner, he wondered if he would see them again. As the week progressed, he realized that he wanted to see Eileen again. It was difficult to explain. He certainly was not in love with her. She was not an extraordinarily beautiful girl. But she made him feel comfortable. Then, remembering that he wanted to be an outsider, he decided to forget about it.

He did not, however. On Saturday morning he arranged to rent a car from an officer who had week-end duty and he telephoned Eileen.

He arrived at six o'clock, with a box of candy for her mother, a bottle of Bourbon for her father, and flowers for her. A big operation. Her father was pleased and her mother suspicious. She probably feared he was out to seduce her daughter. He wasn't. He was simply taking her out for dinner and a dance.

While they were dancing Eileen said, "This means a lot to me, Drew. I guess I'm awfully vain. I had a fine time last week end, but I thought you were doing it all for *them* and I—I—" Her voice trailed off and she flushed, fearing she had said too much.

He let her know that she hadn't. He told her he'd been thinking of her all week. Then, fearing that he had said too much, he quickly changed the subject. She and her family led a wonderful life, he said.

"No," she said, "we don't. You can't see it now because you've been away so long and this seems—different from what you've ever known. It's not a wonderful life. Mother's inclined to be a worrier and nagger. Dad is—well, he's really a defeated man with that little business of his. He had a good job, he could have another, because he's a first-rate printer. But he wants to run his own business and he has no business sense at all. They need the money I bring in from my job at the Prudential in Newark. We all have to work awfully hard and we don't dare look too far ahead."

"If you did look ahead, Eileen, what would you see?"

She smiled at him. "The same thing. The same kind of life in Orange or one of the towns around. And I'm not being bitter, either. You seem to think that when you dislike something you can change it. But you can't. You can only become so adjusted to it that you can't see anything else. And after a while you even sort of like it—as I do."

"But haven't you ever wanted to *be* something different?"

"Of course I have. I wanted to go to college. And before that I wanted to be a great dancer and a great actress and marry Clark Gable or somebody. But I never went to college or took dancing lessons or went to dramatic school or did anything except go to work for the Prudential as a file clerk after I finished high school."

"Maybe you'll meet a handsome young executive who—ah, the hell with it."

"Maybe I will," she said. "But I'm not looking to it any more than I'm looking to marry Clark Gable. I'm not bitter and not unhappy. The trouble with you, Drew, you have a tendency to—romanticize things, or at least us Gannons and our very ordinary lives."

About one o'clock he drove her home, stopping at Eagle Rock high on the hill when she pointed it out to him. They got out and walked to the dark and deserted pavilion and stared out at the dim-out of the forty towns below. In the still morning there rose the distant throb of trains and airplane engines. She told him how she used to hike up here with Joe, bringing lunch and climbing straight up over the rocks from a street in Montclair below. Then a police prowl car cast a light on them and a cop told them to move on. What dirty minds cops had. They were just standing there, not touching each other, gazing out at the dimmed lights while she told him about the old days. And then the law said move on and you had to move. He wanted to come back in daylight. How about tomorrow? Would she like to hike all the way up here and maybe bring lunch?

"Let's do it." Her voice rose in delight. "Right after mass I'll fix us a lunch and we'll start out."

He refused her invitation to spend the night at the Gannons'. He drove to Newark and slept in a hotel, returning at nine o'clock in the morning. They set out, she wearing slacks and he carrying their lunch and a thermos of coffee in an old knapsack they'd borrowed from Francis, who pointed out to him that he must be nuts, a guy in the infantry going hiking on a Sunday off.

Eileen led him by the long way, through Glen Ridge and Montclair, along streets of large houses set in large yards.

"Would you like to live in one of these some day?" he asked her.

"Of course I would," she replied, "but I'm not going to, so I'd better not start thinking about it. You have to have an income of something like twelve or fifteen thousand a year to live in places like these. And how do you make that kind of money?"

"In stuff like the junk business," he said. "There's big money in junk. I don't mean just scrap to melt and mold and shoot at each other in a war. That too, of course. But I mean any kind of junk you can sell. Like cheap gadgets or clothes. Or suppose you're a writer. You can write junky stuff like you hear on radio soap operas. They'll pay you enough."

She was smiling at him as he ranted on. Finally she said, "You aren't sore, are you?"

"Of course I'm not sore."

"I know," she said, still smiling. "You aren't the least bit sore. You aren't jealous of these people or anything. You're just talking, and what you say is absolutely true. But you aren't sore, and that's what I like about you."

"You bet I'm not sore. I wouldn't mind living in one of these places, but I wouldn't want to pay the *price*. Take that big house right *there*. I'll bet the guy who lives there is a vice-president of the Cheese and Feed Store National Bank. I respect that man, I really do; like I respect a work horse on the farm. But I feel sorry for him. Where's he been all his life? Just to the bank and home again. He never went to the races—and I don't mean the horse races. He can keep his house, I don't want it."

And then, presumably, I laughed inanely. It was the way I used to act.

She was laughing too, and she caught his hand without self-consciousness, and they walked hand in hand.

After a while she said, "So if you don't like this, you maybe plan to stay in the Army?"

He told her profanely that he did not, and apologized for his profanity.

"But what are you going to *do?*"

"Well, I'll tell you, Eileen. Sometimes when I read what I think is a good book I think I'd like to write a good book. But I know I won't. It's like sometimes when you go to the theater and see a good actor. Then I think, God, I'm going to be an actor. But I won't any more than when I see a terrific dancer on the stage or in the movies and I think I'm going to take lessons and become a professional. What it comes down to is that I'm best at *appreciating*. And the world can always use lots of appreciators. . . . Listen to that bird, for instance. It's a cardinal. How do I know? Because for a short time when I was a kid I wanted to be an ornithologist and go up the Orinoco River or somewhere. I wanted to be one just long enough to learn a lot of bird calls, and my life has been a lot more pleasant ever since. Much more pleasant than if I'd become an ornithologist with no time for anything but birds. Listen to that cardinal!

"Anyway, it's not so much what I *want* to be as what I think I would like most for the longest time—meaning, probably, the rest of my life. I'd rather be a teacher. If I could, if I have the brains and patience, I'd like to teach American history like my Uncle Judd did. In a college, I mean, because I think that the older people are, the more interesting students they are. And if I can't make it into college teaching— See, I've got to begin from scratch and go to college myself first— If I can't make it into college teaching, I'd like to teach high school. But from teaching the stupid things the Army makes its buck privates learn, I think I like teaching so much that even if I couldn't qualify for high school, I'd take on grammar school. I mean away down with the squirmy little bastards. I'd like that too. It's not a good sign. A real outstanding scholar type would never settle for hauling overshoes on fat little squirmers. But I would. That's why I'm just an *appreciator*. They don't drive hard bargains with themselves. They settle for low prices. Not like the high-powered creative types who must drive some terrible bargains with themselves until they get used to it and probably sort of like it. Not even like the junk men or the vice-presidents of the Cheese and Feed Store National Bank."

She caught his hand again and they walked a distance until he said, "I guess you don't think much of it."

"Think much of it?" She looked at him wonderingly. "I think it's wonderful! You know something? There's a teachers' college in

Upper Montclair. For high school teachers, I mean. There's a bus line goes to it from Orange."

"No kidding?"

"No kidding."

It was strange how good that made him feel. Like a tree must feel if its tap root found a deep hidden well during a hot dry summer.

If we could have left it there or I could even leave it there now, it would be a happy ending. And that's something any life can stand: More happy endings.

He never recalled an exact moment when he decided that he loved her. Three weeks after he met her he was assigned as a casual at Camp Kilmer. And four weeks after that he was on his way. At some time in those weeks they touched, they kissed, they believed that their lives would not be the same again. At least he believed so. And it certainly seemed that she believed so too.

Perhaps his error was in taking her to New York that Saturday. Yet how could genuine love err? How could it turn a wrong corner or make an incorrect introduction? The fact that it happened all the time was of no solace to a victim of the emotion; afterwards he rationalized in terms of "false" and "genuine," as if the emotion could be measured by the ounce or carat on arbitrary evaluation. Which was as fallacious as you could be. Of course their love was the genuine twenty-four-carat article itself, if you must measure it so. When eventually lost overboard in the sea, why say the article all along had been meretricious? The gold was good, as only gold can be. Eventually, however, it simply was lost.

He was up from Kilmer, hoping for time, as so many hoped for time late in that spring. He was pressing her, rather frantically. He wanted her. And he knew that she wanted him. But it had to be *right*, so little time be damned. No quick and covert act under assumed names in a cheap hotel. This was the real thing, till death us do part.

Yes, he was pressing hard. With the arrant cleverness of the young lover he had arranged for a small and not very expensive diamond ring from a jeweler recommended to him by a brother officer and suffering lover at Kilmer. He took her to New York on the pretext of just another date. And then the jewelry store and the little vignette, so charged with emotion then, so pathetic in retrospect. The ring. The eager young soldier. The shy and tremulous girl. The benign salesman, fatuously enacting his role of Cupid. The young soldier had slipped the ring on the proper finger of the girl and then taken it off and showed her the engraving inside: A.J.D. to E.M.G. 5-2-44. Tears came to her eyes. He kissed her gravely. The salesman and a customer beamed at the tableau of all being so well that ended so well.

Outside the store, holding her hand tightly, he said, "And now we're going to the Stork Club to celebrate with a drink."

"The Stork Club!" she said. "They'll never let us in. I'm not dressed right."

"They'll let us in. When I was on that hero detail I had to go there once and I met the guy who runs it, what's-his-name, and he slapped me on the back and said, 'You come around any time, it's on the house.' I won't let it be on the house, but I know he'll let us in."

"No." She halted and looked at him. "That's not the sort of place for us to go right now. There's something you can do for me. I want to meet your mother."

He was shocked and rather frightened. He began to tell her reasons why they should not try to see his mother today. But she looked at him sadly, believing he was ashamed of her. He certainly was not, but how could he make her understand what a difficult person his mother was? He could not, of course.

She went to a telephone booth with him and waited while he looked up his mother's number. Momentarily he was tempted to dial a wrong number and tell her no one answered. But she stood there, smiling at him through the glass, and he would not betray her trust by even the movement of a finger in a dial. For this must be *right*. He opened the door and beckoned to her as his mother's telephone began to ring. His mother, alas, answered immediately. Oh, darling! Where had he been? Why didn't he ever call?

Well, he was calling now. There was someone he wanted her to meet. Would she have a drink with them? But naturally, he and whoever it was must come to the apartment immediately.

"Mother, I don't like to be brutal about it, but frankly I don't feel like facing old Clarence right now."

She was silent for a moment. Then, "Clarence isn't home, Drew. He's in the hospital."

"I'm sorry to hear it, Mother. His liver?"

"No. He—he sort of had a nervous breakdown. He's in the Hartford Retreat."

"I'm sorry, Mother. Remember me to him when you see him. It will do you good to get out. We'll meet wherever you say."

"The Plaza," she replied quickly. "I'll meet you in the lobby of the Plaza in twenty minutes."

Eileen's arm linked in his, they walked slowly up Fifth Avenue through the blue ground shadows of late afternoon, glancing up often at the golden light that gleamed among the towers. He was vaguely aware of passing people who looked at them, at first casually, and then with delighted apprehension of the two very young lovers. It was, he thought afterwards, as if they walked in halo.

His mother strode into the lobby a few minutes after they arrived. She looked quite handsome wearing a sable cape and curious hat and her hair done in some new fashion. It made him aware of Eileen's inexpensive spring coat and plain dress and her long hair that possibly needed something done with it. But then, close up, he saw the ineradicable mouth lines and flesh pebbles that marked his mother's aging. He felt sorry for her, but not for Eileen, who was young.

"Mother, I'd like you to meet Eileen. Eileen Gannon."

His mother smiled radiantly as Eileen hesitantly extended her hand. "It's awfully nice to meet you, child." She turned to Drew, her lips pouting. "Will you please tell me where you've *been?* I've hardly seen you and you never call."

"I've been very busy, Mother."

"Well"—she smiled on Eileen again—"maybe you have at that. Let's go in and have a drink."

He saw, troubled, that his mother had categorized Eileen to her satisfaction in a single all-encompassing glance from bare head to inexpensive shoes. He saw that she requested a table in an obscure corner of the room. And he saw that she was not pleased when Eileen ordered orange juice.

"*I'll* have a Martini," she said to the waiter.

"Mother," he said, "this is a very important day to us. Show her, Eileen."

Smiling tremulously, Eileen extended her left hand.

"Merciful heavens!" His mother fell back in her chair. At last, "You never *told* me, Drew." And then quickly, "Congratulations to you both." Tears started to her eyes. "Forgive me, child." She touched Eileen's hand. "It's all so sudden."

"It really is." Eileen looked as if she were going to cry too.

"It's such a pretty ring. And you got it just today?"

"Yes. It was such a surprise." Eileen flushed and looked vaguely around the room.

"It certainly is to me, Eileen." She looked reproachfully at Drew. "I'd always hoped that when the time came he'd give the one and only girl *my* ring, the Huntley ring." She indicated the smaller of two diamonds on her left hand. Talking now in her southern accent, which had lapsed momentarily in the shock of learning the news, "My grandfather, Colonel Huntley, bought it in Paris for my grandmother before the War Between the States. My father gave it to my mother when they were engaged. My mother gave it to me. When I became engaged to Drew's father, the General, I made him give it to me as *our* ring. And I wanted Drew to give it. It always goes to the one and only girl."

Apparently, Drew thought, she saw no fallacy in the fact that she and his father had not turned out to be the one and only to each other. And now she was off, telling about the Huntleys, dazzling poor Eileen with her old moonlight and magnolias story of her family. On and on she went, her voice purring the litany of her faith in the greatness of the Huntleys. The ambassadors and senators, the soldiers and planters. Eileen listened, her eyes wide, her mouth carefully resisting the impulse to fall open. If only she were more experienced, he thought, she would be faintly amused or bored. But she was young, and while youth should not be a fault, it made her judgment of his mother faulty.

"How I do carry on," his mother said suddenly. "Forgive me, Eileen. I haven't even given you a chance to speak. But"—she smiled sharply—"when a girl has nailed her man, she should know just how good a man she's got."

"For heaven's sake, Mother, your *verbs*. Eileen hasn't *nailed* me. If there's been any—"

"All right, all right, darling." She patted his hand. "Don't be so *sen*sitive." And she patted Eileen's hand on the table. "Are you in school somewhere, Eileen?"

Eileen, coloring, shook her head. "I've finished school, Mrs. Drummond— Excuse me, Mrs.——" Her voice trailed off in confusion.

His mother blinked and remained silent.

Eileen, swallowing, said, "I live in Orange. Orange, New Jersey. I've finished school and I work in Newark."

"Eileen is a secretary," Drew said. "She's a sister of—"

"I'm not a secretary." She frowned at Drew. "Why do you exaggerate? I'm a file clerk."

"I see." His mother sipped her Martini.

It was time they got out of there, he thought. Eileen looked as if she were about to cry.

Fighting down the impulse, however, she said calmly, "It's much better if we don't pretend I'm something I'm not. I graduated from high school last year. I'm a file clerk for the Prudential Insurance Company. My people are quite poor. My father is a printer. My brother Joe and Drew were in the same company in the Pacific. When Drew came back, he came to see us and . . ." She did not quite shrug. She looked down, listless, at her orange juice.

Drew quickly began telling his mother about Joe Gannon. But she was not listening to him. She waited for Eileen to speak again. And Eileen waited for her to speak. He looked at his wrist watch with an elaborate gesture and said it was about time they went along.

"Relax," his mother said. "I want another Martini. . . . Waiter!" When the waiter had taken her order, she said, "So you're engaged and you plan to be married." She had, unaccountably, lost her southern accent.

"That's right," Drew said. "And soon, too, I hope. That's something we haven't had a chance to talk over."

Eileen raised her eyes and looked at him miserably.

His mother sighed. "So you're in a hurry. And I suppose you're in a hurry too, Eileen."

"Look, Mother—"

She said sharply, "Be quiet and stop treating me as such a fool. I simply said I presume you're both in a hurry and I did not infer there's anything wrong with that. It's natural when you're young and there's a war on. I do not say you're foolish, either of you. I am not telling you to wait. I'm only telling you—and I think you understand this better than Drew, Eileen—to make it a proper marriage. I won't cry on your shoulder." She gazed levelly at Eileen. "I won't tell you the sad story of having one son and him gone from you so quickly. Gone so fast and gone you'll never know why. But I won't cry on your shoulder. I only say to make it a good and proper marriage, as big an affair as you can have, with everybody possible there. Make it in a church and try to make it last. Do you have a church, Eileen?"

"Yes." Eileen spoke indistinctly, her head lowered. She lifted her head. "I'm a Catholic, Mrs.—— I'm a Catholic."

His mother, about to light a cigarette, grew still. Then, unsteadily, she lighted her cigarette.

"And that doesn't make any difference to me, Mother," Drew said. "If the fact that I'm *not* a Catholic doesn't make any difference to Eileen. Look, we shouldn't talk about it now. We haven't even had a chance to talk about it together. But I will say this. I'll say that if I ever see the Catholic faith could mean something to me, I'll become a Catholic. And kids of ours can be raised as Catholics."

His mother said, "It won't work. It never works. Nobody knows better than Eileen that it won't work."

"Okay, Mother." He got to his feet quickly. "You've had your say. Now we must go."

Eileen, staring at the table, rose slowly.

"So you're going." His mother gazed up at him. Her voice rose. "Where are you going? What are you going to do? When will I hear from you? Why won't you ever *tell* me any more?"

"Because," he said quietly, "any more you never want me to be what I want to be."

Eileen said, "Good-by, Mrs.——"

"Huddel, Eileen. My full name, in fact, is Dorothy Pinckney Huntley Drummond Huddel. It's a hell of a name, isn't it?" Tears glittered in her eyes. "Would you have lunch with me some day? Bring your mother and we'll—"

"Thank you, no, Mrs. Huddel. We'd better not—"

"Run along both of you," she said and turned away so they would not see the tears running down her cheeks.

There was, and still is, a fountain in a small square outside the Plaza Hotel. When Eileen reached the steps leading up to the fountain, she sat down on them and cried. He rested a hand on her shoulder, trying to comfort her. After a while she asked him to take her home. He tried not to think about the one thing his mother could have done for them: Take off her Goddamn Huntley ring and give it to Eileen.

He had two more weeks before he was shipped to England. In that time she steadfastly refused to marry him. She would only say:

"I'll wait for you. When you come back, I'll be right here. I love you and I'll wait for you forever. . . ."

Chapter XVII

And always, Jane thought, you could tell if a woman loved a man by the way she looked at him. You could see that Marcia loved Drew when she looked at him.

Bathed and dressed at last, she stepped back and studied herself in the mirror. Could I, she wondered, ever look at any man the way Marcia looks at Drew?

As she left her room, she thought happily that Drew and Marcia could not be having an affair, however. A woman who was having an affair with a man almost invariably gazed at him with some degree of possessiveness. She had observed it, at least, in the few positive instances of women she had known in New York and Rome. But the sense of possessiveness was lacking in Marcia's glances at him.

When she entered the living room, General Drummond rose, his face flushed. Marcia gazed at her bemusedly. Drew, sprawled on the sofa, raised his Martini to her and smiled.

"I hope I haven't held up dinner," she said.

"Only Ugo can hold up dinner," Marcia replied. "Half-past nine is his fixed notion of the dinner hour. It's smart to stash crackers in your room or you'll starve to death around here."

"Your wrists," General Drummond said as he handed her a Martini. "They must be very sore."

"Why, yes." Surprised that he would realize it. "They are."

He shook his head. "At any rate, you're all right." He turned to Drew. "What possessed you anyway? You should have seen that ladder wasn't safe."

Drew smiled at him. "You know I'm full of these mad impulses, Father. We saw this tower and I said to her, 'Race you to the top of it,' and up we went, the whole thing quaking and shaking. But what did we care? See, we were racing and—"

"Ah!" General Drummond raised a hand, annoyed, yet amused in a measure too.

"Really, as I told you," Jane said, "it was all my fault. *I* wanted to go up and Drew—"

"It doesn't matter what *you* wanted to do Jane," the General said. "Drew was there and he should have seen it wasn't safe and prevented you. If I'd been there I wouldn't have let you go up."

And she would have obeyed him meekly, she thought in surprise. She would have had the utmost faith in his judgment, as she had always had faith in Daddy's judgments while half believing that all other men were fools.

Marcia said, "See how nice it is to be a woman, Jane? You don't have to *think*."

"Has anybody seen Harry?" asked Drew. "I think it would be nice to send him a drink or invite him in or something."

197

"Don't always be worrying about Harry," his father said. "He gets around and has a time for himself. I think he tied one on last night in Florence while we were at the Sabraccios'. He looked a little green around the gills this morning. Besides, he always has his model boats to play with."

"His *what?*"

General Drummond frowned. "He makes these tiny model sailing ships. Very expert craftmanship. He took it up a year or so ago. He sits by the hour at it, perfectly content. I saw him sitting down there in the bailey this afternoon working at one."

"I'll be damned." Drew looked from Jane to Marcia. "Does anybody besides me find that extraordinary?"

She wanted to agree with him. Now, as she had not before. There was a special pleading about him, a warm and smiling quickness that must draw something close to worship from many of his enlisted men. She could see that now, as she had not seen it before this afternoon. Nevertheless, she could not agree with him in the inconsequential matter of Sergeant Bannister making model sailing ships.

"I think it's pretty extraordinary," Marcia said, looking at Drew with that tender expression. "Harry's a soldier, or has been one for years. Probably he didn't like boats or want to go near the water. I mean . . ."

She had been an actress, she'd said, a rather unsuccessful actress. At least her candor was refreshing. She had the looks and the figure, but perhaps she'd had trouble learning her lines. It was said, however, that that did not make much difference; it was said that if you got to know the right people and were not unwilling to put yourself out a little . . . It was not pleasant to think about. It really was not fair to Marcia. And yet there was something about her indolent movements, the way she carried herself, the way she looked at Drew. It made you wonder. It made you think, Here's a woman who's had a time for herself and is still looking to have a time. Then, too, there was the really mysterious business about her husband. And she'd been married before this. You couldn't tell— It was not pleasant to think about.

She sat down beside General Drummond. "I forgot to mention that I had a letter from Dad the day I left Rome. He wanted to be remembered to you. He understands his promotion is going through and he expects to be transferred to First Army."

"Good." The General nodded. "It was a shame he was cut back from his star after the War and frozen. Your father is the best G-4 in the Army. Brad himself said so. I heard he was being recommended for a second star when the civilians yanked the rug from under all of us. Did your father ever tell you about his bad luck?"

"Bad luck? No."

"It's like Dave never to mention it. Your father didn't go to Command and General Staff at the point in his career when it was important, you know. He was eminently qualified. Everybody knew it. But in those days you had to have a consistent record of superior to enter C and G. And it was your father's misfortune to serve under an officer who didn't believe there was such a thing as a superior officer—except himself. He was, if you will pardon me, a bastard. His name was Calhoun, and he was known everywhere in the Army as Cat-tail Calhoun. He—ah"—the General's expression grew abstract—"I—uh—don't know why."

She could imagine why. Dimly she remembered her father mentioning an officer named Calhoun years ago. But not complainingly, and certainly without any hint of what old Cat-tail had done to him. That was like Daddy. She could almost cry at the thought.

"He never told me," she said indistinctly.

"Naturally. You don't discuss things like that. At least Dave and I don't."

Yes, General Drummond would not discuss such a matter either. Except with his wife. But probably he had not been able to discuss such things even with his wife; Colonel Follansbee had remarked in Rome that General Drummond's divorced wife had been a heller. Poor man. And poor Daddy too. It was doubtful if he and Mother had ever discussed such things. Not that Mother had been a heller. She simply had not liked or ever really understood the Army.

"I think," she said slowly, "that when Daddy moves to his new post I'll go home and keep house for him."

General Drummond stirred and looked at her curiously.

"My mother died a year ago, you know. He's been living in a little apartment while at the Pentagon. I hate to think of him rattling around in a big post house all by himself."

"Well"—General Drummond hitched one leg over the other and summoned a cheerful smile—"it's nice of you to think about your father. But—well, you have your own life to live. You may run into somebody who— You might fall in love and decide to get married."

What does he mean?

"Maybe I will." She felt herself flushing, aware that Drew and Marcia had stopped talking and were listening to them. Then, impelled

199

to say it and knowing that she should not, as she had been impelled to climb the tower this afternoon and known that she should not: "But how will I know when I do?"

Drew said, "The guy will tell you, Jane. The guy will tell you and you'll believe him."

"Yes." General Drummond cleared his throat. "That's right. The guy will tell you and you'll believe him."

But what does he mean?

He could not mean, for he did not know, that she never had been in love. None of them could know. Surely, please God, it did not show. For it was, she understood, an impoverished state in which she found herself. And it must be her own fault. Oh, she'd imagined she was in love a couple of times. As with Dan, who'd been in the Class of '50 at the Academy and who'd gone off to Korea and died there. She had imagined, but she had not truly been in love.

"The egotism of you men," said Marcia. She mimicked Drew's casual tone: "The guy will tell you and you'll believe him." She smiled at Jane. "How about all the times they've told you and you didn't believe them?"

Did Marcia know? She was not, after all, a fool. Did she detect what eluded the men? Undoubtedly, however, she did not see how strange it was that General Drummond had mentioned love and marriage. It recalled the remark of Betty Moresby, her roommate in Rome, after the Embassy cocktail party for the General: "The old boy looks crushed when he looks at you, Jane. I mean he has a crush." And later, after she'd happily accepted the job with him: "If you can out-run him around a desk, Janie-doll, you'll keep your precious reputation, but you may not keep the job." She had disliked Betty's remarks. Betty had been absolutely wrong. General Drummond was a friend of her father and he had acted most properly.

But what does he mean now?

Ugo stood in the doorway. "Dinner is served, signora." He glanced without emotion at the barbarians who failed to dress for dinner. Shrugging slightly, as will a civilized man who has fallen on barbarous times, he turned to the dining room.

It was a good dinner: a *pasta,* a roast of lamb, a green salad, a sweet tart. And food, when you are young and hungry, quiets the tender, the troublesome emotions. Ugo permitted Harry to serve them coffee and brandy in the living room. Then General Drummond proposed a rubber of bridge. The ritual, so pleasantly familiar, enabled

Jane to feel *organized* again. And to feel organized, she thought, was, after all, to feel happy.

After General Drummond and Marcia won the rubber, he excused himself and went to bed. Drew was right, Jane thought; his father did make her feel tense. For she felt relieved after he had gone. In a few minutes, however, she realized that either Drew or Marcia was making her feel ill at ease. It was curious; she could not understand why she felt this way, or even which one of them troubled her. Finally it occurred to her that she simply wished to be alone. Rising, she said that she was going to bed. Marcia rose and said she was going too. Drew looked from one to the other, his expression baffled, when they said good night to him.

As they climbed the stairs together, Marcia said, "Stop off in my room, Jane, and I'll give you some liniment for your wrists." She wished to speak to her about something, Jane believed as they stepped into her room.

The orderliness of the room surprised her. Now that she came to think of it, she would have imagined that Marcia's room would be carelessly maintained. Her indolent manner would indicate it. Also it was said that actresses lived in confusion. But this, even to the exact array of cosmetics and bottles on a dressing table, was as orderly as she always kept the rooms in which she herself lived.

Marcia went into her bathroom and returned with a bottle of liniment. "Maybe this will help, Jane." She smiled and patted her arm. "Good night."

She left, oddly disappointed that Marcia had not wished to speak to her. As she crossed the hall to her own room, she heard Marcia lock her door. It was significant, and Marcia intended her to note the significance. Marcia had been waiting downstairs for her to leave. She was constantly engaged in sending her signals, but Jane could not half read them. She was confused. Drew might understand her confusion. But if she went down to him now, what would she say?

She stood before the full-length mirror of imperfect glass in her dimly lighted room, rubbing liniment on her sore wrists. Observed in the mirror, she seemed to be wringing her hands. It was so unlike the image of the self-possessed woman she tried to place before the world.

Near the fireplace stood a huge armoire of dark wood. Its big door would not stay shut; it had swung open, exposing the dresses and suits which she had carefully hung up. Reaching out, she slammed it shut. Slowly, silently, it fell open again. Undressing, she stood, naked, gazing at the taut, rounded perfection of her young body in the old and imperfect mirror. Then, shivering, she quickly pulled on pajamas.

After she lay down in the wide, cold bed, she continued to shiver. It was strange. She never minded cold. But now she could not stop shivering. There were muffled sounds: the slow tread of feet somewhere; the distant barking of a dog; a scurrying within the walls, perhaps of rats or falling plaster. She was not afraid; she never was afraid of anything, her friends and family said. Brave Jane, bold Jane. Then why didn't she stop shivering?

I wish, she thought, there was someone to love me.

She slept fitfully, dreaming and starting nervously. Once, turning on the light, she saw that it was half-past three. Then she sank into a deep gray channel of sleep, drifting down it deeply, covered over and gone. She was rising, the grayness vaulting up in a lofty dome, and she rising with it, detached and unaided. There were lifted white faces far below. Someone suddenly clutched her wrist. General Drummond stared down at her bemusedly, holding her by the wrist, while around the dome ran Drew, calling to her. General Drummond's fingers began to slip and she screamed.

Her scream awakened her. She started up, her heart racing, her scream seeming to echo in the high-ceilinged chamber. Her right hand groped for the light and found it. Twenty minutes after four. The ghastly night was not yet over. Turning off the light, she fell back, her heart still racing. Wide awake now, she thought she heard a strange sound somewhere in the castle. Her body grew rigid as she strained to hear it. But it was gone, there was silence.

Suddenly deciding that she could not lie longer, she turned on the light and rose and dressed quickly in a warm sweater and skirt. As she opened the door, she sensed rather than distinctly heard someone in the dark hall.

"Who's there?" she asked sharply.

"It's me, Harry, Miss Raleigh," he whispered hoarsely. "Let me get you the light."

In the dim hall light which he turned on she made out his embarrassed grin. He wore a T-shirt and an old pair of GI pants; his feet were bare.

"I thought I heard the General call," he whispered. "I sneaked in and looked at him. He's sleeping like a baby."

As she passed him, going toward the stairs, he said, "You getting up so early, Miss Raleigh?"

"I can't sleep. I'm going to read." She smelled sweat on him and glimpsed his touseled hair, the ugly scar that ran down his neck into his hairy shoulder. She walked faster.

"Miss Raleigh, you want some coffee?"

She paused, looking back at him. She wanted a cigarette, but she believed it unhealthful to smoke a cigarette in the morning before she drank coffee. "Why, yes," she said. "I'll make some."

"Don't you bother. This Hugo, he hides everything, but I know how to get the coffee. Soon as I dress I'll serve you in the library."

He was quick. Soon after she had laid and lighted a fire in the library fireplace, he appeared with a tray of coffee and bread and a small pot of jam.

"You made the fire yourself, miss," he said in surprise. Then, smiling, "There's something to being raised in the Army, isn't there?" And then, fearing he had been forward, "I'm sorry about there not being any fruit juice. Hugo has a big padlock on the refrigerator and I thought I'd better not bust—break it open."

"This is fine, Harry." She smiled at him. "You're very kind to get up. You needn't have."

"I'm a light sleeper, miss. I don't sleep well at all. I get along on very little and I'm always glad to get up. This is condensed milk, I'm sorry, and the butter's locked up too."

"Thanks, you needn't have bothered with bread. I just want some coffee."

He poured coffee into her cup from a silver pot and then stepped back, smiling, his head cocked attentively. He was lonely, she presumed. She might ask him about his model sailing ships, but that could lead to her having to look at them. It was pointless, and she wanted to be alone. She wished to sit here by the warm fire and sip coffee and finish reading old General Drummond's Civil War journal.

"Thanks very much for everything, Harry."

"You're welcome, miss." He backed away reluctantly. "You want anything, I'll be around here somewhere. I hope the Major remembered to put his shoes out to be shined . . ."

She unwrapped the journal and opened it to the place she had marked yesterday and began to read.

It has ever grieved me to hear my great and good friend, General George Thomas, referred to as "Old Slow Trot." General Grant himself has not been loath to perpetuate the appellation. Between these two there ever existed a mute antagonism that I am hard put to explain. I saw it at Chattanooga, when they came close to snarling at each other, and when in truth I did for a time doubt Thomas. But I could not doubt him long, for I had been at Chickamauga. Napoleon said that history is a fable agreed upon, so I will not say what history will try to prove—I will only say that I believe the Union had two generals greater than all others, Grant and Thomas. Thomas's blood ran cold whereas mine ran hot. I was a driver, often sleepless and ever restless, while Thomas had the ease, often mistook for phlegm, of the great leader who does not rail against Nature but works diligently and carefully in the dimensions of Nature, resting his case calmly before her tribunal after having pled it as best he can.

I do not say that Thomas was greater than Grant; I do but say he was different. Because of the action at Chickamauga history will doubtless judge Thomas as a great defensive general. When, however, in the course of time the battles are studied closely it surely will be observed that only twice in the War did a Federal Army drive a Confederate Army from strongly prepared positions in total rout. This occurred at Chattanooga and again at Nashville, and on each occasion the Army was commanded by George Thomas.

There is so much that generalship can do in campaign and battle, and then campaigns are waged and battles fought by men. Thomas always took care of his men, and when it came to battle it could be said that his men took care of Thomas. I have written how after Atlanta, when I learned of Sherman's intentions on his proposed march to Savannah, I begged to be relieved of command and sent elsewhere. I am a Federalist, but I am Southern, and I never could bear the wanton destruction of my people's homes and livelihood. As a Southerner, a Virginian, Thomas understood my great reluctance when I presented it to him and kindly arranged, as I have written, my transfer with him back to Tennessee. The gesture was typical of him and, perforce, made me more eager than ever to be numbered among his best soldiers. Again, after Nashville, when we had broke Hood's army and Wilson's cavalry was pursuing and harrying its remnants southward, Thomas showed his great understanding by permitting me a week's leave to go north into Ohio to try to settle personal affairs. I speak of the madman Jeremiah Baker, who had sent his Jezebel daughter south to Nashville apparently to threaten the honor of the Drummond name. I need only tell Thomas it was an affair of honor and he bid me go, for he, a Virginian, understood without asking the particulars. It was a futile journey, for Baker had disappeared. I mention this but to illustrate Thomas's understanding as we come to my last large engagement of the War, at Nashville.

204

Having come up to Nashville with Schofield after the Battle at Franklin, I . . .

Jane paused in her reading and went back and read again, "I speak of the madman Jeremiah Baker . . ." Who was he? Old General Drummond had not mentioned him before. And who was his Jezebel daughter?

She hurried on, through his account of the Battle of Nashville, to the ending of the journal:

So, at last, I came home to my plantation and found it only a farm, its acres run down, its house in ill repair. True, the house and outbuildings had been spared by the armies which marched through here, the Federals knowing it as my home and the Confederates knowing it as the home of my wife, whose brother rode with Forrest. I came home to this place we know as Burning Brook, a name which I as a child unwitting gave it when, seeing the westerning red October sun shine on the brook, I said to my mother, "See, the brook is burning," and my mother, who smiled seldom and spoke little, smiled and said, "It needs a name; we shall call it Burning Brook." I came home and found my two young bairns run wild and fit to be tamed only by the military life and education of the Academy and my dear wife sunk deep in the apathy of her defeated cause. My slaves were gone, all but four faithfuls whom I scarce had funds to pay, for I had freed all in 1861. I came home, I say, and found much gone, but I missed more than anything the affection and respect of old friends and neighbors. We had tested our differences on the field of honor and the cause for which I fought had been ascendant. It had ended and I wished us to remove our gauntlets and clasp hands, but I had not reckoned on the bitterness that outlasts war and makes of peace a state of siege. I hope that in my lifetime the wound may be knitted and our divided cause reunited.

This is the simple record of a soldier in the War. I would preserve it for my sons and for all the Drummonds who come after for whatever interest and edification it may hold for them. I hereby direct my heirs and executors that this remain the personal property of the family, never to be published in the vanity that necessarily accompanies such an action, and never to be removed from the possession of a member of this family, and to be destroyed at such time as the last Drummond shall die.

ANDREW JACKSON DRUMMOND
12th July, 1867

Rain, which had begun falling earlier, lashed against the windows. Rising, Jane went to the desk where she had placed her portable typewriter. As she inserted paper and carbons, she felt a vague futility about her task of copying the journal. What purpose would be served? The General obviously would not permit it to be published. As she copied, however, and the firm handwriting began to summon vivid images, a strange excitement seized her. She was so absorbed that she did not hear approaching footsteps and she started when General Drummond spoke.

"You're up early, Jane."

She saw, with concern, that his face was drawn with fatigue. "I couldn't sleep. I'll get you some coffee, General."

"Harry's bringing some. I didn't sleep well either. When I finally fell off something wakened me and I couldn't get back to sleep again." Turning to the window, he pulled back the heavy curtains and stared out at the splash of rain on the balcony, the dreary grayness of early morning. "A terrible day."

"Yes." She spoke with conscious cheerfulness. "I'm copying the journal. It's fascinating."

"Yes," he said absently.

"General, who was Jeremiah Baker?"

He looked at her quickly. "I've always wondered myself. Judd says he was an old evangelist who settled near the corners back around 1845 or so and became a friend of General Sam's. Though how Judd knows I've never found out." He frowned. "It doesn't really matter. That personal reference of Grandfather's really doesn't—"

"Of course it doesn't matter. It was idle curiosity on my part. I—"

"Put the coffee down there," General Drummond said to Harry as he stepped into the room. "That's all, thanks."

Harry set the pot of fresh coffee on the tray and left quickly.

"It's not idle curiosity, Jane." General Drummond poured coffee unsteadily into her cup and his. "It's a strange reference to come across in a journal that is really quite impersonal." He sipped his coffee and grimaced. "I want a cigarette."

She held out her pack.

"Thanks, I have some here." He lighted one, inhaling deeply, and then sat down, staring at the cigarette in his fingers. "It must be the God-awful weather. I feel discouraged this morning."

"Discouraged?"

"Yes. With that." He nodded to her typewriter. "The whole project. I don't think I can pull it off." He sipped coffee and stared at her moodily. "Have you guessed why I wanted to try it?"

She shook her head, wondering what he meant.

"Then I'll be blunt and tell you. It was the only way I could think of that could get me close to Drew. He's never had any great interest in the family's history. The—tradition just hasn't meant a thing to him. But he is interested in history. And he has a—a kind of stubborn honesty in trying to get to the—the truth of things. I hoped that— Do you like him, Jane?"

"Drew?" Surprised. "Oh, yes, General Drummond." He looked at her closely until she felt ill at ease. "I like him very much."

"I'm glad." He smiled faintly. "And do you see, can you possibly see, how important it is that he recognize his responsibility in the world? I mean the way my grandfather recognized it and turned his back on all the comforts and acted *responsibly*. The same, I think, was true of my great-grandfather, old General Sam. He left Burning Brook as an aging man and went off and died in the high country toward Mexico City because he wanted to act *responsibly*. I can't document his reason for volunteering, but I'm sure of it." He hesitated. "In a way I think the same might be said of me. I—I've tried to—to act responsibly."

He had, she thought. He truly had. She wished she could comfort him, for he seemed troubled, and it was unjust that he should be troubled about anything.

"The troubles of our times are just beginning," General Drummond said. "I wish I were young enough to have a responsible role in them. But I'm old."

"You're not *old*," she said quickly.

He said with heavy irony, "I'm sixty-three, Jane. And while sixty-three isn't old for many, it's very old for me."

It was difficult to think of him as sixty-three. Rather, she thought, he was simply more mature than all the green young men.

"I'll tell you something about growing old, Jane. You lose control of the most ordinary situations. Your life is built on control. You direct yourself and it is done. Gaining strength from that, you direct others and it is done. And then, sometimes it seems it happens in a single day, you've lost control. Not of yourself. But suddenly others seem to think the force has gone out of you. They do not listen, as Drew will not listen to me now. Probably you are wiser than you ever were. Possibly you have not even been divested of your official office. You never know whether it was some single thing that set it off. But people stop listening to you and you realize that you're old and really quite alone."

Instinctively she reached out and touched his hand. Realizing too

207

late that she should have checked the impulse, she felt the color rising in her face. Then his hand turned spasmodically and gripped hers so tightly that she wanted to cry out. She saw his eyes widen and heard the quick startled intake of his breath. Letting go her hand, almost flinging it from him, he swung to his feet and walked to the window.

Chapter XVIII

Out there the massive castle walls curved in two strong arms and came together at the eastern bastion which looked, through the rain, like hands clasped in prayer. Beyond, the world was lost in mist.

Goddamn my heart, thought General Drummond, it hammers so. Out of control. He had not believed it could happen. Then he thought, It has not happened, nothing has happened, I'm still in control.

He turned from the window. He should not have looked at her just then, he realized. She gazed up at him, her face still flushed, her eyes wide in the dismay of discovery. But there was nothing for her to discover, he told himself. Nothing had happened, nothing would happen. It had been an old man's moment when control had momentarily lapsed.

Turning back to the window and staring at the oppressive walls in the bleak morning, he thought, I'm in control now.

"A bad morning." He must talk, though he did not want to speak. He must never mention that moment of lapse. A bad morning. When and where had it looked so?

"It reminds me of Normandy." He clasped his hands behind him and stiffened his back. "I was speaking of being in control. Grandfather's journal made me think of it, I guess. You mustn't think I'm feeling sorry for myself, Jane. I'm not. I was thinking of Grandfather, who really wrote quite a study in control there. Didn't he?"

He faced her, wondering just how he could steel himself to be unaware of her.

She lowered her gaze. "Yes," she said indistinctly. "He did. Your grandfather, I mean. I hadn't thought of it, but he did."

He paced across the room and back, his hands clasped behind him.

"I was speaking of Normandy yesterday when we were interrupted. You might take some of this down, Jane. You begin to see my purpose, I presume. I want Drew to read it. I want him to understand about command, bigger command than he has yet had, though the sort of command which—I believe—he will have some day. I'm speaking of when the responsibility is all yours but you have, of necessity, lost touch with your—call them the agents of your responsibility. There is a sense of great confusion. You can direct and order, but you cannot be everywhere at once. Your responsibility never is greater, yet at the same time you feel you've lost touch. Drew must understand this. It's a human situation, most dramatically expressed in war, which should be discussed with young men more frequently. You see my purpose? You understand this is directed to Drew? You understand that everything I'm attempting in these few days is for his sake?"

She nodded. Her dark hair shone dully in the light of the desk lamp as she lowered her head over her dictation pad. He turned and gazed out the window and said:

"The Battle of the Hedgerows in Normandy during the month of July, 1944, is often misunderstood by civilians. They are horrified by the heavy losses suffered by the twelve American divisions eventually involved in it. They think the purpose was to capture a town. They think that men were sent carelessly against impenetrable German defenses. They think there should have been some way to go *around*. They do not understand.

"The battle of July had limited objectives. Its purpose was to attain favorable jump-off points for a bigger effort: Breakout from our Normandy pocket. We had to have more room for our build-up of strength. We had to overcome great handicaps in moving troops and concentrating supplies. Our attack in July was designed to solve these difficulties by giving us space. But we faced heartbreaking terrain problems in our attack to the south. We had to advance in relatively narrow corridors between sluggish rivers and across marshy plains devoid of cover. The Germans, on the other hand, had lots of room for defensive maneuver and excellent communications for a flexible defense. However, their greatest advantage was the hedgerows. Those damnable, thick, matted hedges grow out of massive embankments sometimes ten feet high. They're usually flanked by drainage ditches or sunken roads. There never was terrain more ideally suited to a clever defense of concealed strongpoints and dug-in emplacements. I remember one aerial photograph typical of the Normandy terrain showed thirty-nine hundred enclosures in an area of less than eight square miles. You can imagine what it's like to fight in such country.

"Well, as I have told you, I had what I'd been begging for. I had a division. It was mine. I had not trained it. I did not know most of its officers well. In its brief previous combat trial in Normandy it had proved to be pretty—fouled up. As I said, I had made what command changes I could within a few days. An infantry division is interesting. You think of it as a huge juggernaut. It isn't. It advances only as far and as fast as its front line advances. And what is the front line? On your overlay map you arrow it in—X Regiment going here and Y Regiment going there, and Z Regiment, say, in reserve. Take, theoretically, X Regiment. The divisional commander tells the regimental commander, Advance two miles to this ridge, make a ninety-degree turn on the ridge and establish contact with Y Regiment which will be coming down there. So X Regiment takes off, moving as its commander elects, maybe two battalions abreast and one in reserve. Maybe he gets to the ridge and maybe he doesn't. Maybe unlooked-for trouble develops on his left and he has to peel off one battalion to try to take care of it, to say nothing of what's in front of him. Just possibly some remnants of some companies of his two battalions reach the ridge. Take a ninety-degree turn, he's been told. So he does, exposing his flank against all the basic precepts of warfare. He has to scrounge up something to cover his flank and he thinks about Z Regiment sitting back there in reserve and he signals Division, how about some help? The divisional commander, sitting back there chewing his nails and smoking cigarettes, may have the utmost faith in his regimental commander, he may *know* the guy is right and needs help. But Z Regiment has been committed to Corps reserve. He signals Corps and says in effect, Listen, I want *my* regiment. And the Corps commander, if he's a good one, will be sarcastic and say something to the effect of, What's the matter, General, are you in trouble *again?* even though you've never been in trouble in your life. You may have spent years playing golf and bridge with the Corps commander, you may have loved him like a brother, but right then you hate his guts.

"Then you try to understand. If you fail to understand then, all the years of discipline, all the getting to know as many people as possible as well as the getting to know as much as possible of the long peacetime drag—all this is lost if you do not understand. You have to understand that the Corps commander is thinking of trouble you know nothing about that's developed with the division on your left. He *needs* Z Regiment, not to get himself a promotion some day, but because he has two or three or four divisions to think of instead of you with your measly three—pardon me, two, in this case—regiments. So you learn quickly not to yell quickly for help—if you didn't already know it. If you want a corps yourself someday, you think of Corps and beyond that of Army, even when things are pretty sticky in your own paltry division.

"But all of this is no help to X Regiment up there on the ridge with its flank dangling, is it? If the situation sounds very bad and you haven't much faith in your regimental commander, you send the assistant division commander up to have a look around—or you go yourself if you have the time and everything else is well buttoned up. But the chances are that you won't have the time, because this is only one of ten thousand things that are happening simultaneously. Your problem is to decide constantly what is most important. In my division, when I first took over, I did a lot of going up and looking around personally. For one thing I didn't have a very good assistant. When I took over I had the choice of a good assistant commander or a good artillery officer. I took a good artilleryman and never regretted my choice. I figured I was smart and shifty enough to think of things without needing an assistant to think for me. My assistant, before I got rid of him, never was keen about going out and looking around. That's what was wrong with the Division. Too few officers going out and looking around. It's foolish, when you're a general officer and figure how much money the American taxpayers have invested in you, to act with bravado and try to get your ass shot off — Please excuse that crudity and delete it. But I did some of it because I found it gave the men a lot of confidence in their various situations and made them feel I was a worthy commander.

"Well, we still have X Regiment's flank dangling up there on the ridge, don't we? As a matter of fact, it's the actual situation that developed the second day we were engaged in the Battle of the Hedgerows. Only I didn't call Corps for help to release my precious third regiment. I knew what would happen. I'd been in Sicily. I'd read and studied and listened and learned. And it wasn't any two miles to the ridge. It was, as I recall, about a thousand yards from the regimental jump-off that morning. X Regiment was on the left and Y on the right and Z in Corps reserve. Y was a couple of hundred yards short of its target and plugging hard. I never worried about Y. Its commander could be a three- or four-star general some day if he has learned to control his temper. But X worried me. I mean its commander did. He graduated second in his class at the Academy and could have had a brilliant career in the Engineers, thinking up new ways to dredge the Mississippi and things like that, but it was his misfortune to command an infantry regiment in Normandy just because somebody somewhere must have thought it advisable for him to have combat in his record.

"I couldn't quite believe X was on the ridge in the first place. We were deeply echeloned, for we'd had easy going the day before and the division on our left had not kept up with us. Our left flank was protected by a river to a point where the river bent and crossed our front. That is, our cooks and bakers were covered on *their* flank, but our *line* was moving out unprotected. Oh, theoretically, the division on our left was exerting enough pressure to cover us, but I didn't like much the salient we were developing. It was a day like this, rain and no visibility to speak of. There hadn't been any air missions. Artillery was doing its best, of course, but they were temporarily rationed. Stocks were especially low for 105-millimeter howitzers, I remember. We were limited to one unit of fire for attack and one-half unit for each subsequent day of attack and one-third for a 'normal' day, whatever in hell 'normal' meant. Do you understand that unit business? It doesn't matter; Drew does.

"Anyway, in the morning German armor was heard rumbling around on our left flank and by the time word got back it was supposed to be a lot of German armor and my assistant commander and my G-2 had it all doped out how this was the big German counterattack. They were coming right into *us*. You know, that ill-fated division complex. I'd sent out two platoons of my tank company, which was all I had at the time, to investigate. They zipped up on the left of X Regiment and got lost and fouled themselves up one hundred and eighty degrees and came charging back at one of our companies which understandably mistook it for German armor and opened fire and knocked out one of our own tanks before everybody got straightened out and the armor turned around and headed in the right direction again. Well, *they* hadn't found any German armored attack developing. In fact, they proved what everybody should have been able to see: This just wasn't a country where armor could maneuver.

"By early afternoon I'd received so many conflicting reports about what was happening with X that I decided to go up and see for myself. If you'll hold out your left hand and spread your fingers you'll see how it was with X. Your little finger is third battalion exerting pressure on the left. Your middle finger is second battalion, or at least two companies of it up on the ridge. Your thumb is first battalion exerting pressure ahead and to the right. They were spread over a couple of square miles of gently rising hedgerow terrain. Clench your right fist and place it near your left thumb and that is Y Regiment driving hard against strong German defenses. Forget about Y. It was doing what it was supposed to on just about the time schedule anticipated. It was X that worried me. It had gone too fast. The problem was to decide whether the German intended to suck it in so fast and then to pinch it off or whether we really had a soft spot here which should be quickly exploited. In short, it was a problem of offensive and defensive thinking. Thinking offensively, the idea seemed to be to pour everything possible onto the ridge and then to the right along it to flank the defenses which Y was grinding against. But if you did that, you left a big fat hole for the German.

"So I jeeped up to the bridge which we'd taken yesterday. Harry always drove me and I had an aide, a good kid though rather a nuisance. But the T/O said you had an aide, and so you had one. We went up there to the bridge which had been under German artillery fire all night and all day, but was still standing. The Germans laid it on at three-minute intervals, which was rather unimaginative of them, because you just waited until they'd laid it on and then trotted across the bridge. That was the way we kept men and supplies moving.

"Harry and Lieutenant Dickey and I got across and followed the tape line forward across the fields. There was no road to the regimental command post, but a few heavy supply trucks had ground through the mud and we followed the tracks, Dickey running ahead like an eager young beagle. Suddenly we were on the Regimental C.P. I didn't like it. It wasn't where I'd thought it was. On your left hand it was down near the base of the thumb when I'd thought it was somewhere up on the middle finger. The C.P. was a deep, timbered hole dug under a hedgerow which they'd flushed the Germans out of, and at the bottom of this hole sat the regimental commander. He was rather startled to see me. He'd run telephone lines to his three battalion command posts and there he was, a big executive, forever talking on the phone.

"Well, I listened to the Colonel and then I talked personally to third battalion on the left and found its companies were not trying to move ahead, but were just holding, as they were supposed to. I talked to first battalion on the right and finally squeezed out the information that two of its companies were downright idle. Then I talked to second battalion up forward. Its commander was a National Guard lieutenant colonel named Cabot, I remember. He was direct and explicit and understandably explosive and profane and I liked him. He'd gotten two rifle companies up on the ridge, one turned to the right and trying to push ahead and the other fanned and trying to cover the flank and rear. He'd just come down from the ridge himself and he was trying to get his heavy weapons company up, but they were having trouble on the left and he didn't see why the so-and-so third battalion couldn't detach a company to help him. Neither did I. So I told the Colonel to detach one company from the third and move it over to help second and I told him to move one company up from the first. He did not like the idea. He was thinking defensively. He wanted to hang to what he'd taken and not budge until the war was over, I guess. I decided to go up to the second battalion C.P. myself and have a look, and when he tried to dissuade me I knew he was scared. He went with me, of course, but he was scared and I knew that sooner or later I'd have to nail his hide to the barn door.

"I remember thinking about it as we snook and ran up to second battalion through a little mortar fire. I make no bones about the fact I was impressed because he was second in his class at the Academy. But that didn't make him fit for combat. On the other hand, just because he wasn't fit for combat was no reason to disgrace and ruin an otherwise brilliant career. I've heard Drew make sarcastic remarks about the Benevolent and Protective Association. It's not the Academy ring that counts. It's what a man's done overall. You know what he's put into it because you've put it in yourself. If he hasn't put in much, the Association won't help him much. It's like a savings account. You pull out only a little bit more than you've put in. And the Colonel had put in a lot. He just wasn't right for his job. I knew I'd have to remove him delicately so that nobody but he would ever really know why he got a new job. And when we got to second battalion and I met Cabot, who was big and tough and practically uneducated militarily, but who had horse sense combat guts—when I met Cabot, who would go back to selling cars or something after the war, I knew he was the man to command this regiment. He did before we were out of the hedgerows and its former commander became a superb intelligence officer.

"Well, I couldn't fool around up there long. I knew Cabot would do his best on the ridge now that he had additional strength, and I

214

told him to keep plugging along it, don't worry too much about his flank and rear. I got artillery and told them to forget everything else and lay it on the farther side of the ridge. Then I shot back to Division C.P. as fast as I could. The assistant was upset because Corps had been on the phone twice asking for me. I called Corps and told him, Look, I've got something here, I'm tired of fighting this war with platoons, I want *my* regiment back to exploit what I've got. He laughed and said it certainly did look as if I'd got something with that hole, didn't I think they could read maps back there? Then he said Army himself had dropped down to Corps and was quite impressed by the fact I'd been able to make this division *go*. Army himself was there and wanted to talk to me. The Man came on and complimented the division in his gentle voice and then he said he wanted us to hold the high ground and not push on, but clear the roads because he was sending in armor first thing tomorrow morning.

"You do not know such a moment. The Man was a genius, but in this instance he happened to be wrong. Armor couldn't operate effectively in that terrain. I'd been there and seen it while The Man had been studying maps and aerial photographs and possibly talking to Georgie Patton, who'd just come over from England rarin' to go. But we hadn't gone far enough yet to give George's pet armor the country it needed. Tanks we needed in co-operation with infantry to clear the hedgerows, but not tanks clattering all over the landscape. I voiced my dissent and my reasons briefly, which was the way The Man always wanted it. He's a sweetly reasonable man until crossed by a fool, and he listened attentively and said he could see my point, but he wanted to *try*. He wanted to try anything that would save casualties, which were mounting badly. He wasn't thinking merely in terms of our strength and certainly not in terms of public criticism; he just always hated seeing men die. And then, as a kind of afterthought, he said I could have my regiment back.

"So nothing was to work as I had visualized it. I countermanded my orders to Cabot and could imagine him cussing me up there on the ridge. And I countermanded my orders to the regiment commander and could imagine his self-satisfied smile and his wondering if I had any sense at all. X to re-group and hold. Y to continue exerting the utmost pressure. Z coming in from reserve to reinforce X. It looked beautiful on paper. But all battles look beautiful on paper until they're fought. We had one road and one bridge and along it and across it must go all our supplies to the front, all our reinforcements, and in the opposite direction came all our wounded. Now to its constant traffic was to be added half an armored division. If anybody ever asked me what I did in France I'd be tempted to say I directed traffic. That's one thing a division commander is. A grand traffic cop. Others are supposed to take care of it, but nearly always it gets balled up and the division commander has to decide how it will be done. That and being a kind of a grand certified public accountant is more than half his job. See, you know approximately how many men you have up front and how many tons of supplies they require daily and you compute that against the capacity of your transports. Then you know approximately how many trucks are going to have to make how many runs in a specific time over a specific road or road-net. You can time almost to the hour when your men would stop fighting if the transports stopped running. You do it by a slide rule, and it is the only positive thing about war—when the transport conditions are ideal. All the rest of war is imponderable. And so is transport when the roads are clogged.

"Well, my point in these reflections is that there is no supreme commander, no total control. You move most of the time barely in control. You hand orders down, but half the time they aren't your orders. They're handed down to you. It was true in a division and I later found it true when I had a corps. And I saw enough at Army to know The Man was barely in control too. He had SHAEF. And SHAEF had God knows how many pressure groups working on it. You might trace it to the President, but he had the people on his back. And on the conscience of the people I suppose there was the private on the farthest point of the farthest squad. So it was and always will be in war. A huge ring. Around and around. You fit in as best you can where you best belong and there's no point in being too crafty about it. You ride with the system and shelve most of your precious plans.

"I was learning there in the Hedgerows with my one road and one bridge in my sector. I wanted to get in my reserve regiment. But The Man had told me to get in his half division of armor. So I got in his armor. I also sneaked in one battalion of my regiment, but it was all I dared. I figured the thing on a slide rule, basing my premises on my knowledge of the local conditions. Luckily it worked, for I needed that battalion. I knew I would. But I didn't need the armor, I didn't want it in my sector. I have, heaven knows, the utmost respect for armor and I later worked with it most satisfactorily, but I wasn't happy watching it churning down the road in the darkness of the next morning.

"It was what was called a combat team of an armored division, divided into three task forces, each task force composed of a battalion of tanks, a battalion of armored infantry, and a platoon of engineers. I got an hour's sleep in my tent and at 0400 I was down at the bridge as the stuff came lumbering in on schedule. Its commander, a brigadier, was with me. The Germans had luckily stopped shelling the bridge and we sweat the armor across at the rate of forty-five vehicles an hour. In four hours they were across. Meanwhile, the brigadier and I sat down and looked at each other. I had been supplied with a copy of his division's field order and he had been supplied with a copy of my division's field order. My order was that the infantry was to stand aside and let armor through. We were pretty well coordinated when *his* commander appeared and changed everything. *He* had received intelligence from Corps that the Germans were closing heavy reinforcements on the hole that I wanted to develop along the ridge. I checked with Corps and Corps said yes, that appeared to be the case.

"My sense of dismay and almost outrage is understandable to me now. I had been feeling like a man who had somehow *created* something. I'd been thinking of it in static terms, as if it would be there indefinitely. But battle is never static. There had been an opportunity and I had not had the forces to exploit it. Had I had my reserve regiment yesterday I would have run the risk and echeloned my forces deeply and made a penetration which Corps would have supported all-out. It would have been quite a coup and thinking would have been revised up the line. Just possibly, though other students of the battle might disagree, it could have been a major break-through. The Man saw it and Corps saw it and I saw it and we all did our best. But there was only one road and one bridge and now it was too late. At least the armored division commander thought it was too late and Corps was going along with him. The commander, whom I'd known a long time ago as Buttons, said he was Goddamned if he was going to let his armor go up on that ridge and turn its flank and back to the enemy and so get clobbered. I pleaded that if he'd go along with my plan I'd hold his flank. He scornfully and rightfully demanded, With *what?* And there he had me. There was the reason Corps had scrapped my plan for his plan.

"Buttons' plan made me hold my head. He was sending his tanks southwest, diagonally across the attack zones of my regiments to hit what he and Corps now considered the likeliest soft point. At first I was inclined to be sore because they hadn't let me in on their thinking. But there was no reason why they should have since it did not involve any major change in the effort of my division. So I didn't get sore. I set out to learn another in those hard lessons of never thinking you're Napoleon. Just go along and keep the transport moving as best you can.

"I shall not bore you with the details of the next two days. Eventually we had magnificent co-operation between infantry and armor. But that was after everybody had learned for all time that armor cannot attack diagonal to infantry in hedgerow country. Confusion is a mild word to describe the result. At times in those days I felt I was presiding over a debacle. Not presiding, but caught up in it. I became so disgusted that I thought once of requesting to be relieved of command. A long time afterwards Buttons told me he felt the same way. The patience necessary in these situations is incredible. As I observe it now, a commander in battle comes to have a kind of creative sense and so a creative temperament. He rails out against the forces that he thinks are seeking to frustrate his creative acts. Try as he will, he cannot achieve a completely Olympian view of things.

"During those two days my infantry was almost completely immobilized. And Buttons' combat command got hopelessly crossed up in the hedgerows. The trouble was basically one of higher thinking. My infantry positions were thought of as goose-eggs on a map—as lines, if you will. But the infantry is spread out away behind its front line position. It has supply lines, wire lines, mortar positions, vehicles, supply dumps. Telephone lines don't stay in operation with tanks constantly running over them. Neither does much else. For two days it didn't even occur to many people to be sore at the Germans. The infantry was sore at the armor and the armor was sore at the infantry. Everybody practically stopped fighting and started a great exchange of accusations. On one thing I was determined: I didn't want Corps to have to settle our disputes. By conceding and temporizing and requesting we finally worked it out. On the third day we began to put things in perspective and get on with the war.

"But I felt less than perfect about what had happened. There again I think we have the creative instinct of the commander in war. I know little about artists, but I've read something about them and I've observed that they are perfectionists. The same characteristic is true of the best field commanders, I think. I'm not talking about spit and polish. I mean perfection of group effort. You aren't that way because you're bucking for something personally. You're that way

218

because you can't help but be so, just as the artist cannot help but be what he is.

"I felt, as I said, far less than perfect. I felt that I hadn't really retained control during those two days. It had slipped from me despite my greatest efforts. So I was surprised, several days later, when we were going again and The Man came through and said to me, 'You handled the armor situation very well, Jack. Too bad it didn't work, but we had to *try*.' And then he went on to talk of something else. That episode of confusion was totally forgotten in the progressive confusions that constitute war—and possibly constitute life itself. So, in retrospect, I see that I really did retain control simply because I never stopped trying to."

Chapter XIX

Somebody was tickling Drew's lips with a dandelion. He could see it, a great yellow orb. Opening his eyes quickly, he clapped a hand to his cheek. The nerves were jumping all right.

His body grew rigid as his fingers probed the fluttering flesh. Leaping from the bed, he sprang to the dresser mirror. He saw himself, clad only in shorts, rushing to meet his reflection. He saw his face, pressed close to the mirror. From his right temple to the corner of his lips the nerves jumped rhythmically. Dimly he became aware that it was morning, that it was raining, that someone was walking along the hall. Rooted before the mirror, he stared at his quivering face with horrified fascination.

"Goddamn it to hell!" he cried.

Footsteps coming back now. A tap at the door. "Drew," Marcia said.

He was still.

"Drew! Are you all right?"

He suddenly remembered Mr. Hyde locked in his laboratory trying to make himself Dr. Jekyll again.

"Drew!"

Gripping the edge of the dresser tightly, he said, "Come on in and meet Mr. Hyde!"

She opened the door and saw him in shorts. "I'm sorry. I thought—"

"Come in," he snapped. "You've seen a man before. Meet a *jumping* man."

She stood in the doorway, staring at him. "Drew, what is it?"

"Sorry about the melodramatics," he muttered. "I'm scared, that's all. So scared I can't even remember the name of this psychoneurotic what's-it I've got." He pointed to his face. "See it jump."

She came to him slowly, her expression troubled. Reaching out, she gently laid her left hand on his cheek. "You poor doll," she said.

She was such a magnificent girl. The most beautiful piece he'd ever seen. He wanted her. He was not so scared that he failed to want her badly even now. There was a burning behind his eyeballs, indicating tears, indicating that there must be some self-pity involved with these pulsing nerves.

He turned from her, hunting his trousers. Thus, he realized, she saw the deep and interesting scar on his back.

"It's a self-pity morning," he said, looking around for his trousers. "You'd better go now."

"I'm sorry," she said. "I didn't mean—I was just going downstairs and I heard you. Not what you said, but the tone of your voice and I thought—oh, Drew!" She rested a hand on his arm. "What did they do to you?"

Don't let her pity me, he thought. Pity was for a mother, and he did not want a mother. He faced her. He was not embarrassed to stand there in his shorts. And she, he saw, was not embarrassed either.

"*They* haven't done anything to me," he said.

Her gaze, lowered from his twitching face, passed casually over his body. If she looked closely she would see the white Normandy scar on the muscles of his chest, she would see the pebbles of the Pacific wound along his right side above his shorts. But the physical wounds had nothing to do with the twitching of his face, not as far as anyone had been able to determine.

He saw his trousers on a chair then and he pulled them on. "This twitching began one day in a little town in Germany after the war was over. It went away and didn't come back until after I was shipped home from Korea. It went away again and I'd forgotten about it, I'd forgotten it ever happened until just now when I woke up with my face twitching."

"Lie down," she said. "I'll bring you some breakfast and—"

"My face!" He laid his palm along it carefully. "The twitching's stopped! Look!"

She smiled at him. "It has stopped."

"You needn't have known about it at all."

"I'm glad I know," she said. "I'm glad I came in."

"Marcia?"

"What?"

"What are we waiting for?"

She looked away. "You must know. We're waiting until we can *live* together."

He took a step toward her, but she stepped back.

"I wanted to be sure, and now I am sure. I didn't want it to be just rebound, like I've had so much rebound. But you have to be sure too."

"I'm *sure*." He touched his face. "Let's get out of this gloomy joint and go off somewhere together."

She shook her head. "You aren't sure at all. You're sure of how you feel right now and maybe next week. But how about a year from now? A year from now you might be thinking of the one who got away."

He frowned at her, puzzled.

"I mean the girl your father brought here," Marcia said evenly. "The nice girl. The—virginal girl. Because that's what she is and you know it. And that's what I'm not and you know it." Turning suddenly, she left the room and closed the door behind her.

Strolling to the mirror, he studied his face again. Good girl and bad girl, he thought. What a yak. Here in the middle of the twentieth century Marcia had decided to adopt a romantic Victorian illusion. In a sense he had suffered from the illusion ten years ago. But he'd discarded it after finding it was only illusion. A girl was a girl and a brawl was a brawl and a war was a war, but what had made his face begin to twitch again? Theory: Physical strain, Major Drummond, induced when you hung to Jane in the tower. The hell you say, Bud. Hysteria. But who's hysterical now or was hysterical away back then?

It was ten minutes to eleven when he came downstairs. Marcia had coffee heating over a candle in the living room. She looked up at him quickly and then poured him a cup. His father sat beside a lamp near the fire, reading a letter; on the floor beside him was a small stack of letters.

"Good morning," General Drummond said and looked at his wrist watch.

"Morning," Drew muttered and took the cup of coffee from Marcia.

"What do you want to eat?" she asked.

"Nothing," he said, staring at his father across the rim of his cup. The old man looked terrible this morning, drawn and gray, as if he had not slept at all.

"I'm organizing the correspondence I brought along," General Drummond said. "There are some interesting letters from Uncle Chad . . ."

Dear God not now, he thought. No wonder I've got a twitching face. Strolling to a window, he looked out at the heavy rain. The old man talked on. He was *reading* from a letter. From the library came the clatter of Jane's typewriter. Clatter on one hand, yak on the other, the General's machine lumbered on. He moved slowly toward the library door, sipping his coffee as he went. Right out of his father's life and into the life of the Virgin Jane.

Her hair, he thought, was interesting; it had blue lights, like the heroine's hair in some novel or other. There was a mirror here too; there were a hell of a lot of mirrors in this castle. He saw his reflection and made a face at himself. He began to duck and weave his head, daring the twitch to come back.

The sound of the typewriter stopped and Jane stared up at him incredulously. "What on earth are you doing?"

"Making like a punch-drunk prize fighter," he said. "One who's seen too much of civilization."

She laughed, a real peal of laughter. He could not have been that funny. This girl came complete with coiled spring that had to be released once in a while. Young lady, may I release your coiled spring?

"You're crazy," she said.

"Real crazy," he said. He felt pretty good now. No twitch. Maybe tomorrow, maybe in five minutes, but right now there was no twitch and he felt pretty good.

"I've just finished typing up some dictation I took from your father this morning," she said. "It's wonderful."

Is it, he wondered, really wonderful, Jane? But yes. Her eagerly raised face, the long-lashed and blue shining eyes told him so. He wanted to pat her head and tell her it was indeed wonderful that she should find his father's words wonderful.

222

"What's it about, Jane?"

"The Battle of the Normandy Hedgerows."

Oh, God!

"About the problems of command there. I took it down just as he talked about it and I think it's better than if he'd made a kind of formal essay of it. It's—instructive."

Instructive of what and for what? A handbook of how to conduct yourself as you march through the Urals in 1972? Correction. The wars, the General had said, were to be little ones. This, then, might be helpful when you went ashore in Madagascar in 1964.

She rose and swung to the door. These girls with springs moved beautifully. Each poet and painter should be supplied with one to teach him grace in these times that troubled the Olympians.

"General Drummond," she said in the living room, "I've finished typing the Normandy section. Drew would like to read it."

My dear young lady, he thought, you misquote me entirely. Not only misquote; you misconstrue. Now she had thrust the typescript upon him. He could sit here and read it. But he would not, thanks, because she was leaving the library and he did not want to sit here alone and think of his twitching face. He followed her slowly, holding the typescript and sip-sip-sipping his bitter coffee.

The General looked at him eagerly and Marcia watched him carefully and Jane merely watched. So he could not read it here either, not while they watched him. As a matter of fact he didn't plan to read it at all. Putting down his coffee cup, he wondered where Harry was.

"I'm going off to read it by myself," he said to his father, "and I'll tell you what I think."

"Good," said General Drummond. "We'll discuss it."

You'll discuss it, Father, and I shall nod and nod. He went down the stone stairs. Down to the engine room, he thought, the place that drives this castle through time. There was a fragrance of onions cooking down here. He stepped into the kitchen where Ugo hovered over a large pot on the stove.

"Good morning, Ugo."

Ugo looked up and bowed coldly. "Signor."

"Where's Harry?"

Ugo gestured contemptuously to a doorway off the kitchen.

"Thank you, Ugo."

He passed into a small cold room which was used for storage. Harry, wearing an old woolen sweater such as the Red Cross used to hand out, sat on a small box under a light bulb. Knives and sandpaper and bits of wood were spread on a large crate before him. He glanced up at Drew in surprise and got to his feet.

"Good morning, sir."

"Hi, Harry. I heard about your model ships and came down to see one."

Harry grinned, vastly pleased. "I'm just starting a new one. I finished one yesterday. They're little bitty ones, these ones I've been doing on the trip over here. Balsa wood. It's light to carry and—see, I'm going to wax the sails."

From a shoe box he took a three-masted schooner about five inches long. It was fully rigged, its sails set. Harry closed one eye and heeled the model over in his fingers. Drew saw it through Harry's eyes: a running sea, a star to sail her by, and Captain Bannister at the helm. Harry handed it to him.

"I didn't know you liked the sea, Harry."

"I don't. I mean I didn't think I did, Drew. Every time I get on a ship I get sick. But I'll tell you what's a fact, sometimes I wish the General would move near salt water. Up in Nashville one day I bought one of these kits that you put the boat model together yourself and it was so much fun I . . ."

It was fun. He stretched on a bench and told Harry to go on working while he watched. When a kitten crept around the crate, he dragged a bit of string in front of her. When she came close, he lifted her and stroked the silken hair of the bony skull. He watched Harry's concentrated expression, the dextrous movement of sharp knife and soft balsa in his blunt fingers. After a while he picked up the typescript.

He scanned the pages rapidly. Unquestionably his father described the emotional and intellectual tensions of divisional command accurately. Something was missing, however. Somehow he could not identify himself with it, although Father obviously wanted him to find a close identification. The missing element was the agony. *But I don't want to think about it.*

Yet that had to be a part of it. Any time you went up forward, and the General had gone up forward frequently, you saw—*but I don't want to think about it.* The General must have seen and he positively knew what it was. He simply exempted himself from the suffering. That, obviously, was essential to command. *I know that perfectly well.* But human agony was quantitative. It was, quantitatively, much harder to issue an order that would result in a thousand casualties than an order that would result in twenty.

The General had failed to describe it the way it really was. He told it by the slide rule, and it was too much for a slide rule to equate. *I don't want to think about it, but* . . . And he was thinking about it.

Rain began to fall about seven o'clock in the evening. By nine o'clock it was a steady downpour and men slept in the dugouts along the sunken road. Presumably the posted guards were on duty and presumably they would awaken the men who were to relieve them, though their function seemed useless; the land was a sodden morass under the driving rain and the night was so dark that you moved by feel and sound rather than by seeing.

Company A, to which Drew had reported about seven, was in a line along the hedgerows. The companies of the battalion and the battalions of the regiment extended the rough line, so that on the map it looked like the trench lines of the last war, which had been known as the Great War until this one came along, and you could imagine a Hollywood director in a tower ready to shoot the grand sweeping scene when the troops went "over the top." You could imagine it on the map at the Regimental Command Post, but down here on the sunken roads you could not imagine anything once the rain began and darkness fell.

The commander of Company A, which was still one officer short, assigned Drew the First and Second Platoons on the left. He called in the platoon sergeants, Papracki of the First and O'Shea of the Second, to meet him. Both were big men, older than he, and they stared at him impassively, figuring he was fresh from OCS and something new for the meat wagon. They stumbled together along the sunken lanes which composed the platoons' lines behind a dozen hedge-enclosed fields. It was not a solid straight line, of course. There were gaps, theoretically covered by fire points, and there were forward and rear positions. They had been assigned their territory and they were covering it as best they could. Papracki and O'Shea knew their business.

He tossed his gear into Papracki's dugout because there was room for him and Papracki invited him. By the dim light of a lantern suspended from a beam he saw a man, a boy actually, asleep. He lay on his back, spread-eagle, his mouth open. You could not see his breathing; you would have thought him dead if his hands had not fluttered occasionally.

They went out of the dugout into the rain and darkness again. O'Shea came too, even though the First was not his platoon. There was no shelling or small-arms or mortar fire; there was no sound except the rain and the mud sucking at their feet. Occasionally Papracki would pause and silently indicate a darkened dugout to Drew. He stepped down into most, he did not know exactly why, except that Papracki seemed to wish him to. You could not see the sleeping men, but you could hear them. Few snored, but there was much whimpering and moaning, as in a hospital ward. Occasionally one would cry out or mumble a few incoherent words or fart loudly in his sleep. When a man parted his lips suddenly, seeking air, it sounded like a bubble popping. But the worst sound was of men grinding their teeth as they slept. You could not see them, but you could hear them and you could smell them too. Wet clothing and sweat and the rank smell of dirty wet feet and urine and, here and there along the sunken road, the stench of human feces. For they had fallen in here about five o'clock and they'd gotten out their wounded and gotten in ammunition and cold rations. But they weren't digging straddle trenches or doing all the folderol the book prescribed because they had had three days of hard fighting and they were exhausted. They pitched down in the places the Germans had left and they slept, for tomorrow they had to go ahead again.

Once they came on a sentry who had fallen asleep and lay in the mud with his rifle across him. Papracki shone his flashlight in the boy's face and kicked him awake and cursed him dispassionately and said to Drew, "You want his name, Lieutenant?" Drew said no and they went on. It was the only word he spoke until they returned to Papracki's dugout where the boy still slept spread-eagle, with his mouth open and his hands clenching spasmodically.

Papracki was a very good man, Drew thought. He had given him an excellent review of the troops, a review which would have been instructive to the top-side rulers of the world. Without a descriptive word Papracki had said, in effect, "These are your men, Lieutenant. This is *man*." O'Shea asked him if he had any questions and Drew said he had a couple. Turning, he groped in his bedroll and pulled out the bottle of Johnny Walker Black Label he had brought from England.

"I was saving this," he said, "but I see that if I hang onto it too long it may be wasted."

Papracki and O'Shea stared at each other, and then Papracki produced three canteen cups. The two sergeants sank down, with their backs against the hard earth wall, and watched Drew open the bottle. Their eyes, raised to him, were white in their dirty, beard-stubbled faces. O'Shea almost, but not quite, licked his lips.

Drew poured three large slugs and nodded to the sleeping boy. "How about him?"

"Let's not be democratic, Lieutenant," Papracki said. "His name is Provost and he's a good kid, but he's gonna be a preacher, when and if he grows up. He don't approve of drinkin' and such. He don't even swear except sometimes in his sleep." Papracki sipped his whisky, holding it in his mouth a moment and then swallowing slowly. He smacked his lips and swore gratefully and asked O'Shea for a cigarette.

Then, most civilly, he asked Drew when he graduated from OCS. Drew told him he hadn't gone to OCS, he'd been a Company First in the Southwest Pacific and been commissioned directly. O'Shea swore and got to his feet elaborately and shook his hand and said maybe the Goddamn Company finally had an officer. Papracki, frowning, asked him why in hell he'd wanted a commission. When Drew told him he *had* to take it, Papracki didn't see how it was possible. But he took a cigarette from a pocket since O'Shea had failed to oblige him with one from his own hoard, and he held it out to Drew.

"Thanks, I'm loaded," Drew said. "Like a Red Cross caravan. You short?" He held out a pack of Luckies.

Papracki wrinkled his thick face against temptation and said, "Not yet, Lieutenant, but you stick around." He lighted the cigarette and drank again and sighed and said, "Now I see why you didn't ask stupid questions. So I see what you wanna know. You wanna know the best way to stay alive in this place. Right?"

"Right."

"Well," said Papracki, "there ain't any good way. It's mostly luck. See, there's three ways to get through this hedgerow stuff. You can walk down the road, which gets you killed. It's like goin' naked to the birth control ball. Or you can squirm through holes in the corners of the hedgerows an' crawl up along the row leading forward or rush through the holes in a group and spread out in the field. This also gets you killed—or only wounded, if you're lucky. Because the krauts been here before us. They know where the holes is and they got machine-gun reception committees waitin' all lined up on the holes to greet you as you come through. The only other way is to rush a skirmish line over a hedgerow an' across the field. This is a beautiful military idea like they think up at West Point. The only trouble, at West Point they never heard of hedgerows."

He ran the back of a hand across his mouth and said, "Jesus, it's gettin' hot in here." He unbuttoned his fatigue jacket, exposing a thick hairless chest on which had been tattooed a large nude female.

"Mostly," he said, "you got to hack a way through a hedgerow. While you're doin' this the krauts get pretty busy workin' you over. Any time you go over a hedgerow the krauts get busy. What you need, natcherly, is a machine gun, but what you gonna do with a machine gun on a hedgerow? By the time you get it set up you're dead. Or you can cart one along, firin' from the hip. Once in a movie, I think it was Wallace Beery, I seen him mowin' 'em down firin' a machine gun from the hip. What crap. You don't hit nothin'. So mostly you lay a machine gun on its belly on the bank, no tripod, and you don't hit much that way either."

Drew said, "Do you think we should save the rest of this Scotch?"

"There don't seem much chance of drinking it tomorrow," O'Shea said with a crafty expression.

Drew poured three more slugs.

Papracki said, "The way a polite lieutenant we had put it, the men here are *reluctant*. Everybody is *reluctant* to go over a hedgerow first. Not only that, they disappear the second you turn your back."

O'Shea said, "They gotta do things like go to the bathroom or go off to tie their shoe or something."

"I should've said *nearly* everybody is reluctant," Papracki said. He looked at the sleeping boy, Provost, whose hands kept clenching, clenching. His broad, thick face reflected a mixture of pride and tenderness. "Provost ain't *reluctant*."

"I had one like him until this afternoon," O'Shea said. "He got killed one field back. His name was Rinaldi. You know who I mean, Pap. He was an idiot or something. I think he'd been in a nut house. He couldn't read or write or anything. He'd been a permanent KP at Pickett on the Peninsula and he did something and they shipped him as a replacement. Rinaldi, he was never scared of anything, he—"

"Rinaldi!" Papracki said scornfully. "He ain't no Provost. You said yourself Rinaldi was an idiot. Provost—his first name's Richard an' I call him Richard because—well, because that's his name an' he likes to be called by it. He had a year of college somewhere an' he's gonna be a preacher an' everything. He's got a mother an' a sister an' everything an' he carries their pictures an' he comes from this little

228

town in South Carolina. I'll tell you, it's just like God has told Richard to kill Germans an' by Christ he goes out an' kills 'em. Hey, Lieutenant, you got any candy on you?"

"No," Drew said.

"That's too bad because Richard likes candy. But what I wanted to tell you, Richard keeps this platoon moving. I mean, of course, I gotta haul my fat ass out an' say, 'Let's go' an' 'come on,' an' all that crap, an' Richard he's right there with me. The guys see Richard going an' they haul ass too. It ain't *me* they're followin'. It's Richard. So that makes two an' by and by there's more and finally there's a mob and on we go. Lieutenant Endicott, he was a replacement, he got it in the belly yesterday— Lieutenant Endicott was a good enough guy though sort of dumb in some ways, he didn't understand about Richard. At OCS they told Lieutenant Endicott he had to *lead* his men, so by Christ he did just what they told him. Off he'd go, thinking everybody loved him so good that they'd come along too. Nobody hated him, you understand, they just didn't love him so good that they'd get their asses shot off because he was holdin' his up for a high sling. But guys sort of love Richard, even though they think he's a punk kid. Yesterday, when Richard wasn't around at the moment, off went Lieutenant Endicott an' everybody just watched him, an' next thing he'd gotten it smack in the belly. But Richard, I'm recommending him for the Congressional or something."

Once, during the night, Richard Provost cried out in his sleep, awakening Drew. He slept again and was brought wide awake by the earth shaking under him. His eardrums sucked before a deafening concussion and a stream of dirt fell on his face. He was on his feet as Papracki's flashlight stabbed the darkness. By its light Drew seized the field phone. The line was dead.

"It's cut!" Papracki shouted. "They sent through a patrol an' cut it. It's a box barrage, eighty-eights and one-o-fives." The barrage lifted suddenly and Papracki's voice came loudly, 'They're comin' through, Richard!"

"I'm lacing my boots, Sarge," Richard said plaintively in the darkness.

Drew flashed his light about, hunting his carbine. He did not see it, but in a corner of the dugout he saw an M-1 with bayonet fixed. Snatching it up, he sprang from the dugout into the gray mist of early morning, and Papracki came after him.

"Lootenant!" Papracki shouted as a figure leaped from the bank above him.

He whirled, sinking low, and drove the bayonet up at the man. It passed into his belly softly and then jarred as the man doubled, screaming piercingly. A grenade fell from his hand as Drew tried to pull out the bayonet. It was stuck. The man was not a dead weight on it, but writhed and twisted, plucking at it ineffectually. He raised his face, a young face, horribly contorted, the mouth wide, the eyes wide. His voice lost in agony and horror, he did not cry out. But somebody was crying out, a low-pitched *Ahhhh,* and Drew dimly realized it was his own voice as he fought to pull out the bayonet. Slowly, as if to help him, the German straightened himself, screaming now, and Drew pulled out the bayonet.

"Lieutenant," Richard said calmly, "you have my rifle. Here's your carbine."

Drew continued to stare at the German, who writhed in the mud of the sunken road, crying.

Papracki hit his arm hard, yelling, "Skip it!" Raising his whistle, Papracki blew it shrilly. As the men stumbled from their dugouts, a machine gun began to chatter, spraying its tracers along the sunken road. They flattened in the mud.

But you couldn't stay there. You had to *lead.* He heard his voice, surprisingly calm now: "Come on, Richard." He clambered up the bank and fought a way through the thick-matted hedgerow into the open field beyond. Three men trotted across the field through the mist, carrying their rifles at port. Seeing him, each dropped to a knee, like perfectly co-ordinated mechanical toys. He dropped too and aimed his carbine carefully. Bullets clipped the hedge on his left. On his right a rifle crashed above the sound of his carbine. Richard was prone there, firing methodically. Two of the Germans fell. The third, prone, continued to fire until he died.

Papracki appeared and men were clambering out of the sunken road and fighting through the hedgerow. As they ran along the row toward the machine gun a weaponless man burst from the hedge, wailing, his hands pressed to his face. Blood spurted through his fingers from a hole in his jaw. They passed him, running on until they were close to the machine gun in the lane below. The machine gun stopped and they heard men shouting to one another in German. Papracki halted and threw a grenade. As it exploded, a man screamed.

There was a loud slapping sound. Turning, Drew saw Papracki sitting on the ground, his expression surprised. He sank back slowly, his hands fluttering at his chest. His hands dropped, twitching, and then were still. Kneeling beside him, Drew tore open his fatigue jacket.

The bullet had passed through the female tattooed on his chest. He was dead.

They killed three Germans near the machine gun and two fled. He counted up fourteen members of the platoon then and disposed them in a rough perimeter. Four were dead and six wounded; the others had dashed across the fields to the rear. The Germans concentrated heavy mortar and machine-gun fire on them for ten minutes. When it slackened, he began withdrawing the men along the lane toward Second Platoon. But Second had pulled out, and they had to pause and fight again.

About eight o'clock the firing ceased and he sent Richard to find the Company C.P. It was almost ten o'clock before Richard returned, bringing orders from Battalion to withdraw four fields to the rear. The Company Commander and the Exec were wounded, Richard said.

They walked back, carrying their wounded, to the shell of a farmhouse. They sprawled there under a lowering sky in which a few shells whined. Men wandered into the farmyard and silently flung themselves down. Medics came. A truck lumbered in with ammunition and C rations. O'Shea appeared with the Company Clerk. Eighty-one men answered roll call.

The Battalion Exec bustled in cheerfully and told Drew to take the Company *here*. He pointed on the map to the positions they had just left. So they went back, arriving about three o'clock. After they re-established their fire-points Drew took off his helmet and climbed up to a gap in the hedge with hands raised. Stepping onto the field and keeping his hands raised, he walked to Papracki's body and lifted it. Across the field unarmed Germans walked out and carried back their dead. They buried Papracki and the others, marking their graves carefully. After a while the Germans fired a few mortar bursts at them. They returned the fire and the war continued.

A few replacements came in that evening. In the morning more arrived, including a new company commander who questioned Drew searchingly. After all, Drew was by then an old hand in the hedgerows.

He felt like a very old hand two days later when they came to the lip of the draw. Word was handed down from Battalion and the Company Commander handed it down to Drew. They were *here*. They were going *there*. The platoons moved out abreast behind four medium tanks, and there was nothing difficult about it until they came to the draw.

Its sides were too steep for the tanks which lined up at fifty-yard intervals and began methodically firing at the hidden strong points across the draw. The fire was not returned. The Company Commander led two platoons to the east of the draw to flank it. A third platoon was sent to the west. The thirty-two members of the First Platoon lay in a ditch behind the tanks and stared at Drew. He stared at his watch.

I don't even remember what I thought about. The sun was out, I remember, and yellow smoke curled back from the tank guns. The noise of the guns hurt my ears.

At three o'clock, the time agreed upon, he got to his feet and said, "Let's go, Richard." The men watched them as they climbed out of the ditch and then they began getting to their feet slowly. He passed so close to one of the tanks that he could hear a man cursing inside it. Through a port he glimpsed bloodshot, startled eyes staring at him. He looked around. The men were out of the ditch and spread in a skirmish line. Gesturing to them, he turned and trotted down the steep slope into the draw.

Now I remember I was thinking about the Goddamn Drummonds, all of us, and because some of them had done such a thing before, it gave me strength to do it then. I must acknowledge and remember that. But what about Richard, who had no tradition for it? And what about all the others, the saints and sinners and ex-pacifists and mugs who came running into that draw? How does every war manage to keep on mustering its charges of horseless light brigades?

At the bottom of the draw the earth erupted, geysering in dirt and a rain of pebbles and a cacophony of screams. He was down, his face bruised and his body numb. But the terror had not erupted from the earth; it came from above and one side, a hail of artillery and mortar and machine-gun fire which had been previously registered on this spot and now saturated it as the noon sun saturates earth. He staggered to his feet, his only purpose to get out of it—not *back* out of it, but *on* out of it, because it seemed easier to go on than back.

Head lowered, he stumbled on up the farther side of the draw. Pausing, he looked back and saw men rising and coming on and then falling and some rising again. Somewhere a man screamed endlessly. Several yards to his left he saw Richard rise and drop his rifle and not bother to pick it up. He clapped his hands to his groin and walked in a small circle, looking down at his hands with a puzzled expression. From between his hands slipped a gray and mucous substance which slithered snakelike down a leg. His hands tried to seize it and press it back into his abdomen, but it slithered from him in an anaconda winding down and around his leg. He turned, trying to look at it, disregarding the eruptions of earth around him as he stared, baffled, at the incredible unraveling. Suddenly he sat down and began to cry. In a momentary lull Drew heard him crying like a baby.

I did not go to him because I knew he was dying and there was nothing I could do for him. We went on up the side of the draw, those of us who could. Eleven of us got up there and joined with the two platoons flanking from the east. Of the eleven, eight of us were wounded. No wonder my face twitches sometimes.

Chapter XX

He came from the cold storage room, that port of Harry's dream-boats, and glanced in the living room. His father was not there, he saw with relief. Marcia, too, had gone off somewhere. From the library came the clatter of Jane's typewriter.

When he entered the library, she looked up at him and smiled. "Isn't your father's discussion of command in Normandy interesting?"

He sat down slowly.

"I think it's fascinating," she said.

She had begun typing the Civil War journal, he saw. If not one war, then another.

"It's an account of events as Father saw them," he said measuredly. "Probably no other commander saw it exactly the same. I suppose each saw it differently."

She looked at him searchingly. "But doesn't it—stimulate you?"

She dismayed him. Stimulate him? To what end? A few artists of the Renaissance had stimulated him with a sense of life. But death, the medium of his father's art, could not be stimulating.

"I mean," she said, "you must surely be interested in tactics. You must surely . . ."

He could tell her a thing or two if he wished. Yes, in his desire to be a good soldier he had become interested in tactics, as a good mechanic is interested in engines. He had, as a matter of fact, been first in his class at Benning on the subject of tactics. Furthermore, he had applied tactics most practically and quite effectively in Korea. Oh, he understood what his father had said all right. Undoubtedly he visualized it more clearly than she, even to the slide rule, which he had learned to use almost as ably as his father. But why the mystique? Why the fervor?

He interrupted her, his voice low. "The trouble is, Jane, that it's merely mechanics. Interesting mechanics, yes, but—"

"But don't you see what he's saying about—control?" She spoke with intensity. "He's trying to explain the great tensions, the great responsibility between trying to win a battle on the one hand and the cost in human lives on the other."

"The responsibility in trying to win a battle, yes," he said. "But he ignores the cost in human lives. That's the trouble with him. He insists on closing his eyes to the human element except in terms of efficiency."

"But every general has to close his eyes to the human element beyond a point," she said quickly.

He smiled faintly. "And there you've expressed the reason why I have no burning desire ever to be a general. That's what's wrong with soldiering. I decided, after some things went wrong for me, that I'd try to be a good soldier because there didn't seem anything else for me to be. So I tried and I think I was a pretty good one—"

"And you'll continue to be," she said. "Your father sees your great potential if—"

"My father." He regretted the scorn in his tone, but he could not help it. "My father! Why doesn't he leave me alone? If he'd let me live my own life—if he'd let me feel the Army was *my* life, *my* choosing, and not *his*—"

"Drew." She extended a hand pleadingly. "Don't be that way. Don't —ever let him know how you feel. He's a fine man. He—"

"I know he's a fine man, Jane. He's had his problems. But in all his insistent talk about *tradition* he's trying to make *his* problems *my* problems." He paused, seeing with amazement that tears had come to her eyes. What was wrong? She was not the kind of girl who cried easily.

"I'm sorry. It's just . . ." She turned her head, blinking back the tears.

"Just what?"

"I don't know exactly how to put it," she said indistinctly. "I—I'm not sure I know what I mean myself. It's just that I feel he's terribly

234

worried about something we don't know anything about. I don't know why I feel that way, but I do. And he seems so—well, so very much alone." She looked away.

Her sympathy for his father was touching. It was, he thought, an admirable quality. It's a long time since I've admired a woman, he thought, and here I am admiring two on the same day. But equally? And that was a question. Come, Hamlet, he told himself ironically. But irony, this self-kidding, did not resolve the question.

"Your father—" Jane's voice was almost a whisper—"your father needs someone to love him." She turned her back to him and faced her typewriter.

Yes, his father needed to be loved, as all the Drummonds—like all men—had needed to be loved. But, he wondered, is Father capable of loving? And there you had a question about many Drummonds. Including me, he thought.

As Jane began to type, he laid the back of a hand against his face. The flesh was still. But he remembered the first time he felt it quiver.

The war in Europe had been over for six weeks and he had come through it without cracking visibly. His First Sergeant, Arnold, knew that. Arnold had been with him for six months and knew him intimately. He knew that Captain Drummond had guts and a disciplined company who liked him and a girl at home with whom he corresponded regularly. He knew that the girl caused the Captain to refuse to play around—which was not incredible to Arnold. He knew that the Captain had gotten stinking drunk last night—which was rather incredible. But he did not know about the letter which the Captain had received yesterday.

The Captain had simply been sitting there at his desk, staring into space, when his face began to twitch. Naturally, Arnold mentioned it to him. Then the Captain wheeled to the open window behind him and vomited. When he drew his head inside, his face was twitching worse than ever.

"Okay, Arnold," he said, "put me in the jeep and take me to the vet's. I've had it."

As they sped up to the hospital in the city through the warm bright morning, Drew took the letter from a pocket. Tearing it into tiny pieces, he tossed them away. Turning, he watched the white bits of paper blown by the backwash of the jeep. Tearing up the letter did not make him forget what it had said, however. He never did forget.

DEAR DREW,

This is a hard letter to write, but I must write it. The war is over and you have come through it safely. Joe is dead, as you know, and my parents are more dependent on me than ever. I can never leave Orange and I know, no matter what you say, that Orange is not the place for you. Tomorrow I'm marrying a man here I've known for some time. Please do not write me or try to get in touch with me again. I mailed your ring to your mother.

All best wishes,
EILEEN

All best wishes. My God! What did she mean when she said Orange was not the place for him? He *liked* Orange. He hoped to attend Columbia in New York, which was close to Orange. But what had really happened? He did not know and he could not find out.

So you might say that the letter had made his face begin to twitch. But he doubted it. Miserable as he felt that day riding up to the hospital through the German countryside, he doubted it.

So did the Army psychiatrist who examined him doubt it. The psychiatrist was Major Michele Sabraccio. (What a knotted skein life was. Had he come to Florence and subconsciously wished to stay because Sabraccio was there? For Sabraccio had helped him; Sabraccio had treated him as an individual and become his friend. They had corresponded, especially when Drew was in Korea and the circumstances of combat had begun to work the emotions of the Second War again.)

During the two weeks he spent in the hospital his face stopped its infernal twitching. He slept fourteen and fifteen hours a day and talked at length with Sabraccio. He saw himself through Sabraccio's eyes and eventually began to understand himself.

I even remember some of the jargon:

The letter, announcing his loss of Eileen, was something. But it was not everything. Eileen had, however, represented his ego; she was himself, about the only self he felt he had as the self, that ego, inevitably regressed under the stress of combat. For, as a good soldier, the group military superego had necessarily become ascendant in him. But now the war was over and the importance of the military superego lessened, bringing emotions of anxiety and guilt. Eileen, the future, his normal peacetime hopes and desires should now assert themselves in him and become his new superego. Yet Eileen, the one who had come to mean peace and serenity to him, had unaccountably deserted him. So he was left, seemingly, with nothing.

Sabraccio did not attempt to explain the association between his

236

troubled emotions and his twitching face. Thus, when the twitching stopped, Drew did not feel that Sabraccio had cured him. Sabraccio, in fact, abhorred the word *cured*. Once he said, "Today you may feel better than yesterday. Tomorrow you may feel worse than today. Enjoy today and endure tomorrow and it will be interesting to see what happens on the next day." So he was dismissed with a vague notation on his medical report about being returned to full military duty after two weeks of rest following physical exhaustion. Sabraccio said he did not like the word *illness* any more than the word *cured*. "Go along, pal," he told Drew, "and maybe find yourself a pretty fräulein. When you get up this way again drop around and I'll buy you a drink."

He went along, back to the town where his company was stationed, but he didn't try to find himself a pretty fräulein. The fräuleins were hungry and he had food, but it was not his notion of a fair bargain. He drove up to see Sabraccio several times and they drank wine and talked and wandered around the city together. He was interested to observe that Sabraccio did not have a fräulein; although Sabraccio did not say so, it apparently was not his notion of a fair bargain either.

Late one afternoon in mid-July Arnold glanced out the orderly room door into the street as a jeep braked to a halt. He swore in surprise and got to his feet as Lieutenant General Drummond strode in. The General was in a jovial mood. He wrung Drew's hand and patted his shoulder. Since Normandy Drew had seen him only once, before the Ardennes break-through, when they had happened on each other in a small village and the General had invited him to dinner.

Stretching out in a chair and smiling at him, General Drummond said, "I'm your new boss."

"Congratulations," Drew said. "How about a raise?"

The General meant, it developed, that he had been named the area commander. He had spent a few days in Washington late in May. When ordered to report there he'd hoped it meant a command in the Pacific. But the war in the Pacific was about to end, he said authoritatively, and they had called him back with other officers to indoctrinate him with administrative plans for Germany. He would be, Drew gathered, a big wheel in administering the defeated enemy.

"I managed a day in New York when I was back," General Drummond said. "Saw your mother."

"Oh?" Drew looked at him in surprise.

"She sent her best to you."

"Well—I know her husband's dead. Does that mean, Father, that—"

"No." General Drummond frowned and shook his head. "It doesn't mean anything—except that I looked her up and saw her briefly." He looked around the room of the requisitioned house. "How's everything going?"

"Okay."

"I hear you picked up the Silver Star and the Bronze Star too and I know you added a cluster to your Purple Heart. You should wear your ribbons, Drew. It impresses the Germans."

"I don't care about impressing the Germans, Father. They've made an adequate impression on me. All I'm interested in now is getting *out*."

General Drummond frowned. "Don't be foolish. You've made a remarkable record and now you have a splendid future in the Army. The fact you didn't graduate from the Academy doesn't make any difference now. You were born to the Army and you're a natural at it. So forget about quitting. Uh—tell me, are you having any fun?"

"With the fräuleins? No."

The General cleared his throat. "I didn't exactly mean that. Do you have a girl at home?"

"If you saw Mother I'm surprised she didn't tell you. I *had* a girl. She ditched me."

"She ditched you?" The General gazed at him attentively.

"I don't want to talk about it, Father. I don't even want to think about it."

"Okay. I understand." General Drummond rose. "I've got to get along. By the way, I have a big old barn I'm living in up in the city. How about coming up for dinner Saturday night?"

He didn't think he'd go. But he went. The big old barn turned out to be a huge mansard-roofed house which had escaped bombing; it was the former home of a Nazi official, now in prison. The door was opened by Master Sergeant Harry Bannister.

"Harry!" Drew balled his fists and did the old duck and weave.

Harry grinned and then braced himself and said, "It's good to see you, sir. May I take your cap?"

"The door detail." Drew smiled and handed him his cap. "Do you really like it, Harry?"

"Just fine, sir."

As he followed Harry, he could see why he'd like it. The substantial spoils of the insubstantial conqueror. The deep carpets and thick walls, the tapestries and heavy dark furniture were a long way from Schofield Barracks. It could make you believe that you had arrived some place.

He passed through a long, richly appointed room toward doors which were open on a terrace. The doorway framed a girl. She had good legs and she was slender. She turned and he saw that her hair was blonde and close-cropped, fitting her small head like a golden helmet. As he stepped onto the terrace, she faced him. Exquisite, he thought, in the way a sculpted face could be exquisite. She wore the uniform of the American Red Cross.

"Pamela," General Drummond said, "this is my son Drew. Pamela Bayler, Drew."

But cold, he thought, bowing to her, as marble was cold. It was strange, however, that marble could warm you. He glanced at his father. Although his expression remained immobile, General Drummond managed a rare communication. She's not mine, his eyes told Drew, and he turned away.

"Harry! Let's bring out those Martinis."

Pamela continued to look at Drew without speaking. It was a rude and difficult trick that must have required long practice. She succeeded in her objective; she made him uncomfortable. He would shortly do or say something she considered stupid, and then she could realize her wish to dismiss him. Thinking that and half-wishing to snub her, he turned from her and addressed his father. General Drummond, in some alarm, directed his attention back to Pamela.

She spoke, then, in a low and amused tone. "Where did you get so many ribbons, Captain?"

"I bought 'em, Pam," he replied, thinking that he hated her already. "Do they call you Pam?"

"When they know me real well they do."

"Then I'll bet everybody calls you Pamela."

Smiling suddenly, she said to General Drummond, "How about that? Is it a compliment or an insult?"

"Upon my honor I don't know." The General looked both alarmed and mystified. "I mean," he added quickly, "it's supposed to be a compliment, but—"

"What's that one?" She pointed to the red and white-fringed blue field of the Distinguished Service Cross. "I recognize the others, but not that one."

"The Indian Campaign Medal," he said. "I saw it in the PX and it's pretty and I bought it."

"That's the Distinguished Service Cross," General Drummond said hastily.

"You have one too," she said to him. "That must be significant, don't you think?"

The General looked pleased. "It could be, Pamela." He took a Martini from the tray which Harry held out to him and said, "Cheers."

Pamela wrinkled her nose and smiled at Drew and sipped her cocktail.

"Now that you know the story of my life, tell me yours," Drew said. "What brings you to occupied territory?"

"The will to serve," she said deadpan. "The desire to lift up the down-trodden and alleviate the anguish of my fellow man." She was pretty arch, but so was he. "Do you have a cigarette, Drew?"

A bell chimed somewhere. General Drummond, looking relieved, excused himself.

"I just got here this week," she said after Drew lighted her cigarette. "I haven't been playing around in Paris, if that's what you're wondering. Your father came to the office this week and paid his compliments. It seems he met *my* father in Washington several weeks ago and when I came here *my* father sent him word. *My* father is nuts about generals, maybe because he was a draft dodger in the First War."

Drew looked at her with interest. "How do you know?"

"My mother told me once when she was sore at my father."

"So," he said, "for the sake of the family honor you decided to don the noble gray and—"

"No." She sipped her drink and grimaced. "I was just bored purple. And before that—" She turned abruptly and looked over the terrace wall and down a garden of fruit trees to a litter of bombed-out houses. In the evening shadows an old woman with a large wicker basket on her back crept among the rubble, as if hunting something. "What do you think of that?" she asked.

"You mean and us beautiful people standing up here?"

She nodded.

"I don't like it much," he said. "I don't like it at all. It had to be, I know. I mean *they* started it and I guess we had to do something about it. But I don't like being here now. It makes me uncomfortable. I want to get out."

"You're a nice guy." She looked at him levelly. "I haven't talked to a nice guy in a long time. It's good to—*talk*. I ought to warn you that I'm pretty bitchy. Let me tell you what I mean. I've been watching that old woman down there for some time and I've been watching us up here. And I know it's a scene. Contrast and all. And I ought to feel some pity for the old woman. I don't hate Germans, and I don't hate anybody just because they're something or other. But I don't pity the old woman, I just don't feel anything about it. That's what I mean when I say I'm pretty bitchy."

General Drummond stepped onto the terrace with an aging colonel and a civilian. The colonel was a military government officer and the civilian had come from the State Department in Washington. Pamela greeted them courteously and made small talk affably, Drew observed. Why, he wondered, had she acted differently when introduced to him?

It was a downhill dinner party. The colonel and the civilian obviously wanted to talk about important affairs with the General, but felt constrained by the presence of Pamela and Drew. The General realized it and was vaguely amused, thereby displaying a pleasing sophistication that Drew had not observed in him before. It was a simple matter to extricate Pamela and himself after dinner. His father had presumed that they would leave. His motive in planning the evening was transparent—and kind.

"God," Pamela said after they left, "that's what I mean by being bored purple."

"Do you want to go to the Officers' Club for a drink?"

"No. I've been there once and I won't go again. I *hate* it. All those horny, sweaty, drunken men sitting around ogling you."

"Don't be too hard on them. They can't take fräuleins in there and they have to refresh themselves at a bar with comrades in arms once in a while."

"Let's go to that outdoor café down by the square," she said. "The one that sells bootlegged Scotch in coffee cups."

They sat down at a table under a eucalyptus tree and ordered the bootlegged Scotch in coffee cups and watched the American soldiers roaming, roaming and the fräuleins passing in pairs. In a moment someone spoke to Drew. He looked up at Sabraccio.

"Mike!" He introduced Pamela. "Pull up a chair and have a Scotch in a coffee cup."

Sabraccio, a book tucked under an arm, smiled at them benignly. "I wouldn't think of it. I've had my beer and finished my book and I return now to my cell. Stay there, looking young and handsome and hopeful, both of you, and I'll dream of you. Good night, Miss Bayler."

"Who's he?" Pamela asked after he walked away.

"My psychiatrist."

"No kidding!" She leaned toward him. "You mean you had to go

241

to the psychiatrist? That's wonderful. It shows you're an intense, complicated, mixed-up guy. In short, you're interesting. What happened?"

He told her. He did not mention Eileen at first. Then he told her about Eileen too.

"That's priceless." Her gaze soberly absorbed his. "I don't mean priceless like a joke. But a real priceless thing to have happen to you. And not many invaluable things do. Mostly just cheap and mean little things happen. Do you still think of her?"

"Sometimes."

"Suppose she said she was sorry, it was all a mistake. Would you forgive her?"

He frowned thoughtfully. "I don't know. Maybe I would. I wouldn't know unless it happened."

She nodded. "That's the honest way to be. Something like that happened to me. I had this terrific thing with a guy. It was broken off. I guess it's over for good. My father pulled out the old cliché about foreign travel. He's a terrific cliché artist, the very best. He's made pots of dough at it, running his own advertising agency in New York, and he believes every single last word of his copy. That's why he's made so much dough at it. He's kidded himself so long that he believes what he says. I really hate him. I mean I used to hate him. Now I just mildly loathe him. Do you love your father?"

"Not especially."

"It's much easier if you don't," she said. "Anyway, as I told you, my father pulled this old cliché about foreign travel being good for a girl after she's had a thing with a guy. It didn't matter that I'd been abroad before without noticeable beneficial results. It didn't matter that there was a war on, making foreign travel impossible. See, that merely challenged the old advertising copy spirit. What was the answer? The Red Cross, of course. It was simple. He knows everybody. He even knows Harry Truman. He's a Republican, but he and Harry are the best of friends. At least that's what he's always saying. He asked me if I'd mind. I told him not at all." She shrugged. "Anything was better than hanging around New York staring out at Central Park. They couldn't *school* me any more because I managed to graduate from Bryn Mawr, which is a pretty good school. They couldn't *marry* me off because I'm over twenty-one and I'll marry when and if I want to. The only thing they could do was *travel* me, even though there was a war on. So here I am. I can't say I like this place much, but it's better than hanging around New York wondering where your next mink is coming from."

"So you have pots of dough," Drew said.

"Not me." She shook her head. "My *father* has pots of it, but he's the stingiest man in town. He hasn't spoiled me, if that's what you're thinking. I didn't just sit around my parents' humble duplex. I worked." She smiled at him wryly. "I made myself *useful* at my father's agency. I helped plan some pretty good layouts. It was the sort of useful well-paid job with a future that made me happy to quit and join the Red Cross."

They drank several cups of diluted Scotch before he paid the exorbitant check and drove her to the house where she was quartered. He would have liked to put his arm around her as they rode through the deserted streets of the city. He did not, however, for he knew she'd think it an obvious and therefore a corny gesture to ride through a German city acting like a couple of high school kids.

When he stopped at her door, he asked if she'd like to take a drive to the Forest tomorrow. She said indifferently that she wouldn't mind. The next morning he returned, bringing sandwiches and bottles of beer in a knapsack. They drove fifty miles and walked up a hill and examined a castle. They ate their lunch and talked and drove back to the city.

She was a great girl, he decided. Having decided it, he carefully confined himself to the company area for the week. On Friday she sent him a curt note by a courier. She had a mission to a town sixty miles away on Saturday; did he want to ride along? "Yes," he replied on her note, and he was at her office at nine o'clock the next morning. This time he carried a fifth of Scotch in his knapsack—and no sandwiches.

She came out to his jeep carrying a knapsack too.

"What's in it?" he asked her. "Scotch?"

"Yes," she said. "Don't drop it."

It was, he thought, an auspicious start. But the day dragged. When they reached the town, they could not find a decent restaurant and had to scrounge from an officers' mess. Then she was gone about Red Cross business interminably. One thing he observed: she performed her work thoroughly and efficiently. When they started back, it was late. He made a wrong turn and became lost. It began to rain and he had forgotten to bring side curtains for the jeep.

Unaccountably, she began to laugh. He had not heard her laugh before.

"It's priceless," she said. "Here we are absolutely lost and it's priceless. Stop the jeep and we'll have a drink. I love the rain."

They had a drink on the deserted road, passing the bottle back and forth a couple of times, and then they drove on slowly. The gasoline level was low, but they didn't care. They could leave the jeep and report it stolen and some day they'd reappear in recognizable surroundings. It didn't matter. There had been a war and the war was over and they were wandering in a forest with two bottles of Scotch. They felt magnificent.

As it grew dark, they passed a sprawling, lighted building near a small lake. Drew stopped the jeep and looked at a sign: HOTEL HELD.

"That means hotel, doesn't it?" he asked.

"Hotel means hotel," she said. "It's a useless piece of information I picked up somewhere, but hotel means hotel in French, German, Spanish, Swedish—with two l's—and even in Yiddish, with a single l. Only the Italians insist on calling it an *albergo*."

"What does Held mean?"

"I don't know. I don't speak German."

"Let's go in and try to get something to eat and maybe we can get directions."

Carrying their knapsacks, they dashed through the rain from the jeep and plunged into a low-ceilinged room. An aging, white-mustached man stared at them in astonishment. Then he expressed profound joy and, finally, deep obeisance. In German, however. He summoned an elderly woman and a young woman and three children to behold the wonderful Americans. They did not speak English either.

"What's the German word for eat?" Drew asked her.

"I told you I don't speak German," she said. "The French verb is *manger* and the Italian *mangiare*, but we're now in Germany."

"I remember the word," he said. "It's *essen*." He grinned at the old man and said, *"Essen?"*

The old man beamed and nodded and spoke to the women and children. Then he lighted a lamp and led them up a short flight of stairs and into a large, low-ceilinged room where there was a fragrant smell of pinewood. The old man lighted many lamps in the room, which contained several comfortable chairs and a low table before a fireplace and a large bed in one corner and a single bed in another corner. He opened a door and lighted a lamp in a small bathroom and then he knelt before the fireplace and struck a match to the tinder and logs which had been laid there.

Pamela, standing in the middle of the room, looked drolly at Drew. "You're really hell with the language, Captain. All I want is a ham sandwich and you throw in a double room with bath."

"Danke," he said as the old man bowed and backed from the room. "It's the only word I really know," he said to Pamela, "and an important one. I didn't want to hurt his feelings."

"Of course," she said drily, sitting down in a chair before the fire and curling her legs under her. "He has a lot of dignity and he means well. He's probably not seen more than a couple of Americans and already he's very perceptive about them. He figures that when two of opposite sexes come into a place at nightfall they want to shack up together."

"Well?" asked Drew, as he poured Scotch into two glasses.

"Please," she said, "let's not be corny. It could be priceless. The setting. The sound of that rain on the roof and the fire crackling." She sipped her Scotch meditatively and looked at him. "You look bronzed and downright handsome in the firelight. And I look positively beautiful, don't I? And smell the pine."

"And we sitting here," he said, "such dear platonic friends."

"But of course. That's what makes it so priceless." She sipped her Scotch. "Why mess it up by trying to drink the whole bottle? I've tried that and you must have too. You tilt the bottle till the floor tilts. The animal panting and cries of ecstasy. The rumpled bed and the hangover. Afterwards you feel like a whore, and I don't want to feel like a whore."

He stared at her. "You're an extraordinary girl, Pam."

"No, I'm not. I'm just like the girls I know and like. We've all read *The Sun Also Rises* and been frightened by the image of Lady Brett."

"So you want to live just beyond the suburbs and have a lot of babies?"

"Some do. But not me. I detest babies. I want to stay in the city and try not to be a character in a novel."

The old man and woman served them dinner on the low table before the fireplace. It was a palatable meal, accompanied by a bottle of cool dry wine. Afterwards they had another Scotch and they did not talk much.

At last she rose and said, "I'm going to take a bath."

He continued to stare into the fire, his back to her, listening to her moving about and running water in the tub. She was a new kind of girl to him and this was a new kind of contest. But he thought he understood. She wanted to be able to take it or leave it alone, whatever it might be, whether one of the so-called vices or renowned virtues. She wanted to be in control, of herself rather than of another.

245

Thus, when she decided it was right, it would be very right. She sought, actually, a perfection of character.

She came from the bathroom, holding an enormous bath towel loosely about her, and began drying herself before the fire. This was rough, he thought. She must be, after all, merely an exhibitionist. For there was little modesty in her movements as she stood there, rubbing herself dry and talking casually about the people she'd interviewed on her mission today. Her slim body, like her face, was exquisitely formed, her feet small and perfect, her breasts small and taut. Carefully folding the towel about her, she sat down on the floor and lighted a cigarette.

He took a bath too. When he came out, she was lying in the big bed smoking another cigarette. As one exhibitionist to another, he thought, and wandered around the room drying himself without modesty while she watched him indifferently.

"I turned your bed down," she said.

"Thanks," he replied. "It was very thoughtful of you." He turned out the lamps, except the one beside her bed, and dropped his towel on the floor and got in his bed. "Good night, Pam," he said.

"Good night, Drew."

He lay awake for a long time after she turned out her lamp, thinking what an extraordinary girl she was.

She had gone when he awakened in bright morning. Downstairs he found her sitting at a table with the old man, a map between them.

"I've figured the way back with his help," she said. "It's simple."

They drank some tea and Drew paid the bill and they drove away in the warm sunlight. Following the old man's sign directions, they turned onto a narrow dirt road which wound through the forest about four miles to the highway.

As they crossed a wooden bridge over a small rushing stream, she said, "Let's get out and walk in the sunshine."

He parked the jeep off the road and they walked up the stream, following its winding through bright clearings and dark stands of pine where no birds called. They did not try to speak above the brawling of the stream. He followed her, watching her sure-footed, lithe movements over slippery needles and outcroppings of rock.

They came to a place where the stream poured whitely into a sun-dappled basin. You had to shout to be heard above its rushing. Taking off her jacket and shoes and stockings, she stepped into the stream and cried, "It's cold!"

246

She slipped and he steadied her, grasping her arm strongly and pulling her back. Raising her face to his, she stared at him fixedly and then closed her eyes. Drawing her to him, he kissed her. She moved both of her hands slowly, one to the back of his head and the other to his thigh, as she held the kiss. They were lying on the pine needles then, and the rushing stream made it unnecessary for them to try to speak. What had not been right to her last night she made very right for both of them beside the stream.

Chapter XXI

Sometimes, when he was most positive that he wanted to be a civilian again, he tried to remember what had been attractive about those years before he returned to the Army.

"You'll hate being a civilian," his father had said with intensity. "Stay where you belong, Drew."

General Drummond tried hard to persuade him to remain in the Army when Drew called on him one evening late in August and told him he was getting out.

"I know you're going around with Pamela," the General said. "She's a nice girl. She told me the first time I met her that she likes the Army and thinks it must be an interesting career. Does that mean anything to you?"

How gullible his father could be sometimes. When he stood be-before her, a lieutenant general, did he expect her to tell him that she actually hated the Army?

"What are you going to do if you get out—marry Pamela?"

"I don't know, Father."

And he did not know. He wanted to marry her. He had asked her, but she did not answer him directly. She said he had a *thing* on her, as she had a kind of a thing on him. And then she changed the subject.

"But what are you going to *do*?" demanded General Drummond.

He told him, then, the surprising thing he had done and how surprisingly well it seemed to be working out. Early in June he'd written the Dean of Admissions at Columbia College in New York a long and eloquent letter, applying for admission on the chance he would be discharged by fall. He had enclosed transcripts of his Army records and told the Dean where he could document his civilian background. The Dean, amazingly, was willing to gamble on him. Now, since he had more than enough discharge points, all he asked of his father was help in expediting his return to the States.

In reply, General Drummond ranted against *privilege*. He took Drew up on the mountain of the Army where he surely hinted at privilege in assuring him of a fine career. Then he dropped him into the abyss of civilian life where, he said, there was nothing, nothing. He wore himself out with arguments. When he had finished, Drew was unmoved. There was, in the end, nothing the General could do except bargain. He would see that his discharge was expedited if Drew would remain in the Reserve.

"You'll never regret it," he said. "Some day you'll tell me— No, I suppose you'll never tell me, but some day you'll be glad."

Drew agreed to the bargain; he would have agreed to almost anything, he believed, in order to get out. And then, to his amazement, tears clouded his father's eyes.

Although he wanted to get out, he dreaded to leave Pamela. For she wanted to go home too. Apparently, however, it had been easier for her father to get her into Red Cross foreign service than out of it. Drew tried to believe that she wanted to go home because he was leaving, but he knew he was kidding himself. She was an independent girl, so self-sufficient that she declined to sleep with him after that morning beside the forest stream. Presumably, he told himself, she did not love him. Yet why were there tears in her eyes when she kissed him good-by?

He was late in entering Columbia, but he made up the lost time quickly. The classes were vaguely disappointing, perhaps because the subjects were so elementary and easy. Nevertheless, he worked hard. Everybody worked hard; everybody wanted to get ahead; everybody wanted to make money. He often felt old and bored among the incredibly young and enthusiastic freshmen.

He found a cheap room in the Village and rode the subway to and from the campus where he had a part-time job in the library. He dressed carelessly and read omnivorously and drank beer with veterans he met in the Village. Once he considered going out to Orange to see Eileen, but he checked the impulse. She was through with him and so he was through with her. He had written her once after receiving her letter, but she had not replied. It was futile to speculate over why she had dropped him; it was worse than futile to think about her.

He thought constantly of Pamela, however, and wrote her regularly. She responded infrequently and finally ceased writing him early in November. Just one more girl to forget. But he could not forget her.

The Christmas season loomed depressingly. There would be dinner with his mother, the Widow Huddel, as she wrily called herself, and that was all there would be to Christmas. He considered making a trip to Burning Brook to see Judd and Mildred, who kept urging him to visit them.

Then, one morning in mid-December, as he read the *Times* while riding uptown in the subway, he glimpsed the name of Mrs. Roger Bayler on the society page. When he left the subway at 116th Street he checked the name in a telephone book. Roger Bayler, Inc., Madison Avenue. Roger Bayler, residence, Fifth Avenue. He called the residence and asked to speak to Miss Pamela Bayler. The servant told him she was not at that address, but to call a number which she gave him.

His heart beat quickly as he dialed the number. Pamela answered and recognized his voice immediately.

"Drew! It's good to hear you."

"I'll bet. Why don't you ever answer your mail?"

"I hate to write letters. They finally let me out three weeks ago. Why don't you have a phone in your place?"

"I can't afford it. But I can afford to take you out for dinner. When do you want to go?"

"Not tonight. My roommate and I are asking a few people in for drinks about six. Come on around."

He went at half-past six to an East Side apartment house. A honey-haired girl who wore harlequin glasses opened the door and said, "I'm Gloria, the roommate. You must be Drummond."

Across the room he saw Pamela. He had remembered accurately the golden helmet of her hair and the lithe beauty of her body. But he had not realized his legs could become leaden when he looked at her. It was, he thought, more than just a thing with him.

"Hi." She detached herself from the men who surrounded her and, coming to him, she presented a cheek to be kissed.

Such dear friends. She introduced him to other dear friends, men mostly. Men who had survived the war under one or another yoke. Men who worked in agencies. Individuals, certainly. But, as far as

Drew could discern after an hour of listening, not individualists. They wore the uniform of Brooks Brothers instead of olive drab Some vehemently protested their Madison Avenue service; others were apologetic; a few endured it silently; a very few, who must be high on the promotion lists or never had had it so good before, obviously relished their duty. He felt that he had met all of them before. Yet he knew from experience that if he came to know any one of them well, his first generalized judgment of him would prove to be not quite true. So he tried to become better acquainted with two or three of the men at Pamela's party. They would not let him, however. And he understood that too. He did not wear their uniform.

Bored at last and despairing of ever being more than an outsider looking in at Pamela, he decided that he'd better go. He'd take his Pamela-induced symptoms with him, the leaden legs and racing heart and moist palms, and he'd bolt out of there, never to return. Farewell all. You too, Pamela.

As he went to look for his coat, she came after him. "Where are you going?"

"I have to go," he muttered.

"Yellow-belly."

"Oh, sure." He did not look at her.

"I thought you were taking me to dinner."

"I want to, but—"

"Then come on." She pulled a coat from the closet and called back to those who still lingered, "You're overstaying. We have to go." People looked at her, some startled, others amused. She bared her teeth at them and went out with Drew.

"That was pretty nice of you," he said. "I—"

"Don't be grateful. I can't stand grateful people. You never were grateful when you were in the Infantry. It was one thing I liked about you." As they stepped onto the street, she said, "You don't know where to go, so I'll tell you. A good place where they won't clip you."

She told a taxi driver the name of a restaurant and sat close to Drew. He put an arm around her and pulled her closer.

"Please," she said, and he withdrew his arm.

In the restaurant she silently raised her drink to him and gazed at him levelly. This, he thought, is where she tells me off.

But she said, "I'm going to have to teach you a lot. Not *have* to, but I'm going to anyway, I don't exactly know why. First of all you're going to have to learn to recognize a phony. A phony is always *nice* to you because you've got something he wants or else he's so scared and unsure of himself that he doesn't dare be anything but nice."

"I don't agree with you," he said. "I—"

"You have to agree with me." She smiled at him. "Or you won't learn anything. You can unlearn it afterwards, but first you have to learn it my way. Otherwise you'll be"—she shrugged—"lost. Take that party. It was full of phonies. Most of them work at the agency. I went back to work there a week ago. It seemed right to ask them in for drinks after I'd been away so long. They came, figuring I wanted to make a hit, I wanted something. When I walked out with you the real ones knew that I was real too, that I don't give a damn. A phony is shocked by something like that. A real is amused. He doesn't give a damn either. Do you understand? You have a lot of other things to learn, Drew. Little things and big things. Your clothes aren't right. Be sloppy if you want to, but be expensively sloppy."

"Look," he said, "I haven't much money."

She frowned. "You told me once your divorced mother lives in town. Doesn't she have any?"

"I guess she has, but—"

"Borrow from her. And don't worry about paying it back. She'll love it. At least I'll bet *your* mother will love it. Look, it's almost 1946. All the young men who went out and got their tails shot off are owed something. Parents are going to have to start help supporting their children. I frequently put the touch on my old man. He *expects* it. Those bourgeois virtues died with the war. Everybody knows it. Don't be naïve." She lit a cigarette. "What do you want at Columbia? What do you want to become?"

"As I told you in Germany, I'd like to be a teacher of history in a college somewhere. And I'd like to write some books. Eighteenth-century America interests me. Just the other day—"

"God!" She shook her head wonderingly. "You still want that. When you told me in Germany I thought you were still a little punchy from the war. You want to be a teacher just because that uncle of yours was one. You think of him as a rebel. And you want to rebel against your family tradition too. I'm all for rebellion. But why imitate your uncle? Why not be something on your own?"

"I figure, Pam, that I can be something on my own by being a teacher. I know I'll like it. I even like the smell of library stacks, the quiet and the note-taking and the—the thinking."

"Maybe," she said, "I can't teach you anything after all."

Looking at her steadily, he said, "Maybe you can't, Pam. But I'd like to try to learn a little from you."

She grimaced. "What a morbid conversation. Order me another drink and let's skip it."

Why did she ever bother with me? I didn't know then and I don't know to this day. What did she really want? She wanted . . .

There was, of course, the physical attraction, the *thing,* as they thought of it. He did not conceal it. She tried to. For a long time she succeeded so well that he decided he did not attract her physically. In the spring he learned differently. One night, after they'd spent the evening listening to a jazz combo in the Village, he took her to his room and they made love passionately. After that night they frequently slept together.

She was, he realized, a burning girl. But she did not want to be a tramp. She loved luxury. But, hard as she worked at the agency, she did not expect to pay for her tastes. She admired independence in anyone and sought it for herself. But she neither wished nor tried to free herself from social dependence on the numerous places and faces that had become familiar to her. She wished, above all, to be honest. But she suspected or detested any manifestation of the so-called simple virtues in others. Viewed through the prism of her complexity, what normally seemed right to him could appear to be quite wrong while a thing he used to consider wrong could seem absolutely right.

Early in June she announced that the agency was sending her to South America for three months. It was the end of their affair, she said. He asked why. She told him. It was the second time around for her, she said. This was the way it had been with a man at the agency before her father broke it up. He fired the man and she went to Germany for the Red Cross. She was disgusted with herself for being such a tramp. "Then marry me," he said. How could she? He was a *freshman.* And she went away and did not write him.

He continued to work hard at Columbia. His grades were high and he would be able to complete his undergraduate course in three years. A professor hired him to do research for a military history he was writing; it was a high honor for one who was technically a sophomore. He learned much about methods of research and even about writing, since the professor wrote lucidly and interestingly.

I began to develop confidence in myself that summer. I thought that Pam was out of my system and I was finding the way to the things I wanted.

On an afternoon early in October, as he crossed Fifth Avenue from the Public Library, he saw Pamela coming toward him. She saw him and her eyes darted away, seeking a means to avoid him. He realized, suddenly, that he wished to avoid her too. But they could not. They came on, each borne on the tide of pedestrians crossing with the green light, until they met in the center of the Avenue. They paused, staring silently at each other, as people jostled around them. Then he took her arm and turned in the direction she was going.

They were married in December at a church on Park Avenue. Judd and Mildred came up from Burning Brook and Judd acted as his best man. His mother cried at the ceremony. His father sent a big silver tea service from Germany. Pamela's mother became mildly drunk at the reception. Her father wrote them a check for five thousand dollars.

What did I really like about it? Well, I liked the way Pam and I made love a lot in that expensive two-room apartment. I liked lying around on Sundays, reading and listening to recordings. But I didn't like being a kept man. I went back to Columbia physically, but I really didn't go back at all. After we were married it wasn't the same. I felt it would take too long to earn the degrees I needed. I was in such a hurry. Why I was in such a hurry I don't know, except that I didn't like being a kept man. And Roger Bayler made me feel kept.

It takes only one generation to create a tradition, he sometimes thought. One can accomplish it in the course of a few years simply by living in a certain manner and insisting that there is no other way to live. It was not necessary to go to the lengths that the Drummonds and the Huntleys had, he decided wrily: many generations, roots in a specific place, son following father in the same profession. Roger Bayler accomplished the same effect in a brief time.

He was, it was true, an imaginative man, more imaginative than any of the Drummonds or Huntleys had been, and probably more talented too. He had, for example, invented a father. Actually his father had been a bankrupt druggist in a small town in southern Illinois. From this humble material Roger Bayler created the exalted image of a country doctor. When he was a young man working on a small Iowa newspaper, he wrote a book about this noble country doctor father of his. It was a very popular book because it expressed a lot of platitudes that made people feel "warm and comfortable," as many readers told Bayler.

On the wings of his book's success he sped to New York. He had no illusions about becoming a popular professional writer. He realized, at an earlier age than most men, the exact limitations of his facility. His facility with words, he saw, could best be applied to things that people *bought*—and how many people bought books? He had been very poor and he wished to be very rich. In the sun glare of the Mid-Western prairies his imagination had seen the glories of the fabulous East. So he went to work as a copywriter for a New York advertising agency, transmuting some of his vision to soap and fabrics and practically anything that anyone might be stimulated to buy.

He was so facile, so quick to learn, so adaptable and shrewd, that within two years he stole the two best advertising accounts from the man who had hired him, and opened his own agency. Then he soared. He learned about wines and rare books and he consorted with people who were mentioned favorably in the newspapers. Within a few years people believed when they met him that he never had lived in any but his present circumstances. Bayler, always collecting illusions and seldom being disillusioned, believed it himself. Thus he created the tradition of Roger Bayler.

When Drew married Pamela, he felt that he was fortunate in his father-in-law. He did not understand why Pamela said she disliked her father. And then, gradually, he began to see why she did. Finally, to his dismay, he discovered that she did not really dislike him at all. She merely saw through some of his characteristics which, to her annoyance, reminded her of traits she possessed; and she wanted, as do many people, to believe that there was no one quite like herself in all the world. She sometimes argued or quarreled with her father. But always over trivial matters, and never over basic principles.

Drew's dismay at this came quite late in their relationship and only after he discovered that the basic principle of Roger Bayler's life was to promote the tradition of Roger Bayler. That is, he did not wish his daughter and son-in-law actually to lead their own lives; he wished them to lead his life. He wanted them to live as he and his wife did and he wanted them to succeed him in the management of his business. Although this made him sound generous, he actually was not. He was simply trying to perpetuate the tradition of himself which he had created. He would have been generous only if he had helped Drew attain his educational goal in every possible way.

He did not. In subtle ways he made Drew feel ill at ease about being a student at Columbia while Pamela worked at the agency. (He was so capable at subtlety that Drew did not realize how he accomplished his purpose until long afterwards.) The autumn after they were married, when Drew had completed three years of his college credits, he left Columbia without much regret and went to work for Roger Bayler, Inc., as a copywriter. Bayler was elated. When he proved to be a capable copywriter, Bayler was extravagant in his praise. He was Bayler's boy, as Pamela was Bayler's girl, and others at the agency courted them and feared them and (probably, Drew realized) hated them.

Recognizing that he did not basically like the work, he trained himself never to think whether he liked it. Liking it was unimportant. Performing efficiently and, when possible, better than others was the only important thing. It was, in a sense, like the Infantry.

Six months after he joined the agency he was put in charge of an account. His job was to handle the advertising of a manufacturer of men's toiletries. It was an easy account. The only irksome aspect was the fact that he had to entertain officers of the company frequently. You began drinking with some of them around noon and you continued to drink until they released you, whether it was three o'clock in the afternoon or three o'clock the next morning. You did things you did not want to do and you said things you did not believe. It was, in a sense, like the Infantry.

He began to understand Pamela's complexity. Her protests against her father's driving ambition for himself and for them were of the lips and not of the heart. She wished them to be *graceful,* but it's difficult to be graceful when you're always *running.* And she could not stop running. She protested that she did not really want a career, but she could not bear the prospect of being "just a housewife." She wanted to *be* somebody, yet she often was angry because that end could not be achieved effortlessly. Paradoxically, she drove Drew hard at his job—almost as hard as Bayler drove him and he drove himself. He trained himself not to protest.

I was protesting, though—and so was she. We simply didn't realize it at the time. What was it that troubled us? I think it was always being in such a hurry. In a hurry to make money, in a hurry to get ahead, in a hurry not to be thought a slob. When, sometimes, we realized that we didn't have the vaguest idea where we were going, we were still in a hurry to get away from where we were. Alcohol is always the quickest passage from the place you are. We drank too much and so we quarreled too much, over nothing really, except being in a hurry and not knowing how to slow down gracefully.

It seemed, at the time, that it ended with a bang and not with the whimper reported by Mr. T. S. Eliot in the poem so greatly admired by many of the people Drew and Pamela called their friends. Afterwards, however, when you stepped back and inclined an attentive ear, you could hear the echo of the long protesting whimper of their marriage. You could remember Pamela drinking too much and yourself drinking too much. You could remember the lies they told in public and the lies they told each other. You could not say, however, that it was Pamela's fault any more than your own. You could not say it was Roger Bayler's fault. Neither could you say it was the fault of a particular way of life in New York at a particular time. If you had to make a big, juicy generalization about it you might say that they had failed to try to live without fear of others' opinions.

At the time, however, he did not fully understand the basic causes of the breakup. He simply became involved in a series of brief situations.

There was, to begin with, his state of mind. He was sick of the job and the life on Madison Avenue. But he had trained himself not to admit it. His sickness with it showed, however, when Bayler put him to work at the "creative level," planning the advertising for an important client. An agency executive named Abe Heineman worked with him on it. That is, Heineman worked and he did practically nothing. He tried. But he discovered that he actually did not care about the client or the account. And, not caring, he could not bring himself to produce any ideas.

Bayler insisted that Drew present the plans to the client's representatives at a conference which Bayler himself attended. Heineman was there too, listening to Drew's presentation of his ideas. He tried to make it clear that it was Heineman's plan, saying frequently, "I think Abe has a good idea here—" Each time, however, Bayler laughingly deprecated Drew's "modesty" to the client's representatives, who were delighted with the plans. At the end of the conference Heineman strode from the room and Drew followed him quickly. "Look, Abe—"

"Skip it, Drew." Heineman stared at him without rancor. "There's no place for people with my kind of name in this outfit. I'm going down the street and get another job. Dave Starke can use me."

Dave Starke! Now he understood. Dave Starke still was remembered at the agency with a kind of awe. Like Abe, he was a brilliant Jew. Once, when Pamela had been angry with Drew, she had brought up his name. He was, she told him, the man with whom she'd had the affair before her father had induced her to go abroad with the Red Cross. When Pamela told him about Starke, he'd felt resentful of him. But now, suddenly, he sympathized with him. Probably Starke had genuinely loved her and wanted to marry her. Because he was a Jew, however, he had been unfit to perpetuate the tradition of Roger Bayler. He saw it clearly now: Bayler's dictation and Pamela's acquiescence—and her resentment, which she hid even from herself. But he, who lacked Abe Starke's talent, had been acceptable to Roger Bayler because his name was Andrew Jackson Drummond, 4th, and he came from a fine old southern family of soldiers. . . .

He told Pamela about the Abe Heineman incident that evening. They had a scene. He was acting like a fool, she said, and he had to "get on the ball." The next morning he told Bayler that Heineman had done all the work on the new account and should receive credit for it. Heineman had resigned, Bayler said gravely, and then, with fatherly kindness, he urged Drew to "get on the ball."

But he didn't get on the ball. The person who did was a new man at the agency, Eli Chadwick. The interesting thing about Eli was that he hurried so gracefully he did not seem to be hurrying at all. Eli was handsome and intelligent and well connected and well educated and socially charming. These attributes were not what made him attractive to Pamela, however, Drew decided eventually. She liked Eli Chadwick because he hurried so gracefully that he made her haste seem graceful too.

She saw much of him. They worked together on a couple of accounts at the office and Eli was forever dropping in at their apartment or taking them out for dinner. Throughout that summer of 1948 it was Eli, Eli, Eli, until you'd have thought you were at a Yale football game. All good friends, of course. Such very good friends. When Drew finally told Pamela he was tired of seeing so much of Eli, she laughed at him and said he was jealous. When he insisted that she not see Eli so frequently, she grew angry. They quarreled childishly. They patched up—and quarreled again.

At the end he acted childishly. In retrospect, however, he did not see how he could have acted otherwise.

He came home late one evening after a trying session with a client and found Eli stretched gracefully on the sofa with a drink in hand while Pamela sat on a hassock beside him. It was quite a domestic scene, especially when Eli asked Drew, without rising, whether he'd have a drink.

"No, thanks." Drew stared at him, fighting back his anger. Then he said, "Eli, old boy, I have to ask you something. I have to ask you to leave. I want to talk to Pam."

She whirled on him. "*I* asked Eli to come in . . ."

Yakkity-yakkity-yak. Eli saying he was going. Pamela saying he was *not* going. Drew saying . . . Yakkity-yakkity-yak. Drew left the apartment and spent a sleepless night in a hotel.

The next morning he was summoned to headquarters: Roger Bayler's office. Pamela had preceded him there and pleaded her case. She sat on one side of her father's enormous desk. Drew sat down on the other side and Bayler asked him what it was all about.

"I've *told* you what it's all about," Pamela cried at her father. "I told you I want a divorce and Eli and I want to get married."

Drew stared at her dazedly. Going under the anesthetic, he thought vaguely. And then, No, coming out of it.

Bayler, after asking Pamela to leave the office, loosed his great talent for rationalization upon the subject of their marriage. He said it had become obvious that they could not live together happily. Better that they should be "civilized" and Pamela get a divorce. Better that they should start again while they were still young. He, Roger Bayler, would personally make certain that Drew got another job in another agency . . . Yakkity-yakkity-yak!

Long afterwards Drew heard that Eli Chadwick made an ideal son-in-law and perpetuated the Roger Bayler tradition.

It was odd how unemotionally I left New York. I thought I'd sunk a few roots in it, but I found that I was like a traveling salesman who had spent one night in a hotel room.

He considered going back to Columbia. But he realized that his desire to be a teacher was as dead, at least for the moment, as his desire to work for an advertising agency.

He bought a one-way airplane ticket to Nashville. As the airline limousine took him across the Jersey Meadows to Newark Airport he found himself thinking not of Pamela but of Eileen. What had happened to her? When he reached the airport, he looked up the Gannons' telephone number in Orange and stepped into a booth. There he paused, a coin in his fingers, while he wondered what he would say. Gradually he realized that there was nothing he could say to Eileen. For a time their relationship had been perfect. But it had ended quickly and it could not be revived. He could only remember its fleeting perfection.

Leaving the telephone booth, he sat down to wait for the airplane which would take him to the one place the Drummonds always returned when they had nowhere else to go.

Chapter XXII

"Burning Brook," said General Drummond, "was a place where the family always felt happy and secure. The family—most of its members—uh—were home-loving . . ."

Oh, please, Father, Drew thought and listened to rain pelting the windows of the castle. They lingered at the luncheon table, Jane and Marcia watching his father attentively as he cracked a walnut. He had held them spellbound with his talk about the earlier Drummonds' patriotism. He had joined mother and home with country, leaving only God to complete the oratorical quadrature. It was malarkey.

"We don't know too much about General Sam," said General Drummond. "But we can see from what we know that he was a fine man, patriotic, home-loving . . ."

We can see nothing of the sort, Drew thought. The assumption was completely wrong. His father should be told the truth.

"I have here"—the General took a slip of paper from a pocket, like a lecturer reporting on a foreign place—"a copy of a notation of General Sam's in 1821 after he'd married and taken over the management of the plantation his wife inherited."

He passed it to Jane and she read it thoughtfully. Nodding, she handed it to Drew. He barely glanced at it and passed it along to Marcia. He knew what it said.

> Plantation Catalog. Cotton yield poor last yr. 12 niggers, 9 field hands & 3 domestics. 2 field hands old & fit for 1 yr. longer. 4 mules, 5 horses, only 1 fit for Genlmn to ride, 3 milk cows, 2 sows. Acreage 850 approx. Will buy more hands & then 200 acres south when monies avble.

"And here," said General Drummond, passing another slip to Jane, "is a copy of an entry my grandfather made on Christmas Day, 1855."

> God has been good in this year. Acreage stands now at 1,500. 550 cotton, 200 corn, 500 fallow, the brushland now 200. Field hands, 58 of whom 9 indigent. Sold 4, bought 7, deceased in year

6. Dismissed Mr. Farrell as overseer; need strong young man. The whiskey distillery was most profitable this year. Mules 16, horses 12. My three-year-old, General Knox, won at Nashville and is now standing stud in Williamson County. Our great sorrow of year was death in November of baby Judith, aged 6 mos., of inflammation of the lungs. A good yield and fair cotton prices enabled us all luxuries—chocolate, spices, red & sugar almonds, muscatel raisins, Madeira, Sherry, Claret, Lisbon & Port wines, French & Spanish brandies. These & salt, tea, coffee, clothing & some wheat flour & implements. Nearly all else we take from our land.

Drew, watching Marcia read the notation, saw her expression grow puzzled. Bless you, Marcia, he thought, if you wonder what solemn conclusion my father will try to draw from this. He looked at Jane. She watched the General expectantly. And bless you, too, Jane, he thought, for admiring him so. He has been too little admired and he needs it, for he looks terribly old and sad.

There was, after all, much to admire in him. He had endured the long monotony and risen to the sudden arduous duty of war. Because of him, and men like him, the nation had won a great war. Yet what had been his payoff? A wife who left him, a son who mostly had scorned him, and then retirement. No wonder that he groped so desperately now to explain to himself—and, incidentally, to them for whatever benefit they could find in it—the tortured sources of his strength.

Jane should be his daughter. Jane could become his daughter if she would agree to a marriage. There's only one small trouble, Drew thought. She doesn't love me and I don't love her. Not quite yet. Perhaps eventually and possibly never, but certainly not quite yet. He had been living today with Eileen and Pamela, and his imagination was incapable of living with a third at the moment.

Not even with Marcia, who knew the secret of his twitching face. She returned his gaze inscrutably, a modern woman holding an ancient notation in her hand. She was understandably baffled as to what the General meant, except that the acreage of Burning Brook had increased and the land had prospered. She should not be baffled, for that was absolutely all the notation meant. The General should leave it at that. The mystique he was now creating about the meaning of the land to the later generations was absurd. Burning Brook had not helped him endure the twenty years of peacetime Army routine. Worshiping his ancestors had not helped him. As a young man it was doubtful if he had given much thought to his ancestors. But now, growing old, he turned to them as if they could explain what he could not explain himself.

General Sam tantalized him. He painted him enthusiastically until he stood in heavenly high light, like a Benjamin West heroic figure on a field of honor. What his father was trying to say, Drew knew, was that blood will tell. He disagreed heartily, though silently; who, for example, had been Joe Gannon's great-great-grandfather? If, however, the General was right and blood would indeed tell, what had it told in the case of the Drummonds?

I can't tell him that he's absolutely wrong. Yet now he's speaking truth about this feeling a man can have for the land. I felt it when I went back to Burning Brook that fall.

A few days after he arrived from New York he heard Judd shouting in the yard and he rushed outside, as once, in that country, they had rushed at the cry of Cherokee or Creek.

"Geese!" Judd pointed up to a floating skein pulled south by a leader. There came down to them a faint melodious gabbling that chilled Drew's neck. "They're early this year and off their main flyway. I wonder why. It's years since I've seen geese here."

After Drew lowered his gaze from the sky, the yellowing land, dying frostless in autumn, looked different. For several days afterwards, as he rode and walked about the farm with Judd and talked to him, he felt that he saw the land as it once had been. There had been, he and Judd knew, a great joy in it.

Honey stolen from the wild hives in the sycamores. The bear cornered in the canebrake by the pack of dogs. In the early summers of those days wild strawberries grew everywhere, staining horses' legs scarlet. It was a land of wild plums and black haws and grapes and chestnuts where wild pigeons often darkened the sky with thundering wings. By day the partridges drummed and deer stepped softly in the glades; at night the panthers screamed like women. The land of plenty and opportunity, the land of danger and desire.

Drew saw it, through Judd's eyes and his own imagination, as he had not before. The land moved in and filled the void of his life. He was suspended, bemused, land-struck. If most of the people he had known in New York could have seen him then they would have said that he was dead. But dead, he thought, only as the seed seems dead in the dark earth before it turns and sprouts upward. He felt on the verge of something, though he had no idea what that something might be.

Then, on a chill gray Sunday morning, as he rode forth with Judd, he believed he knew what it was. He was not on the verge of something. Rather, he had arrived. He was here forever. The countryman. The good farmer, skin reddened and roughened, muscles hardened. The rustic reader and philosopher, given to the pleasures of the senses. The pleasures were all about, as the wild plums once had grown all about. The changing of the seasons, the horse between the knees, the good food, the pretty young woman who stopped her car on the road yesterday and smiled at him and introduced herself as a neighbor.

They cantered up the side road and finally, when they walked their horses, he said to Judd, "It's a wonderful life. I could stay here forever."

Judd reined in, and so did Drew. The horses nodded and flicked their tails, rubbing against the alder underbrush below a crest in the road.

"You can." Judd looked at him gravely. "If you're happy here, you know that Mildred and I will be happier than we've ever been to have you stay."

"I know, Judd. I—"

A car, which they had not heard, roared over the crest and plunged at them. The horses reared in fright. Drew had been sitting loosely; he pressed his knees and grasped the saddle in time to save himself being thrown. An alder bough lashed his cheek painfully. He glimpsed the face of the Negro driver, grinning up as he hugged a woman to him.

"Goddamn—b—b—bastard!" he yelled after the car. "Who does he think he is?" he cried to Judd.

Judd, quieting his horse, sidled her from the underbrush. He held her in tight rein, stroking her neck, and stared at him.

"That was Lester Cross," he said quietly. "Avery's brother-in-law." Avery Johnson was Judd's Negro farmer, an able and amiable man.

"I'm sorry," Drew muttered. "Not because he's Avery's brother-in-law. But for what I almost called him."

"You mean the way you choked off 'black'?"

Drew nodded.

"It no longer is the age of the horse," Judd said, "and this never was the country of the white man."

"I know. I guess it was the *tradition* approving of my yelling from the superiority of horseback that a man is a Goddamn black bastard."

"Don't blame the tradition for everything," Judd said. "I've heard the phrase as often in the sanctified Puritan tradition of New England. Why not just blame yourself?"

Smiling suddenly, he touched Drew's shoulder. They turned their horses and galloped back to Burning Brook.

After they had unsaddled and rubbed down the horses, Judd said, "Come on in the library. There's something I want you to read."

In the library he opened a combination wall safe and took out an old calfskin notebook. He held it in both hands and gazed thoughtfully at Drew. "For some time I've thought you should read this," he said slowly. "I've talked about it to Mildred. The time has never been right. But now it is."

"What is it?" Drew took the notebook and opened it curiously.

Testimonial of Genl. Samuel Drummond to the Rev. Jeremiah Baker was written at the top of the first page in a small, stiff hand.

"Jeremiah Baker," Drew said. "He's the one your grandfather mentioned in that journal of his. That ambiguous reference nobody has ever been able to—" He stared at Judd. "*You* know who he is. You must have known for a long time."

Judd smiled faintly. "I've known. But your father doesn't know and your grandfather never knew. It's not something that would ever be of any—use to your father. I wish you'd never tell him. But it might, in a strange way, be of some use to you to know."

"Who was Jeremiah Baker?"

"A Yankee preacher who went west. A great evangelist. Henry Ward Beecher described him glowingly in a letter once. You know Sinclair Lewis once called Beecher 'a combination of St. Augustine, Barnum and John Barrymore.' Maybe the description fits Baker too. He must have been around sixty when he settled down here at the Corners in 1845 or so. I guess he figured his evangelizing days were over and he was content to live by the creek down there and preach in the Methodist Church. He had a wife, a young woman. He somehow got to General Sam."

"*Got* to him?"

Judd shrugged and pointed to the book. "Look at what's written there. Sam didn't write it. Jeremiah did. Jeremiah *got* Sam to tell it to him. It must have been a struggle of giants, Jeremiah wrestling the words out of Sam's soul. He should have called it the *Confessions*. But the word obviously had a Catholic connotation to him and so was heretical. He preferred the evangelical word of *Testimonial*. In a way, I suppose, old Jeremiah was one of our first psychiatrists. But read it."

"But—"

"Read it," said Judd, turning away.

I read it. It was difficult, in places, to separate Sam's confessions from Jeremiah's judgments. But later, with Judd's help and my own imagination, I was able to understand it completely. I could see Sam sitting with Jeremiah in the yard of his cabin under the locust trees, down there where the creek still rushes. Was Sam seeking a return to heavenly grace while morbidly relishing his sins? Was Jeremiah trying to return him to grace while equally relishing his sins—or why did he document them so thoroughly? I remember its beginning . . .

I, Rev. Jeremiah Baker, do here set down the Testimonial of Brig. Genl. Samuel O. Drummond, his Years of Sin placed before the Judgment of Almighty God through Jesus Christ Our Saviour. He comes to my house at evening & speaks of the Past but will not Pray with me. Thence I come to the peace of my Church & by candle light Pray for him & enscribe what he hath told me that I may read back to him the enormity of his Sins when they are all set down. Then shall he surely throw himself on the Merciful Judgment of Almighty God . . .

The imagination fleshens skeletal facts.

There was a last feather of smoke in a clearing arched by blue sky and then the trail plunged down. The Cumberland Road from the former State of Franklin to a bluff on the Cumberland River was opened in September, 1788. In the spring of 1790 a man and a woman, walking, with their belongings lashed on a horse, took to the road in the company of an undetermined number of others. The man's name was Nathan Drummond. His antecedents are unknown. The woman's name is unknown, but she was, presumably, his wife, for at some time on the hundred-and-eighty-mile walk across Cherokee country he conceived a child in her.

They came, eventually, to the place called Nashboro or Nashville where a few cabins and bark tents sprawled around a log courthouse, two taverns, two stores and a distillery. It was much as an earlier traveler of the road, named Andrew Jackson, had found it when he arrived in the preceding fall. Presumably the man, Nathan, began clearing land south of the town and feeding his woman and himself the game he killed. On February 1, 1791, there was born to the couple a son they named Samuel Obadiah. Or perhaps he named himself. For there is no existing record of his birth. We have only his own word as to the date of his birth and his name.

He told Jeremiah that his mother died when he was three months old and he remarked piously on her staunch moral character. His filial devotion, while touching, was spurious, since he was only three months old when she died and he did not know her name or he would have recorded it. But he wished it to be known that he was born good. Whatever evil he committed, he seemed to be saying, was the result of the world in which he lived. He made a point of his father having fought with Nolichucky Jack and other leather shirts at the Cowpens, and then, he told Jeremiah, "When I was 3 yrs. my father went West into the Indian Territory & disappeared." Seldom has a parent been dismissed so laconically.

He was left in the care of a settler named Bowen or Bowman, who had a blockhouse north of the river. There was a bad season when he ate only potatoes and slept on leaves, when the settler cut open the crop of a hen that had eaten melon seeds laid out to dry and picked out the precious seeds and then sewed up the crop of the precious hen. There was a bad night when Cherokees raided and he smelled the sweat and urine of fear.

At the age of ten he was on his own, a stable boy employed in Nashville at Talbot's Tavern, which faced the square at the end of Market Street, overlooking the new stone courthouse, the jail and whipping post and stocks. Sam Drummond often stabled Andy Jackson's horse when the great man rode in to the courthouse or to tipple in Talbot's or enjoy the cockpit nearby. He slept on straw and grabbed what he could from the kitchen and dressed himself in whatever rags he could filch or find.

One spring day in 1803 he boarded a keelboat at Johnson's Landing under the bluff and put off for New Orleans with a consignment of cotton and skins. His wages were three dollars a month and keep. He did not reach New Orleans, however. The boat put in to Natchez and there, as Jeremiah zealously editorialized, dropping Sam's direct quotations, "One Timothy Buxton the Sweep Man led him into Carnal Pleasure & his Downward Path did begin. There he was led to a House Under the Hill & given up to a large Mulatto Woman."

Why our hero did not continue to New Orleans is not recorded. Neither do we know how he happened to be taken into the home of a certain Mr. Wilberforce, a planter, who lived a day's journey north of Natchez. He described him to Jeremiah as "a veritable Dandy, tall & elegantly attired, wearing leathern boots & fine ruffled lace at his throat. He was in truth my Saviour & represented Opportunity such as can come to any in Our Country. I am always telling my two fine sons to keep an eye open to Opportunity . . ."

Sam Drummond lived with Mr. Wilberforce and his wife for five years. Mr. Wilberforce taught him to shoot with pistol and rifle and gave him a horse to ride. Mrs. Wilberforce taught him to read and write and cipher. "They kindled in me the desire to be a Gentleman, such as after much travail I have become. I learnt Honour, which permits judgment of Self only by your Peers, they being none but Ladies & Gentlemen. I learnt the Code, which demands rectification of wrongs on the Field of Honour & prefers death to Dishonour."

Jeremiah, of course, could not let pass such an opportunity for moralizing. Parenthetically he remarked, "I remonstrated at length this evening with Genl. Drummond over the Code, which is but a form of Murder. He would not budge." Again, Jeremiah remonstrated with him when Sam Drummond said that after five years he left the Wilberforces at night without farewells and rode away up the old Chickasaw Road, a route of dark legends which by that time was often called the Natchez Trace. "I ask him why did he leave so? He would not tell me. I tell him that if he would be Saved he must confess all his Sins and throw hisself on the Mercy of Almighty God through me His Minister. He say it nothing. It being dark then, my good wife come to the door & says she going to bed. Genl. Drummond left, bidding us both good night most civilly, & I come here to the Church to Pray & write by candle light. He is a fine Gentleman & must be Saved."

In his evening conversations with Jeremiah, Sam Drummond passed lightly over the next three years spent trading in the Creek Territory. He lets us see him next in 1811 as he rode up to the Nashville Inn from Knoxville. He reports a fatuous conversation with Andrew Jackson when he sought a commission in the Tennessee Militia from the politically appointed Major General. Although his report of the conversation may be meretricious, there hangs in the library of Burning Brook today a framed letter, dated December 4, 1811 and signed by Governor William Blount, commissioning Samuel Obadiah Drummond a Captain in the Army of Tennessee.

Shortly thereafter Captain Sam Drummond steps under the proscenium of recognizable history. His grasp of history was small, however, in the remarks recorded by Jeremiah. He made much of the sense of patriotism that led him to seek a commission. He also made much of the fact that he was seeking his "Fortune, & whither Destiny led my steps Fortune did not always await." Certainly it is obvious that he believed his captain's commission would not impair his search for fortune, and he was mightily fond of a saber he obtained in Knoxville and a red sash and buff coat with which a Murfreesboro tailor outfitted him.

Attired thus, he entered the operations in the northwest. The perspective of time makes those operations seem almost comic. They were real enough, however, to the soldiers led from one military disaster to another by names now long forgotten: Dearborn, Hull, Van Rensselaer, Smythe, Wilkinson, Harrison, Winchester. In Tennessee, Andrew Jackson beseeched and cursed a dull-witted government which failed to see that only he could win victory in Canada. Ignoring the untried genius of the Hermitage, the Government sent Brigadier General James Winchester north with two of Jackson's regiments. At the head of one company rode Captain Sam.

Brigadier General William Henry Harrison, to whom Winchester relinquished command, had got himself in a mess. By October, 1812, the forces of the speechifying Harrison, who had pledged himself to recover the entire lost northwest, were fouled across half of Ohio. In three widely separated columns they lolled in a great crescent from Defiance on the Maumee to the tributaries of the Sandusky. They were plagued by the immemorial difficulties of short supplies, ill discipline, dysentery, ignorance of terrain and general indifference to the outcome of the whole campaign. But the immediate difficulty was the great swamp that stretched from the Auglaize River on the left to the Sandusky on the right athwart Harrison's intended victorious passage. It seemed impassable as the Alps. Harrison couldn't get through it and he didn't know how to go around it. He sank back, writing letters and delivering speeches to anyone who would listen, and a good many of the militia had a bellyful and trailed off home.

Captain Sam, with Winchester at Defiance, recalled that "We had no flour or beef in December & we eat our horses & hickory roots. Scores died each day of the typhus & there was no discipline. The Genl. was an easy-natured man & I darent discipline my men elst I lose them all." On December 20 Harrison bestirred himself to concentrate his forces. The Tennesseans and Kentuckians and the 17th U.S. Infantry under Winchester were ordered to prepare sleds and move to the Maumee Rapids. They did so, fortifying themselves on the north bank, and awaited the arrival of Harrison.

Winchester thus found himself with about thirteen hundred men in an extremely exposed position far from any reinforcements and about forty-five miles from two strong concentrations of his enemy. While his men were raising log works at the Rapids two Frenchmen drifted into camp from Frenchtown on the River Raisin, which was thirty miles forward and within the British lines. Frenchtown, they said, was held by only a couple of hundred Canadian militiamen and a hundred Indians.

"We were eager for a dash at Frenchtown," said Captain Sam. "We come North to fight but we had only sat & starved & died & we would Fight elst why had we come at all. So I spoke up boldly at a Council of War which most Officers attended. I was of persuasive tongue & found my sentiments echoed on all hands, espy. Col. Allen of the Kentucky Rifles, & so we carried the day & the Genl. agreed we would have a go at it." Far from being critical of Winchester's incredible action, Sam gloried in having helped precipitate it. Winchester, with a weak detachment, proceeded to split his forces further. Off to Frenchtown through the blue-shadowed snows and leafless timber of winter marched six hundred and sixty riflemen commanded by Colonels John Allen and William Lewis of Kentucky. They moved onto the ice, along the shore of Maumee Bay and Lake Erie, until nightfall. At two o'clock the next afternoon, January 18, they saw smoke rising from log cabins along the River Raisin.

The men deployed in a long skirmish line at the forest fringe on the east bank and moved forward slowly as the Canadian militia on the west bank of the frozen river opened up with a three-pound howitzer. "It was the first time I & many heard a Piece in action," said Captain Sam. "I drew my Sword and cried, Follow me, Boys!" The troops passed over the frozen Raisin through the patter of small-arms fire. Men fell, wounded and killed, and the Canadian militia withdrew in good order, while the Indians covered their flanks. The Americans pressed them about two miles into the woods, until darkness fell, and then retired to Frenchtown.

Lewis sent a message to Winchester, saying he had Frenchtown and asking what he should do now. Winchester, having split his small force once, split it again and personally marched forward to the Raisin with two hundred and fifty men. Harrison, coming up to the Rapids the next day, found about three hundred riflemen and many sick huddled behind unfinished log works. Uncertain what his next move should be, Harrison sat down and wrote a letter to James Monroe.

When Winchester arrived at Frenchtown, he was mildly distressed to find his troops had taken up the most comfortable quarters they could find and had strung out a very thin picket line on three sides of the town on the western bank. Despite his distress, he ordered his reinforcements to bivouac outside the snake fence of the picket line and he personally retired to a house on the eastern bank. He figured it would be a good idea to withdraw, but he didn't know how they could get out the fifty-five wounded. A man came in and reported the enemy was preparing an attack in strong force, but everybody allowed he didn't know what he was talking about. The General said they'd better start getting out timber to raise a log work and then he went to bed.

At dawn on the morning of January 22 a force of six hundred Brittish regulars commanded by Colonel Proctor and about seven hundred Indians commanded by Chief Round Head appeared within musket range of the snake fence.

"We heard the skwaling of their fifes & by the morning light we see the winking of their brass & their green & scarlet uniforms as they formed into line. ——— the British, Boys, cried I, let's have at them . . ."

Rhetoric and blood and thunder along the River Raisin. Its fear and pain forgotten so many years later, the glory burst over Sam Drummond like a rocket and lighted the words Jeremiah put down. The British came with a bang-bang and the Indians whooped and scalped and the old General slipped and slid across the ice, waving his sword and hollering, "Hold up hyar, boys, hold up!" Jeremiah was the recorder of a tale that night rather than a moralizer.

It was a century before Judd and Drew moralized about it, placing Sam accurately in historic time and place and incident which he had not bothered to describe—doubtless because he did not understand it. They saw him clearly, as Jeremiah had not. A man in a brawl, brave enough, but without a trace of military genius. Shifty, however. Very shifty. Able to hide himself under a log as the Indians hunted the forest for scalps. Able to make his way through deep snows back to the Rapids. But uncritical of the fact that Harrison, terrified by the disaster, retreated fifteen miles from the Rapids. Unmindful and indifferent, too, that Proctor, as terrified in victory as Harrison in defeat, deserted his wounded prisoners and scurried thirty miles to the rear. Sam was convincing as well as shifty. Otherwise, how had he been able to detach himself from Harrison's army and talk himself into possession of a horse and ride back to Tennessee?

He must have been a mighty convincing talker to take in Jeremiah so completely. For pages the book that had started out to be Sam Drummond's confession of sin was simply his tale of derring-do in war.

He joined the cavalry force of Brigadier General John Coffee, that "strong, encircling arm" of Andrew Jackson. After the crimson war clubs dangled in the squares of many Creek encampments and Red Eagle rose to defend his land against the encroachment of the whites, Sam rode south with Coffee in September of 1813. He came to know the arid Georgia upland pine barrens and the Alabama swamps. He crossed the Raccoon Mountains to the Ten Islands of the Coosa River and in November he was at the massacre of Red Sticks at Tallushatchee, where no warrior escaped the inexorable law of frontier war.

He was one of the fifty-four men who answered Coffee's call at Emuckfaw Creek to go forward and try to flank the attacking Creeks, and, like his commander, he was wounded there. Jackson commended him for courage displayed at the Horseshoe Bend of the Tallapoosa where nearly eight hundred warriors were surrounded and slain. He was present at Fort Jackson when, in solemn council with the chiefs, his commander in chief stripped Indian allies and foes alike of twenty-three million acres and so destroyed the Creek Nation.

"Many of us who had fought & bled for these lands were much interested in them. I was in frequent communication with Mr. Davon of Knoxville who was forming a new Land Company . . ."

A major then, he was at Mobile and in Jackson's madcap dash on Pensacola. Coming to New Orleans, he was in each major development of the battle there.

> On that cold Jan. morning when a God-sent breeze lifted the mist we see by dawns light the pride of the British Army advancing toward our parapets. There was a hard frost in the night & in the dawn the cane stubble stood like silver spikes & across the field far as eye could see into the rising mist moved a solid mass of red tunics & white crossbelts. Off in the mist came the orange flashes of the British guns & our own answered, sending off such billows of smoke that it spoilt the aim of our riflemen who could see nothing. When the smoke cleared we see the British only 300 yds away & coming at a run, bayonets held at the charge winking & wavering in dawns ghostly light, for as I have told my sons, the bayonet is never steady in the charge despite the will to make it so but wavers in the strain of the advance.
>
> I rapped out the Orders Ready! Aim! Fire! Load! & the first rank stood down to reload & the second took its place & then the second rank stood down from the parapet & the third rank stood up to it. The solid British line grew thin but still it come on & the lines behind it was broken & jagged but they come on. O my Boys was good Boys, firing & reloading calm as you please as the British come on. Of a sudden I see a Splendid Figure in sash & cape ride

to the front, sword as light as a willowstick in his hand, beside him his aide on a black pony. I did not know then it was Sir Edward Pakenham himself but I knowed that he was a great man & a brave man, riding there before his thin front rank urging them on . . .

Remembered dreams of glory in the long evenings thirty years later. A Splendid Figure on horseback. The symbol of what Sam Drummond would be. The symbol of what the family believed he actually had been as the tradition grew.

But Jeremiah Baker was not a fool. He finally realized that he was being hoodwinked. He had fastened on Sam Drummond as a soul to be saved. He sought confession of sin and he was hearing a proud tale of glory. He protested strenuously.

This evening returned from my week's visit to Nashville for which Genl. Drummond kindly lent me a horse. The General called, in morose mood. I ask him, Brother Drummond what troubles you? He would not answer, but sat silent, smoking a cigar, as darkness fell. The moon was up early & he got up & I thought he was going to where his horse was tethered but he passed on to the road & paced there in the moonlight. I joined him & paced with him, waiting for him to say what troubled his Soul. At last he spoke, saying it had troubled him long.

While they paced in the road that evening Sam Drummond spoke of the wilderness north of the Ohio as it had been in the winter of 1813 after he left Harrison's army. In that year it still was coursed by the almost invisible highways of the Indians, whose time had nearly run out. For narrow roads had crept into the wilderness and beside the roads the clearings increased like threaded beads. When war came, the whites paused, peering ahead into the uncertainty. The Indians, dispossessed and seeking repossession, glared back. War parties of both sides raided and burned, killing and scalping. In the flux of war some whites and many Indians tried to maintain the ways of peace.

Somewhere north of the Ohio an almost invisible trail crossed a narrow track.

You can imagine Sam riding south along the track in the twilight of a winter day, head tilted against a keening west wind that skimmed the snow puddles. He was hungry and his horse was tired and he did not know if there was shelter this side of the Ohio ferry. The faint trail crossed and he did not notice it. Then his horse raised her head with pricking ears and suddenly his own woods-keen nostrils caught the scent of cooking meat. He pulled up and looked for sign of smoke or shelter, but there was no sign and no sound except the west wind rubbing the bare upper boughs. He rode on and the scent was gone. Turning his horse, he paced back to the scent and then he saw footprints in the snow at the crossing of the trail. He traced the party in the snow. One, two, three. Two and a half, really. For the feet of the third were small. Two men and a boy. He should go on, he knew, but he did not know how far it was to the Ohio and he smelled meat. Dismounting, he tethered his horse. His rifle at ready, he followed the footprints along the trail cautiously, up a draw and over a crest.

Someone spoke behind him and he whirled. An Indian stood there, an aging man, unpainted, head unshaven, a trader's thin blanket drawn about him. Sam covered him with his rifle. Slowly the Indian unfolded his arms, opening the blanket, and held up his right hand in the sign of peace. Sam lowered his rifle, but he looked about alertly. Then the Indian raised a cheap iron cross suspended on a chain about his scrawny old neck. So he was a Catholic Indian. From the Canadian East probably, but going West. Where was he going?

Sam tried his scant Creek on him, but the Indian did not understand. Perhaps he was an Ottawa or a Mohawk who understood French. Sam sniffed the meat in the air again and rubbed his belly. The Indian nodded and led the way into a hollow where a haunch of venison hung over a smokeless fire before a carefully concealed lean-to.

> Then I see the Indian was in trouble. His old squaw lay in the lean-to under a blanket with her belly all swelled up & her legs drawn up & the death look on her face. Moreover I see a girl who was young & most comely. I could not take my eyes off her, but she would not look at me.

Sam led his horse from the road and unsaddled her and stamped out a place in the snow for her to crop dead grass. He sat down by the fire and cut off chunks of unsalted venison with his knife after the Indian had tasted it first and nodded. He offered the girl a chunk of meat on the point of his knife, but she would not take it from him; she took meat only from the man who presumably was her father. And the old woman, who refused to eat, lay and watched, her black eyes gleaming in the firelight. As he wolfed down the meat, Sam thought that the old woman had gone as far as she could and waited now for death. The Indian could have left her, but he had not. He was stuck in a bad spot, near a road, where any passer-by could smell or hear his camp. That was why he had been watching the road. But watching it, oddly, unarmed. There by the fire were his bow and quiver. Sam knew that the Indian could have winged him in the back. But the Indian had watched unarmed and brought him to his camp and offered his hospitality.

By signs he tried to ask where they came from and where they were going. But all he could learn was that they had come far from the East and were going far to the West. When he'd eaten his fill, he got to his feet. He smiled at the girl and reached for her hand. She drew back. Doubtless grinning owlishly, he made the sign of sleep and pointed to the lean-to. She moved backward from the circle of fire-light. The Indian spoke, not to her, but to Sam. He held up the iron cross which hung from his neck.

"I fell to bargaining," Sam told Jeremiah, "for I could not set the girl from my mind. She was not the ordinary stumpy Indian squaw. Neither could I set from my mind that the Indians have no moral sense like us but let their women do what is expedient . . ."

We do not know exactly how it happened. We have Sam's word of how it happened, as he paced the clay road in Tennessee beside Jeremiah more than thirty years later, but we question his good faith. Certainly he was troubled. But was he sufficiently penitent to confess honestly? It's doubtful. For he was sly. One can see that he arrived at slyness naturally; without it there would have been many times when he might have been destroyed. Yet, knowing how he arrived at slyness does not enable us to condone him.

The Indian attacked him, he said, and in self-defense he drove his knife into him and killed him.

Though I hate Indians I felt a horror at what I done. I turned to the girl who had shrank down beside the old woman & I pulled her to me. I meant no harm as God is my witness but the great rage in which I live overpowered me & I cried out Love me, Love me, Love me for I had lived without love & I wanted to be loved. O, had she loved me I would have tooken her with me across the Ohio & into my own country & I would have found a place where we might live and love. But she stood against me like a young tree & would not love me. Of a sudden she moved fast & I see a knife flash. It cut me from temple to jaw. I cried out in pain & seized her throat in both hands & when I let go she was dead & the old woman never stopped her wailing. I packed snow on my wound & rode on in darkness. I have always said this scar on my face is a wound from the War. To those in the Southern Campaigns I let it be known my wound was rec'd in the North & to those in the Northern Campaigns I let it be known my wound was rec'd in the South. But that is how I rec'd my wound.

And Jeremiah, writing in the quiet of his church, added, "May God have Mercy on his Soul. But how can He unless the Genl. will repent of his Sins which are of Lust and Rage. . . ." Pray, Jeremiah urged him. Repent! Perhaps there were times when he did repent. If he did, however, Jeremiah does not record it.

Lust and rage drove him. And some of his lust spilled through Jeremiah, who was only mortal, as he set down with morbid relish some of Sam's enjoyment of women in New Orleans.

Aided by Jackson and Coffee, he obtained a lieutenant colonel's commission after the war ended. For six years he drowsed among the bayous and along the blue Gulf. He knew the monotonous routine of the small forts, punctuated by two occasions when he challenged under the Code for insults of unknown causes. On each occasion he was mollified by an apology. There came, finally, a march into Florida. He might have stayed there forever, watching the changing patterns of sunlight and rain on the pride of China trees, if it had not been for Captain Robert Torrey of Tennessee.

The Code demanded that I reply to a base insult by Capt. Robert Torrey at Pensacola. I issued the challenge thru my Exec Officer, Maj. Robertson. A friend of Torrey's interceded, saying he was young & soon would be going Home because of death in his family. I replied we could drop the Matter if Capt. Torrey made a public apology. Torrey replied he would see me in —— first. We met at dawn in a place above the town & fired simultaneously, Torrey's shot going wild & mine striking him over the heart. He expired 2 hrs later & I prepared my Resignation from the Army.

Sam Drummond followed the spring of 1821 north, drawn to the hills of Tennessee. His speculations in land had ended in failure, his assets included little besides a horse and a uniform with gold braid. "As I rode I pondered how I might recoup my Fortunes. Destiny led me . . ."

It would appear, however, that his own will rather than destiny led him to the home of Jocelyn Boyce, who had served with him in the Creek War. It could not have been coincidence that Boyce's large farm lay not far from the "plantation" of Martha Torrey, sister of Captain Robert Torrey.

On my first day at Boyce's I rode much in the vicinity of the Torrey Plantation & saw much potential in its spacious acres which were in disrepair.

In some respects that is the most chilling sentence in the record. The young man shot above the heart in Pensacola and the older man leisurely riding close to his home. What lay behind the insult delivered or imagined in Pensacola?

Shortly he penned a note to Martha Torrey, the inheritor of the land, since her father had died a couple of months before her brother: *Lt. Col. Samuel O. Drummond of the U.S. Army requests the Privilege of a Few Words with Miss Martha Torrey at her Convenience.*

The note, its ink faded, was found among her effects after she died. It was preserved by the family as evidence of the courtly gentility of Sam Drummond and of the enduring love that Martha bore her husband. For the family did not know that Samuel Drummond had killed Robert Torrey in a duel. Martha Torrey Drummond never spoke of it. Word traveled, however. There was a vague hint of scandal connected with Sam's resignation from the Army that persisted into the days of his grandson, Colonel Andrew Jackson Drummond, Jr. Probably that was why his grandson always spoke of Sam Drummond as a great gentleman and would show the note as evidence of it to anyone interested.

Apparently Sam never mentioned killing Robert Torrey until he told Jeremiah. Then he spoke with extraordinary candor.

Martha finally sent word that she would see him and he rode to her house:

> The house was not imposing at first view & quite unworthy of Miss Torrey's acreage, being two storeys of brick with a chimney at each end & lacking a portico. Yet it was pleasantly situated in white oak & beech trees which well could have surrounded a finer house. A Mammy led me into a small parlor where Miss Torrey sat on a settee with fanciwork on her lap. She was rather a plain young woman with brown curls over her forehead & a shawl about her, even tho it was a warm day. She did not extend her hand but only looked at me & said, Col. Drummond what is your business in this house? I dropped to a knee before her & said Madame I have resigned from the Army & traveled a thousand miles to seek your forgiveness. At this she burst into tears & it was some time til I could calm her.

Five months later Sam Drummond married Martha Torrey. Jeremiah expostulated with him those many years later:

I ask him did he not see the enormity of his Sin. Bow down, I told him, & worship the Lord & pray for His forgiveness. It will come to you, even as it came to David after his evilness toward Uriah & Bathsheba. Yet he only looked at me & I understood that he did not know the Book nor even the beginnings of knowledge, he was an ignorant man.

The last entry in the record of Sam's visits to Jeremiah apparently was written several evenings later.

Genl. Drummond was sorely troubled when he visited me to-night after returning from Nashville. The War with Mexico, de-clared in May, has been much on his mind. His elder son, who graduated from the Academy at West Point two years ago, has gone to it. His younger son, who graduated this year, will go. Now I believe he will volunteer also. He would not come to my house this evening but met me at the Church. I thought that now he wished Salvation, since he came to the Church. Yet when I spoke of it to him he turned on me greatly vexed. I answered him calmly & in truth felt sorry for him, he is such a perplexed & troubled man. Why do you drive at me so, Sir? he cried. And you Sir, I replied, why do you come to me if not for help? He fell silent, his head bowed, & I wished to be kindly. I spoke of his outer accomplish-ments, his family & plantation.

And Sam said to Jeremiah:

Now you speak sense. I have been good husband & father, my wife sits up there tonight a Lady in the new fine house I builded. I have increased the land & made it yield & made profit in cotton & slaves & tobacco. I have sat in the Legislature & become a Brig. Gen. of the Militia & my name is well spoken of in this my State. I have took what I found & done the best with it I could.

That was "the outer man," Jeremiah replied. But what of the "inner man," who loved his sons and his wife. What of the soul?
Sam Drummond cried:

What is the soul when it is not loved? I have took my pleasure in a hundred strange places but I am not loved. My wife does not & never has loved me. On the night of our marriage she locked her door on me & whilst I could have carried it off its hinges on my shoulder a Gentleman does not act so. I went below & drank heavy of whiskey which failed to dim my rage until I smashed a wall & nigh broke my fist. A week later I forced my way into her room & had my way with her & in my rage I cried out Love me, Love me. But she did not answer until later when she said, I only

276

can ever Hate you. It has been so always, I forcing myself upon her that we may be of family & our name increase, until I have give up & we seldom speak.

Jeremiah started to write, "There is—" The line is incomplete. That is the end of the record.

Chapter XXIII

When Drew had finished reading Jeremiah Baker's record of his conversations with Sam Drummond, he sat and stared out a window of the library.

I remember seeing the white-painted fences out there and a couple of fat steers in a field and leaves blowing across the yard. I smelled chicken frying for dinner and I heard old Celeste, the Negro maid, laughing as she swung through the pantry door, and I heard the tocking of the big clock in the corner. I could have awakened blind after years of sleep and known that I was at Burning Brook. And I thought, This isn't the Drummonds' place, it belongs to the Torreys.

Then Mildred came to the doorway and said, "Dinner's ready." She smiled at him. "Wake up and eat, dreamer."

He realized, as he got to his feet, that she'd called him before. You're lucky, Mildred, he thought, that you're not a Drummond. And then, What do I care about my great-great-grandfather? What does anybody care about his great-great-grandfather?

As he plunged a spoon into his fruit cup, he looked at Judd gravely and said, "Where on earth did you get it?"

"Get what?" asked Mildred.

Judd smiled at her. "He means Jeremiah Baker's record. He's been reading it."

"Oh?" She grew still. "Oh," she said.

"I came across it in New England," Judd said. "A coincidence. An almost incredible coincidence."

"It could have been faked," Drew said. "How do you know it wasn't?"

"I *know* all right." He looked at him quizzically. "Would you like to believe it was faked?"

277

Drew shrugged. "It doesn't matter to me. General Sam's dead and it all happened a long time ago."

"You mean it doesn't matter at all?" asked Mildred. "You don't care that he was—the way he was?"

"Yes, I care." He fell silent and ate.

He did care, though not to the extent of feeling depressed. The truth about Sam's character, which he had heard his father praise so glowingly, troubled him. He understood, however, why Judd wanted him to know the truth. His almost calling Avery Johnson's brother-in-law a black bastard, minor in itself, had been sufficient to impel Judd to a long-contemplated act. Judd wanted him to realize that— How would you put it? We are not who we think we are, Lord. If that wasn't in the Bible, it should be. There were responsibilities to living in this land of pride. Black could be as white as snow. And snow-white grew from black earth. There were responsibilities here. Things were not always what they seemed to be. Judd wished him to understand the dangers of pride and prejudice. And he did. But understanding did not make him comfortable. To the contrary, he felt uncomfortable. Yes, Judd wanted him to stay here, but he was trying to point out that there were responsibilities here too, this was not paradise.

"But why," he asked suddenly, "would General Sam admit all those things? It's not—credible."

Judd, his fork suspended, looked at him gravely. "You won't be satisfied? You won't simply take my word for it?"

"Why should he, Judd?" asked Mildred. "What you start you have to finish."

"All right," Judd said. "I'll tell you after dinner."

Celeste served them coffee in the living room. Mildred began knitting and Judd lighted a cigar.

"I advertised for it," he said.

"You *advertised* for it?"

Judd nodded. "I began teaching history at the University of Chicago in 1930. And I'd started working on a book. I wanted to do a big"— he made his tone wry—"definitive work on the effects of religion on the American frontier. And I also fell in love with a girl and wanted to marry her." He smiled at Mildred. "But in the course of research for my book—which I never finished—I came across some remarks by Henry Ward Beecher about Jeremiah Baker. I recognized the name at once, of course, from having read my grandfather's Civil War journal. Well, I'd always been fascinated by that reference of Grandfather's, which was so obviously a slip. And when I came across Baker's name in another context I got quite excited. I checked everywhere for further information about him.

"There was nothing. Only those references by Grandfather and Beecher. But it plagued me. Sheer curiosity. Or maybe suspicion. I smelled something and I wasn't sure what it was. Then I decided to send out some notices and ads. I tried to be smart about the notices. I identified myself and said I was working on a book about Jeremiah Baker. I offered to *exchange* information about him. No luck from a couple of ads in the Cincinnati papers, which is the largest city near Pendennis. I tried other places, like *The New York Times* Sunday Book Review. And then, after I'd given up ever hearing from anybody, *luck*. A letter from Providence, Rhode Island, written in an aged, shaky hand. But a prim hand and expensive note paper. It was signed by a woman named Melissa Carson. She sounded suspicious— but eager. She wanted to know whether I was a member of a Tennessee family of Drummonds. She said that when she was a young girl in Pendennis, she'd known Jeremiah Baker.

I wrote her, of course. It was like fishing. She *knew* something, I felt. I hit on the right bait. I said that my grandfather had spent many years hunting Jeremiah Baker and his *daughter*—which was a lie of sorts. But I was fishing. She wrote right back asking me to come to Providence and see her. I didn't have the money to go gallivanting around, but it was nearing the Christmas vacation in 1931 and"—he grinned—"we went."

Mildred smiled. "We were married and went to Providence on our honeymoon. He'd thought we couldn't afford to be married yet, but all of a sudden he decided we could afford to visit Providence. So we were married and went. I had a school friend living there. She told me who Melissa Carson was. She was in her eighties and widowed and her children dead. Her husband had owned cotton mills. Melissa was a character. Stubborn as steel. She lived in a salt-box on the hill in Providence and drove herself around in one of those electric cars. One of those high, square, glassed affairs you operated with a long bar. My friend said every policeman in Providence was scared to death of her."

"I could see why when I called on her for tea," Judd said. "A frail, white-haired woman. But her eyes. They were very dark and—aggressive. She was suspicious of me. *Why,* she wanted to know, would anybody want to write a book about Jeremiah Baker? I told her about my original project—and how I thought Jeremiah typified a kind of frontier preacher. She rocked a while, and then she said, 'Young man, you're just curious.' I admitted it. She said she'd known Jeremiah's daughter and Jeremiah in Pendennis when she was a girl. Then I told her that my grandfather had gone there looking for them after the Battle of Nashville and that he'd referred to Jeremiah's daughter as a Jezebel.

"She stopped rocking and leaned toward me and she asked in a low voice, 'Do you know *why?*' I confessed I didn't. She changed the subject. I thought what a waste of time my trip had been, how foolish ever to get involved with your ancestors. But as I was leaving, she handed me a package. 'Read this,' she said. 'You'll want to talk with me when you return it about four o'clock tomorrow afternoon.' It was Jeremiah Baker's record of Sam's confessions."

Mildred said, "He sat in our hotel room and held his head while he read it. He had me read it. I didn't really care what his great-grandfather had been, but I confess it rather chilled me."

"I decided it must be faked," Judd said. "I told Melissa Carson that the next afternoon. She said it was not. She'd known Hannah Baker, Jeremiah's daughter, and Hannah had given it to her years later just before she died. She said that Hannah was born in 1847 when Jeremiah was sixty-one years old and his wife, who was also named Hannah, was thirty-four. When Hannah was four years old, her mother died and Jeremiah raised the girl. I remembered her eyes filled with tears. He raised her with 'devotion and love and kindliness,' she said. When the girl was fourteen and Jeremiah thought he was dying, he gave her Sam's confessions.

"But how, I asked her, could my grandfather have known about this during the Civil War—or even cared? She rocked a while, and then she said she didn't know. She asked me about Burning Brook. I told her it had gone to rack, but it was still in the family. Then I said an odd thing, something that had been in my mind ever since reading Jeremiah's record. I told her that after reading about the *evil* at Burning Brook I somehow wished I could go back there and make it *good*. It was a curious feeling. Can you understand it?"

"Yes," Drew said slowly, "yes, I understand that, Judd." It was strange, he thought, that he had dimly felt the same way since reading Sam's confessions.

"Well," Judd said, "old Melissa looked at me and said, 'So you do believe this is the truth?' I told her that I did. Which was true. I believed it. She smiled and after a while she dismissed me. We went back to Chicago and"—he grinned—"I thought what a hell of a way to spend a honeymoon. What a waste of time.

"In April a law firm contacted me. Melissa Carson had died.

A young lawyer came to see me. He brought me Jeremiah's book, sealed, and told me Mrs. Carson had bequeathed me five thousand dollars in her will. I was stunned. When I opened the sealed package, which contained the notebook, I found a letter."

Judd got to his feet leisurely and left the room. When he returned, he handed Drew a letter and said, "Read it."

On stationery which bore the name of Melissa Carson she had written:

DEAR MR. DRUMMOND,

I offer you a few memories, gleaned from my girlhood friend, Hannah Baker.

You must often wonder why Jeremiah Baker would give his daughter this record of Sam Drummond at the age of fourteen. People are not rational. They can only be, at best, reasonable. It seemed reasonable to Jeremiah to tell her the truth because he believed he was about to die. The desire for confession is strong in everyone. Jeremiah was seventy-five and he'd had a heart attack. They were very poor. You cannot understand what it was like to be poor in a hamlet like Pendennis, Ohio, in the 1860's. Jeremiah had quit preaching. He did not even attend church. He tried a little schoolteaching and clerking in a country store. The things that had happened to him had been too much. He was not Job. But he had, as he approached death, an overwhelming desire for the truth. He wanted the ledger to balance. He wanted Hannah to know that she was not his daughter. Her father was Sam Drummond . . .

Drew, blinking, looked up at Judd.
"Read it," Judd said.

. . . Jeremiah told her that he knew he could not have been her father. Her mother had confessed to him that Sam Drummond had been the father. You should know, too, Mr. Drummond, that Jeremiah forgave his wife. He was a good man. It is not pleasant to reflect on the evilness of Sam Drummond, but reflect we must. Jeremiah's wife was young and comely and each evening Jeremiah went to his church to pray and write. . . .

While Sam, thought Drew, returned to Hannah Baker. He must have seen and desired her as he rode about the countryside, as he had seen and desired Martha Torrey's land. An unregenerate schemer who must have taken gleeful satisfaction in his plan.

. . . The record has reverberations, Mr. Drummond. Even while Sam Drummond was sinning, he wished to confess his past sins. Black as he was, he still had the glimmerings of a conscience. Yet

281

his apparent bravery was a form of cowardice. At the very end, when he realized Hannah was going to have a child, he simply ran away. The Mexican War was his excuse. He volunteered and ran off to it as fast as he could go.

I was very interested in your grandfather's remark about Hannah—his half sister—being a Jezebel. She was a pretty girl, a remarkably pretty girl, though not a lady as a lady was then defined. Jeremiah had given her much more book-learning than most girls then had. But she had to go to work as a hired girl on a farm nearby. The people on that farm were very kind to her. Remember that. Remember that in remote and unhappy places like Pendennis there are kind people. Jeremiah did not die immediately, as he had expected to. He lived on and she took care of him as best she could while she worked as a hired girl at that farm nearby. But she knew the secret and she was bitter. She felt cheated. She wanted what most girls want: to be somebody. On Christmas Day, 1864, she read in a Cincinnati paper about the Battle of Nashville, which had been won ten days before. She read the name of General Andrew Drummond and she knew who he was. Her half brother. He owed her something, she felt. So she schemed her way to Nashville.

That wasn't very hard for Sam Drummond's natural daughter. She was only seventeen, but she was quite fearless. And pretty, too, as I have said. She left in her best clothes and along the way she told a carefully made-up story about going to Nashville to find her wounded brother. People were most helpful. She made her way to General Drummond quite easily.

Your grandfather was a tall, proud and handsome man, Mr. Drummond—so, at least, his half sister told me. On sight she was —quite taken with him. And it seems fair to say now that he must have been rather taken by her since he called her a Jezebel. But he was most proper. A real gentleman. You must understand that. Still, she found herself quite shy when she identified herself as the daughter of Jeremiah Baker, whom your grandfather had met once at Burning Brook. Remember, she was a country girl, only seventeen—but she was, she thought, in love with him on sight. And then she was overwhelmed by the enormous sinfulness of her feeling so. She remembered the story of Tamar and David's son, Amnon. She was afraid and she blurted out her story to General Drummond. She asked him for money to help Jeremiah, who was sick, she said, though she wanted money for herself too. She wanted— It doesn't matter now.

General Drummond became very angry and said he did not believe her. She was afraid and fled back to Pendennis. But since you've told me that General Drummond traveled all the way to

Pendennis I can see he must have wondered, after all. I believe now that he was attracted to her—and frightened and troubled. He did not find them in Pendennis because Hannah took Jeremiah to Cincinnati immediately upon her return from Nashville. She was afraid that her half brother might come looking for her and she could not forget the story of Amnon and Tamar. Jeremiah Baker died two days after they reached Cincinnati. In time Hannah married a man of means and left Ohio and never returned.

Below her signature there was a date about a month later and a few more lines written in a tremulous hand.

MR. DRUMMOND:
I have thought upon my letter for a month and now I do not find the truth painful. You will receive it after my death, whenever that may come. You will also receive a small bequest because I like you. I hope you will use it to improve Burning Brook. Your grandfather spoke so warmly of the place that day in Nashville—before I identified myself as his half-sister. You see, I was born Hannah Baker.

Drew stared at a car droning along the blacktop road beyond the fields. A shaft of sunlight, breaking through the clouds, glinted on its metal. It disappeared, but he continued to stare after it, wishing dimly that he could go away as swiftly.

"You came back," he said dully to Judd. "Even though you knew the beginnings of this place, you wanted to come back."

"Yes. We had a variety of reasons. One—not the only one, mind you, but one—was the vague wish to make this a—better place."

They had succeeded, Drew thought. They had not just created a productive farm, a comfortable rural retreat; they had become known in the countryside as people who worked for any good and just cause, whether or not it was a popular cause. Thinking of this, Drew remembered the image of himself he had conceived only that morning: the sensual country squire, the rustic rationalizer. It was so like the way in which General Sam must have visualized himself that he wanted to shudder.

"You realize," Judd said slowly, "that your father doesn't know the truth about General Sam. I wish you'd never tell him. It would hurt him. There's nothing wrong in being hurt if it does you a little good, but I don't think it would do Jack any good. I know it wouldn't."

"I suppose not. Father's always been a great one for the family tradition and he just couldn't stand the truth. After all, it's mainly the tradition that made him what he is."

"You're wrong," Judd said. "Your father made himself. He's a prime example of a self-made man. He simply won't admit it, even to himself. He's always had great virtues—intelligence, tremendous loyalty, a real feeling for justice, a strong sense of obedience. So obedient that when Father told him he was going to the Academy, he went to the Academy. But don't ever think your grandfather made your father—except in reverse."

"Except in reverse? What do you mean?"

Judd stared at another car passing on the road. He sighed and said, "Your grandfather was a drunk, Drew. Not a tragic figure, mind you, though he made himself an object of great self-pity. You remember hearing often enough that story of Teddy Roosevelt and him in the Spanish-American War. Mother told me once that because he didn't get to the war he hit the bottle hard. She wanted to believe that was why he drank. But I don't know, I doubt it. It takes more than a single incident to create a drunk. Mother loved him and kept him going. If it hadn't been for the thousand and one ways she bolstered him, he'd surely have been eased out of the Army. He'd never have made his colonelcy if it hadn't been for the First War when the Army was so desperate for experienced old housekeepers."

I remember that the truth about Grandfather hit me hard. I was surprised that it did because I'd always believed I didn't care anything about the family background. But apparently I did care, for I began counting over the Drummonds and wondering if I was as bad as the worst of them.

"From the time Jack and I were youngsters we recognized how weak Father was behind all his bluster," Judd said. "As we grew older we wondered, from small incidents, if he didn't have a streak of cowardice. At least I wondered. And I know that Jack did, even though he wouldn't admit it. I mentioned it only once to him, when we were in our teens. He jumped up, his face actually pale, and I remember he muttered, 'I don't know, Judd. I don't want to talk about it. I don't ever want to *think* about it.' And we never spoke of it again.

"My point about your father is simply this. He received most of the impetus to become what he has in a kind of recoil from *his* father. I don't say that Jack hated Father. As a matter of fact, in later years he was always very kind to him, much kinder than I. He was simply determined to be as unlike him as he could possibly be. So determined

284

that I don't think he'd had a half-dozen drinks by the time he was thirty. So determined that he set out to be the best soldier possible.

"I've told you before how he won the D.S.C. in the Argonne doing that foolish and really unnecessary thing against those two German machine-gun nests. But I haven't told you before *why* he did it. He's never once mentioned it to me, but I know why. It was the one thing his father was most unlikely to have done in the Argonne Forest."

Judd looked thoughtfully at the dead cigar in his fingers. "Action and reaction, coil and recoil. That's the Drummonds. You noticed that General Sam didn't have anything good to say about his father. And you've seen that the first Andrew Drummond obviously was prepared to believe the worst about *his* father, General Sam. And I can tell you for a fact that my father, for some reason, had little use for *his* father, the first Andrew Drummond, but was forever rhapsodizing his grandfather, General Sam, whom he never saw and about whom he actually knew nothing. Now you know what a poor opinion Jack and I had of our father, but you have heard us extol our grandfather, whom we never saw. You know how you have sometimes felt about your father, but do you remember how you used to plague me with interested questions about your grandfather when you were a child? So we go. I hope that your sons love you deeply some day. I say I *hope*. It's too easy for a man to judge his father, as you judge yours and I have judged mine. It's easy—and futile. The important thing is how are you going to judge yourself?"

I began, then, to judge myself. I did not want to stay at Burning Brook. Judd and Mildred had come to terms with it; they'd lived it and made it. But I had not. I had not worked my passage to any place, least of all Burning Brook. I did not want to return to college. I knew I never would return to the one civilian trade I'd ever practiced, the advertising trade. Father, with his strange facility for entering my life at crucial times, came to Burning Brook the following week. He had returned from Germany for reassignment. He made me feel that I had best judge myself as a soldier. So I went back to the Army. For there was no place else for me to go. I would be a good soldier. . . .

Chapter XXIV

And now I have been a good soldier. I've worked my passage, perhaps even back to Burning Brook. But I cannot go there because it is Father's place. And the Army? That belongs to Father too. The difficulty, the tragic difficulty, of the sons and the fathers has been explained to me. My mind understands it but my heart is not big enough to encompass it when Father tries so hard to make me be him rather than myself.

He stood on the balcony, watching the setting sun of this seemingly endless day shine brightly on Castello di Falcari. The rain had passed and now the castle gleamed brightly on its high hilltop, as if it had been washed. From the library came the sound of Jane typing, slowly and hesitantly.

Going inside, he paused in the library doorway. Jane started and looked around at him, and he saw with consternation that she had been crying.

"Haven't you had it for one day, Jane?" He held out a pack of cigarettes to her.

"No." She turned quickly to her typewriter.

He lighted a cigarette and sat down, wondering what troubled her. He would not ask; there was little sense in a man asking a woman why she cried because, if and when she wanted him to know why, she would give a false reason and expect him to guess the truth.

Her fingers faltered and two keys jammed. She raised her hands to her face. When she faced him, eyes filled with tears, he was holding out a cigarette again. "Thanks," she said unsteadily as he lighted it.

"Take a break," he said. "Take ten. Put it away for the day and forget it. It's a hopeless job anyway."

"It's *not*," she said. "He—he has so much to say. His—his feeling for the past and the family is wonderful. . . ."

But he doesn't know the facts, Drew thought, because he became so set in his idealistic notions that we didn't want to tell him the truth.

"He's been a soldier all his life," she said, "and it's unfair to expect him to use words as if— Don't you see, Drew?" Her eyes appealed to his.

"Up to a point, Jane. But Father's trying to parlay it too far. He's trying to find something—esoteric in the commonplace fact of a family. Everybody has had one. Psychiatrists these days urge you to forget your family background as much as possible and—adjust. To me Father's talk about the past is an attempt to justify his—his own unhappiness."

She lowered her gaze. "He is unhappy. I can see it." Looking up at him, "He needs somebody—"

Yes, he needed somebody who loved him. Like Sam Drummond, he must have often privately cried for someone to *Love me, Love me.* Pitying him suddenly, he wondered, How can I comfort him without being exactly what he wants me to be? Looking at Jane, he thought, She might have been able to do it. If she—if I—if he—

"Don't you see," she said, "that he's doing all this for you? He wants you to—to take pride in who you are and what you are."

It was time, he thought, that he got out of this room. She appealed to him too strongly. She made him think he was young again and ready to begin for the first time. Although statistically thirty-one, he felt very old. Too old to begin for the first time. Too old ever to see the world as she now saw it. But she and her view worked a strange appeal on him. So it was time he got out of there. He'd better go looking for Marcia who never could begin for the first time either.

He got to his feet and she looked at him in surprise, unable to understand why he was leaving so suddenly. Stick around, Jane, he thought. Wait a while. Give me a little time to think.

When he passed into the living room he was relieved to see that Marcia was not there. Then he heard his father's voice in the hall.

"Just set it down in the usual place, Harry." General Drummond came through the doorway. He looked more cheerful than he had an hour ago at five o'clock. The reason was apparent when Harry appeared behind him bearing a tray of Martini ingredients.

"It's very early for a drink under the abominable customs of this country," General Drummond said. "But I'm going to have a quick one." He cocked his head at Drew. "Will you join me?"

He didn't want a drink, but he nodded.

Did the mere anticipation of a Martini relax his father? He would have been outraged if anyone had called him alcoholic, yet sometimes it seemed that he merely existed from sunup to sundown, when, briefly, he came alive. But what else was there for him? Had Grandfather felt that his life was empty too, and was that why he'd drunk so heavily?

"I used to make 'em three to one and then four to one," the General said. "And then one day in Washington a friend of mine made me a five to one. And so it's been ever since." He dropped ice into the pitcher. "But there was a good reason for it—at least that first time in Washington. It was immediately after the Germans surrendered."

"I remember," Drew said. "They flew you back to Washington and you thought you might be going to the Pacific."

It had been shortly before the time his face began to twitch. Suppose he said, "Father, did you know that I sometimes have a twitching face?" What would his father say? "Nonsense," probably. He'd probably say, "A cold must have settled in the facial nerve," and go on pouring gin.

"Ah, Jane"—General Drummond looked up, smiling at her, as she came from the library—"just in time. Will you join us?"

She looked at him oddly. As if, Drew thought, she wanted to stay and felt she must not. "No, thanks," she said. "Later. I want to change."

They watched her go and then their eyes met hurriedly and General Drummond busied himself stirring.

"I remember your telling me afterwards that you saw Mother on that trip back to the States," Drew said.

He stopped stirring. "It's curious you should remember that."

"I thought it was curious that it happened."

He filled two glasses and only ice remained in the pitcher.

"I thought maybe there was going to be a—reconciliation."

He handed Drew a glass and raised his own and said, "To you." He sipped his drink reflectively and said, "No, nothing like that. When Dorothy divorced me that was the end as far as I was concerned. But she wrote that she wanted to see me if I returned. Something urgent."

Something, thought Drew, that's none of my business.

General Drummond muttered, "I am smoking too much," and then he took out a cigarette and lighted it. He sat down and crossed his legs. "As a matter of fact, it concerned you." He frowned at his drink. "I never mentioned it. But a lot of water has run over the dam since then, it's a long time ago. I know it doesn't make any difference to you now. And sometimes, when you're inclined to think harshly of your mother, remember that she's always had your best interests at heart. Do you remember that girl, I can't think of her name?"

Drew, standing, carefully set his drink on a table. "Eileen? Do you mean Eileen Gannon?"

288

"That's the one," said General Drummond. "The little Irish girl from Orange. Well, your mother was greatly alarmed because you were engaged to her. She wanted to see it broken up."

Drew lifted his glass and stared at it. "What did you do, Father?"

"Nothing."

His tone was too casual, Drew thought.

"You won't find me going around busting up romances."

And now his tone was too defensive.

"I didn't really do anything, Drew. I had two days in New York and I agreed with your mother that we'd better—that it might be a good idea to go out there to Jersey and—and meet the girl. So I telephoned out first and got a car from Governor's Island and your mother and I tooled out there . . ."

He could see it. The Army limousine driven by a sergeant pulling up to that dingy house, the distinguished general with stars on his shoulders and bars on his chest stepping out with the proud southern lady, the frightened faces of Eileen and Mrs. Gannon behind the lace curtains. What did he mean he didn't do *anything?*

"You were well out of it, Drew. And I don't mean just because they were poor. There's nothing dishonorable in being poor. And not just because they were Catholic. A lot of my best friends are Catholics. But I don't think a Protestant can ever marry a Catholic happily and I think a true Catholic wouldn't marry a Protestant. . . ."

Well, General, she didn't. Not because I was a Protestant. But because you and Mother went there in all your glory and looked at them askance.

"It doesn't matter now. We called in all courtesy and tried to talk. It was pretty hard to make conversation with them. That's the point I'm trying to make. There was no—common interest."

And it was the point that you and your divorced lady were careful to make to them, General, when in your foxy wisdom you saw that Eileen was sensitive and the Gannons timid and uncertain. Because of you, my wonderful parents, I lost Eileen.

"Well," said General Drummond, "you were lucky. It's all over now."

"Yes, it's all over now," he muttered. Lifting his glass, he drained it and strode from the room.

He found himself in his bedroom, thinking, *Sometimes, when you're inclined to think harshly of your mother, remember that she's always had your best interests at heart.* Swearing, he flung himself on his bed and lighted a cigarette. It could not have been only his mother's doing. His father had plotted with her. Together they had had a sure instinct of how to do it, his mother furnishing exact intelligence on the nature of Eileen and the Gannons, his father planning and leading the bold stroke. If that did not work, they must have agreed, they'd try something else. The fact that they were divorced meant nothing to them then; all that had been important was that they believed the *boy* and the *name* in social peril. Unquestionably they had not protested the marriage to the Gannons. They had known that if they handled the situation carefully the Gannons would protest the marriage. They had given Eileen and her parents the opportunity of saying, in effect, "It will not work." And Eileen, within a day or two, had decided it would not work. She had returned the ring and written him the letter in which she'd said she was marrying someone else, thereby saving the General and his divorced wife the necessity of breaking it up in some other manner. Eileen could not have been in love with anyone else when she wrote him; she merely had known that she would find someone—Lord, anyone. At the time, and ever since, the General had been thoroughly convinced of the righteousness of his act. So convinced that he had not felt much hesitation in mentioning it now.

His father was shrewd. He knows that after eight years I'm not in love with Eileen, Drew thought. I'm not carrying the torch for her now. But because I do not love her now does not make what happened then of no consequence. That, however, was the sort of truth that eluded his father.

After a while he became annoyed with himself for lying there in his room like a hurt child. He did not, after all, now love Eileen. Why he had lost her had been revealed to him, but it was not a great revelation of his father's and mother's characters. They had acted most consistently with his knowledge of them. It had always been so, and it would be so as long as they lived.

Getting up slowly, he took a shower and dressed. When he started downstairs he suddenly felt he could not face his father. Not for a while. Not for another of those monotonous Martini sessions. He went down to the ground floor and through the port into the castle bailey where sheep grazed in the lengthening shadows of the walls.

"Hey!"

He turned at the sound of Marcia's voice. She sat on a huge flat stone where Harry had spread out material for a ship model. He crouched on his heels beside the stone, sandpapering a bit of wood and staring raptly up at her.

"Harry's making me a boat," she said.

A dream-boat, Drew thought. Harry had dreams too, and they were not simply of boats along the shores of the Antipodes. You could trace them in his expression as he looked at her. The lovely woman in slacks and sweater on the rock, sculpted and nude in Harry's Antipodean dreams. Then, looking at her, he thought, Why see her through Harry when I see her so clearly myself?

Harry glanced at him, not altogether pleased to see him. "Good evening, sir."

"Hi, Harry." He hunkered down on his heels beside him and stuck a blade of grass between his teeth and looked up quizzically at Marcia.

She smiled at him gravely, quite aware of men's dreams. "You'll be late for the cocktail hour."

"I may miss it altogether," he replied. "I'm tired of cocktail hours."

"And so am I."

"Me too," Harry said. "I mean, ma'am, I've gone on the wagon."

"When?" asked Drew.

Harry looked at him deadpan. "Last night."

They talked aimlessly until she said she was going to dress for dinner. She vaulted lightly off the stone and they watched her walk away admiringly. They did not stir and they did not speak. They sat upon their heels as Harry shaped a sailing ship; they could sit thus comfortably for as long as an hour.

The boy had seemed a bit miffed, General Drummond thought after Drew left the living room. Perhaps he'd been unwise to mention the incident to him. Yet it had happened a long time ago and he obviously did not love the girl now, if he had ever loved her. It was incredible that he could have wished to marry her. That dingy house, and those narrow streets all leading nowhere. She had been a pleasant girl, but not the girl for Drew. Going there with Dorothy had been an unpleasant assignment. But he *had* to go to try to save Drew. The girl realized her inadequacy. Even she must have known that the breed counted. It need not be famous, naturally, but there must be a strong breed to win the important races. There must be a tradition of winning. And she simply had not had it.

So, regrettably, it had been necessary to eliminate the girl. To save Drew, to keep him in the Army, to make him fulfill the promise of the tradition. But then, thought General Drummond, I somehow failed him there in Germany after the War. I did everything I could, but I could not make him see the wisdom—even the downright necessity—of a service career. I must not fail him again.

He sipped his Martini and sighed. A red wave of weariness washed upward from his knees and pressed about his chest while he waited fearfully, staring at the glass trembling in his hand. Then it was gone, up and out, and he sat lethargically, the trembling of his hand stilled. Gone, but it would return. For an instant he'd been afraid. If only he could rest, it might be a long time returning. But he could not rest. The task was not done; it was scarcely begun. God give me a little time, he thought. God? He smiled to himself. I don't think that I believe in Him, and it would be more graceful of me if I did not keep calling on Him. Especially now. But the job was not done. Drew gave no sign yet that he comprehended his responsibility to stay in the Army, his truly enormous responsibility.

He heard the click of heels on the stairs. Jane's footsteps. He drained his glass and looked at the door expectantly. Then she came toward him, smiling, and a small bubble seemed to burst in him. It was alarming. No, it was human. But Drew must be inhuman not to see . . .

He was on his feet, speaking cordially, grateful for the preoccupation of mixing Martinis. She stood near him and her perfume penetrated the smell of gin. Gin and perfume. It reminded him, irrelevantly, of Dorothy. Most irrelevantly. Or was it? If only Dorothy had been like Jane. But she hadn't been, and so he had stricken her from the record. Courage, he thought dimly, stirring the drink. Above all, courage.

He handed Jane her glass and raised his own to her and said something. He was not sure what he said, for he suddenly was bemused, close up, by the pupils of her eyes. The word, he believed, was patulous. They seemed to spread widely, and around that infinitesimal detail surely was created her remarkable beauty. It was a crazy notion. He wished that he had not looked at her so closely. For she had observed his look and was gazing at him oddly.

Then she was making kind remarks about the glut of words he'd poured forth today, her mind winnowing all that chaff for a few kernels which he despondently believed she would not find. Oh, he was full of irrelevancies today. When she questioned him about Burning Brook, he realized that he might never see it again, and that thought, more than any other of the day, depressed him. But he didn't show it. Naturally. He heard his voice flowing warmly. He was even mildly amusing about the fact that he had been named to membership on the board of directors of a large corporation in Chicago. It was the fashion these days, he told her, to appoint retired generals and admirals to boards of directors. Thus far he had functioned only once. A company airplane flew him from Nashville to Chicago where he attended two meetings and merely listened, and when they had lunched and dined him for two days, the company airplane flew him back to Nashville. It was a dull and empty business, he said, but it had become almost a civic obligation of retired generals to serve on boards of directors. His irony eluded her, for she dwelled on the subject as if it were somehow sad instead of mildly absurd.

As they finished another Martini, he wondered where Drew was. He should be here, he thought. And then he was glad that Drew had stayed away this long because it afforded him the enjoyment of talking relaxedly with her. Finally, somewhat bitterly, he realized that he could not afford that enjoyment. He did not have enough time. He should be utilizing precious time in subtly and skillfully turning her thoughts to Drew. But each remark about the boy that occurred to him he had made before.

Rising, she walked to the balcony doorway. He watched her, absorbed by her extraordinary gracefulness as she passed through the open doorway into the blue and golden glow of early evening. Drawn to her, he followed her slowly to the balcony, shedding weariness behind him and stepping lightly into the fresh rain-washed air. Neither seemed to lead the other. They were simply walking effortlessly and slowly in step along the balcony and then along the wall.

In the bailey below a sheep bleated.

"Look at that cute lamb."

She raised an arm to point. As he turned abruptly to look, his arm brushed against her. He felt the rounded strength of her arm and the soft warmth of her breast. Unaccountably they were turning, turning toward each other and he thought, Goddamn my heart, this is it. And reaching out, as if to support himself, his arms went around her. He felt her arms pass around him, as if she too needed support. Dimly he saw her raised face, the blue and patulous eyes half-closed, her lips parted. Bowing his head, he kissed her.

He raised his head quickly, as if to rise above the dreadful racing of his heart, and she said tremulously, "I love you, General Drummond."

My name, he thought vaguely, is Jack; she doesn't even call me by my name. And then, stunned by the total rout of his plans, he dropped his arms and stepped back from her. Reaching out blindly, she rested a hand against the parapet, breathing quickly, her head

293

lowered. But this, he thought, can turn into a victory for me. Then his heart knocked his chest like a mailed fist and he remembered that nothing was possible for him now. He did not even have a present, let alone a future. He was finished. If only she had not said she loved him, there might still be some way to salvage something.

Leaning against the parapet, he stared down. With growing horror he saw that there was absolutely nothing left. For Drew and Harry stood down there, staring up at them, witnesses to this tragedy. Drew had seen. But, he thought wildly, he does not *see*. He does not understand. He would call him up immediately to explain the incredible folly. But as he opened his mouth, Drew turned away quickly, his head lowered. He tried to cry after him, but he had no breath.

He turned to Jane, not looking at her, speaking past her. "It's an impossible situation. You will forgive me. You'll have to leave immediately."

She uttered a low cry and turned from him, walking away, and then suddenly running.

Leaning over the parapet, he tried to shout at Harry. But he could only form the name with his lips and whisper.

Harry sprang up the stone stairs and raced along the wall to him. "General! You take one of your pills!"

"Listen to me," General Drummond muttered. "You will help Miss Raleigh get her things together and drive her to Florence immediately. Come to my room and I'll have a check for you to give to her. I don't want to see her again."

"General—"

"You heard me, Goddamn you!"

"Yes, sir." Harry's right hand was half raised in a salute before he checked himself and trotted away.

General Drummond walked haltingly toward his room, plucking at the crumbling masonry of the parapet.

Drew started up the stairs slowly. His feet moved faster until he was racing. In his room he collected his things and packed his bag.

He heard footsteps in the hall and someone knocked on his door. "Drew!" His father's voice.

He stood still and did not answer. General Drummond groaned and walked on.

The Drummonds, he thought vaguely. They take what they want and they do as they please. That's the tradition. I've had it.

Closing his door quietly behind him, he tapped lightly on Marcia's door. There was no answer and he went down the stairs, carrying his bag. As he stepped into the living room, Marcia came from the balcony.

"Where is everybody?" she asked. "What became of the big cocktail party?"

He smiled at her wrily. "It was a big flop."

She looked at his bag and her eyes widened. "Drew, what is it?"

"I'm getting out, Marcia. Do you want to come with me?"

"But *why?*" She came toward him, a hand outstretched pleadingly. "What happened?"

"I've had it, that's all. It's too complicated to explain right now. I don't want to see my father and listen to any more of his myths. I'm getting out. Do you want to come with me?"

"But"—she looked around dazedly—"I can't just walk out on guests."

"This guest is walking out."

"Drew, do you—feel all right? I mean—"

"Of course I'm all right. At least my face isn't twitching, is it?" Leaning toward her, he kissed her forehead. "You're a good girl, Marcia. Do you want to come with me? I don't know where, but it will be a long way from Florence."

She gripped his arm. "Drew, does it have something to do with—with Jane and you?"

"Not Jane and me," he replied. "Jane and Father. They just had a big love scene out on the wall. Harry and I had grandstand seats."

Her lips trembled. "Then—then it does have something to do with you and Jane."

"No, it doesn't," he said impatiently. "If you think—ah, let's forget it. I told you it's too complicated to—"

"Okay." She blinked her eyelids quickly. "Okay, Drew. I'll drive you to Florence, leave you there, and that will be that."

"No, I'll leave you here." If that would be that in Florence it was simpler to end it now. There had been too many complications for too many days. He smiled at her, unwilling to leave her, yet unwilling that they should drift on pointlessly. "I've had fun with you, Marcia. Thanks for everything."

"Drew." Her hands fell helplessly.

"Well?"

"No," she said bitterly. "But I'll drive you to Florence."

"Thanks, Countess, I have transportation." He picked up his bag. "So long, Marcia."

As he went down the stairs, she called after him. He did not answer. He took the double turning of the drawbridge and swung down the road between the rows of cypresses.

Swallows darted, crying, in the twilight. A rising wind bore the fragrance of pines. After a while he told himself that he felt pretty good. He felt better than he had in several days. He was free again.

When it was almost dark he heard a car descending the road behind him. Pausing and looking back at its headlights, he wondered if Marcia had changed her mind. He hoped so, for she would not destroy his sense of freedom. Only his father was able to do that with his constant application of pressures, his constant assertion of his own egotism. Well, let him lead his own life, he thought, and I'll lead mine. Then, with barely contained hysteria: But I won't call Jane Mother if he marries her, I won't ever go near them at all.

He saw, when the car was close, that it was the English Ford his father had rented. He looked about quickly for a place to hide, and then he realized that he was thinking like an angry, runaway child.

The car stopped and Harry looked out at him. "Where you going, sir?"

"Florence. How about a lift?" He made out luggage piled on the seat beside Harry.

"Drew," Harry said in a strained voice, "why don't you go on back. Your father—"

"I don't want to talk about *him*. Are you giving me a lift or aren't you?"

"Get in," Harry said.

When he opened the back door, the overhead light flashed on and he saw Jane. He paused in amazement. She turned her head and did not speak.

He climbed in silently and shut the door and Harry drove on. At last he said, "I thought . . ." His voice trailed off. Now he believed he understood. The old man was not such an old man after all. Or, you might say, he was a very old man who had let his instincts get out of control there on the wall.

"Cigarette?" He held out his pack to her.

She took one. By the glow of the match he held to her cigarette he saw that she had been crying again. A strange girl. A kiss was only a kiss and a pass was only a pass. Yet she must have been so repelled by the old man's action, after having admired him so, that she felt she had to quit and leave. And then he thought, What about yourself? Why did you leave? Could it possibly be, as Marcia believed, that you were jealous?

Inhaling deeply, he looked out and up at evening stars. No, he thought, he was not jealous. If he had been, he now might be willing to go back and might even urge her to return too. If he loved her, he would be filled with joy at discovering she'd walked out on his father. And he did not feel great joy. He felt, oddly, a little sorry for his father.

At last he said, "Don't hold it against him too much, Jane. It was —just an impulse."

She was silent.

"I didn't leave because of—of what happened," he said. "I was simply fed up with his—his trying to make things seem what they never really were. And I'm tired of his always trying to make everything go his way—even to grabbing a kiss because he apparently felt like it. He seems in such a hurry. He just doesn't give you any time."

That's it, he thought. I need time. Jane needs time. Maybe, if we had enough time, as Eileen and I never were given enough . . .

"Where are you going?" he asked her.

"There's a night train to Rome," she said.

They were on the highway then and driving fast through the darkness. Staring up at the dim shadows of the hills, he asked, "And then what are you going to do?"

After a while she said, "I'm going home just as fast as I can."

"Why?"

She did not answer. She did not speak until they saw the lights of Florence ahead. Then she said unsteadily, "There's something you ought to know. You probably can't understand it, but you ought to know it anyway. I—I love your father. What happened was —my fault. He did not mean to do it. He sent me away."

He believed at first that he had not heard her correctly. And then he knew that he had. He simply had not wanted to believe what she'd said. It was too—incredible. It was true, however. And he could, with a great effort, understand how it could have happened. But the bastard sent her away.

He knew that she was crying silently. "I'm sorry," he muttered, "I'm terribly sorry."

He bought her ticket at the Central Station. As he turned from the ticket window, he saw her backing from Harry, who held out an envelope.

"Please, Miss Raleigh," Harry said as Drew approached. "The

General ordered me to give it to you. It's a check for three hundred—"

"I told you I won't accept it," she said evenly. "If you persist in making an issue out of this I'll rip it in two."

"I'm just trying to follow the General's orders, Miss Raleigh. If—"

Turning, she strode after her porter. Drew caught up with her and Harry tagged behind them, through the gate and out to a platform. On the steps of her car, she turned and held out her hand to Drew.

"Good-by, Drew. Thanks again for saving my life yesterday." She tried to smile. "Maybe we'll run into each other some day on some post or other. I hope so. It would help me keep believing in the Army."

She swung up into the car and disappeared.

Harry slowly ripped in half the envelope which contained the check. "I had to do it," he said apologetically. "I'll tell the General she did it. She would have anyway if . . ."

A whistle blasted shrilly somewhere. Drew stared up at the train, wondering if she would lower her window and wave. He felt Harry plucking at his arm.

"Drew"—Harry gripped his arm tightly, he voice intense—"if I was you I'd get on that train and go with her. Stick right with her and go on back home to the Army and she'll marry you. It would make your father a happy man."

"My father!" Drew said scornfully. "She doesn't love me, Harry, and I don't love her."

"That don't matter," Harry said. "It would all work out." He said something else, but Drew couldn't hear him as the train began to move.

Chapter XXV

You can ride from the Beverello Quay in Naples to the island of Ischia in two hours aboard a little steamer which is seldom crowded on weekdays. As the steamer pants toward Cape Mysenum, past the yellow hotels of the Via Partenope and the Posillipo Hill, the squalor and confusion of Naples disappear in the illusion of a beautiful city. Astern, Vesuvius refuses to recede slowly.

If it's a dazzling bright morning, as was the Monday when Drew took the steamer, there are few more pleasant voyages anywhere. Hard by Cape Mysenum the steamer changes its course and bears toward the island of Procida. The wind freshens, dappling the sea, and far to port Capri detaches itself from the blue mass of the Sorrento peninsula. There is much conversation and laughter and eating among the passengers, who are principally Italian, with an occasional grave English couple or a lonely German wanderer, but seldom an American. For not many Americans go to Ischia, even now.

Procida is a sun-drenched island with pink- and yellow- and blue-faced houses above a strip of beach where swarms of brown, laughing boys haul blue, lateen-rigged fishing boats from the sea. The steamer backs to a quay in the lee of a breakwater and it's tempting to go ashore, especially if something has been troubling you and you wish to be distracted. So, at least, thought Drew. He felt that he could wander for weeks among the strange islands which seem to have been cast outward by the widely flung arms of that coast.

He did not linger on Procida, however. He went forward on the steamer and watched Ischia rise from the sea, its extinct volcano turning from gray to brown as the boat approached it. Green terraces formed and white, flat-roofed houses took shape against dark volcanic soil. A castle stood up and a white beach lay down and in the bright, windless morning chestnut trees and umbrella pines hung motionless above the sea.

Do not go ashore at Porto d'Ischia, Sabraccio had told him, and do not go ashore at Casamicciola. You can visit those places later. Go on to Forio, the last port of call on the western coast. At last Forio glared whitely in the noon sun between blue sea and treeless, yellowish-gray volcanic slopes. He disembarked and collected his luggage on the quay and selected an old man from the clamoring carriage drivers.

"Casa Vastano," he told him and helped load his luggage into a four-wheeled carriage which was drawn by a bony, white-plumed chestnut gelding.

The Casa Vastano was a small *pensione* lovingly operated by a philosopher named Francesco Vastano, Sabraccio had told him when Drew went to Fiesole to say good-by the morning after Jane left for Rome. Sabraccio spent two hours with him on that Saturday morning. He did not offer advice and opinions; he offered, rather, a receptive ear and an attentive mind as Drew described the events of the previous two days. Finally, when Drew said he was leaving Florence immediately and thought he'd spend the rest of his vacation in France, Sabraccio shook his head. By all means leave Florence, he said, but there was nothing better than the sea and the sun when you were troubled; and nowhere was there a finer sea or a brighter sun than on the southwestern coast of Ischia. While Drew waited, Sabraccio telephoned his old friend Vastano, who said there would be plenty of room in his *pensione* beginning Monday.

The carriage left Forio and climbed a narrow sunken road which twisted up the slopes. It was a land of vineyards terraced from the hard volcanic earth, a country of wine where small gray donkeys pulled huge casks on two-wheeled carts from cellars honeycombing the roadsides. A happy island, Drew observed, where everyone smiled and spoke to everyone else, a place of patience where even the right-of-way on the narrow road was negotiated calmly. They came, in early afternoon, to a high ridge of the volcano and saw the blue sea far below. Then they went down, iron brakes screeching on the turning carriage wheels, until they came to a turnout, still high above the sea. There a smiling young boy leaped off a wall and cried, "Casa Vastano!"

Drew paid the driver and let the boy take one of his bags. Carrying the other two, he followed him down steep stone steps. The way leveled in a path around a cliff and then descended again in flight after flight of hollowed steps until, quite suddenly, there was a flat white roof and a yellow wall where bougainvillea flamed. Beyond, the sea stretched infinitely.

Francesco Vastano was plump and bald and spoke English as he had learned it while working in a Brooklyn restaurant. After introducing Drew to his wife, Vastano led him to his room, which was high-ceilinged and whitewashed and overlooked the sea. On the communal terrazo-floored veranda, where scores of exotic plants grew in brightly painted pots, Vastano served him a lunch of pizza and salad and a large bottle of the pale, sweet wine of the country called Tears of Christ. Vastano's reputation as a philosopher seemed an irony, for he simply had a large supply of truisms which he liked to display. Yet he took such genuine pleasure in displaying them that he made them seem almost new, so perhaps he was, after all, a philosopher. In most matters he was inclined toward pessimism. He warned Drew of the dangers of the sea and the menace of the sun.

He said regretfully that there was absolutely nothing for Drew to do at Casa Vastano in the evenings now because there were only three guests, a Roman couple on their honeymoon and an elderly Englishwoman who read all day and half the night.

After lunch Drew put on swimming trunks and moccasins and walked down to the small pebble beach. At one end of the beach the elderly Englishwoman sat reading a book under a black umbrella. At the opposite end the young Roman couple lay in the shadow of a rock, arms entwined about each other. Spreading a bath towel on the pebbles in the center of the beach, Drew stretched out and listened to the wash of the surf. After a while he waded into the warm water, dived, and swam out quite a distance. Floating and looking toward the shore, he was surprised to see that the Englishwoman had risen and was watching him, and the honeymooning couple had disentwined themselves and were watching him, and on the cliff above stood Vastano, one hand shading his eyes while he beckoned wildly. It was curious. The sea was warm and there was no current; he felt that he could swim and float for hours. He swam back leisurely.

Vastano came down to the beach and reproached him for swimming out so far. It was dangerous, he said, though he did not explain why. Then, warning him not to stay in the sun too long, Vastano walked back to the *pensione* and the Englishwoman resumed reading under her black umbrella and the honeymooning couple lay down and indulged themselves in a long and presumably passionate kiss.

Drew, lying face down in the sun, felt invulnerable. He was a good swimmer and he tanned rather than burned and he was not wedded to a book or a young woman from Rome or a package of platitudes. I come and go as I please, unafraid, he thought, and the place where I now find myself is better than any place I have been. In a sense he had run away, he knew. Try as he would in the past three days, however, he had not been able to decide what he was fleeing. Sabraccio had not suggested an answer; Sabraccio had believed that he'd figure things out for himself eventually and had simply offered an environment conducive to thought in the solitude of the Casa Vastano. But if he were running from something, he should feel more vulnerable now.

As he came down through Rome and Naples to Ischia he had thought of the obvious things. His father's iron will. His disappointment in Jane. His frustration with Marcia. Altogether, they added up to *something*. Altogether, perhaps they were enough. He had been in Tuscany and now he was in Ischia and eventually he would be—where?

Raising himself on his elbows, he lighted a cigarette. Perhaps he ran not because of where he had been but because of where he was going. Destination unknown. Like a good many others in his time he seemed to have been absolutely every place. To war, to school, to bed; to the city and to rustic retreat in the country; to love and marriage and loneliness. But he never had really found anything that lasted much longer than Tuscany had lasted and Ischia would last now. He had, unquestionably, lived in a state of rebellion. He did not regret it; he regretted, rather, that his revolution had been so poorly organized. He had not resisted his father's way of life with anything better or stronger. If the lot of a policeman in Army uniform was shallow, why had he not inundated it with something deeper? He had not returned to college because he'd found the pursuit of theoretical knowledge unsatisfying. He had not returned to his Madison Avenue trade because he'd found it even more empty and illusory than the policeman's trade. He had not returned to anything because he seemed to have lived through everything and, if there were a hell, it would be a place where you repeated your life with exactitude. His fault had been in not going on to something when he'd found he could not go back to anything.

But on to what? The memorable people in the world were those who had passionate convictions—about art or science or human nature or religion—to which they applied themselves assiduously. But the great majority of people did not have passionate convictions. So, he thought, I am not memorable. But who wants to be memorable? Still, I would have liked to raise one sonnet or painting or test tube or well-taught student against my unmemorableness. But it's too late. Not because I'm thirty-one, which is really young. But because I lack any strong convictions, which joins me to the vast unmemorable majority.

Snubbing out his cigarette, he lowered his head and closed his eyes and thought, At least I'm not afraid.

He dozed and dreamed fantastically of blood-red figures on a yellow landscape across which he moved fearlessly. He saw Judd trying to hammer a silver spike into a black anvil at Burning Brook. When he started to speak to him, Judd looked up, his face weary. Awakening with a start in the blinding sunlight, he sat up and rubbed his eyes.

Recently he'd been thinking much of Burning Brook, he realized. Subconsciously he must have been telling himself, I can always go back there. But he could not, he thought now. Not because his father and Judd and Mildred lived there, but because all the Drummonds all the way back lived there and would forever remind him of his inept rebellion.

Gathering up his towel, he walked up the path to the Casa Vastano. He took a shower and dressed. As he put on his wrist watch he realized that just a week ago at this time he had walked into Harry's Bar and met Marcia for the first time. Suddenly he missed her acutely. Thinking that he never would see her again and wondering what to do with himself, he went to the veranda and let Francesco Vastano mix him a Martini.

He ate alone at a table, facing the sea. At a table to his left sat the Englishwoman reading a book. At a table to his right the honeymooning couple murmured and laughed. Once, glancing from one table to the other, he thought he was so completely a member of the unmemorable majority that he was finding solitude hard to bear.

It had not been so before Marcia and his father and Jane had appeared in Florence. There had been long, good days when he was content to walk and eat and read alone. But solitude did not suffice now, even though he had come to this island believing that he desired it.

He read until a late hour that night and awakened early the next morning and took a swim. After breakfast, he climbed the long flights of steps to the road and followed it for a couple of miles to a small village where he wandered through narrow streets and twisting alleys, as if looking for something. The fact that he did not know what it was, he thought, did not mean he would fail to recognize it if and when he found it. Walking back to the Casa Vastano, he ate a light lunch and put on trunks and went down to the beach. While dozing, he dimly heard Vastano's son, Armando, shouting excitedly. Turning over on his belly, he slept.

The crunch of feet on the pebbles awakened him. Looking up, he stared incredulously at Marcia walking toward him. She wore a robe and carried a swimming cap and she smiled at him rather bleakly.

"Hi," she said.

"Hi!" He got to his feet.

Silently she spread a towel beside his and stretched out. She stared up at him, her expression inscrutable behind sunglasses. Then she said, "I thought of a lot of things to say on the way here. I mean things I was going to say when I saw you. And all I said was 'Hi.' "

"Well, hi." Smiling, he lay down beside her, leaning on his elbows and looking at her.

She turned, resting her head on an arm, and looked at him. At last she said, "Sabraccio told me where you were. I went to see him Saturday afternoon when I found you'd cleared out of your apartment for good. I—I sold my car. I mean I practically had to *give* it away. Anyway, I got rid of everything and I'm down to four bags —and a hatbox. I'm going home."

"When?"

She did not tell him. She said, "That's pretty good cutting, four bags and a hatbox—for a woman."

"That's very good." He lighted a cigarette. "Do you know what's become of my father? I was going to say I don't care, but I do."

"I don't know where he is, Drew. But you ought to try to get in touch with him." She sighed. "It's sad. A real sad story, I think. He talked to me for half of Friday night after he found that you'd cleared out of the castle. Do you know what? He *wanted* you to marry Jane. That's why he hired her. He hoped that—"

Drew said slowly, "He thinks he can order human relationships as if they're duty rosters. He didn't hurt me, but he certainly hurt Jane when he ordered her to leave. Harry gave me a lift back to Florence with her on Friday evening and she told me she loved Father."

Marcia sat up. "It's terribly sad. When he realized that she loved him he felt he had to order her to leave." She spoke slowly. "I think you got hurt too. I think you were looking for a chance to fall in love with Jane and you felt your father had spoiled it."

He would not deny it. Probably she was right.

"So I was hurt too," she said. "I wanted to make the—the first team just this once. I wanted to break my long-time run of second-string luck. But I changed my mind after you left and I talked to Sabraccio. I decided it's better to—"

She meant, he thought, that she loved him. She had followed him to Ischia because she loved him. She had hoped, pathetically, for the old idealized notions of courtship and marriage between them. That having failed, she was willing—I love her, he thought, but I cannot tell her now because she wouldn't believe me.

Crossing her feet under her, she rose. "Do you just lie around here all day long? Don't you ever go in the water?" She took off her robe and desire stirred in him as he looked at her lovely body in a scant two-piece swimming suit. "Or don't you know how to swim?" She buttoned on her cap.

"Come on," he said, rising, "and be careful of the rocks on your feet."

She was a strong swimmer, keeping his leisurely stroke beside him as he went straight out. He watched her each time he swung his head, expecting her to look back at the shore or to stop and say that they'd gone far enough. But she did not look back and she did not stop. She'd try to swim to Spain with me, he thought, and that's one reason why I love her.

He stopped at last and grinned at her. "Hey!" he cried.

"Hey-hey!" She raised her face to the sun and laughed. "It's wonderful!"

They floated for a while, their finger tips touching, and then they swam slowly back to the beach.

As they waded through the shallows he looked at her longingly. She was a most desirable woman, her face and body so beautifully formed. He glanced down at her slim waist, her rounded legs. On her hip, just above the briefs, was a mole. On her left hip. On her left hipbone.

He halted, staring after her incredulously, feeling that cold November Korean morning as the warm Mediterranean wavelets washed around his knees. He could hear LeRoy Tate saying, "She has a mole on her left hipbone, Captain, and it moves when she moves."

Now she was on the beach, taking off her cap and flinging back her hair. She had not been Tate's girl, he thought numbly. He knew she had not been. Here, instead of evidence, was the extraordinary coincidence of life. How often was mere coincidence misinterpreted as solemn evidence? How often, even with the Drummonds? But even if she had been Tate's girl, he thought as he gazed at her, it would not make any difference in my love for her. Welcome to the human race, Drummond.

She brushed at her hip. She touched the mole and it was gone. She held it up on a finger. It was, he saw, a bit of seaweed which she flicked to the beach.

Throwing back his head, he uttered a sound that was half whoop, half laughter, and he plunged on through the shallows.

"What's the matter?" she asked.

He touched her shoulder gently. "Philosophy," he said. "Illusion and reality. Moles and seaweed."

She looked puzzled. "I'm not very bright. I like the sound of everything you say, but sometimes I don't—"

"I'll tell you a story," he said, "a true story."

"I love stories," she said, rubbing her hair with her towel, "especially true stories. But dry yourself first or you'll burn. And you'd better let me put some sun-tan lotion on your back."

"Okay." He dried his face and back and stretched prone beside her, closing his eyes contentedly as she rubbed the lotion on his back. He felt her fingers avoid the scar and he said, "Put it on that too, it doesn't hurt any more."

"Okay." She dabbed the scar tenderly. "Now tell me the story."

"Let me put some of that stuff on you."

"Thank you, no. Not just now. I'll take care of myself. Tell me the story."

"Do you remember me asking you if you ever knew a guy named LeRoy Tate?"

"No. Wait a minute, yes, I do. I remember everything you ever said. That first night at the castle—go ahead."

"And you said you didn't know him." He craned around. "And I *know* you didn't. You have to understand that."

"Yes," she said patiently, "we understand each other. But why don't you begin at the beginning?"

As he told her the story, they lay facing each other, not touching. After he had finished, she moved quickly and sat up, her eyes filled with tears.

He moved quickly too and touched her arm. "I told you I *know* that you never knew LeRoy Tate."

She turned her head. "How do you know? Because I don't have a mole on my left hipbone?"

"Of course not. You could have one and I still wouldn't believe the—evidence. But it set me to thinking how we—we live by such illusions."

"But suppose," she said, "that I told you I really was the girl who loved Tate? How would you feel then?"

"That's part of my point about illusions. It may not please you to hear it, but it wouldn't make any difference in the way I feel about you now. What might have been real then has nothing to do with what is very real to us now."

She gazed at him pensively. "You're very clever, Drew. I wish I had the words to say how clever. What you're saying is to forget my

—my illusions about—us playing it straight. You mean that I'm foolish to keep on thinking I must try to play it by the rule book now after having—broken so many rules." She looked away. "You don't have to go to so much trouble. I knew when I came here I was—going back to the old way of things. Don't go to so much trouble, Drew. When I asked Mr. Vastano if you were here, he smiled and gave me the room next to yours."

"You're wrong," he said slowly, "if you think I'm saying that everything is an illusion. To be what you consider—decent, to—to observe that paper marriage to Edoardo until you can un-paper it, I don't say that's an illusion. That's just a—a place for us to make a good beginning."

Her eyes widened. "You mean—"

"I mean," he said, "that I love you. I want to marry you. But you'll never know how much I love you unless we wait."

About one o'clock the next afternoon they walked to the village. There under the sun-mottled leaves of an olive tree in the courtyard of a tiny inn, they ate a lunch of bread and cheese and cool, pale wine.

"Yesterday," he told her, "I came to this village as if I were looking for something. And today I know I've found it. I tell you everything now, don't I? I never stop talking."

"We stopped talking to sleep," she said. "We slept five and a half hours last night. That is, I lay down that long, but I didn't sleep at all. Did you?"

"I think I did. I'm the peasant type who can always sleep." He smiled at her, admiring her beauty in the mottled shade of the olive tree. "And you're a peasant too."

"Yes," she said, "I'm a peasant even when I'm not wearing this peasant-style dress. But you're not. You're—"

"Old Professor Drummond. I'm old Professor Drummond sitting under an olive tree in my sabbatical year. And you're old Mrs. Professor Drummond, hair gray and body gone flabby from bearing our fifteen children."

"You, old Professor Drummond," she said, laughing, "do you still love me?"

"More than ever, my dear." He reached across the table and squeezed her hand. "More than when we sat under this same tree thirty years ago and you consented to be Mrs. Professor Drummond."

"So you would be Professor Drummond," she said.

He looked at her alertly. "Unless you don't want to be his wife. If you don't want me to—"

"No," she said quickly. "I want what you want. If you want to run a filling station at the edge of the Mojave Desert, that's what I want too. I'll learn to fix flats and happily spend my life looking for nails in punctured tires. But tell me, old Professor Drummond, how have I been as a faculty wife all these years? Was I—"

"You've been grand, Marcia. You've been quiet at the right times and vociferous at the right times while I wrote all my books . . ." He stared beyond her through the archway of the courtyard at a distant blue patch of the Mediterranean. He doubted suddenly that there were any books in him. "I guess," he said in a low voice, "I could only teach in high school."

"No." The pressure of her hand seemed to buoy him toward whatever goal he desired, even if it were only a filling station goal. "You're Professor Drummond and I have a question to ask you. Do you ever regret quitting the Army thirty years ago when you were thirty-one?"

"Never once." He said it promptly.

"But how," she asked, "has being a professor been different from being a soldier?"

He pondered that. While he pondered, she asked, "What were the things about a soldier's life that made you quit?"

At last he said, "The main trouble was that I never really wanted to be a soldier. I'm opposed to war. But the times weren't convenient for opposition. And I'll tell you something interesting. All soldiers are opposed to war. They spend their lives getting ready for it, but they never are ready, and finally they go out and fight even though they're opposed to it and not at all ready for it. That's the chief trouble with being a soldier. You can't say it's the monotony— though I've said it often enough. Actually, though, I know that soldiering is no more monotonous than working for any big corporation. But I still haven't told you why I quit it thirty years ago, have I?"

"No," she said, "you haven't told me, darling. Did you think I wouldn't like the life? Or did you think I somehow wouldn't measure up to it as would that girl, I refuse to try to remember her name, that sweet but rather strange girl whose life you saved in a tower in San Gimignano?"

"You'd have been fine at it," he told her. "You were very beautiful, and a beautiful woman can be anything she wants to be any-where. You were smart, too, though you used to deny it. But most important of all, you were never mean. So you'd have been as good at it as at being a professor's wife. The worst thing would have been having to leave you sometimes."

"But I'd have gone wherever you went," she exclaimed. "I'd have gone absolutely everywhere with you."

"Not on maneuvers," he said. "Not to study the secret missile at the secret proving ground. Not to all the little wars my father fore-cast, to say nothing of the big one."

"At least being a professor you didn't have to go to war any more. You'd had your wars and proved yourself brave."

"I was never brave, Marcia. I was often scared. I did what I had to do and I was often ashamed. I saw bad things and did bad things and had bad things done to me. And sometimes I was so ashamed that it made my face twitch. At least I think that's why my face twitched."

"Now," she said, "you've told me why you quit the Army."

"No, Marcia, I haven't. It would make me sound noble if I said that was the reason. It would make me sound good and military serv-ice bad. But on Madison Avenue I saw and did and had done to me just as many bad things as ever happened in war. Morally speaking, that is. I once saw a man's testicles shot off at a client's meeting. Morally speaking. Once, in an office, when a man who considered me his friend turned his back, I stuck a knife between his shoulder blades. Military service is like any form of service in any organiza-tion. There are quite a few absurdities connected with it. But in general you merely seek your rightful compensation and deal with the human condition, both personal and political. The measurement of you as a man is the same and maybe even a shade finer than in other pursuits: honesty with yourself and fairness with others. I'll tell you something. I had a qualm or two before I quit the Army—before you got your divorce and we were married. I'll tell you now, these thirty years later, I was a pretty good officer. I was efficient and I liked to try to get to the heart of things. I knew and followed the simple rules that make even a railroad section gang function well: Never get mad, never issue an order you can't enforce, never ask any-body to do anything you won't do yourself, talk to everybody, listen to everybody. That's all there is to this functional life. But I'll tell you something. Before I quit I was egotistical enough to think that I did the thing so well that it would be better if I instead of somebody else was doing it."

"Then why," she asked, abandoning the pretense that they were living in a hypothetical future, "do you want to quit?"

"Because," he said, "I can't shake off the feeling that it's not *mine*. It belongs to Father. And it should not. The United States Army belongs to as many men, as many good men, as there are in it. Let me give you an example. A very good friend of mine, a major named Pete Oliver, is a Colorado miner's son. He went to the Academy and he's making the Army his life. He's a smart, nice guy, and he has a wonderful wife and a couple of cute kids— You'll like the Olivers when you meet them some day. Well, my point is that the United States Army belongs to Pete Oliver—to all the Pete Olivers. It doesn't belong to his father or his grandfather or his great-grandfather. I'm pretty sure, in fact, that Pete hasn't the vaguest idea who his great-grandfather was. Which is the best way for anyone to be. Which is the way it is in the Army—for most of our best men. And it's the way I wish it could be for me. But wherever I go in it I feel my father's presence. For instance, I did a crazy thing in Korea when I refused rotation home. But I was trying to *prove* something. I was trying to prove I was a better man than my father or any of the Drummonds. And I shouldn't be trying to prove anything."

"But you don't have to prove anything, Drew."

"I know I don't. But I *feel* that I have to with Father always hovering near. Ever since I went back to the Army in '48 he has found excuses to come and visit me wherever I was. He even wangled himself an observer's junket to Korea. It killed him that he couldn't get a command in Korea. I think he'd have taken a reduction to brigadier just to be there. But they figured he was too old for the job. At any rate, he wangled a trip to Korea and he came to visit me and it took a while for the men in my outfit to forget my father was a lieutenant general. They forgot it, though, after I refused rotation. And when I spent all those months at Valley Forge Hospital, even after he'd retired, he would come to visit me and sit and talk and talk about the Army. It was the kind and natural thing for him to do, but the people at the hospital stopped thinking of me as *me*. They thought of me as the Lieutenant General's son. So that's why Italy was wonderful to me. I was myself. I was free. But he came even here to Italy, following me."

She pressed his hand again. "Now, perhaps, it will be different. After we're married perhaps he'll—"

"No." He looked at her bleakly. "It will always be the same until the day he dies. And I don't mean that I wish he'd die. I just wish that his hold on me would die so that I could . . . I could . . ." His voice trailed off.

"Stay in the Army, Drew?" she asked quietly.

"Yes. It's the place where I belong."

They wandered through the village, looking up alleys, gazing down at the sea. He followed her into a tiny ceramic shop when she exclaimed, "I'd like that great big blue bowl. I don't know what I'd do with it, but I'd like it."

"How would we get it home?" he asked her.

"I'll carry it," she said. "I'll carry it all the way under an arm." She paused. "But I don't need it. It's foolish. I don't want it."

"Of course you want it. I'm going to buy it."

"No," she said positively, "I don't want it."

"Then look at this little ashtray. It says 'Ischia' and look at the crazy figure of that fish on it. It's cheap and corny, but I like it and I'm going to buy it for you."

"But I don't smoke," she said.

He smiled at her. "But I do. Every time I flick an ash I'll remember Ischia."

"I love it," she exclaimed. "I want it. We'll keep it on our coffee table and you can flick ashes in it. Buy it for me, please."

Hand in hand, they walked from the village, following the road that curved around the flank of the dead volcano. Silent at last, as if they had finally exhausted their seemingly inexhaustible thoughts, they gazed from the terraced slopes to the shining sea.

They passed many carts of wine casks pulled by small donkeys. The drivers invariably halted, smiling delightedly at recognition of the two lovers, crying, *"Buon giorno,* signor, signora! *Come sta?"* And they, hands locked, smiled and replied, *"Buon giorno,* signor."

They did not speak to each other, however. It seemed, Drew thought, that each waited for the other to break the silence. Then he realized that they found ample communication in the pressure of their hands.

When they came to the turnout, they paused for a moment, gazing far down at the Casa Vastano. They went down the steps, still holding hands, and around the path to the next flight.

Marcia suddenly squeezed his hand hard. He looked at her. She pointed down silently.

Beside the wall of the Casa Vastano General Drummond stood, gazing upward. Seeing them, he raised an arm and waved.

"Even here," Drew muttered. "He's followed me even here."

"Drew." She looked at him pleadingly, the pressure of her hand intense. "Please. Don't let anything happen to spoil it for us. It's so perfect. Don't let him spoil it."

"He won't spoil it." His tone, he realized, was almost savage. "He *can't*. I'll—"

"Then wave to him," she said quickly, releasing his hand and raising an arm to wave to the General. But General Drummond did not see her. He had started up the long flight of steps, his head lowered, his legs knifing quickly.

"Look at him come," Drew said. "Two at a time. Double-time. He just can't wait to sink his hooks in me."

"Don't think of it that way," she said, starting down the steps.

"I can't help it." He followed her reluctantly. "It reminds me of a time when I was a little kid and we lived on Luzon. I took it in my head one day to crawl under our bungalow and hide. I don't know why. Everybody knew I was there and I wouldn't come out. So he came in after me. I remember him squeezing in on his belly after me. He didn't say a word and neither did I. As soon as he touched me I crawled out after him. I thought he'd whop me hard. But he didn't. He just asked me why I did it and I said I thought of it as a kind of game to see if he could reach me. He stood there, all covered with dirt, and all of a sudden he grinned. He just ruffled my hair and turned away."

"Remember that," Marcia said over a shoulder. "Remember it was a game and he showed that he loved you when—"

"He and I are getting rather old to be playing games."

"General Drummond," she called down the one flight of stairs which now separated them. "Welcome to Ischia."

He had halted, his head lowered, his left hand supporting himself against the retaining wall. His right hand fumbled in a pocket and then he raised the hand to his lips. At last he looked up at them descending the stairs. His face appeared gray, as if he were in pain, but his lips twisted in a smile.

"Drew." The word came in a quick gasp. "Marcia." His lips twisted harder in his strange smile. "Happy to be here," he gasped.

"Father." Drew hurried ahead of her. "What's wrong?"

"Nothing." General Drummond gripped Drew's hand tightly. "My damn wind. Bit of indigestion. I'm okay now."

"General! General Drummond!" Harry was racing up the stairs.

"My keeper," the General said bitterly. "I wandered away from my keeper. Send him back, will you?"

"Your keeper, Father?"

"Send him back!"

"Harry!" Drew shouted. "Halt there!" Harry halted, staring up at them. "Go on back!" Turning slowly, his head bowed, Harry descended toward the Casa Vastano.

"Good boy." The General grinned at him, gripping his arm tightly. "Good voice. You rap 'em out. The orders, I mean. Real snap in it. Your voice, I mean."

"But why did you call him your keeper?"

"Old joke," the General said. "Not funny any more." He stepped between Drew and Marcia, taking each by an arm, and they walked down slowly. "Sabraccio told me where you were. Very kind of him to tell me. I know you didn't want to see me. But I wanted to come. I wanted to explain—"

"There's no need to explain anything, Father. Everything's all right."

General Drummond halted, clutching Drew's arm and not releasing Marcia's. His tired old blue eyes glittered momentarily as he searched Drew's face. Then he said, "Yes. We've had too many explanations." He smiled. "I finally follow you. I finally believe that everything will be all right."

He walked on down slowly, still holding each by an arm. He breathed heavily and he did not speak until they reached the last flight of stairs. There he paused again, gazing out at the Mediterranean. "A beautiful sea. A beautiful day. Reminds me of the Atlantic off Sandy Hook on a clear day. When I was a boy at Hancock on such a day—" He squeezed Drew's arm more tightly and his tone became dry. "But as we agree, we've had too many explanations, too many reminiscences."

"On such a day, General," Marcia said to him, "you'd go swimming and—"

"Yes." He smiled at her. "And I'd lie on the beach and stare out to sea and think of all the things that— Ah, there's Harry." He called to him in a warm voice, "What d'you say, Harry?"

Harry smiled at him uncertainly. "I made the arrangements with Vastano, General."

"Good. Thank you, Harry. As always, you're a good man." He looked from Marcia to Drew. "It's almost five o'clock. I'm not tarrying in this place. But it's almost five o'clock and I want a Martini."

He smiled. "I guess you'll always remember me as a man who took to Martinis in his old age."

"I'd enjoy a Martini, Father."

Marcia looked at him, her expression urging him to say he'd remember more than that about his father. But he could not think of anything to say. How could he have memories when his father was right here?

"Run up those stairs ahead of me," General Drummond said to them. "We'll have a Martini on the veranda and look at the sea. Harry's made the arrangements with the fellow who runs this place."

He followed them slowly, heavily, gripping the rail. When he reached the veranda, his face was contorted, as if in pain.

"General Drummond," Marcia said, "do you feel well?"

"I worked up a blister," he muttered. "I have this damn blister—"

"Sit down, Father," Drew said, suddenly concerned. "Sit down here and I'll mix the drinks."

"No, sir." General Drummond twisted his lips in a grin. "Nobody can mix 'em like I do." He moved slowly to Vastano's bar and stepped behind it. "This is fine," he said. "I can stand here and look out to sea and— Good. Harry set everything up here, I see. Where is Harry?"

"Right here, sir."

It was strange, Drew thought. Harry had been standing right there all the time.

"Good man, Harry," the General muttered, not glancing at him as he dropped ice in a pitcher. "It's a funny thing," he said. "Whenever I mix a drink I remember my father, I don't know why. When my father poured a drink he used to say, 'Courage. Above all, courage.'"

General Drummond poured gin over the ice. The bottle slipped from his hand and he fell. When they reached him, he was dead.

Chapter XXVI

Through the red light of dawn the four-engined Air Force transport flew home at approximately two hundred and seventy miles an hour. Within the cabin, surrounded by the muted rumble of the engines, there was no sensation of movement except for the slow, steady oscillation of Drew's blouse on a hook above their seats.

Wide awake now, Drew looked at Marcia's face on his shoulder. Smiling at him abstractedly, she rose and took down his blouse.

"Are you chilly?" he asked. "I am."

"No. I just want to look at your jacket."

"You mean my blouse."

"Your blouse," she said. "I'll remember that. I have a lot to learn. First I want to know about these." She touched the ribbons.

"It isn't necessary." He glanced around. Across the aisle Harry slept with his mouth open. In the seat behind him a young Air Force sergeant was curled embryonically in sleep.

"It may not be necessary, Major," she said, "but it's nice for me to know as much as possible. This must be the important one, this first one with the doohickey on it."

Aft, the baby daughter of a young Air Force captain and his wife gave a low, waking wail, and passengers began to stir. There was the click of a lighter and the pungent morning smell of a cigarette.

"That's the important one," Drew said, getting to his feet and pulling on his blouse.

The two-star Air Force general who had boarded at London last night rose from a seat forward and stretched. Closing an eye against the smoke from his pendant cigarette, he grinned. Drew, smiling in reply, noted his command pilot wings and the Distinguished Flying Cross and Legion of Merit among his ribbons.

"Morning, Major." The General held out his hand and introduced himself.

When Drew introduced him to Marcia, the General smiled at her appreciatively. His forehead and cheeks were heavily lined, his cropped hair gray; he no longer was a young general, but when he looked at Marcia something boyish came to his face.

"I was sorry to hear about your father, Major."

The crew had informed him, Drew realized. After the plane was airbound from England the General had gone forward to the flight deck. The pilot probably had told him he was outranked on this flight by a retired three-star infantryman riding from Rome in the trunk. Somebody named Drummond who'd died of a heart attack in Italy and was getting a free ride to Arlington. It was a funny setup, the pilot might have told him. His son, an Infantry major with a weird set of TDY rest and recuperation orders; and his batman, an old doughfoot; and his secretary, a dame. Get a load of the dame, General, the pilot might have said, and you'll never feel sorry for the Infantry again.

Now the General was getting a good appreciative load of her as he said to Drew, "I never knew your father personally. Only by reputation."

Malarkey, probably. But courteous.

"I worked for Ninth Tac for a while. That's where I learned about your father."

Then it was not malarkey. If he'd worked for Ninth Tac he undoubtedly had heard of General Drummond.

"It's mighty kind of the Air Force to give us a lift." Drew smiled faintly. "Though I'm not sure Father would have approved of either him or us taking up the space."

The General grinned. "Unification," he said, studying Drew's ribbons and insignia.

Wearing your history on your breast and sleeve was often misleading. It was, however, something communicable. It had helped him in Rome yesterday, for example, when the Association had taken over. The Association would always arrange a ride to Arlington for a member—and for a member's son who wore the uniform. But he knew that his ribbons, more than anything else, had helped to arrange a ride for Harry and for Marcia, whom he had identified as his father's secretary. He was, after all, familiar with the machine; he knew where to oil it and when to tinker with it and how to keep it rolling smoothly.

The crew chief stood there with a thermos of coffee and paper cups. "Coffee, sir?" he asked the General.

"Ladies first, Chief. Miss Dale?"

The General scarcely looked at her as he studied Drew's ribbons. I wish he wouldn't read me, Drew thought, because he draws a partially false conclusion. But partially true too. More true than false. They're the marks of my trade.

The sense of sadness returned. If only Harry had told him or Judd had written him that his father had only a short time to live. It was too late now. Yet if he'd known, how would he have acted differently? He would not have left the castle. If he hadn't left and Marcia had not come after him, however, they might not be going home together now.

Across the aisle Harry lighted a cigarette and looked at the coffee longingly. Drew passed him his cup and asked the chief for another.

"You want to watch them drive an airplane, Miss Dale?" the General asked suddenly. "Bring your coffee and come on."

In a moment the co-pilot came back and told Drew that there was room on the flight deck and the General had asked him to come up too.

He went forward and stood with his hand on Marcia's shoulder behind the pilot. The General sat in the co-pilot's seat, explaining throttles and levers. Sunlight flooded through the astrodome and the airplane rolled gently in a perpetual dead center of space.

Not listening to the General, Drew stared through the astrodome. The rising red orb of sun lighted eastern cloud-heads with crimson and gold, shaping them into castles and towers on the crests of lavender mountains. It seemed that he was looking back at Europe, to the evanescent mountains and castles and towers. But the sun was rising fast and the pictures fading. Soon they would be gone forever. The frescoes and paintings, the books and quiet piazzas, the amorphous ideas and faint hopes would be ancient dreams. And now it was gone. Now only the sea shone down there through a bright morning haze.

Pointing to the graph above his head, the General talked about the governing factors of altitude and temperature. He was talking of something he understood and liked. Here in the gleaming metal under the astrodome, among the mysterious gadgets and predictable human tensions and skills, he felt at home. And he wished them to feel at home too.

Here under the astrodome, as the olive-brown continent took shape before them, he invited their passing friendship. Not for the sake of his dead father riding back there in the luggage compartment, Drew realized. Not for the sake of the ribbons on his chest which were supposed to be so significant. Rather, the General invited their friendship because he envied them their youth and because he believed that they wished to comprehend their flight through space.

Functional, he said in effect to them. No magic. If he had seen the evanescent castles and towers and mountains in the rising sun, he had not remarked on them. His mind had been preoccupied with calculations of distance and time and speed, his hands moving efficiently over the control pedestal and the great instrument panel.

This literally was the new world as they passed over the white-fringed coastline onto the continent. The old world vanished in the morning sun.

They returned to their seats and sat close, looking down at the continent speeding under them, watching the familiar patterns of American towns and farms and highways. Marcia's hand was in his as they looked down. And he found that they were talking quietly of plans: of a funeral, a divorce, a marriage. Beyond that they did not plan. They did not need to. For they knew, without discussion, where they would be.

"Down there," he said, leaning forward and looking out the port as the airplane descended over Maryland. "Down there is one of the posts. See the precise geometric pattern. See that curving road and those cottages. We'll be living in one of those."

"Where?" She leaned forward eagerly. "Oh, there. I see. I can hardly wait to be living down there."

"If only," he said, "Father knew it." Incredibly, tears came to his eyes.

Her eyes filled too and she gripped his hand harder. "I think he does know. I'm positive he knew that last day on Ischia that we'll be right down there."

Down there, he thought. And some day I'll be back up here, going some place I don't want to go. But I will go.

As the ground rose to meet them, he glimpsed a man raking leaves in a yard.

"The lucky dog," he said. "Raking leaves in his own back yard."

"If that's what you want," she said, "you can—"

"It's not a matter of what I want," he said.

She looked at him. "Why isn't it?"

"It's a matter of being like the airplane," he said. "Funct. nal. Moving efficiently and predictably as specified by construction."

"But how do you know how you're constructed?" she asked.

"By knowing what you're going to do even when you're not at all sure you want to do it."

She pressed his hand. "Some day we'll have our own back yard. Some day we'll go back and lie on beaches and walk on hilltops."

"I wonder," he said as the airplane settled toward a landing.